THE PERFECT FAMILY

Visit us at www.boldstrokesbooks.com

Advance Praise for *The Perfect Family*

"*The Perfect Family* is the perfect read, a poignant and realistic look at the things that take a family apart, and the way love can bring it back together. Written with grace and sensitivity, this novel celebrates the healing power of forgiveness and understanding."
—Susan Wiggs, *NY Times* Bestselling Author

"*The Perfect Family* is a novel, yes, but also a tool for change. It should be in school libraries, psychologists' offices, and on teachers' bookshelves! Parents and students alike can learn from the Davidson and Crane families. As described in the manuscript, love and support can defy discrimination!"—Stacy B. Killings, PhD, Certified School Psychologist, Gates Chili High School

"The image of the 'perfect' family is shattered when the youngest son announces he's gay. Warmly poignant, realistic, dramatic, and honestly presented, Shay's story is an engrossing family saga for the modern world."—Pat Cooper, *RT Book Reviews*, 4½ stars

"After 20 years of educating on gay issues, *The Perfect Family* provided me with a fresh, soulful, and enlightening coming out story. I would recommend *The Perfect Family* to anyone who wants to understand the innumerable issues that face a family when a child's reality collides with a family's expectations."—Scott Fearing, Outreach Director, The Gay Alliance of Genesee Valley

"Kathryn Shay has written an emotional, dramatic, and engrossing story relevant to our times, our lives, and our perceptions about love. This is a tale that had to be told, and it will enrich everyone who reads it. I read with rapt attention."—Stella Cameron, *NY Times* Bestselling Author

"It's been a long time since I've read a novel that so comprehensively and compellingly speaks to a teenager's coming out experience. Societal, religious, and family system factors are beautifully addressed in Shay's narrative. As a UCC minister, I particularly appreciated the help given to the family and the solace they find in churches like ours. I will recommend *The Perfect Family* to any family with a gay or lesbian child or to anyone who wants to learn more about what life is like when a gay youth has the courage to come out."
—Reverend Lee Ann Bryce, United Church of Christ Minister

"How does a family redefine itself after its identity has been shattered? How can love survive when the people we love most reveal that they aren't who we thought they were? In *The Perfect Family*, Kathryn Shay explores these questions with fierce honesty, courage, and abundant grace."—Judith Arnold, romance and women's fiction author

Praise for Kathryn Shay

"Kathryn Shay never disappoints!"—Lisa Gardner, *NY Times* Bestselling Author

"Kathryn Shay is a master at her craft, deftly weaving emotion, romance, realism, and intrigue to create a love story that you'll never forget."—Catherine Anderson, *NY Times* Bestselling Author

"Kathryn Shay's storytelling grabbed me on page one and her characters held me until the very last word. A definite keeper!"—Barbara Bretton, *USA Today* Bestselling Author

"Poignant and compelling, this novel reinforces Shay's well-earned reputation as a first-rate storyteller."—Shelley Mosley, American Library Association

THE PERFECT FAMILY

by

Kathryn Shay

A Division of Bold Strokes Books

2010

ISBN 10: 1-60282-181-X
ISBN 13: 978-1-60282-181-1

THIS TRADE PAPERBACK ORIGINAL IS PUBLISHED BY
BOLD STROKES BOOKS, INC.
P.O. BOX 249
VALLEY FALLS, NY 12185

FIRST EDITION: SEPTEMBER 2010

CREDITS
EDITOR: STACIA SEAMAN
PRODUCTION DESIGN: STACIA SEAMAN
COVER DESIGN BY SHERI (GRAPHICARTIST2020@HOTMAIL.COM)

Author's Note

Dear Readers,

Several years ago, in between my other contracted books, I started writing *The Perfect Family*. Then, however, it was titled *A Mother's Story*. It didn't take me long to realize this tale was everybody's story, so the book was renamed. It also went through many iterations. Believe it or not, the first draft was in first person. The first three drafts didn't have a secondary storyline. And with each version, the characters kept getting more complicated and deeper, the plot more complex, and the themes more life-changing.

The reason for this is because what happens when a kid comes out to his parents is more complicated, deep, and complex than anyone can imagine. The disclosure doesn't have to be painful, but it does change a family's life. At least that's what happened to me. My son is gay and when he told us, all I wanted to do was assure him that I loved him and handle the situation well. I didn't know then it wasn't all up to me. Extended family, the church, school, the neighbors, best friends were all affected by his coming out and they affected our family during that time. The book isn't autobiographical. It's fiction. But many of the events in the story happened to us, or happened to families of other gay kids I knew. Some of it is gleaned from what I read after my son's disclosure. I don't think it should matter how much is true or not for our family because all of it is true for some gay teen, somewhere, who comes out.

I love this book with all my heart and soul because it tells a story I badly wanted to tell. I want the book to offer hope to teens and parents who are going through the situation we experienced. I want both teens and parents to learn something about the process. I want to alert people to the fact that with love, sincerity, honesty, and a little help from their friends they can experience the ups and downs of the coming-out process with grace, integrity, and hope. I think my family did it this way and I couldn't be prouder of them.

I hope you enjoy the book. You can contact me via e-mail at kshayweb@ rochester.rr.com to let me know your thoughts.

Or visit me online at:
www.kathrynshay.com
kathrynshay.livejournal.com
www.myspace.com/kathrynshay
www.facebook.com/pages/Kathryn-Shay-Fan-Page/241178789369

To get a free copy of a CD by the real person Jamie's character is based on, order *The Perfect Family* from www.BoldStrokesBooks.com and receive it with your order. Or check out www.kathrynshay.com/current. perfect.family.html for availability from the author.

Dedication

For my son Ben. I love you.

CHAPTER ONE

The Cancun sun sparkled on the surface of the Caribbean Sea while a cool breeze wafted off the water and played peek-a-boo with Maggie Davidson's dark hair. She struggled to tie it back, but the wind won.

"It's a lost cause, Mom. Put on your hat." Her son Brian bent over, picked up the straw monstrosity they'd bought at an open-air market, and handed it to her. Bronzed after only a few days on the island, he grinned down at her. His shoulders were as wide as his father's but he hadn't quite reached Mike's six-foot height.

"Thanks." She patted the chaise. "Sit a minute."

"Can't. I'm playing catch with Dad and Tim down on the beach. Gotta keep my arm in shape for my last season."

Brian was the star third baseman on his high school team and hoped to get a baseball scholarship to college. Before he took off, he kissed her cheek. He smelled like sunscreen and Maggie was hit with a memory—she and Mike and their best friends, Gretta and Tim Chandler, vacationing in Myrtle Beach every spring break. The adults had to physically corral all three small kids to coat them with lotion.

"Then go play with the guys."

As he swaggered off in a way that had girls falling at his feet, Maggie gave in to her nostalgia. The reminder of time passing was the impetus for this whole trip. She and Gretta wanted to bring their two families together before their now-grown children dispersed. Gretta's daughter Amber was in college and would graduate in May. In nine months, Brian would go off to a yet-undetermined university. Then after next year, Maggie's younger son Jamie would be on his way, leaving her and Mike empty nesters. Already.

Another shadow fell over her. "You okay, Mommykins? You got that, 'Oh, I wish they were little again' look on your face."

Ah, her intuitive child. Jamie seemed to know when something was bothering her. If she had a fight with Mike or a problem at work, he'd guess all was not well. Even when she was simply down in the dumps, Jamie sensed it.

In many ways, Maggie had a special affinity for him. He liked to do what she did—they went to plays in downtown Rochester, preferred the same movies, and recorded their favorite TV shows to watch together later. Interestingly, Brian and Mike frequented car shows, did weights in the basement, and went to sports events in the area. Their family was lucky, she'd always thought, that they could fill the kids' needs this way. It had never been a problem because, of course, Mike spent alone time with Jamie as she did with Bri. And the boys were each other's best friends.

"Mom. You're spacing out."

"I was thinking about when we used to go to Myrtle Beach all those years ago."

Lanky and slim, but with broad shoulders like all the Davidson men, Jamie flopped into the chaise next to her. His dark hair, thick and wavy, fell into his eyes. It was the exact color of hers. "This trip was an awesome idea. I *so* can't believe we're here on Christmas."

"It's the only week we could coordinate our schedules to get away."

"It's great, especially now that Brian's stopped sulking 'cuz he had to leave Heather."

Heather Barone was the pretty junior who'd become the love of her older son's life. Maggie liked the girl right away, and that hadn't changed in the two years she and Brian had been together.

Grasping Jamie's hand, she gave it a squeeze. "Didn't leave anybody special behind, honey?"

"You'll be the first to know." He dug into the backpack under Maggie's chair and drew out a slim book. "Wanna run my lines?"

She couldn't help but smile at the child of her heart. His stunning baritone and acting talent had scored him the lead roles in all the high school plays since his freshman year. Nothing made her happier than to hear her son belt out one of his solos. Mike and Brian went to every performance, every year to cheer Jamie on.

"I'd love to run lines with you."

"Let's start with scene two. Where they get to Brigadoon. You play Jeff." His dark eyes narrowed on the script. "Man, is this plot lame. An imaginary city. Falling in love in one day."

"But you enjoy playing Tom, don't you?"

Emotion flitted across Jamie's face—sadness, maybe? Periodically, she caught a glimpse of that look, but every time she asked him about it, he told her he was just being thoughtful. Though she believed intellectually it was better not to push him to reveal what he wasn't ready to talk about, as a mother, staying silent was hard. "Yeah, sure I do."

"Jame?"

His expression lightened. "Come on, let's do this. I'll even sing 'Almost Like Being in Love' for you."

They read lines for a half hour before Jamie said, "I'm good. I'll be off book easy when school starts again." He leaped out of the chair and grabbed her hand. "Come on, Mama, let's go ride some groovy waves," he joked.

Maggie wasn't crazy about waves, but the guys always tried to coax her into them. "Can't, I have to study." She nodded to the chair.

He frowned at the book, *Gender Issues In Society*. "What's this for?"

Maggie worked at Rochester Community College as a psychology professor. She'd taught there for twenty-two years and loved her job. "It's part of Psychology 102. We've added a unit on sexual orientation and gender identity."

"I didn't know you were teaching that stuff." His tone was odd.

"Don't think it's interesting?" she asked.

He shrugged. "Maybe to some kids. I'm all for live and let live."

"I believe that, too. But—"

With a man's strength, he tugged her up and started to drag her away. "No school talk, Mom." He held her hand all the way to the shore, where the sun was so searing it hurt to look at the water.

Gretta and Amber were waist deep in the ocean when she and

Jamie joined them. A wave whooshed up, knocking Maggie back. She was five-four and solidly built, but she fell down and sucked in a mouthful of salt water. She surfaced, coughing. "Yuck."

"Gotta plant your feet, Mom," Jamie yelled around cupped hands, just before another wave hit.

This time she came up sputtering, with hair in her eyes and seaweed tangled around her ankles. "Now you tell me."

Fifteen minutes later, Maggie begged off and she and Gretta trudged out of the Caribbean. Amber and Jamie jogged to the shore, retrieved the Styrofoam boards they'd left there, and dove back into the ocean. The two women detoured to the swim up bar and settled in pool lounges. As the water lapped around them, they clinked glasses and knocked miniature umbrellas askew. Gretta's blue eyes, framed by auburn hair, twinkled like jewels. "Merry Christmas, Mag."

"To you, too."

Maggie smiled over at the woman who'd been her best friend since they met at the college where they both taught. Maggie was the newbie in the psychology department and Gretta was a rookie in graphic arts. After a few years, Gretta quit teaching to start her own business. She ran a thriving art gallery in Rochester where she exhibited and sold her own work, as well as that of other local artists. They'd been as close as sisters for twenty-plus years and Maggie often mused if she could talk to Gretta for a half hour every day, she'd stay sane.

"This trip was a great idea, Gretts."

"Glad you came?"

"Yeah, even if my mother started World War Three over it."

"Gertrude Lorenzo is spending Christmas with her son Jimmy in Connecticut. And you did your duty by entertaining mom, sis, and baby brother at your house last week for a holiday. So no more bad thoughts."

If only it were that easy. Maggie was raised in a dysfunctional family, though the term hadn't been coined when she was growing up. Living with a chronically depressed mother and a never-at-home father with a gambling problem, all the Lorenzo children suffered from their parents' stern outlook and exaggerated self-absorption. That view had driven them so far as to disown their oldest child Caroline when she was eighteen and Maggie eight.

"Mags?"

"You're right. We're in paradise and I'm going to enjoy it."

The midday sun beat down, and as they sipped icy rum-rich piña coladas and caught a glimpse of their kids frolicking in the water, Maggie banished thoughts of her difficult upbringing, of the sister she'd lost, and concentrated on the much more pleasant here and now.

❖

"Oh, God, that feels good." Mike lay face down on a padded chaise while Maggie rubbed sunscreen on his back. As they were under a canvas awning that shielded them from the sun on the beach, she was also giving him a massage. Strong fingers dug into tight muscles, making him moan.

"I told you we didn't need to pay eighty bucks for an appointment with the salon masseuse." She leaned in closer and he could smell the salt and sea air on her skin. "I can finish the job up in the room, if you like."

"I'd like."

When she was done and moved to the other chaise, Mike stayed where he was, relishing the warm afternoon breeze drifting over his body. Maggie had worried about the expense of this trip, but he'd been determined to find the money in their budget. They didn't make as much as the Chandlers, and had college tuition looming, but as two full-time working spouses, he and Maggie could afford the break. And she and Gretta were right. This was probably one of the last vacations their two families would take together. The thought made Mike's heart knock hard inside his chest.

He heard the boys come up to them.

His older son said, "Man, we're wiped. We're going up to the room to crash."

"Speak for yourself, Mr. Jock. I'm ready to rock," Jamie put in.

Mike chuckled. He could picture his kids playfully socking each other in the arm, like he and his three brothers used to do. Contrary to Maggie, Mike had grown up a happy kid and adored his mother, father, and siblings. "Be sure to be ready by six for church."

"Church? Aw, come on, Dad, this is vacation." Brian's voice held a whiny edge.

"All the more reason to thank God for what we have."

A long pause, then Jamie said, "God wouldn't care if we missed once, Dad."

"I'd care."

Dead quiet.

He opened an eye to see the boys had gone still and Maggie was sitting in the chair, her shoulders stiff, her head angled, which was her signal that she was unhappy. Rolling over, he sat up and straddled the lounger. "What?"

The guys glanced at their mother. He hated when they did that, waited for her to intervene with him.

"I guess I agree with them. I think we could forgo Mass down here."

"Well, I'm on the other side of this issue, so how do we decide?"

"Three against one?" Jamie joked.

"I got a more powerful force with me, Jame."

Maggie sank back in her chair and sighed. Her hair was up in a knot on her head and bangs accented eyes that were now filled with a familiar resentment. But she said, "All right, if it's that important to you, I'll go."

He cocked a brow at the boys. They tried to let Brian and Jamie make their own decisions, but Mike encouraged them—Maggie called it pressure—to stay involved in the Catholic Church. His pastor, Father Pete, told him he was doing the right thing.

"I'll go, too." This from Brian.

"If I have to." Jamie's answer held a trace of bitterness, which Mike had come to expect in matters concerning the church.

"Then it's settled. Go sleep now. We'll wake you up in time to dress."

The boys headed to the hotel and Mike turned to his wife. Now her expression was inscrutable. "Thanks for backing me on this."

"I don't want to spoil our trip, Mike. But at some point, we need to talk about *this*."

"You're moving away from the Catholic Church." He'd found out inadvertently that one Sunday when he was away on business she'd attended a Unitarian church in downtown Rochester. They'd had a major fight about it, and the issue was still unresolved.

"So is Jamie."

"Because of *you*."

"No, because his rational thinking and liberal beliefs are in stark contrast to your church."

"It breaks my heart, Mag. I've been praying about it." He took her hand in his. It was soft, small, supple, like the rest of her. He loved every inch of this woman, even her faults. "But let's wait till we get home to hash this out." He ran his fingers over hers. "The guys are right about one thing. There's plenty of time for a nap before Mass."

She smiled like she had when they first met at SUNY Geneseo. She'd been running around the track and lost her footing. He'd come up behind her and saved her from falling. She joked that he'd continued that role all their lives together. They'd married as soon as they graduated, then moved back to Sherwood, a small town on the west side of Rochester, New York, where Mike had grown up, near his mother and father, her sister, and two hours away from her parents.

"Okay. Let's go up to the room and finish that massage."

"Music to my ears." He winked at her. "We were *so* right to get the boys their own rooms."

With a surge of energy, Mike bounded off the chaise and grabbed their towels and bag. He tugged Maggie up and she nestled into his chest. They made their way to the room, their differences forgotten in the warm glow of the Caribbean sun and anticipation of sexual closeness.

❖

The inside of the Mexican cantina could have been a Warner Brothers movie set. Jamie expected to see Brad Pitt saunter through the swinging doors and shuffle across the sawdust floors. The three-piece band played some Mexican sonatas, and the smell of free-flowing booze and cheap beer permeated the air. The place was packed with mostly people his own age and of varying ethnic backgrounds, but there were a lot of *gringos* here. Apparently, this bar was the hot spot for kids vacationing in Cancun. Amber sat at the table with him, her third shot of tequila in front of her. Brian had downed a shitload of those and had moved on to a pitcher of beer. As always, Jamie was the designated driver of the van their families had rented.

Amber motioned to Bri, who was dancing with a little Mexican beauty. "Heather isn't gonna like that."

Stretching his legs in front of him, Jamie shook his head. "I don't get him. He mooned over her for two days, and now he's drooling over some other hottie."

"It's the male gene, buddy." Amber, who was twenty-one, treated him and Brian like brothers because they'd been raised together. "Except for you. You been pretty tight with Julianne for years."

He sipped his Coke. "We're good friends."

"No romance in your life?"

"Maybe." He hated everybody drilling him about not dating. Hell, a lot of the kids he hung out with, from the play especially, hadn't hooked up with anybody either. "I don't kiss and tell," he said playfully.

"Hmm." Amber scanned the bar and Jamie watched her. Talk about a hottie. Her curly brown hair, currently with red highlights, framed a flawless face with slate blue eyes. "Hey, Jame, that *chica*'s eying you."

"Where?"

"By the wall. The one in the pink skirt."

The girl in question smiled at him. He smiled back. Her looks were classic—chiseled facial features, waist-length, midnight-colored hair—and Jamie could appreciate the package in a detached sort of way. She headed over when she caught him checking her out. He pasted on a grin.

"*¿Usted desea bailar?*" she asked. He didn't need Amber—who was majoring in Spanish—to translate for him.

"*Sí, señorita.*"

Jamie took her hand, escorted her to the floor and began to dance which, contrary to most guys, he was good at. The music relaxed him and soon he forgot that this was just another one of his performances.

❖

The Cancun airport was jam packed when they arrived Tuesday morning for the early flight home. Announcements over the PA system and the excited buzz of travelers filled the open space. Gretta's family had gone ahead of them in line. Maggie, Mike and the boys had shown their IDs and answered the standard questions. Then the computer at their counter had frozen and the guys went to sit while Maggie and Mike waited for the boarding passes and baggage claims to print out.

Sliding an arm around her, Mike tugged her close. His dark blond hair had been bleached by the sun, and his tan made his blue eyes stand out. "The vacation was great, wasn't it?"

She nosed into him, inhaling the familiar scent of his aftershave. Though there had been blips in the past week, she felt really close to him now. "It was nice having some alone time, too."

His chuckle was very male, warming her. "Four times in one week. It's been a while."

"Hmm. Nice." She let out a sigh. "Back to the real world."

He frowned over at the boys and Maggie tracked his gaze. Brian slouched on a chair next to Amber. "He had too much to drink last night." Mike's tone was worried.

"I know. We need to talk about that with him again."

"He drinks sometimes at home. He says he never drives, but it's a problem, Mag."

"A lot of kids drink, Mike. The most we can do is try to contain it. I hate to see him hung over like this, though."

"Serves him right." He nodded to Jamie, four seats down, headphones on, fiddling with his iPod. "Jamie didn't have any alcohol."

"I don't think he drinks at all." Mike stared at his other son. "In some ways, like that, I'm glad he's different from most kids. In other ways, I wish he wasn't."

"Be careful, Mike, you don't want him to know that you wish he wasn't who he is."

His face closed down. "If you're talking about the church, Mag, I have to be honest about what I want for him."

Maggie had some suspicions that he wanted Jamie to be different in more ways than his beliefs about church. Despite how close she and her husband were, there were some things they didn't talk about.

She stood on tiptoes to kiss his cheek. "Think about it, okay?" To change the subject—because this wasn't the place to get into any of that—she asked, "Did you check our voicemail at home?"

Mike pulled out a slip of paper out of his shirt pocket. "The dog sitter left a message saying she's bringing Buck home this morning." Their chow/shepherd mix who was a full-fledged member of the family.

"The boys missed him. I swear they would have brought him

along if they could have." She watched the man behind the counter fiddle with the computer. "Anyone call for me?"

"A Teresa DeAngelo."

"I don't recognize the name."

"She said you didn't know her, but she needed to talk to you, that it was personal."

"Huh. So she wasn't from school?"

"No, and she didn't leave a number for you to call her back. She said she'd phone you again."

They were distracted by a commotion at the ticket counter next to them, where apparently a computer was working. "I'm sorry, señor," the attendant said to a family of three she was waiting on. She glanced at the employee helping Mike and Maggie. "Could you come here a minute, Elena?"

Elena excused herself to assist her colleague.

Rapid Spanish rolled off the man's tongue. His wife, clearly distraught, clutched a baby to her chest. The parents weren't much older than Brian. Their attendant spoke to them gently, and the woman burst into sobs.

Elena returned.

Mike asked, "What's wrong?"

"Those poor people. They're going to visit family in America. Her father sent two tickets."

"And?"

"They need to pay for the little one. She's too old to ride for free." Elena shrugged. "No Happy New Year for them, I guess."

"They don't have the money?"

"No."

"Is a seat available?"

"Miraculously, one solo seat is available. We could shift people around, too, to get them together. But they'd have to pay."

Mike studied the family then he pulled out his Visa card. "I'll pay for the child's ticket."

The woman behind the counter dropped her pen. "Excuse me?"

"I said I'll pay for the third ticket."

Maggie watched her husband, her eyes misting. He was such a good man, an unselfish one. At times like this, all his flaws faded away.

Open mouthed, the attendant took Mike's card. "That's really nice of you." She went back to the other counter. Words were exchanged, and the father's head snapped up.

Mike nodded. "*Feliz año nuevo.*"

The man flushed and whispered in his wife's ear. She started to cry hard. "*Gracias tanto. Dios le bendice.*"

Mike acknowledged the blessing, took his card back, and grasped Maggie by the hand. "We have so much," he said.

Standing on tiptoes, she kissed his cheek. "Me, especially."

CHAPTER TWO

A few days after they returned from Cancun, Maggie headed into her office at the college to clean up some paperwork and prepare for the upcoming semester. She dumped her books and bag on a side table and sat behind her big maple desk. After being away from school for winter break, she took pleasure in her surroundings. A window overlooking the snow-covered trees behind the building allowed natural light to spill inside most of the day. High shelves stuffed with books she'd collected through the years flanked them. Potpourri in strategic places scented the air. Her life as a teacher had been fulfilling and rewarding and had formed much of her adult identity. Closing her eyes, she savored the moment of belonging and stability the room provided.

"Hey, sleeping on the job?" She looked up to see Damien Kane, also a psychology professor, in the doorway. His loose-limbed, rangy body slouched against the doorjamb, and his brilliant smile gave him oodles of charm. That, and the face of a movie star.

"I'm just enjoying the quiet time."

"I saw you come in." He held two cups. "And brought you coffee with a bit of cream, like you drink it."

Maggie shifted in her seat, disconcerted by how much Damien seemed to know about her preferences. Disconcerted *and* flattered, she had to admit. Gretta said he was interested in her, but he flirted with most of the women at RCC, so Maggie tried not to worry about the... intimacies he exhibited. "Um, thanks. Come on in."

Dropping down on the couch, he motioned her over. She sat next to him and accepted the cup. The coffee was hot, taking the edge off the chill of the January day in upstate New York. "Mmm."

"Obviously the Caribbean agrees with you. You look fantastic with that tan."

"Sun's bad for your skin. I tried to keep covered with lotion, but it washed off in the water."

He propped his feet up on the coffee table. "Isn't it funny how the things that are bad for you feel the best?"

She ignored his comment. Damien seemed to relish double entendres, and it was best not to give him any encouragement. "How's your vacation been?"

"So-so. I've got the girls this week." He was divorced and his daughters lived two hours away.

"Then why are you here?"

"Missy and Emma wanted to go to the mall. I dropped them off."

"Wouldn't kill you to traipse around with them."

"You think?"

"I do. Kids love it when you take part in their activities."

Steel gray eyes focused across the room. "I don't relate to them as well as you do to your boys."

"Start with the mall, Damien."

"Maybe. They want to go to some concert next month. I might be able to manage that."

"Sounds like a plan."

He trained his gaze on her. "So, was it all fun and frolic in Cancun?"

"Uh-huh. Mike got the rest he needed."

"The perfect husband and father took time for himself? I'm shocked."

Cocking her head, she asked, "What does that mean?"

"Just that he always seems to do the right thing, pays enough attention to you and spends time with the whole family. Do you ever fight?"

"Of course we do."

"About what?"

"How did we get into this?"

"I'm feeling nostalgic, I guess. I spent Christmas alone."

"I'm sorry."

"Maggie?" Her department head, Nancy Schultz, had come to the doorway. About forty-five, with unabashed ambition, Nancy wanted the chair post and had gone after it with verve. Maggie had voted for her. "I didn't know you were coming in today."

Glad for the interruption, Maggie stood. "I wanted to get a jump on paperwork and planning. Did you need to see me?"

"Yes, if you have time, I'd like to discuss some budget issues with you." She gestured to Damien. "I already corralled our Dr. Kane."

Damien, like some others at the community college, had a PhD. Maggie had settled for a master's degree when she'd gotten pregnant with Brian and then Jamie.

"When would you like to get together, Maggie?"

"I can do it now."

A scowl shadowed Damien's face, but he was his charming self when he stood and bade her and Nancy good-bye.

As Damien left, Maggie felt bad for him because he was alone. She thought about divorce and what it would be like to spend Christmas apart from her kids. She shivered with the prospect of that happening in the family she'd worked so hard to build, especially after the fight she and Mike had that morning about a church event she refused to go to.

"You okay?" Nancy asked.

"Yes, sure. Let's get to that budget."

❖

Holding a marker, Mike stood in front of a whiteboard on an easel in a meeting room of St. Mary's Catholic Church. As chair of the Contemporary Issues committee, he'd gathered the members around an oval oak table. Even in there, the smell of candle wax and incense from a funeral yesterday lingered. "As you know, Father Pete's asked us to come up with topics for discussion in the next six months, issues which the contemporary Catholic Church faces. We'll study the biblical basis for these areas, then branch out from the texts into analysis and our own opinions."

Father Pete, a tall, powerfully built man of about fifty-five, sat forward. "Remember, the purpose of these studies is to learn the church's stance on the issues which confront Catholic men and women today."

Anita Ruiz straightened to her five-two height. Her turbulent expression reflected an innate intensity. "I have a few questions."

"No surprise there," the woman next to her mumbled good-naturedly.

The group joked with her. Anita was a nurse for underprivileged kids in the city and a devout Catholic who struggled unendingly with some of the harsher stances the church took on contemporary issues. Yet she had one of the strongest faiths Mike ever encountered and he admired her for being able to balance both. Things tended to be black and white with him, especially about his religion, a fact Maggie constantly reminded him of when they disagreed.

"Go ahead, Anita."

"Who's going to interpret these passages from the Bible?"

"I will," Father Pete said firmly.

"And whatever you think they mean is what we have to agree with?"

"No, Anita," the priest added gently, though his gray brows were furrowed, "the church's stance on the issue is what we'll accept and talk about how to do God's will within her parameters."

Mike hitched a hip up on a table to the left. "What's your concern, Anita?"

"I've got a lot of them. One is how horribly women were treated in the Old Testament." She cited Hagar's suffering at the hands of Abraham's wife. She mentioned Lot's offering his virgin daughters to the men of Sodom. "I always worry in studies like these that we're going to conclude physical abuse is acceptable. Or prejudice is all right. That maybe because they're in the Bible, we have to allow them."

"I think everybody struggles with passages like that, Anita." Mike's own wife did, not that he faulted her for that specific questioning. "It's one of the reasons we're here. To gain more insight. Shall we keep that in mind and forge ahead?"

"All right."

"First, we'll brainstorm topics. Then we can vet them. We're hoping for five or six subjects, which would take us through June."

Lively discussion among the six men and ten women in the group followed. By nine, Mike felt filled with the spirit of God and exhilarated by the enthusiasm of the group. He surveyed his notes on the board. They had their work cut out for them: divorce, the place of women in the church, homosexuality, papal infallibility, and abortion had been chosen.

Father Pete gave the closing prayer. "Dear Lord, be with us in the coming weeks as we examine these issues. Holy Spirit, guide us to know Your word, Your meaning, and do the work of Your church. Help us to accept what the holy fathers hand down on matters of faith, even when it's difficult. Let us remember You are the most important one in our lives."

After the prayer, Craig Johnson approached Mike. A stocky man with a receding hairline, he was Mike's golf partner and best friend. The four of them—Maggie and Craig's wife Judy—socialized often, worked on church committees together, and spent time at school events, since they had a son Jamie's age. "Where's Maggie tonight?"

"She's not coming to the study group."

They'd fought about it that morning, and he regretted diminishing their vacation closeness…

How are you going to rectify these issues if you don't analyze their biblical basis?

Mike, you know I'll get angry when people say divorce is wrong, but annulments aren't. When they say homosexuality is a sin against God. And when they profess women have no right to make decisions about their own bodies. I don't believe in any of that.

As he'd told her in Cancun, Maggie was drifting from the church, and it nearly broke his heart. In some ways, he felt like he was being forced to choose between her and his God. Father Pete assured him that God wouldn't let that happen and that his role was to keep his wife in the fold.

Craig's expression was sympathetic. "I'm sorry. I know you wanted her here."

Mike's gaze rested on Judy, petite and blond, who was talking to Father Pete across the room. "You're lucky you're on the same page with your wife."

"Let's have dinner Friday night. Maybe we can bring Maggie up to speed."

Maggie would have a fit if all three of them ganged up on her, and besides, Mike would never put her in that position. "No to the latter. But dinner would be fun. Come to our house, I'll cook steaks. We'll relax and talk about politics and education."

Craig clapped him on the back. "I'll pray for her. And you."

"Thanks, we all need that."

Mike spent the drive home praying, too, for insight on how to handle this divisiveness between him and the woman he loved, next to God, more than anything else in the world.

❖

In Advanced Placement English two weeks after Christmas break, Jamie dragged his desk close to Julianne's to discuss the current topic Ms. Carson had assigned. "So, what did *you* think about why Othello believed Iago?"

His friend's hazel eyes sparked with fire. "He's a guy. His ego gets in the way and jealousy gets the better of him."

"Not all guys are like that, Jules."

"You, James Michael Davidson, are a breed of your own." She meant it as a compliment, but once again hearing how different he was annoyed him. "What do you think?"

Jamie shrugged. "Othello feared Desdemona would reject him, so Iago could convince him she was unfaithful and ready to do just that. People are so afraid of rejection, they don't think straight. And they do stupid things because of it."

Flushing, she tried to be nonchalant. "People get rejected all the time."

For the life of him, Jamie couldn't figure out girls. Julianne was probably referring to the popular jock who'd asked her out, strung her along, and then broke up with her a couple of months later because she wouldn't put out for him. She'd convinced Jamie to fill in for her deadhead boyfriend and take her to the Junior/Senior Valentine's Ball next month.

Jamie had been staring into space and brought himself back to the present. "Some rejections are worse than others."

Frowning, Julianne leaned toward him and grasped his arm. "You okay, Jame? What were you thinking about?"

"Seems to me family rejection would be the worst. If your friends turn on you, I think you can accept it. But if your parents and family reject you, can you bounce back from *that*?"

"As if that would ever happen to you. You've got the best parents in the world."

Jamie's smile didn't come easily. His insecurities always came out at times like this. He thought of his mom, how much he liked her as a person, loved her as his mother. She'd been his unconditional supporter all his life. What would he do if he ever lost that? He wasn't sure he could survive. "It happened with my mom's family. They kicked her older sister out because she married a divorced man."

"You never told me that."

Because Julianne was a fundamentalist Christian, sometimes Jamie had a hard time talking to her. In the last year, she'd gotten even stauncher in her conservative views. "It never came up."

"No matter what, Jame, you'll never be rejected by God."

"Never?"

"Well, not if you're sorry for your sins."

"What—"

Ms. Carson asked for everybody's attention. "Let's come back into the circle and hear what you think about the Moor's reaction to Iago."

After a general class discussion, the teacher handed back their journals. "I enjoyed these. I wrote my responses on the ones I could read. A reminder: only four assignments per month can be confidential. Here's the list of this week's topics."

She gave the papers to Jamie, who sat next to her. As the sheets went around, Ms. Carson bent over so only he could hear her. "Can you stay a minute after class?"

English was the last period of the day. "Yeah, sure. I have a quick blood drive meeting"—he was in charge of the school-wide collection that year—"then play practice, but not until three."

While the kids put the chairs in rows, Paul, one of Jamie's friends who played the villain in *Brigadoon*, came up to him. "Wanna run some lines before practice?"

"I gotta talk to Ms. C first."

"We'll meet you in the cafeteria."

Jamie watched Paul walk out the door and meet up with Nick. The two guys were gay. They didn't announce it, but had confided in close friends like Jamie. And they never said they were together—Jamie thought they were, but pretended they were just buddies. They'd be harassed if they came out as a couple, even today when there were laws against discrimination. Sometimes the little town of Sherwood seemed to exist in another time period, a lot like Brigadoon.

When the classroom emptied, Jamie sat on top one of the desks. "What's up?" he asked Ms. Carson.

"You had another private entry."

"Yeah. My limit for the month."

"How come, Jame? This unit seemed to make you go more into yourself."

His heart started to beat fast. He liked Ms. Carson a lot—so did all the kids, even Brian, who had her for an English Comp class. Every year she was voted the favorite teacher in silly polls the seniors took. Some of the guys had a crush on her. Jamie didn't, but he thought he might be able to confide in her. "I know I've been more into myself." He shrugged. "Stuff has started coming up for me."

She touched his shoulder. "I'm a good listener. Can I help?"

"How?"

"We could start by letting me read those entries."

Fear batted against his chest and he glanced away. "Maybe."

"It makes you nervous for me to do that."

"Uh-huh."

"Then we should wait if you're not ready."

"No, maybe you're right. Can I have time to read them over again? I think I want you to see them, but I gotta be sure."

"I'll go to the teachers' caf to get a Coke. Take your time. Do you want a drink?"

"No, I'm good."

Which was a lie. His pulse was beating a wild tattoo.

After Ms. C left, Jamie picked up his journal, the cover decorated with all his favorite indie bands. Often, he wrote poetry in it because the format helped him to get his feelings out better, to not bullshit himself. The last four entries were in verse.

He scanned the first. Reread the second, as it was more revealing.

Free to Be You and Me

When we were little
Mom read a book aloud to us.
In it kids could be who they are.
William could have a doll
And you didn't have to marry a prince.

She said all people
Were meant to be free,
Men and women fought for it.
Died for it.
Countries split apart
For people's rights.

Even the bird, the whale, the tiger
Have a freedom I don't have.
Why?

Anger gives way to fear
And I don't act.
Yet.

Ah, the all purpose yet.
It should be soon.
It will be soon.

But an inner voice recants,
I *hope* it will be soon.

Swallowing hard, Jamie read the last two poems, which went even
further, which revealed more things he'd never told anybody, not even
his mother. But down deep, Jamie knew when he'd written the entries,
he'd wanted Ms. Carson to read them. Telling her could be like a dress
rehearsal.

She returned in five minutes. "All done?"

"Yeah."

Crossing to her desk, she leaned against it and sipped her drink. "You don't seem like you really want to let me read the entries, Jame."

"No, I do. Honest. Besides, you said during the war unit that the best time to do something is when it's hard for you."

"How smart I am." Smiling, she held out her hand, and it took more courage than David facing Goliath to give his journal to her.

"I'll read what you wrote now. Want to come back after practice?"

"It'll be about five."

"This is important, so I can hang around. Besides, I have papers to grade."

"Five it is." He stood. "I gotta go."

"Jamie, don't worry. I care about you." She did, he knew that. "And I don't judge."

"Gotcha. See you later."

Jamie stepped out of the classroom, and amidst the crowds of kids jostling each other and talking loud, he tried to be cool. But heading down the hall, the fear he was talking to Julianne about caught up with him and he hoped like hell he hadn't just made a big mistake.

❖

Sweat poured off Brian's face as he lay on the bench and hefted the barbell above his head. A fifty-pound weight loaded down each end. Even his hands were slippery beneath his workout gloves.

"Come on, Davidson, go for the burn. One more." His friend Tony Simonetti spotted from the side.

Grunting, Brian did one last rep. The weights clanged as Tony helped hook the bar into its holder. Brian collapsed into the bench, breathing hard.

His buddy glanced from side to side, then bent over low. "If you'd take some of that juice Cummings got for us, this wouldn't be so brutal."

"Eric Cummings is an asshole." The guy did have muscles, but not from hard work. "And you're a fool if you take that stuff."

"Maybe. I'm not sure yet."

Once in a while, Brian thought about using steroids. A lot

of athletes were into them. When he told his brother what he was considering, Jamie dug up some research that scared the shit out of Brian. Heart trouble. Liver damage. But shrunken testicles sealed the deal. He wasn't messing around with his balls.

A whistle sounded from Coach Perkins. Coach was so cool. He shaved his head and wore sweats all day. Brian thought he might want to be a PE teacher, too.

At the signal, Brian headed to the next station. This time he was paired up with Luke Crane. "How's the shoulder?" Brian asked.

"Better. I'm gonna be able to start on opening day."

Luke was a nice guy, the pitcher on their baseball team and valedictorian of the class. The girls hung around him all the time because of his dark blond hair and delicate features, though his body was way more pumped than anyone else's. When Brian joked once to Jamie that Luke was almost pretty, Jamie had told him not to be such a tool.

Brian pointed to the weights. "You wanna go first?"

"Yeah." Spreading his legs, Luke positioned his arms and Brian loaded a barbell with more pounds than he himself could handle. Luke grunted through four squats.

"That's enough, Luke, don't kill yourself."

"Gotta get to five." His face was red and his mouth pinched tight but he didn't stop. Man, the guy was driven.

After they finished and showered, Brian put on jeans and his Sherwood High sweatshirt, hurried out of the gym area and headed down to the locker he shared with Heather. She had cheerleading practice and finished about the same time as him. He found her bending over with her cute fleece-covered butt stuck in the air. Seeing nobody was around, he crept up behind her and palmed her cheeks. She startled, then said, "Is that you, Luke?"

"Like hell. Crane would never move in on me."

Heather straightened and when she faced him, her hair bobbed in its ponytail and her dark eyes sparkled in delight. "Hi, guy."

His heart flip-flopped in his chest. Not only did she give him a boner by just looking at him, but she made him feel all warm and fuzzy inside. "Hey, beautiful." He kissed her on the mouth. "Hmmm."

She drew back when they heard a noise down the hall. Brian turned and saw Jamie approaching.

"Get a room!" his brother said when he reached them.

Brian told him to fuck off, then playfully socked him in the arm. "Need a ride?"

They shared a Prius hybrid, which his mom's brother, Uncle Jimmy, had given them when he'd bought a newer model. Jamie was really into the environmental stuff, too, but Brian never gave it much thought.

"No, thanks. I gotta go over some songs with Ms. Marlo as soon as she finishes with the dancers. I'll hitch a ride with somebody else. See ya later."

Brian shrugged into his coat and was waiting for Heather to do the same when he saw Luke Crane come around the corner and bump into Jamie. They stood and talked for a few minutes and Luke smiled. The guy didn't do that a lot, was always real serious. But Jamie had that effect on everybody. He made people happy, and it was a talent Brian admired in his brother.

❖

"Sorry," Jamie said when he bumped into Luke Crane in the hallway. "I wasn't watching where I was going." Because he was thinking of how he hadn't told Brian about his meeting with Ms. Carson.

Luke gave a half-smile, revealing a dimple Jamie never noticed before. "Me, either. I was thinking about something else."

The guy looked totally cool. He'd obviously just showered and his dark blond hair, short and spiked, was damp. The blue of his sweatshirt accented his eyes. He was bigger than Jamie with broader shoulders and a hell of a lot more muscle.

Jamie shifted his backpack from one arm to the other. "Have a good practice?"

"Yeah." Luke stuck his hands in his pockets and leaned against the wall of lockers. "I hurt my shoulder last year, but it's back in shape."

"Bri told me. Glad it's better." Duh, he sounded like a dunce. Why couldn't he think of something interesting to say? "I don't know how you do it, star pitcher and valedictorian of the class. You make it seem easy."

"That's all a performance."

Interesting choice of words. "What do you mean, Luke?"

The guy's face blanked. "Nothing. It was a dumb thing to say. Speaking of performances, I hear you're the lead again in this year's play. Brian brags about you all the time."

"Thanks. I love acting. I think I might do it out in the world, you know, someday."

"That's great, Jamie. That you do what you want to."

"Don't you?"

Luke's blue eyes filled with sadness and he shrugged as if to say, "I wish."

"There you are."

Jamie startled at the intrusion. He saw Kiki Jones, Julianne's best friend, come up behind Luke. Her reddish hair fell in soft waves around her face and she had delicate features. She greeted Jamie, then said to Luke, "I've been waiting at my locker for you." She sidled in front of him and gave him a kiss on the mouth. A long one.

Luke pulled away, his face red as he darted a glance at Jamie.

Jamie cleared his throat. "I'll leave you two love birds alone."

"Nice talking to you, Jamie," Luke said as Kiki slid her arm through his. "Really."

"See you later."

Jamie hurried down the hall, his stomach in knots. Kiki Jones was pretty and popular. She'd been voted queen for last year's Junior Prom and everybody thought she was hot. Why should Luke be an exception?

Sighing, Jamie went out the side door and was glad for the cool winter air. He'd walk around the building to the auditorium so he could get his head on straight. By the time he got to practice, he'd fall right into the role of Tom. He thought of what Luke said about performances and realized how little people knew about each other.

And he wondered what was going on in Luke Crane's head.

CHAPTER THREE

Wearing a jet-black tux with a blue cummerbund to match Heather's dress, Brian stood in the doorway to Jamie's room and leaned against the jamb. His brother's space smelled like incense. Brian noted the framed pictures on the bookcase, in front of tons of books on the shelves. One whole row was of Greek mythology, which his mother used to read to them when they were little and Jamie still dug. On the bed was a spread their dad had brought back from Mexico. Now their dog Buck slept on it, snoring like hell. The stuff in Jamie's room wasn't to Brian's taste. His own was full of trophies and sports posters—with the slugger Willie Mays in the place of honor—but hey, Brian had always accepted Jamie for who he was.

Yet he had to be big brother sometimes so, as Jamie yanked on the tie he was trying to fix, Brian said, "You can be such a dweeb."

Jamie dropped his hands. "Who the hell invented these? I just got the hang of a bow tie, now guys are wearing ascots. It's nuts. This whole prom thing is."

Brian crossed to Jamie and stood before him. "Here, let me do it." He wiggled his eyebrows suggestively. "Heather says I got magic fingers."

Brian wrestled with the soft green material of Jamie's tie. Tonight was the Valentine's Ball and everybody went to it, including his prom-phobic brother. "What are you doin' afterward?" he asked Jamie.

"Coming back here with the kids from the play. We rented all three installments of *The Lord of the Rings.*"

"Jamie, Jamie, Jamie. Have I taught you nothing? After the prom is *not* a time for movies."

Jamie rolled his eyes.

"There you go."

"Thanks." Jamie faced the mirror. "Where you going after?"

Following suit, Brian stood next to him in the glass. Even in appearance they were different: one dark, one light; one muscular, one slender but solid. "*We're* going to the lake."

"No surprise there." Jamie snorted. "Don't have to ask what you'll be doing."

Brian waited a second. "Can I ask you a question?"

Jamie shrugged.

"Why aren't you taking somebody you like to the dance?"

"I like Julianne."

"No, I mean a girl you'd make out with."

"Nobody's on the radar screen yet."

"Never has been, Jame."

Jamie went to his desk, got his wallet and checked inside. "Whatever." He slanted his brother a glance. "We're not all sex-crazed maniacs like you."

"I love Heather. I'm not in it for the sex."

"Yeah, I know." Jamie's tone turned serious.

"Though it's a perk."

Brian shared a lot with Jamie. They'd had their first cigarettes together. He'd told Jamie when he and Heather finally got horizontal. And they both hated the same French teacher. But some stuff he didn't tell his brother, like the pot he had stashed under his bed. He wondered what Jamie wasn't telling him.

"Did you know Grandma Lorenzo wanted to come tonight so she could see us all dressed up?" Jamie asked. "Aunt Sara was going to go to Cornwall to get her, but Grandma got sick."

"Which is good luck for us."

One of their similarities was their dislike of their maternal grandmother. Because she'd had such a tough time growing up, his own mom drilled into them the importance of family. Brian believed nothing would ever come between him and his brother.

"I'm glad Grandma Lucy and Grandpa BJ are here tonight, though," Jamie said. "They enjoy these things."

"Yeah, and they'll slip us a twenty before we leave."

"Definitely a bonus." Jamie stuffed his wallet in his back pocket. "I guess I'm all set."

"Lookin' good, bro."

"Back at ya."

"Come on, Buck," Jamie called to the dog, who roused and leapt off the bed.

As they started out, Brian grabbed Jamie's arm. "Jame, what I said before about having a girlfriend. I didn't mean, you know, to hurt your feelings."

For a minute, his brother's jaw tightened. "I know, Bri. But I'm down with it. For now, anyway."

"Whatever works for you."

"Let's go before everybody gets here."

Eight couples and their parents were coming to the Davidsons' house to take pictures before the dance. Their pre-prom party wasn't as big and fancy as the ones the Lewises had before the spring balls, but it would be fun. "Mom can get her crying and her 'oh I can't believe you're my babies' over before everybody gets here."

"Poor Mom. She's so sensitive."

"Yeah, I know."

One behind the other, they left Jamie's bedroom, bathed in a feeling of brotherhood and acceptance.

❖

"It's lovely, dear. The spread you put out."

"Thanks, Mom." A sturdily built woman with Mike's smile and a mass of gray curls, Lucy Davidson was the perfect mother-in-law. Though Lucy and BJ had moved to a small lake house two years ago, it was only a half hour away. They got to share in all the boys' events and were an integral part of Mike and Maggie's lives.

"You seem a bit distracted."

"Do I?" She'd been thinking about her talk with Jamie yesterday when he picked up his tux.

You don't seem happy about the Valentine's Ball, honey.

I think proms are lame.

Then why are you going?

Julianne needed a date. Her ex was supposed to take her, so I'm the understudy.

Honey, do you want to talk about anything?

Nope, let's go watch Lost *instead.*

The doorbell rang. "I'll get it," Lucy told her. "You finish with the hors d'oeuvres."

Gretta, who came to every pre-prom event for the boys, as Maggie had done with Amber, brought in more ice from the garage. "I have the punch all ready."

"Thanks. You've been a big help."

She joined Maggie at the counter, setting the bag down with a thud. "Hard to believe, isn't it, the boys are so grown-up."

"In some ways I hate it."

Gretta laughed. "I did, too. With Amber. But we gotta let them go, Mags."

"Easier said than done. You sobbed when Amber left for college."

"So did you. We're a pair." She pointed to the last of the cheese appetizers Maggie was preparing. "Those look great."

Since the ball included dinner at six, this four o'clock repast consisted of light finger food and chocolate-covered strawberries, which smelled decadent. Vowing to not feel nostalgic about the boys growing up, going away, and instead enjoy the night, Maggie smiled at her friend. "I've got to get these out."

"Go ahead, I'll put this ice on the soda in the cooler."

Maggie took the last of the trays to the dining room, where she found Judy Johnson, Craig's wife, rearranging the dishes.

"Tyler's handsome tonight, Judy. And that date of his? Absolutely beautiful."

"I can't believe…" Judy averted her gaze and swiped at her eyes.

Setting down the food tray, Maggie circled the table and slid her arm around her friend. "You okay?"

"It was five years ago. But it seems like yesterday we thought we were going to lose him." She waved her hand in front of her face. "I'm sorry, I'm a mess."

"I don't know if you ever get over a life-threatening illness in your child."

Shakily, Judy drew in a breath. "He had a checkup a few weeks ago. No signs of the leukemia. He doesn't have to go back for a year."

"That's wonderful."

"I thank God every day for it." She shook her head. "And apologize for not having faith that Tyler would be well again."

"I think God would understand."

Judy shrugged off the mood. "Let's change the subject. Your boys are as gorgeous as ever."

Maggie's gaze traveled through the kitchen to the family room. Jamie and Julianne stood in front of the fireplace talking with some school friends. Brian was over in a corner, his arm around Heather.

"What other parents are coming?"

"The Simonettis and the Cranes."

"None of Jamie's friends?"

"No, a group of them are going stag but they didn't want to come for pictures."

Fussing with the centerpiece, an arrangement of blue and white carnations she'd brought, Judy was thoughtful. "We don't know the Cranes well."

"Luke's on Brian's baseball team, though they hang out in different crowds. But his date, Kiki Jones, is Julianne's best friend. I think that's why they're here."

Another peal of the bell. This time, Maggie headed to the foyer to answer it. On the porch were Dr. and Mrs. Lucas Crane. "Hi. Come on in."

Both tall and slender, Lucas wore a meticulous suit and Erin a fur-trimmed coat. She handed Maggie some roses.

"Nice to see you again." The couples ran into each other on occasion at baseball games.

"Thanks for the flowers."

They made small talk while Maggie hung up coats, then she led them to the back of the house, noticing Mike was in the den off the foyer where he'd gone with his father. She called out, "We've got guests, honey."

"Be right there."

❖

Mike occupied the big padded desk chair while his father lounged in a recliner and scratched Buck's head. Mike hadn't seen his dad in a while because BJ had been in Florida with one of Mike's brothers for a month, so they'd come into the den for a few private words after his parents arrived for the prom pictures.

Mike was tall like his dad, but more muscular. Brian had inherited his looks, too. BJ said, "Can't believe the boys are at this point in their lives."

His father spent a lot of time with both his grandsons but was closest to Brian, who was named after him. Once, when Mike's dad broke his arm, Brian went out to their house several times a week, even when he had practice, to help with the chores. His parents never missed one of Brian's games unless they were out of town.

Lucy, on the other hand, doted on Jamie, and he returned her affection. Last year when she'd had surgery, Jamie went to visit her while she was laid up at home. She bemoaned the sorry state of her finger and toe nails because she'd missed her biweekly pedicure and manicure. Jamie excused himself, drove to the drugstore, came back with nail polish, and painted her nails. He said it was one of the few times he'd seen his grandma cry. God bless him, he couldn't figure out why.

"Feeling nostalgic?" his dad asked.

"Very. They'll both be gone soon."

"Some people like it when their kids go to college."

Mike scowled. "I can't imagine *any* benefit from having the boys out of this house."

"I couldn't either. Every time one of you left, I felt like I lost a limb." BJ shrugged. "It's not all bad, though. There are perks to an empty nest, you know."

"You and Mom have a full life."

"Well, we miss your brothers and sisters. But we love having you nearby. You're busy, too, with church, with your friends."

"Yeah." He told him about the Contemporary Issues group.

"Hmm."

"What?"

"That pastor of yours is conservative." Mike had grown up in Sherwood, and all his family had attended St. Mary's. But Father Pete had come to the parish after his parents moved to the lake.

"I agree with his views, Dad."

"Sometimes that scares me."

"Why?"

A knock on the door. Brian peeked his head in. "We're gonna leave in fifteen, Dad. Picture time." He grinned. "Come on, Grandpa. I want one of you and me."

BJ stood and clapped his namesake on the back. "My pleasure, young man."

Mike got the camera out of the drawer and headed for the living room. He caught a glimpse of Maggie in the kitchen, shot her a smile, and took his place in line with the other parents.

First the couples. Wide angle...snap.

Then the girls. "Aw, come on, show some leg," Brian teased.

Finally the boys. They were too far apart, and Mike made them move close. Tony Simonetti quipped, "Keep your hands to yourself, guys. No gay stuff."

Mike didn't like the remark, and Jamie was frowning when the picture was taken.

Finally the kids donned coats and herded out the door.

In the living room, Mike asked, "Now that they're gone, who would like a drink?"

Everyone but the Cranes. Dr. Crane had been checking the time for the last ten minutes. "Sorry you can't stay," Maggie said to them as she and Mike escorted the couple to the door.

Erin pulled her coat tight around her. "Some other time."

Luke's father gave a stiff good-bye.

Mike closed the door. "Chilly."

"Luke seems like a nice boy."

Back in the family room, after everyone had been served drinks, they toasted. "To our children. Ah, to be young again."

❖

At ten o'clock in the downtown Convention Center, Brian came up to Jamie with his coat in his hand. The band had taken a break, and they could finally hear each other talk. "We're going outside on the balcony. Wanna come?"

"You'll freeze your asses off."

"That's part of the fun. Makes the girls cuddle."

"No thanks." He angled his head across the room. "Jules is in deep discussion with Eric Cummings, and I need to keep an eye on her. The guy brought another date and she's still talking to him."

"That's right. He asked her out a while ago, then dumped her. Never could figure that whole thing out."

"He's a loser."

"He's hot for Heather, too. There she is…gotta go." Brian headed off.

At least his brother wasn't drinking. Nobody was allowed outside during the proms, except on the wraparound balcony, which was chaperoned. Kids who were busted with booze suffered major repercussions. Brian wouldn't risk his baseball career for that, at least not here. Maybe at the lake. He wondered if the other guys would drink up there. Would Luke Crane?

Julianne, dressed in a pretty sage-colored dress, rose from the table and came toward Jamie. Her cheeks were flaming and her eyes were wet. He pulled her behind a pillar and hugged her.

"I'm sorry. I shouldn't have talked to him."

"Want me to go beat him up?"

"Oh, yeah, Mr. Pacifist." She swiped at her cheeks. "I must look awful."

"You need to fix your makeup." He smoothed a hand down her hair. It was soft and curled around her face. The other girls had theirs sprayed and set like concrete. He liked Julianne's natural.

Kiki appeared at Julianne's side. "Jules? What happened?"

"Come to the ladies' room with me. I'll tell you then."

Jamie watched them go. His throat got all tight, like he had a sock stuffed in it. He leaned against the pillar and jammed his hands in his pockets, wishing he was going to the lake with all of them, wishing he could be…

"Having fun?"

Luke's deep voice startled Jamie, and he pivoted. Dressed in a dark tux, Luke wore red accents to match Kiki's dress. They were definitely a couple tonight.

"It's okay. You?"

"I'm not crazy about proms."

"Me, either. You look great, though." Hell, why had he said that? Guys didn't say stuff like that to other guys.

"You, too, Jamie." Luke's gaze was direct, intense, and it made Jamie fidget. But he couldn't break the eye contact.

Finally Luke glanced in the direction the girls had gone. "Julianne all right?"

"Cummings keeps stringing her along."

"He's a complete prick. You should have heard him in math class the other day. Mr. Granberry shot him down, but Jesus, he mocks everybody, from queers to girls to black people."

Jamie's hands fisted. He said, "I gotta get some air," pushed off the pillar, and made his way outside to a deserted section of the balcony with a view of the city. The night air felt cold on his heated skin. Damn it, he had no idea Luke was a bigot. He actually thought...

"What'd I say?"

Surprised that Luke had followed him out, Jamie glanced over at the guy. He should lie to Luke like he did to everybody else. But fuck it, he was so tired of pretending. So tired of covering up who he was.

And Ms. Carson had said, *I'm not telling you what to do, Jame, but keeping secrets can make you sick. I know, I've seen it up close.*

Luke asked again, "Jamie, what did I do wrong?"

Okay, he'd do this, but he couldn't look at Luke, so he stared at the Rochester skyline. Gripping the balcony so hard it hurt, he blurted out, "You could start with your use of the term 'queer.'"

A long, long silence. Great, now he'd done it.

Then he felt Luke's hand on his shoulder. Strong, muscular fingers practically seared through Jamie's tux to his skin. "Gay people get to use terms like 'faggot' and 'queer' and nobody can say anything about it."

Jamie's whole body sagged and he felt his eyes sting. Had the time finally come? Circling around, he lifted his chin. On the heels of his relief, something big and rich and potent shot through him. He'd never felt the bolt of lightning-like attraction before. Staring at the cool guy before him, who'd just made his own huge revelation, Jamie's stomach played leapfrog with his emotions. "How'd you know?"

Luke's face was shining with the same feelings churning inside Jamie. And right out there in the open, his hand moved to Jamie's biceps and rubbed up and down. "Same way you knew about me."

Jamie swallowed hard.

"I'm right, aren't I?" Now Luke's voice was throaty, turned on, too, Jamie hoped.

His heart galloping, Jamie took the biggest step of his life so far. "Yeah, you're right."

CHAPTER FOUR

The Monday after the Valentine's Ball, Maggie was sitting on the bed with a book in her hand and watching the president on television—she'd volunteered for his campaign in the last election—when the house phone rang. Since everyone else was out, she was tempted to let it go, but ultimately decided to pick up the extension on one of the shelves of the headboard. "Hello."

A hesitation on the other end. At first, she thought it was one of those irksome computer-generated calls, but then a real voice came across the lines. "Maggie Davidson?"

"Yes, this is she."

"Did you used to be Maggie Lorenzo?"

An ominous feeling went through Maggie, making her tense. "Yes. Who is this?"

"Did you grow up in Cornwall, New York?"

"I'll answer that after you tell me who you are." The woman's voice was soft and hesitant, but her questions disconcerted Maggie.

"My name is Teresa DeAngelo."

"You called when I was in Cancun."

"On Christmas Day."

"Do I know you, Teresa?"

It sounded like the woman took a deep breath. "No, but I know you. Or at least I know of you."

"How?"

"I'm your sister Caroline's daughter."

Maggie dropped the phone. It fell onto the dark green and blue quilt. How many years had she waited for this contact? She took a deep breath to control the swell of emotion inside her.

Finally she picked up the phone. "I'm sorry, this is a shock." Then a thought hit her, making her mouth go dry. "Oh, no, is Caroline…isn't she well?"

"Not like you mean. Mom's alive and physically fine. I know you haven't seen her in years."

"Thirty-seven. I haven't seen her in thirty-seven years." Since the day Caroline was forced out of the Lorenzo household and left Maggie behind with the fallout.

"I know why she didn't contact you," Teresa went on, "but why didn't you ever find us?" Now Caroline's daughter sounded bitter. "Mom said you two were close."

Maggie cleared her throat. "I was eight when she left, so of course I was powerless then. Even in high school and college, there wasn't any Internet, so I had no way to conduct a search for her."

"What about when you got older?"

"I got married in the eighties and my husband hired a private detective. But by that time there was no trace of Caroline. Teresa, we didn't even know the name of who she married. She never told us."

"I guess I understand."

"Please, tell me why you're calling. How is Caroline?"

"Not good, Maggie. Not good at all."

❖

Mike arrived home after a grueling budget meeting at work. His wife wasn't in the kitchen so he climbed the stairs and found her sitting on their bed, phone in hand, a bereft expression on her face. "Mag, what's wrong?"

She lifted the phone. "You won't believe this."

"Is it the boys?"

"No, they're fine." Shaking her head, she seemed mystified. "Remember a Teresa DeAngelo called over the holidays?"

Relieved, he sank down on the bed. "Yeah, I forgot all about it." He glanced at the phone. "Did she call again?"

"Yes. Oh, Mike, she's my niece. She's Caroline's daughter."

Knowing how badly his wife had been hurt by the events in her childhood and how it had affected her adult life, he grasped her hands. "Your sister Caroline?"

Maggie nodded.

"Wow, this is a surprise." Shock was more like it. "What happened to her?"

"She married the divorced man she told my parents about and had one child. By Teresa's account, they were a happy family and had a good life." Maggie shook her head and smiled. "She's a teacher like me."

"Oh, sweetheart."

"I'm thrilled she was happy all those years. I missed her so much and worried about her."

"I know." He waited. "Why did her daughter call now?"

"Because Caroline's husband, the love of her life according to Teresa, died a few days before Christmas. He was quite a bit older than she, and Caroline's been depressed. Her daughter's worried and decided to call her family."

"So they knew what happened to you?"

"Yes, apparently Caroline knew I was married, had kids. Even where I lived."

"That's more than we could find out about her."

"Because we didn't know her last name or the identity of her husband. Actually, I still don't. Teresa wasn't very forthcoming with details."

"Did she say why Caroline never contacted you? You were so close."

Mike's comment was an understatement. Caroline had been more of a mother to Maggie than Gertrude Lorenzo was. And when her older sister left, Maggie's world had been turned upside down.

"No. She said Caroline should talk to me about all that."

"What did Teresa want, honey?"

"Help with her mother. Who, by the way, doesn't know her daughter called me."

"In any case, it's good news. What's next?"

"Teresa's going to tell Caroline we talked. I told her I wanted, very much, to see my sister. I'd fly out there, meet her anywhere. Or she could come here."

Smiling at his wife's excitement, Mike smoothed a hand down her hair. "I'm so happy you've found her."

And, he thought with a sudden burst of inspiration, maybe God was at work here. One of the reasons Maggie had such trouble with the Catholic Church was because the Lorenzos' pastor had been the one to advise her parents to disown Caroline if she went through with the marriage to a divorced man.

Suddenly Maggie's eyes widened. "Oh, Lord, Mike, my mother will have a fit."

"Maybe not. Maybe she regrets what happened and will want to see her oldest daughter."

"That would be a miracle."

He gave her a half-smile. "God does provide those once in a while."

"You know, I always wondered why God deserted Caroline."

"Oh, honey, He didn't."

Maggie stared at him.

"And as far as your mother's concerned, you're forgetting what your counselor said. She can't hurt you anymore if you don't let her."

"You're right."

Mike hoped he was. He hoped and prayed that having Caroline in their lives now was a gift, not a burden, one that might help Maggie forgive a church that took Caroline away from her in the first place.

❖

Despite the snow drifting outside, the atmosphere in Maggie's Psych 102 classroom was warm and bright, with its wall of windows letting in an unusual February sun. Her students normally sat in a circle in the spacious area, but today they were scrunched in front where Maggie had displayed birth-order characteristics on a screen. Maggie had taught this lesson before, but the content had more meaning for her this year.

After about five minutes of allowing the kids to complete their individual tasks, she said, "Time's up. Who wants to share what they've written?"

Susan Blakely, a petite brunette, sweet and smart as a whip, waved her hand. "Me, Mrs. Davidson."

Crossing to the girl, Maggie handed her an eraser. Props helped keep this group, which tended to be talkative and rowdy, in line. The only person allowed to speak was the one in possession of the eraser.

"I'm the oldest," Susan began. "I think some of the traits up there are insulting. I don't feel neglected, and I don't always have to be right."

"Not all the traits are going to apply, Susan. As I said at the start of class, this is a psychological theory we need to assess. Is there any trait up there that does fit you?"

"Yeah, I guess. I do feel responsible a lot of the time. My mom worked and I took care of the littler kids a lot."

Maggie thought of Caroline, who'd bought the Lorenzo children's clothes, purchased Christmas presents for them, and signed school notes when their mother couldn't get out of bed.

But today, at the memory, instead of the hollowness she used to feel when she taught this part of the lesson, an inner joy spread through Maggie. Caroline hadn't called yet, but Teresa said to give her time and Maggie was being patient. Teresa *had* e-mailed her a picture of her sister, and Maggie was dumbfounded by how much they resembled each other. Jamie, particularly, had been fascinated by Teresa's call and Caroline's story.

"Someone else needs to share now."

A boy yelled, "Me, me, me." Cute Tommy Sengle, a star athlete who came to RCC for a year to boost his grades and was dying to play football at for a Division I college.

Susan tossed him the eraser.

"I'm the fourth kid, and I get my own way all the time."

A girl slouched next to him blurted out, "You think, Tommy?"

Everyone laughed. Tommy was one of the reasons they'd resorted to the eraser. He'd dominate the discussion if Maggie let him.

Other students talked about which traits applied to them and which didn't. Despite the preponderance of negative examples in the material, most picked good traits they had because of their birth order.

"What'd you put down, Mrs. Davidson?" asked a young boy who reminded her of her brother Jimmy.

As a teacher, Maggie almost always participated in the exercises she expected her students to do.

Again she thought of Caroline, and how some of her own personality had been formed by her sister's leaving her at such a young age. "I'm the second child and am an overachiever." She shrugged. "I wish I wasn't, though."

"Why not?" another boy asked.

Because Mike hated it and said she was always trying to make their lives perfect.

"It's not an easy trait to live with." She glanced at the clock. "We're almost out of time. Open your notebooks again. Put in the date. Write down one thing you learned today that might help you dealing with life in general."

Maggie was a firm believer that if a class, whether it be psychology, math, or English, didn't relate to her students' lives, the material delivered was worthless. She'd had disagreements over that philosophy with other teachers who claimed it was impossible to make every lesson relevant. But it wasn't that difficult, not if you thought outside the box.

While they wrote, she considered Jamie's and Brian's birth-order traits. They weren't so stereotypical. Jamie was more somber than Brian, who had an easygoing attitude. Jamie examined life and Bri seemed to let events happen without worrying about them. But they were both caring and loving, and they liked to have fun. Last night, they'd played a video game on the TV and jabbed each other the whole time.

When the students left, Maggie headed to her office. Once she got inside, she dropped down in her chair, opened her desk drawer, and took out a picture of her and Caroline that she'd kept since childhood. Both had dark hair and dark eyes. Of course Caroline had matured into a beautiful young woman while Maggie was going through the awkward body stage of an eight-year-old. She remembered when they were trying on clothes, Caroline saying, *I looked just like you at eight, baby. You'll grow out of it.*

As Maggie stared at the photo, she was once again appalled by how Caroline had been taken away from her. It had been the driving force in the family Maggie herself had created. She believed nothing could cause this kind of schism among her, Mike and her boys. But for the first time in years, Maggie felt optimistic about having an older sister in her life again.

❖

"What a day this has been…" Jamie sang the words to "Almost Like Being in Love," for once putting his heart and soul into it. Not because of Fiona, his love interest in *Brigadoon*, but because of a guy in the audience, tenth row, end seat. He was super excited that Luke was there, despite the fact that Kiki was with him. With the lights shining bright on his face, and the packed house enthusiastic, Jamie poured his heart into the lyrics celebrating real love.

Rising from the bench, he did the dance steps Ms. Marlo had choreographed for the scene, then fell into the role and executed a couple of improvised turns and arm flourishes across the stage's wooden floor. The director sat in the audience for every performance, and when he finished the song, he heard her yell out before the applause began and the audience gave him a standing ovation. Jamie basked in the accolades. Even if other areas of his life hadn't yet fallen into place, this one had. He was meant to act.

The rest of opening night, the laughs seemed louder, the songs more dramatic, and when he took his curtain call, the audience once again leapt to its feet. Including row ten.

Still in costume, the actors followed their usual routine of appearing out front to take pictures and greet their parents and friends who'd come to see the spring musical. His mom and dad and Brian were there, of course, as well as his grandparents. Aunt Sara's family was coming Saturday night. Several of his teachers came up and congratulated him, but he kept scanning the area for Luke.

Brian, especially, seemed up for him. "Hell, you're good," he said to Jamie. "I could never do that."

"Thanks, Bri."

After talking with tons of people, Jamie took one last glance around, but didn't see Luke anywhere. Disappointed, he went backstage with the cast.

Ms. Marlo hugged him and his friend Paul as soon as she walked into the room. "You guys! I love you."

"I love you, too, Ms. M." Jamie picked her up and swung her around, as she was little, weighing less than his mother.

"What was with the turns?" Ms. Marlo asked when he put her down. "I've been trying to get you to improvise for weeks."

"It felt right." His grin matched hers. "You know I always do better when I have an audience."

"Aren't we happy tonight?" she said, taking his cheeks in her hands.

"Yeah, we are." He kissed her forehead, then someone grabbed her from behind. Adrenaline pumped through them all after a performance and they tended to be more affectionate.

Happy, Jamie crossed to the vanity area and sat next to Paul to remove his makeup.

"Can I catch a ride to the Ground Round with you, Jamie?" Though the formal cast party wasn't until the last show, they celebrated at a local restaurant after each of the other performances.

Jamie applied some cold cream to his face and wiped off the foundation. "Um, I have to take Brian and his girlfriend home."

"Why? I saw your parents here."

"They had plans and had to duck out right after we said hi. I told them I'd chauffeur Brian and Heather. Can one of the other kids give you a ride?"

"Probably." Paul frowned into the mirror as he cleaned off lipstick. "You're coming to the restaurant, though, aren't you?"

"Yeah, sure. I'll be there after I dump Bri. I promise."

Distracted by the lie he'd told, Jamie finished with the makeup and left hurriedly. In the men's dressing area, he shed his costume and put on brown jeans and a tan light cotton pullover that had taken him an hour to pick out at home. Slipping into a leather jacket, he headed out of school without saying good-bye to anyone. He didn't want to answer any more questions.

It was cold and windy, and light snowflakes had begun to fall, so Jamie jogged to his car. The engine warmed up the interior of the Prius and he sat there for five minutes before the passenger door finally opened. The night air slid inside along with Luke Crane.

"Hey," Jamie said, hearing the nervousness in his own voice, trying to quell it, but he couldn't.

"Hey, Jame."

Luke wore a sharp gray sports coat and navy blue sweater beneath. His shoulders ate up the inside of the small car, and his cologne, one that was both woodsy and musky at the same time, filled the entire space. Jamie wanted to lean in closer, inhale the scent and touch the skin that lay beneath those clothes.

"Man, you were unbelievable. I never saw you perform before. It was awesome."

Had praise ever meant more to Jamie? His heart beat even faster. "Thanks. A lot like you are on the pitcher's mound."

"Maybe." When Luke drummed his fingers on his knee, Jamie realized he was nervous, too. "We have more in common than I think sometimes."

"Yeah." A hesitation. "What'd you tell Kiki?"

"I dropped her off at Julianne's. Some other kids were already there. I told her I had to go pick up soda."

"Mmm."

"Sorry about all that."

Luke had told Jamie he wasn't ready to go public yet, and since Jamie hadn't come out either, he went along with the secrecy. They'd been hanging out since the Valentine's Ball, though, and every time it was more exciting, more physical, more…normal. Now he wanted everybody to know who he was. So Luke still dating a girl felt like they were backtracking. And it pissed him off.

Probably sensing that, Luke added, "I won't be seeing her too much longer, Jame. I promise."

"I guess."

As Luke stared over at Jamie in the lamplight from the school parking lot, his blue eyes filled with excitement. Now, *that* made the lying easier. "At least I get to be with you for a few minutes after that performance. You know, kind of to share in it."

"I know."

Reaching over, Luke grasped Jamie's hand. His was big and callused from throwing balls and holding bats. The texture made Jamie's skin sizzle. That, and the fact that he'd never held hands with anybody in the moonlight.

And when Luke yanked on his fingers, dragging him as close as he could, Jamie realized he was about to get his first real kiss from somebody he was totally into.

Funny, it *was* almost like being in love.

CHAPTER FIVE

Madonna blasted out from the portable CD player in the corner of the laundry room, a big space at the end of a hallway and adjacent to the garage door entrance. Maggie sang along with one of her favorite old tunes from high school, "Papa Don't Preach." The volume was high and she was a little off-key, but the memories came in full force, probably because Caroline was back in her life. She was thinking about her boyfriend, Jack, and necking in his car while this very song played on the radio. But as usual, the positive recollections led to bad ones from her childhood years and she couldn't stop the leap this time…

Physical abuse as a ten-year-old…

Get a switch from the lilac tree. You're going to get it now.

What did I do, Ma?

You know.

Often, Maggie didn't.

Psychological manipulation as a teen…

You can go out only one night on the weekend.

Why, Ma?

Because Amelia Ranaletti is doing that with Andrea.

That doesn't make any sense.

And maybe the worst of all, damaged self-esteem…

You aren't smart enough for college. You'll stay in Cornwall, work at the factory and get married to a nice Italian boy…

It was no wonder that, after Caroline left, Maggie had fled the house with Jack or someone else every chance she got, as well as joining clubs and activities to escape. Thank God life was different with her own boys. They never tried to avoid her and Mike, so she banished thoughts of her mother and concentrated on all that was right with her family.

Jamie had been magnificent in *Brigadoon* and his drama teacher said he'd be a top candidate for a drama scholarship if he sent out a tape of the performance with his college applications next fall. Brian was flying high because he'd been chosen captain of the baseball team, and Mike was happy with his church activities. She and Mike were doing okay, too. Thinking of last night's lovemaking, she sang louder.

Jamie appeared in the doorway of the laundry room. "Rockin' Mama!"

Glancing up from Mike's shirt—she was trying to get a stain out of the sleeve—she grinned and lowered the music. "Hey, buddy."

"You sound happy."

"I am." She angled her head to the CD player. "Reminds me of my old boyfriend."

"Yeah? Do tell."

She shrugged. "Not much to tell. He was pretty well-off. Grandma Lorenzo didn't like him, so I snuck out to see him."

Slouched against the doorjamb, her son cocked his head. "I'm sorry you had such a tough childhood."

"You know what I finally figured out? Some people have wonderful childhoods, then hard times with their kids. I had it bad when I was young, but hit the jackpot with you guys. I wouldn't trade the two."

"And you might even get your sister back."

"I will, Jame. I know it."

"It's so weird, having three people in my family I've never met."

Gertrude Lorenzo's legacy. Though she tried not to ponder what her mother would do when she found out Caroline was in their lives again, fear washed over her like a cold shower at unexpected times like this.

Jamie sank down on one of the two steps that led to the laundry room from the hallway. Buck came up and nosed at him, wedging in the space between the doorway and Jamie's knee. He began to rub the dog's neck.

Maggie stopped scrubbing and watched her son. "You want to talk, honey? You seem, I don't know, sad. Or nostalgic."

"Maybe nostalgic."

"Is it the letdown from the play? You always feel blue after the school musical is over."

"No. It's not that." He bit his lip. "I gotta talk to you, though."

Her pulse rate sped up. Good news never followed that statement. She dropped the shirt on the washing machine and leaned against it. "Shoot."

"I have a date Friday night."

"That's good, isn't it?"

"I think so." His gaze locked with hers. "I hope you do, too."

"Of course I do. Can we meet her?"

"It's not a her, Mom. It's a him."

"A him?" She stared at her son blankly. The sound of the refrigerator across the room, the ticking of the clock on the wall seemed unnaturally loud. When the realization hit, her mother's heart tightened in her chest. "You have a date with a boy."

A long pause. "It's okay, isn't it?"

Please, God, let me handle this right. After a moment of speechlessness, she said, "O-of course it is."

Jamie's fingers tightened on Buck's collar. Suddenly he seemed smaller, more fragile, in his jeans and sweatshirt.

Maggie crossed to him, knelt down, and took both of his hands in hers. His were freezing cold. "Honey, you know there's nothing you could ever tell me, ever *do* or feel that would make me love you less."

A frown. "Yeah, I know that."

Well, she'd done that right. At least he knew her love was unconditional. But oh my God…the ramifications of his admission were far reaching.

"I just…I don't want this to make you sad. Especially now that you're so happy about Aunt Caroline." He glanced down at the linoleum, then back to her again. "Are you upset?"

"That you're gay?"

"Yeah."

You have no idea. "No, honey. I love you for who you are."

"Do you feel bad?"

How honest could she be? With Jamie and herself?

"Only that you didn't tell me sooner." Not quite the whole truth, but part of it. The easier part. Again, she thought of all they'd shared.

Yet, dear Lord, he hadn't told her something so vital to who he was. The notion made her stomach cramp.

"There wasn't any need to tell you. I never wanted to date before. Now I do, which is why I said something today."

"I guess I can accept that, for now." Later, she knew, it would haunt her. Pushing away the selfish thought, she cleared her throat. "Does anybody else know?"

His expression was wry. "The guy I'm going on a date with."

"Who is it?"

"Luke Crane."

Her jaw dropped open. "Luke Crane? Brian's teammate?"

"Ma," he said, sounding like the adult in the situation. "One out of every ten people is gay."

She knew the stats, had brushed up on them for a section of her Psych 102 course.

"Even jocks."

"I know. I never suspected it about him, though."

"Did you, about me?"

Maggie had had some concerns. Once or twice she'd brought them up to Mike. The discussion always upset him, so she kept her worry to herself. One night, though, over a bottle of Merlot, she'd confessed her fears about her son to Gretta. She'd sensed all along Jamie was different, but in the end she decided the best course of action was to let Jamie tell her. "I had some suspicions, honey."

"Why? Because there were no girls in the picture?"

"Uh-huh."

And because he'd been interested in theater, and then started hanging out with a group from the plays. Paul and Nick were gay, she knew from Jamie himself. Also, Jamie had no desire to participate in sports beyond a brief stint at diving. Stereotypical thinking, which embarrassed her but had been there nonetheless.

Maggie moved to sit next to her son on the step. Buck compensated by lying at their feet. "Does Brian know? About you or Luke?"

"No."

"Did you tell any of your friends? Julianne?"

"No, definitely not her. She's so right-wing Christian, Mom, I can't talk to her anymore. Especially about something like this."

"I'm sorry." Maggie knew she shouldn't ask, but like prodding a toothache with your tongue, or taking off a Band-Aid to check a wound, she couldn't leave this alone. "Did you talk to an adult, honey?"

"Um, yeah. Ms. Carson."

A sudden prick of tears, which she mercilessly battled back. He'd told another grown woman and not his mother. "H-has she helped you?"

"Yeah. A lot."

"That's good."

"Luke and I aren't gonna hide being together, Mom. We're not going to broadcast our dating either, but kids will find out."

She groped around her mind for the mother role, one she usually fell into so easily. "How close are you two, Jamie?"

"We've been hanging out since the Valentine's Ball. We got to be friends, then it turned into more."

"Are you happy?"

He nodded. "My first boyfriend." His expression turned sappy and Maggie's heart ached and rejoiced at the same time. Then anger took over—that he'd been deprived of this normal adolescent feeling for so long. "It's fun, Mom."

"Good for you, honey."

They talked about the times Jamie had seen Luke and his giddy feeling was even more evident, making it easier not to think about all he hadn't shared with her.

After a half hour, she glanced at the clock. Mike would be home soon, so she was forced to bring up the mechanics of dealing with what Jamie told her. "How do you plan to handle this at home? With the family?"

"Bri's gotta know before anybody at school finds out. I'll tell him. You tell Dad."

Which they both knew would be the hardest part of all this.

Mike's love for his son was deep. But how on God's earth was he ever going to reconcile Jamie's homosexuality with the Catholic religion? He was so single-minded about the church. The thought of how his attitude would influence this huge benchmark in their lives terrified Maggie. She squeezed Jamie's arm and left her hand there, more for herself than him. "Dad will want to talk to you about all this."

"I know."

"What about the rest of the family?"

Since he was a baby, Jamie always got this certain expression on his face when he was troubled. Maggie could read it like a neon sign. "No."

"No?"

"I don't want to announce to anyone I'm gay, Mom."

"What does that mean?"

"That I'm a son, a brother, a friend and an actor, not just a gay man."

"I understand that."

"And you didn't feel the need to announce to anybody that Brian's straight, did you?"

How wise he was for sixteen. Of course, he'd had time to think this out. And she was still reeling about the effect his disclosure would have on Mike. On all their lives.

"All right. I can abide by that wish, until it's time for people to know."

Like Brian's graduation party, a few months away, if Jamie decided to bring Luke as his date. There were several possibly homophobic people in their lives. Now, however, she had two big secrets to keep from her family.

A half-grin from her son. "We'll tell people on a need-to-know basis." Standing, he reached out a hand to her. She took it and prayed he didn't feel hers trembling. When she got to her feet, she hugged him. He held on longer than usual. "I love you, Mom."

"I love you, too."

"Come on, Bucky," he said to the dog, and they both disappeared down the hallway. She heard his feet pound on the steps, the bathroom door close, and Buck bark at being left outside.

Dazed, Maggie picked up Mike's shirt and stared down at it unseeingly. Her heart thudded in her chest as the ramifications of Jamie being gay flooded her. She picked up the stain spray to apply more to the cuff, but dropped the can to the floor. Gripping the shirt to her chest, she swallowed hard.

"Stop it, Maggie," she said aloud. This wasn't a tragedy. If Jamie had a terminal illness, or hit somebody while driving and killed them, or was into drugs, that would be a tragedy. His sexual orientation was a simple fact of life.

Forcing herself to move, she put the white clothes in the washer, but random images bombarded her: Brian teasing Jamie about not having a girlfriend...Jamie's dislike of proms...discussions about having kids, and Jamie saying he wanted some. She thought about *Brigadoon.* Her son was a boy who'd never experienced longing for the opposite sex, but he always played the romantic, heterosexual lead in the plays he loved so much. What had *that* been like for him?

Her heart ached for her child—what he'd gone through alone, and what he would still go through, even in this day and age. In bigger cities, gay kids were more accepted, but Sherwood was different. And she knew the shattering statistics on gay teen suicide—three times higher than others in the age group.

After she closed the machine's lid, she went to leave the laundry room, but instead, slid to the floor and wrapped her arms around her waist, trying to squelch her negative thoughts—like the wish to go back to how her life was an hour ago. Like the wish that...no, she wouldn't even think about that. It took her a while, but she won the battle and chose instead to figure out how she could help her son. And her husband.

❖

With Buck at his heels, Jamie took the stairs two at a time. He catapulted into the bathroom, slammed the door, and lowered the toilet seat. Dropping down onto it, he buried his face in his hands.

Breathe in, breathe out. Again. And again.

When his stomach settled and he didn't feel like he was going to hurl, he stood and crossed to the sink in front of the mirror. He looked the same. Too skinny. Great hair, now that it was longer; normal nose. Eyes that, some cheerleader had told him, could get him into any girl's pants. Showed how much she knew. But as he stared at his reflection, he sensed he wasn't the same and never would be after what just happened in the laundry room.

He'd told her! Finally, after years of self-doubt that made him sick to his stomach, and when that passed, months of feeling like he was going to bust open from the inside if he didn't let go of his secret, he found the courage to tell her. Luke's last text message said, *If you do, I will.* They'd made a pact to approach both their mothers today.

But, oh God, he'd upset her, this woman who'd been the most important person in his life. He could see it in her face, always filled with gentle love and an acceptance most kids couldn't fathom.

Typical of her, she'd tried to be brave. She said the right things. Yet he knew her almost as well as she knew him, and what he'd revealed would cause her worry and pain. He'd pretended he was good, too, that he hadn't had sleepless nights over who he was, hadn't gone through stages of self-loathing and recriminations. He was, after all, an actor. And he *had* come out on the other side, *had* accepted who he was. Rejoiced in it, even. Finding Luke just brought it all together.

Still, this step was done. Finally, finally done.

After splashing some water on his face, Jamie opened the door and made his way to his own room. Flopping on the bed, with Buck leaping to the foot of it, he checked his text messages. None. He was dying to know how it went with Luke, who was scared shitless of his parents. But like Jamie, being gay had gotten too big to keep inside anymore. It took too much energy to keep the door closed on a closet full of secrets. How would Luke's mom and dad handle it? Would they explode, say awful things that could never be taken back? Luke feared they might, and having gotten to know the Cranes in the last few weeks, Jamie expected the worst.

Linking his hands behind his head, staring up at the ceiling, he thought about his mom again. She hadn't said any of those awful things and she never would. She'd deal with his being gay and any problems that caused inside her and make his coming out easier for him. Yet Jamie wasn't out of the woods. Brian would freak, and Jamie would have to smooth over not telling him sooner. But it was his dad's potential reaction that woke Jamie up in the middle of the night in a cold sweat. Because of the church he belonged to and the religion he embraced, his own father could reject him. His dad might say those things he could never take back.

And Jamie didn't know what he'd do if that happened.

Probably sensing tension in him, Buck barked and moved in to nuzzle him. Jamie petted the dog for a while, then grabbed his phone and sent a text saying, *So, how'd it go telling your parents?*

After a while there was a chime. *I couldn't do it, Jamie. Maybe we should both wait.*

Jamie's hand curled around the cell. "Now you tell me."

Disappointment shot through him, harsh and acute. When he got past it, he messaged Luke that it was okay, he should wait until he was ready. But it wasn't, really. The plan was to share the joy of coming out to their parents. He wanted to share everything with Luke.

"Shit!" he said aloud. Bolting up, he knew he had to get out what he was feeling, so he went to the desk, to his journal, which was the only place he'd been honest for months. Once again, he poured his heart out on the pages.

Alone

I am alone in this.
I didn't think I would be.
He promised he would tell.
It was too much for him.

Fear mixes with joy.
Joy colludes with hope.
Hope brings about expectation.
Was he wrong to have told all?

His real self speaks:
No, no, no.
It's right. No matter what.
Right to be the person you are.

Isn't it?

❖

Drums were beating at Mike's temples when he pulled his Pontiac into the garage. Work had been a bitch because some inventory had been lost and it had taken him all day to find it. Then the slow drive home in the sleet was tedious. Grabbing his briefcase, tie, and jacket from the front seat, he exited the car, glad this day was over and looking forward to a manhattan, conversation with his wife and catching up on the boys' day.

He smelled baked chicken as he entered the house. Maggie was coming down the back stairs and they met in the hallway.

"Hi." She kissed his cheek. She must have taken a shower because he caught a whiff of her bath splash. Dressed in jeans and a long-sleeved white shirt, thick socks on her feet and her hair shiny and a little damp, she looked young and healthy and was just what the doctor ordered.

"Hey, sweetheart." He held her close for second, thanking God for giving this wonderful woman to him, then walked with her into the kitchen, put his keys in the cupboard, and picked up the mail.

As he leafed through the letters and flyers, she asked, "How was work?"

He mumbled, "Fine."

"Any news with your boss?"

"Still making waves about cutting back."

Mike was the vice president for a local software distributor in Rochester. His new boss was downsizing, and one of the people he wanted to lay off was Mike's assistant, Laura Simpson. But the woman was a solid worker and they needed her. He thought that with one more meeting, he could preclude that cut, at least.

Setting down the envelopes, he removed a bottle of whiskey from one of the lower cabinets and began to fix himself a drink. "How was *your* day?"

Maggie poured herself wine from the refrigerator. "Eventful."

"Yeah?" He sank onto a stool at the island counter in the kitchen they'd remodeled when they moved in. "Did Caroline call?"

"No, but she will." Her smile seemed off, somehow.

"Then what's wrong?"

She folded her arms across her waist. "Mike, I talked to Jamie today. About dating."

Oh, Lord, please let this be the news he'd been praying for. When Maggie brought up Jamie's sexual orientation in the past, he couldn't talk to her about it. Since then, though, Mike had had fears about his son. And his son's soul. He tried not to, but they were there, inside him. "Tell me he finally has a girlfriend."

"No." She hesitated. "A boyfriend."

Mike stared at her.

"I'm sorry." Maggie's voice came from far away, as if she was in another room. "We've brought up the possibility before, but I know hearing it confirmed is a blow."

He shook his head, trying to clear it.

After a moment, she came to sit on the stool next to him. "Are you all right?"

Forcefully, he focused on her, tried to use her as an emotional compass as he always did with the boys. "No, Mag. I'm not all right."

She was struggling, too, so he reached for her hand. It was shaking. He needed to deal with this well, for her and for his son.

"Mike, listen, we can work through this. It's going to be fine."

Looking down at the floor, he thought of Jamie, curly haired and teetering when he took his first steps on the tile. Had Mike done something wrong all those years ago to bring this situation about? "Oh, God, poor Jamie."

His wife drew in a heavy breath. "I think it's important not to let him know you see this as a problem."

She had to be kidding.

"He doesn't see this as a *poor Jamie* scenario."

"What else is it, honey?"

"It's who he is. Our little boy is simply different from you or me or Brian."

"The Catholic Church disagrees with you."

"On more than this, Mike."

Familiar angst welled up inside him. Their disagreements about issues in the Catholic Church had caused rifts between them over the years, but compared to what this could do, those were minimal. "Our church says he's still loved by God, Maggie, but his sexual preference is a choice, a sinful one. And he can change it."

"The church is wrong on this, Mike, psychologically and morally. First and foremost, who we love is a sexual orientation, not a choice, not a preference. Any religion that tells you differently is archaic and dangerous."

Why did she say that? How was he supposed to make this come out right if she spouted heresy?

"Second, with that in mind, you've got to handle this well with Jamie." She watched him carefully. "What you say now, when you first see him, will be the foundation of your relationship for the rest of your lives."

His glass hit the counter harder than he intended. "What do you think I'm going to do, cast him out of the house like a leper? For God's sake, Maggie, I'm his father. I love him no matter what."

"I know you love him. But he has to feel your acceptance of him, despite your views on his sexual orientation."

"I realize that. And I wish to hell you didn't think you had to tell me all this."

She didn't take her words back.

He said, "I'll do what's right, and part of that is staying true to God and my religion while I protect my son."

"I'm not sure you can do both."

They heard Jamie moving around upstairs. Fear flashed in her eyes.

"Be honest with me, Maggie. You can't want this for him, can you?"

"I…I'm not going to think in that vein, Mike. It won't help any of us."

"Denial certainly won't help."

Very quietly, but in a slicing tone, she said, "Neither will disapproval." Noise on the stairs. Jamie's feet hit the landing with a thud. "Please, Mike, be careful."

Standing, he gulped the rest of his drink, set it down, and strode to the foyer, saying a quick prayer to God to help him do what was best now. One point his wife was right about—the rest of their lives were at stake.

CHAPTER SIX

Jamie *so* did not want to have this conversation. After his dad hugged him, he'd said, "Let's go to the porch." Jamie had no choice but to follow.

They sat inside the glass enclosure that faced their wooded backyard. His mom and dad had planted two of the trees as saplings when he and Brian were little. Now they'd grown into towering maples. This room was heated, but not enough, and Jamie shivered. At least he thought that's what caused the chill. But it could be Luke's reneging on him and now this heart-to-heart with his father.

"I hear you and Mom had quite a conversation today." His dad's tone was even, controlled. He was always calm in a crisis. And of course this *was* a crisis to him.

"Uh-huh." Damn it, Jamie's voice cracked like it did when he went through puberty. Which was tough enough for any guy, but when you realized you might like boys, *becoming a man* was a nightmare.

His dad squeezed his arm. "I love you, Jamie. Nothing can make me love you less."

"That's what Mom said."

"It's true. For both of us."

Thank God for that, anyway. It buoyed Jamie, though he knew it wouldn't be smooth sailing with his dad. A *but* was coming.

Quietly, his father asked, "Want to tell me how you're feeling about all this?"

"I'd rather know how you're feeling."

Which wasn't quite true. There were caveats on his dad's love, mostly if something conflicted with his unshakable faith in God. Sometimes it hurt knowing God was more important to his father than Jamie was.

"I'm worried about you, Jame."

"I'm okay, Dad."

His father glanced down. "Your hands are shaking."

Shit. He shoved them under his thighs. "It's cold out here. Honest, I'm fine. I told Mom I want to date, so it's time for you to know."

"How long have *you* known?"

"A while."

"Do you want to talk about anything in particular about your sexual preference?"

"No."

"Then I'd like to discuss the gay lifestyle."

Jamie's fists clenched. "Dad, the term *gay lifestyle* is insulting. It implies that all gay people live the same, have the same morals when nobody would ever say all straight people do." A hard ball formed in Jamie's stomach but he went on anyway. "And being gay isn't a preference. It isn't a choice I made."

A muscle in his father's jaw pulsed. "This is all somewhat of a surprise for me. If my terminology offends you, I'm sorry."

Jamie didn't respond.

"Let me try to say it in a different way. I'm worried about what I know, or have heard, about being a gay man in society."

"What's that?"

"Promiscuity. The gay club scene. The danger of sexually transmitted diseases."

Glancing away, Jamie swallowed hard. He loved his father so much and never, ever wanted to hurt him. But still… "You're a bigot if you think all gay men are promiscuous."

"Excuse me?"

Now he faced his dad squarely. "It's a blatant stereotype. There's no more promiscuity among gay people than straight ones, and AIDS is spread by heterosexuals, too."

"But as your father, I need to warn you. Protect you."

Jamie bolted off the couch. "Consider me warned. I don't wanna talk anymore."

Before Jamie could get away, his dad stood and grabbed his upper arms. Broad shoulders that had borne the responsibility of raising a family, nurturing his sons, spanned Jamie's.

"Listen, I'm sorry if—"

"You offended me. I know." He tried to shrug his father off. "I gotta go."

His dad's grip tightened; they stared at each other. Then he yanked Jamie to him and hugged him like he used to when Jamie was a little boy.

And Jamie started to dissolve. He clutched at his father's back, breathed in his familiar scent, let it comfort him. He even buried his face in his dad's chest and stayed there. Old emotions—ugly ones—started to come back. He'd finally come to terms with who he was and he didn't wish it away anymore, but his father's reaction conjured up all those self-doubts. And once again, Jamie felt bad about who and what he was.

Wordlessly, he drew back, fled the porch and raced to the foyer. Taking the stairs two at a time, he slammed the door to his room and fished out his cell phone. He needed to talk to Luke. They were supposed to do something together tonight but couldn't because of a family event at the Cranes' country club. Maybe Jamie could catch him before they left.

❖

Brian shuffled to the door of Jamie's room, where an old folk song by Joni Mitchell played low from his computer. "Something's wrong with Mom and Dad, isn't it?"

His brother was sitting on the bed, writing in his journal. "What do you mean?"

"It's like after Grandma Lorenzo comes to visit. Like they got the wind knocked out of them. Did Grandma find out about Teresa calling?"

"Not that I know of."

"Mom's been so happy about that."

"Yeah. I wish Aunt Caroline would get in touch with her, though." Jamie glanced through the window where rain began to pelt against the panes, then back to Brian. "How's Heather?"

"Pissed at me."

"Why?"

Stepping inside, Brian closed the door. He lifted a pile of books off the chair and set them on the desk. "Big Boobs Barbara flirted with me at lunch. Heather was in the guidance office, so I flirted back. Somebody told her. Probably that prick Cummings."

Jamie asked, "Did Heather ever find out about Mexico?"

"No. Besides I didn't do anything serious."

"Yeah, sure."

He noticed his brother's shoulders were tense beneath his long-sleeved brown T-shirt. "You okay?"

"Uh-huh. Why?"

"You seem edgy."

"Nah. Bored maybe."

"Got plans tonight?"

Again, Jamie glanced at the computer. He could be a real geek sometimes.

"Besides being online?"

"I did. But they fell through. Why?"

"Heather and me are goin' to the movies. Wanna come?"

"Even though she's mad at you?"

"Yeah, she'll be over it by then. Come with us?"

"Maybe."

That was weird. Jamie usually teased him about his taste for action movies. "You can pick the flick. Heather likes what you do, anyway."

"Doesn't matter. I'll see whatever you want." He stood and tossed down the journal. "Maybe I'll even treat with the money Uncle Jimmy sent me for my birthday." Neither of them could work because of sports and drama commitments, so cash was scarce.

"Jame, you sure nothing's wrong?"

For a second, Jamie looked so sad it spooked Brian. Then he joked, "Why, because I'm not a cheapskate like you?"

Brian pulled the trump card. They had some things they used to do when they were little, and though they didn't need them much as they grew up, he used one now. "You promise? That you're all right?"

Neither of them could lie if they *promised* they were telling the truth.

Jamie swallowed hard. "I promise. Let me tell Mom and Dad I'm going with you."

As Jamie headed down the hall to their parents' bedroom, Brian felt better. Jamie promised, so everything was okay.

❖

An hour after the boys left for a movie, Maggie was sitting on the bed in a pink nightshirt, reading Dan Brown's newest book, when she heard the shower go off. A few minutes later, Mike came into the bedroom. Naked. Though he slept in the buff, he almost always put on pajama bottoms or boxers before bed in deference to the boys, who routinely wandered into their bedroom. She watched her husband. There were lines bracketing his eyes and mouth. His whole body seemed coiled. Without a word, he crossed to the door and locked it. Circling around the bed to her side, he removed the book from her hand and switched off the nightstand light. She could barely see him, but she could smell the soap from his shower and feel his hands on her.

"Mike, what…"

He silenced her with his mouth. It came down on hers hard and demanding. Startled, she grasped his biceps. His hand at the back of her neck kept her close, so she slid her arms around him.

The kiss deepened and his breathing escalated. Usually there was stroking, cuddling, teasing in their foreplay. Without letting go of her mouth, he pushed her to the bed, laying her out flat. His hand groped for her nightshirt. When he released her to yank the garment over her head, she said, "Mike, I—"

"Shh. I want it this way."

Fast and furious, it seemed. He touched all the spots that after twenty-some years of lovemaking he knew so well. He made her come with his mouth.

Only when he gripped her arms so hard it hurt and thrust inside her without any gentleness, instead with a frenzy which bordered on violence, did she feel a trace of fear. He grunted his release, loud and long. Then he rolled off her, collapsing on the mattress.

He stayed there, sweaty and spent, his wrist draped over his forehead. She switched on a lamp and the light cast his features in hard planes. Instead of relaxed satiation after sex, his body was taut.

"What was that all about?"

For several seconds, he didn't answer, the branches batting the side of the house the only sound in the room. "I'm feeling a lot now. Truthfully, I don't want to analyze it." He glanced over and said, "I needed that. Can you leave it alone?"

"I guess."

He turned over and in seconds, his breathing evened out. Maggie wasn't as lucky. She tried to read again but she couldn't concentrate. So she switched off the light and lay staring into the dark night for a long time, wondering exactly what had happened here.

❖

The next morning at seven a.m. a noise woke Maggie. She climbed out of bed—Mike was gone—pulled on a velour sweat suit and slippers, and followed the banging sound, worried because they all slept in on Saturdays. She found Mike stacking paint cans in the garage, with Buck cowering in the corner. The early April morning was milder than most, but the air was still cool and she shivered.

"What are you doing?"

He looked over his shoulder. Little particles of dust floated in the air and dirt smeared his cheek. "It was a mess in here. I couldn't stand it anymore."

She scanned the shelves at the back of the garage where junk tended to collect. Every item was in place. He'd dragged bikes and old chairs out of the storage area and put them on the front of the driveway. Running her hands over her upper arms to warm herself, Maggie wandered out to the pile he'd made. In it was a red tricycle, a two-wheeler with *The Flyer* painted on the bar, small lawn chairs, and an odd assortment of toys and games. To her, they were memories of their little boys. "What are you going to do with this stuff?"

"Give it to the church garage sale. I'll take it over this afternoon."

Fishing out a baseball glove, she held it up to him. "Wasn't this Brian's first mitt?"

"Uh-huh."

"You can't give it away." She ran her hand over the cold metal of the bike. "And this is Jamie's first two-wheeler."

"So? They're all grown up. They make their own decisions now. This baby stuff has to go."

"Mike, please, what are you *doing*?"

He whirled around. "Don't start on me."

Stung, she stepped back. After a moment, she picked the mitt up and ran her fingers over the worn leather, picturing Brian's little hand fitting inside it for the first time. Then she walked back into the house and stowed the glove in a drawer in the kitchen. As she made coffee, she pushed up the sleeves of her shirt and noticed a bruise on her arm. Add last night to Mike's manic behavior this morning and Maggie felt like she was standing in the ocean in Cancun again, the sand shifting under her feet.

Unfortunately, her husband's uncharacteristic actions didn't end in the garage. On Sunday morning, he rose early again. The boys got up for church at ten. Mike was showered and ready twenty minutes before they had to leave. "Get a move on," he yelled up the steps as he paced the foyer.

Maggie heard Jamie and Brian grumble amidst the sounds of running water and an electric shaver; some curses filtered down the hall to her, where she was dressing in her bedroom. Hurrying, she was downstairs in minutes. Five more and Brian joined them in the kitchen.

Jamie was the last to finish dressing. He sauntered into the room wearing a striped shirt...and jeans.

"What's this?" Mike asked.

"What's what?" Even Jamie's stance was belligerent. Defiant. Despite how basically easygoing the boys were, Mike and Maggie had had their share of rebellion from them. When Jamie was in middle school, he dyed his hair green for fun and Brian got an earring, both of which irked Mike. Each of the boys went to places they weren't supposed to go and fibbed about their whereabouts, like normal teenagers.

But they'd already fought this *no-jeans-to-church* battle. Mike had won.

"You know the rule, Jamie."

"Yeah, but I don't agree with it."

"You're entitled to disagree." Mike glared at him. "Not disobey."

Jamie flopped down onto a stool. "What? Are we living in the Dark Ages?"

"Go upstairs, young man, and put on some nice pants."

"No. I just won't go to church." He stood and tried to brush past Mike.

Grabbing Jamie's arm, Mike yanked him back. "Yes, you will. Now go change!"

Brian said, "Jeez, Jame, just do it, it's no big deal."

"Do you understand what I'm saying here?" Mike asked.

His eyes simmering with emotion, Jamie stared at his father. "Yeah, Dad, I understand. Loud and clear."

❖

It was too much for Maggie to handle alone. All week, she'd avoided Gretta, who she told her secrets to, because Jamie had made her promise to keep his disclosure to herself for a while. And Gretta would sense instantly something big had happened. But because her emotions were in a whirlwind, Maggie made an appointment to see Melissa Fairchild, her intermittent counselor for the past twenty years.

The therapist's office had always been a haven. Up a flight of stairs, on the second floor of a building in a restored part of downtown Rochester, the three rooms housed teak bookcases and bright airy windows and were painted a soothing peach. On the walls hung two Monet prints and a Renoir drawing. Short couches were opposite each other with a stuffed chair at one end, between the sofas.

Melissa was an attractive woman with brown curly hair, now beginning to gray, wise eyes, and a sympathetic smile. Maggie valued her intelligence, her insight, and her wit.

"Hi, Maggie. Good to see you."

"Same here."

Melissa studied her. "Something's wrong, isn't it?"

Maggie dropped down on the couch where she always sat and Melissa took her usual chair. "I don't know where to start."

Settling in, Melissa picked up her leather-bound notebook. Inside held notes on Maggie. Melissa scanned the top page. "Is this about your mother?"

"No, but there is a looming issue on the horizon there." She inched forward on the seat. "Caroline's daughter called me, Melissa."

"Your *sister* Caroline?"

"Yes."

When Maggie had first come to see Melissa, she'd spent six months dealing with her mother and how Maggie's personality had been formed early on. A huge part of that discussion was the loss of Caroline at such a young age. It had been the most traumatic event of her life. Until now?

"This is good news, isn't it?"

"It is. Of course it is. But no one else in my family knows. I won't tell them until I talk to Caroline, at least."

"That's a lot to take in. You should be going slowly and you have to consider Caroline's wishes, too."

"I'm afraid I won't be able to make this work for everybody."

Melissa sighed. "It's not your responsibility to make Caroline's coming back into your lives work."

"Then who will?"

"People are responsible for their own actions, their own happiness."

"But Caroline just lost her husband. I have to help, to protect her."

Melissa shook her head. "We've been over this before. You can't protect everyone in your life. Sometimes the course of events just have to unfold naturally."

Resting her head back on the couch, Maggie tried to clear her mind. "There's more, Melissa. It's why I'm not thinking straight. Not internalizing what I've already worked out here."

"What is it?"

"Jamie just told us he's gay."

Melissa waited for moment, then said, "And that's a problem for you?"

"It is for Mike. Brian doesn't even know yet. The jury's still out on the rest of our family and friends."

In halting sentences, she told Melissa about Mike's issues with the church and how she was feeling cut off from him. She recounted her worry over how Brian would react. "I just don't know how to help them through this."

"They've got to help themselves, Maggie." Melissa waited a beat. "Don't you see the connection? You couldn't fix everything when you were growing up, and you can't now."

"Is that what I'm trying to do?"

"You tell me."

"Maybe. I feel bad, though."

"About Jamie?"

"Yes, of course. His life is going to be hard now."

"In some ways, maybe. But here's another way to think about it. The gay community is huge in Rochester. You'd be surprised at the number of judges, lawyers, doctors, teachers, and therapists in it. And they support each other. Sometimes, it's a kinder community than the straight one."

"I'd hope that's true."

"The Gay Alliance is very active in the city, too. They offer support for parents, and more importantly, to kids who come out."

"Oh, good. I'll have to research that. But his future is going to be so different. Will he find a partner? What about kids? It's all so overwhelming."

"You know the statistics on divorce among straight people. Jamie's chances of finding a solid relationship and sticking with it are equal to that or maybe even greater."

"I guess. It's the twenty-first century. But life is different in Sherwood. It's such a small town, with such a small school. Most of the teachers are tolerant, but there's a contingent that's narrow minded. Just last year we had a row at a PTA meeting about a pregnant teen being in the prom court."

"Granted, Sherwood High School's not like bigger city schools. I've always thought its quaintness was charming. We forget that conservative views often accompany small-town living."

"This will be a problem." Maggie swallowed hard and leaned back into the couch. "What should I be doing for him? I don't know if he knows about safe sex when it comes to other boys. Hell, Melissa, *I* don't know what to tell him on that account. And Mike certainly won't."

"Does he have an adult doctor?"

"No, a pediatrician still."

"Get him an adult doctor. Maybe yours—the one you like so much—Bea Rubenstein."

They talked more about Jamie's physical safety and Brian's potential emotional upset. They discussed her relationship with Jamie and how Mike was handling her son's coming out.

After a half hour, Melissa cocked her head. "What is it you're not saying?"

Tears welled in her eyes.

"Maggie?"

"He didn't tell me for so long, Melissa. He says he's known for a while. I feel terrible about that. Inadequate as a mother."

"He *did* tell you. In high school, when most kids can't come out to their parents. That usually doesn't happen until college or often much later."

Now tears coursed down Maggie's cheeks. "There's more. I'm ashamed of this part."

"You can tell me, Maggie. I won't judge."

Maggie bit her lip. "Mike asked me if I was sorry Jamie was gay."

"What did you say?"

"I wouldn't answer him."

"But you know the answer?"

She nodded.

Melissa waited.

"I...I wish Jamie wasn't gay, Melissa. I wish my son wasn't who he is."

The therapist said, "So let's talk about that."

CHAPTER SEVEN

Jamie held up his phone, willing a text message to arrive. "Come on, come on, Luke." Just to be on the safe side, he was online, too, his IM up and running.

It was Wednesday night and Jamie hadn't heard from Luke since yesterday afternoon. He was seriously bummed because he feared Luke's silence was his fault. When they hung out on Monday, Jamie had pressed Luke to tell his parents he was gay. Sure, the situation wasn't great at home for Jamie, but it was out now, like it should be. And he and Luke had made a pact to do this together, to be able to date like other kids.

So Luke had told his parents Tuesday after school. He'd sent one text an hour later...

It didn't go so hot. I wanted you to know I did it this time. Gotta go, be back in touch...

But he hadn't called and Jamie had gotten worried so he'd driven over there after dinner Tuesday night...

The Cranes' three-story, cedar-sided house was in an upscale part of town. The big homes on tree-lined streets with manicured lawns always intimidated Jamie. Still, he pulled his car into the circular brick driveway, got out and, with confidence he didn't feel, strode to the front porch. The air was warm today. Maybe that was an omen, a good one, Ms. Carson would say. He rang the bell, which chimed the first few chords of *Ode to Joy.*

Luke's father drew open the door. He was a tall man with stern features and a mouth that almost never smiled. Jamie had only seen him wearing a suit, like he was now. "Hi, Dr. Crane, is Luke here?"

"He's here." The man gripped the doorknob, his fingers biting into the brass.

"Can I, um, see him?"

"Not now."

"Pardon me?"

"I said you won't be seeing my son until we get a handle on this whole thing." Without giving Jamie a chance to respond, he slammed the door. But not before Jamie witnessed the undiluted revulsion on Dr. Crane's face.

Then Luke hadn't gone to school today. Jamie called him all morning but his cell was off. When Jamie tried the house phone, he got the machine. By then, he thought, *Fuck it*, and left a brief message for anybody to hear.

Now, it was almost eleven at night and Luke wasn't online. His own house phone rang and he snatched it up, but before he could speak, he heard his mother's voice. "I got it, guys."

He would have stayed on to see who it was, but his IM chimed so he flew to the computer. The message was up.

Hey, Jame.

He typed back, *What's going on, man? I been worried.*

Got reason to.

What happened?

You won't believe it. They're so freaked, they won't let me out of their sight. I can't find my cell. I think they took it. If I cut off quick, it's because I'm not allowed to use the computer.

Why?

They think it's giving me ideas...making me think this is okay.

This? As in us?

Yep.

Oh, shit.

Look, I—

There was the sound of a door closing and blue lettering came on screen. *CoolHandLuke has signed off at 10:59.*

Stunned by Luke's situation, Jamie heard out in the hallway, "What's going on, Mom?"

Sliding off the chair, Jamie opened the door. Brian, wearing Gap pajama bottoms and a T-shirt like Jamie, was standing in the doorway to his room with Buck at his side. The dog barked at their mother, who was fully dressed.

"Who was that on the phone?" Jamie asked.

His mom's shoulders were stiff beneath her sweatshirt and she ran a hand through her hair. "Um, it was Dad. I'm meeting him for a drink at the golf club."

"At eleven?" Brian asked. "You have to work tomorrow."

"Yeah, I know. Go to bed. I'll see you in the morning."

Brian closed his door, but Jamie didn't. "What's happening, Mom?"

"Nothing you need to concern yourself with, honey."

"You sure?"

"Yes."

He started away, but he hesitated. "If I should be concerned, promise you'll tell me."

"Jamie, people have to work out their feelings in their own way. Dad's grappling with a lot now. We need to cut him some slack."

"Okay." He leaned over and kissed her. "I love you." Then he closed his door.

Between his mother's weird actions and Luke's abrupt sign-off online, it was a long time before Jamie fell asleep.

❖

April first was the launch of the men's golf league Mike participated in every year, and after playing, all the guys met at the bar of the club for drinks. Mike sat in the outdoor area of The Nineteenth Hole and drew a puff from a Marlboro. It was cool out here, but a cigarette was what he needed. Another puff. He'd paid eight dollars for the pack in the vending machine. He and Maggie hadn't smoked since college, and he had no idea how much the cost had gone up.

The price of vice. Oughtta be a song. He started to hum, then realized he must be drunk. Why not? It took the edge off. He could confess his overindulgence to Father Pete. All weekend, Mike made mistakes. He'd tried to pray about it, but he found no solace there, either. He had to get advice on all this from the priest. But tonight, he needed this escape.

The thought of his inadequacies had Mike gulping the rest of his beer and stubbing out his cigarette. None too steady, he rose, walked back into the bar, and sat down onto a stool.

"I'll have another Molson's."

The pretty bartender with brown eyes like Maggie's glanced over his shoulder. He heard dangling behind him. "I've got his keys," Craig said.

Mike took a swig of newly drawn brew when the woman set it in front of him. The pale ale was ice cold and went down smooth.

"Wanna tell me about it?" Craig asked, dropping onto the stool next to him.

Disgusted with himself, Mike ran his finger around the rim of the glass. "You'll wish you didn't know."

"Maggie okay?"

Recalling the sex last week, and the bruises on her arm that she tried to hide from him, he took another swig. "It's Jamie."

"He's not sick, is he?"

Ah, the sixty-four-thousand-dollar question. "No, Craig." Knowing Jamie didn't want his situation made public, that Maggie had promised not to announce his sexual orientation to anyone, Mike nonetheless told his friend the truth.

When he finished, Craig blew out a heavy breath. "Mike, I'm sorry."

"Me, too."

"You and Maggie must be devastated."

He didn't give his wife away. "I am."

"I'll help, in any way I can. You two were there for us when Tyler was diagnosed with leukemia. We'll be there for you now."

Something was wrong with that statement, but Mike's brain was too fuzzy to figure it out. Over Craig's shoulder, he caught sight of his wife threading her way through the crowd at the bar.

Anger rose inside him. "Did you call Maggie?"

"Yes."

"Why the hell did you do that?"

"Because I've got my own car and you can't drive yours. You refused to go home with me and I have to leave."

"Shit, Craig."

Maggie reached them. "Hi, guys."

From the corner of his eye, he saw Craig and Maggie exchange looks, Craig place the keys in her hand and kiss her cheek. Then he clapped Mike on the shoulder. "Take care."

Mike only grunted.

When his friend headed out, Maggie sidled onto the stool next to him. The fresh scent of her—she showered at night—suddenly made him feel grimy. He didn't look at her, but gazed into his beer instead.

Finally, she spoke. "You had too much to drink. It's okay. Craig called because he's worried. And you can't drive."

"I know I can't drive. I'm not an idiot!"

He felt her recoil next to him.

"Craig didn't have to call you." Mike transferred his gaze from the beer to the ballgame on the overhead TV. "I was going to…" He drifted off. In truth, he had no idea what he was planning to do.

A long silence while he sipped his drink. She picked up the pack of cigarettes and surprised him by saying, "Hmm, I'll bet that's fun to do again." They'd given up smoking early in their married life when they became responsible adults, which right now wasn't so appealing.

"It is. Want to go have one?"

"I'd love to. But no."

He smiled. "You're upset, too."

"Of course I am."

"You pretend you're not sorry he's gay."

"That's not what I'm upset about."

"Yeah, sure."

She reached over and took a sip of his beer.

"Want a drink?"

"No, I'll have some of yours."

For a while, they sat there, blindly staring ahead, lost in their own thoughts. It was soothing to him, the two of them together. They'd faced problems through the years like this and suddenly he was terrified of losing his closeness with his wife. When his glass was empty, he threw some money down on the bar and stood. "I'm ready to go."

Inside her car, he stretched out his long legs as much as he could in the front of the Honda Civic and leaned back into the seat. His eyes closed.

The short trip home was made in silence. But when Maggie pulled into the driveway, then the garage, she turned to him. "Both kids were up when I left. They wanted to know why I was going out."

"What did you tell them?"

"That I was meeting you for a drink."

"It won't hurt for them to see their saintly father had a few too many beers."

"I'm not worried about that."

He stiffened. "What *are* you worried about, Maggie?"

The light had gone on in the garage when she activated the automatic opener and the softness of her features shamed him.

"I'm worried you're upset about Jamie being gay and because you've had too much to drink, you'll say something tonight you don't mean, or wouldn't want the boys to hear."

He didn't respond. Instead, he stared out the front window. Before the overhead light went off, he caught a glimpse of the drywall. One summer the boys complained that the inside of the garage was dull and boring. Mike had shrugged a shoulder and said, "Then fix it."

They'd spent weeks doing *artwork* on the interior, covering the entire space. Some of it was simple shapes and letters—their initials, the school Spartan head, Brian's uniform numbers, the logos for Jamie's favorite bands. Other parts were scenes they asked Gretta to sketch out, and they'd painted colorfully within the lines. It was an eclectic hodgepodge that to this day both he and Maggie treasured. Tonight, Mike ached for that time in his life.

So he said, "You know what I've been thinking about?"

"What?"

"That our different views on Jamie and his life are going to split us apart. And we're going to lose the closeness between us because we disagree about him." He paused. "I know it's selfish, that I should be thinking about Jamie, and I am, I swear. But I'm worried about us, too."

Reaching across the gearshift, she took his hand and held it in a way that made his pulse calm. "So am I, honey. I'm afraid of exactly that."

"It's why I drank so much."

No response. What could she say?

"Promise me we won't let this come between us."

"I promise, Mike." She kissed his knuckles, her lips as soft as her skin.

"All right then." He squeezed her fingers. "I don't want Jamie to know I was upset tonight about him."

"We'll tell him we had a fight."

They'd been honest with the kids throughout the years, thinking it was healthy for the boys to see two people in love disagree and work differences out. "That's a plan."

She hesitated. "Mike, maybe you should get counseling to sort out your feelings. Melissa Fairchild could suggest someone. I've got another appointment to talk to her next week."

Melissa was Maggie's therapist, whom she'd seen periodically all of her adult life. Given the way Maggie had grown up, Mike had always been glad she had Melissa, though sometimes he worried what she told the therapist about him.

"I don't need Melissa. I've got an appointment with Father Pete on Wednesday."

"I'm not sure that's going to help us."

"You need Melissa. I need Father Pete. Maybe *she* won't help us either."

The door from the house to the garage opened, precluding further discussion.

It wasn't Jamie standing in the entryway. It was Brian. Silhouetted against the light coming from the hallway, he seemed smaller, more fragile than he really was. They were going to have to be careful when he learned the news about Jamie.

"What's going on?" his older son asked when they exited the car.

Mike stuck his hands in his pockets. Despite what he said earlier about his kids seeing him like this, he hated tainting the boys' image of him. "I had a few too many beers. Mom came and got me."

"No shit."

Now that Brian was almost an adult, they didn't chide him about his language. Both boys cursed, but not to excess and seldom in front of their parents. And they never took God's name in vain.

"Sorry, son. I'm not being a good role model for you guys."

Brian grinned. Blond curls tumbled into his eyes. Mike

remembered taking him for his first haircut and how Maggie cried when wispy pieces hit the floor. "Oh, I don't know, Dad, I could do worse than become a man like you."

Mike's hands fisted at his sides. Finally he managed to say, "Thanks, Bri. But not in this."

Once inside, Mike turned left to go upstairs, but Brian went into the kitchen with Maggie. Out of sight, but in earshot, Mike stopped to listen to their conversation.

Brian said simply, "What's really going on, Mom?"

"What do you mean?"

"The vibes around here have been wacked for a few days."

"Have they?"

"Nobody's sick, right?"

"No, honey. Nobody's sick."

"You and Dad, you're all right?"

"Yes, I promise. But you know what? I haven't had much time alone with you. Why don't we go out to dinner tomorrow night? Just us two?"

"I have baseball practice until six. After that?"

"Sure."

The chair scraped back and Mike heard Brian say, "I love you, Mom."

Before he was caught eavesdropping, Mike stumbled upstairs and into his bedroom. He shed his clothes and fell into bed. He wasn't proud of himself, and Maggie was none too happy either. Worse yet, he'd disappointed God. He said a brief prayer of apology as he drifted into unconsciousness.

❖

The next day, Maggie agreed to go for a walk with Gretta. She needed her friend even if she couldn't divulge the secret she was keeping.

"It's getting warm, finally," Gretta commented as they went down Main Street, her long strides eating up the pavement.

"I'm glad to see spring. It always cheers me up."

They didn't talk for a while. She loved that she didn't have to be *on* with her friend. After a while, though, Gretta spoke again. "I've sensed something's been bothering you, Mags. You know you can tell me anything."

"You're right, of course, I'm upset. But I can't tell you why yet."

"Why not?"

"I've been asked not to."

Her cell phone rang.

Gretta's brows rose. "Why'd you bring that on a walk?"

"I gave Caroline's daughter my cell number." She shrugged. "I didn't want to miss a call from my sister."

"Go ahead, then, and answer it."

"Hello."

"Maggie?"

"Yes, who is—" but she stopped midsentence. And suddenly, she knew the identity of the caller.

"This is your sister Caroline."

Tears welled in her eyes and she nodded to Gretta. "I-I knew it. I knew this was you."

Gretta grabbed Maggie's free hand. Her own eyes were moist.

"Oh, Caroline, I'm so glad you called."

Sniffling on the other end. "Me, too, Magpie."

At the nickname, Maggie began to cry.

"Shh, honey, let's not blubber."

"O—" Hiccups. "Okay."

"What are you doing now?"

"Walking downtown with my friend Gretta."

"Do you want me to call you back?"

"Uh-uh. Hold on a sec." To Gretta, she said, "It's her, Gretts. Oh, my God."

"Want me to stay?"

"No, you go on ahead."

"Call me." She kissed Maggie's cheek. "And enjoy this, honey. Don't worry about whatever else is going on in your life."

When Gretta headed out, Maggie spoke into the phone. "I can talk now. I'm sitting down so I won't fall over."

Caroline laughed and Maggie remembered the sound viscerally. She hadn't been exposed to much laughter in the Lorenzo household except for Caroline's.

"Teresa told me about Derek. I'm so sorry."

"It's awful. The holidays are the hardest."

Ah. Teresa had called at Christmas, and Easter wasn't far away. "I'll bet. You could come here for Easter. Celebrate with us."

"Oh, no, honey, I'm not ready to face the family yet."

"Not even me?"

"I'm sorry."

"I'm rushing this. Like I always do. I'm just thankful you called." She waited. "I will see you though, right?"

"Yes," Caroline said. "I plan to visit in the summer. Terry rented a cottage for us on Conesus Lake. I'll be finished with teaching and you and I can see each other then."

"Will Teresa be able to get away for the summer? Is she a teacher, too?"

"No, she chose to stay home with Chloe. Unfortunately, she and her husband have divorced, and she's at loose ends right now."

"I'm sorry, that must be hard for her and you."

"At least you'll get to meet her and my precious grandchild."

"Oh, Caroline."

"Now, tell me about your husband and those boys of yours."

For fifteen minutes, Maggie regaled Caroline with happy stories about her family, leaving out the most recent strain.

"You could come and watch Brian play baseball. And we have a video of Jamie's performance in *Brigadoon*."

"No, Mags. I need a bit more emotional equilibrium before I churn up my past." A long hesitation. "I'm still trying to cope with Derek's death."

Caroline went on to tell Maggie about her husband, Derek Dean, finally divulging her last name. Derek was the younger brother of Caroline's boss and a partner at the architectural firm where she went to work right after graduation from high school. He'd been separated from his wife—no kids. He and Caroline had met, fallen in love, and after he divorced and they married, they moved to Colorado, intentionally far away from the Lorenzos. He'd died at seventy-three of a heart attack.

"We can e-mail and talk, though," Caroline offered. "But don't tell Sara or Jimmy yet."

No mention of their mother. Caroline and Derek had stayed in touch with Derek's brother, so Caroline knew their father had died in his sleep ten years ago and that their mother was still alive. In his eighties and retired, the brother was the one who'd kept the Deans apprised of the rest of her family situation.

"Phone calls and e-mails will be great," Maggie conceded. "Send pictures, too."

"I'll do that tonight. I'm so glad to be in touch with you, sweetie. So glad. See you soon, sis."

Not soon enough, Maggie thought as she thumbed the off button, but she'd already pushed too much. She was going to take this gift on her sister's terms and, as she said, not try to control what happened with it. Maggie began the hike toward home, vowing to appreciate the good in her life and not mope about the issues her immediate family was dealing with.

But as she walked, memories she'd kept at bay intruded. One in particular, the night that Caroline left...

Her parents were in the front room of their house in Cornwall watching *All in the Family* when the show was preempted by a news bulletin about the Vietnam War. At eight, Maggie hadn't been sure what war was about, but recalled distinctly her father's disgruntlement at the interruption.

Caroline walked into the room. Her sister was so pretty, so kind, that Maggie always smiled at the sight of her. She ruffled Maggie's hair, then sat down on a chair in the corner where she could see both their parents. "Ma, Dad, I gotta talk to you."

"Be quick about it," her mother said. "Archie'll be back on soon."

"Mags," Caroline told her, "go check on Jimmy." Their one-year-old brother.

"He's sleeping, Caro."

"Go anyway, sweetie. I need to talk to Ma and Dad alone."

Maggie had left the room, but instead of heading upstairs, she stood by the doorway out of sight and listened.

"What's the matter?" their mother asked. Maggie heard the sound of a match being lit, smelled the familiar, awful scent of the Chesterfields her parents smoked.

"I'm...I..."

"What, Caroline Anne?" Maggie's father's deep voice rumbled from the couch. He worked odd hours at the Glass Works, and when he *was* home, he wanted peace and quiet. Mostly, he wasn't there, though. He spent nearly all his free time gambling at the race track or playing cards until the early hours of the morning.

"I'm getting married," Caroline said simply.

Silence. Then, her mother shouted, "Jesus Christ, are you pregnant?"

"No."

"You don't even have a boyfriend," her father put in.

"I do."

"Why don't we know about this?" Her mother's tone made Maggie afraid. "You know you aren't allowed to go out with anybody unless he comes here and we meet him."

"I-I was afraid to tell you."

"Who is it?"

Caroline waited a long time. "I'm not ready to say yet."

"What's wrong with him?" Her mother again.

"Is he colored?" her father asked in a horrible tone.

"No, Dad, he's…divorced."

"What?" Her mother bellowed now. "That's a sin. Divorce is a sin."

"I won't have it," her father added. "You stop seeing him right now."

"It's not up to you, Daddy. I'm eighteen." Her sister's birthday had been last week.

"Is that what you were waiting for?" Gertrude snapped. "Sneaking around with some married man until you were legal age."

"Frankly, yes."

"This is fucking ridiculous. I won't have it," he repeated.

Maggie had never heard her father use the word that Caro told her never to say.

"I'm calling Father Bingham." Their parish priest, who was mean, even scary sometimes.

Caroline gasped. "Please don't do that, Ma. He'll make all this worse."

When her mother rose to use the phone in the living room, she caught sight of Maggie eavesdropping. "Go upstairs, you little brat, and stay up there, or I'll get a switch from the lilac bush."

Maggie had flown up the steep steps to the room she shared with her sister Sara, who was asleep in the other bed, and dived into hers, hiding her head under the blankets.

Caroline came in hours later, after the priest had gone home. She uncovered Maggie and scooped her up. They headed to Caroline's room down the hall. The floorboards creaked beneath her sister's feet as Maggie hung on to her neck. When they reached her room, Caroline set Maggie on the bed, then went to a white dresser and opened a drawer. Maggie loved this space with its blue walls and the old dressers Caroline had repainted white. She let Maggie help with both. The air smelled like Caroline, too. When she came back to the bed, she sat down. "Here, Mags, I want you to have this."

Maggie stared down at the chocolate Fanny Farmer Santa each of them got every Christmas in their stockings. They were the best treats ever. She'd already eaten hers. "It's yours, Caro."

"No, you take it." She placed the candy in Maggie's little hands. "I've got to tell you something."

"Ma and Dad are mad at you."

"Yes. I…I have to go away, baby."

Maggie's eyes widened. "For how long?"

"Probably a very long time. I'm getting married, and Ma and Dad don't want me to."

"Why?"

"It doesn't matter."

Maggie began to cry and the chocolate Santa fell to the sheets. She grabbed on to Caro's hands. "You mean you're going away forever?"

"It could be a long time."

"Take me with you, Caro."

"Oh, Magpie…" Now her sister's cheeks were wet. "I can't."

Maggie threw herself at Caroline and got a stranglehold on her neck. "Please, don't leave me here with them."

"I-I…"

"No, no, please. Don't leave."

"I have to. I'm sorry…"

Maggie neared her home, a little breathless, her speed having increased with the memory. Maybe, just maybe, the wound of Caroline's abandonment would finally heal with her sister's reappearance in her life. Now, if she could keep other wounds from festering. She thought about all that was happening with Mike and the boys and once again vowed she wouldn't let her own family fracture as her extended one had.

CHAPTER EIGHT

Waiting to meet Luke, Jamie sat on the floor down the hall from the gym feeling anxious. Luke had come back to school today, but had been so busy getting caught up from a two-day absence that they hadn't had much time to talk. Luke asked to meet him before practice started.

Jamie was upset about how Luke's parents had treated him, about his own dad's reaction to Jamie coming out and the tension at his house. Balancing his journal on his knees, he worked on another entry for English, only this time, he didn't have to keep it private or hide what was important to him.

They were reading Kafka's *The Metamorphosis* and the assignment was on self-identity. Though Jamie wondered if Ms. Carson designed some to the topics specifically for him, she assured him she didn't. He wrote what was in his heart.

Who is this boy?

Who is this boy emerging
From the cocoon of the perfect son?
The loyal friend?
The reliable brother?

Who is this boy
Who wants other boys?

A stranger?

A freak?
Just another scared child?

"No," I shout.
"It's me. I'm the same.
Please see me.
Please love me.
Please accept me.
I'm not so different from you."

Then an inner voice whispers,
"Yes, you are."

After he wrote the entry, Jamie could breathe easier. He checked his watch and saw it was time to meet Luke. Standing, Jamie stowed his gear in his backpack, headed down the hall, went inside the boy's locker room, and found Luke dressed in his gray and blue uniform, leaning against the wall. As he got closer, the glaring fluorescent lights from the ceiling made Luke's face pale. It was also blank. Jamie had learned quickly this was a self-protective mask he wore.

"Hey, Luke."

When he saw Jamie, Luke's expression brightened. That made Jamie feel a little better. Still, he said, "Sorry about your parents."

"Yeah, me, too."

Jamie's gut clenched as he thought about his role in this. "I pushed you to tell them. You knew they weren't ready."

"It's not your fault, Jame. It's theirs. My father is such a bigot. He's so irrational, it's hard to believe, you know?"

He didn't know. Though his own father was having trouble with Jamie's sexual orientation, it wasn't because his dad was prejudiced. "Can I help?"

"No." Luke ran a hand through his hair. "I have to wait it out."

"At least they let you come to school."

"Only because we're doing AP test review." His hand gripped the leather glove he carried. "Have to maintain the old grade point average," Luke said in an imitation of his father.

"I can't believe they kept you home for two days."

Something hard glinted in Luke's gray-blue eyes. "Fuck them."

Though he hated what he was about to say, Jamie tried to sound sincere. "We could do some damage control. If we weren't seen together again, the issue might blow over."

Luke pushed off the wall and smashed his fist into the cold steel of a locker. The tinny sound reverberated through the open space, making Jamie jump. "No. All of this can't be for nothing, Jame."

"Okay, okay." Jamie scanned the area. The rest of the team had already hustled out to the field and when Jamie saw they were alone he grabbed Luke's hand, brought it to his mouth and kissed the abrasion on his knuckles. Despite the circumstances, he reveled in the feel of Luke's skin on his lips.

Leaning in close for a minute, Luke touched Jamie's forehead with his own, then drew back. "I gotta go."

"All right. Text me later."

Jamie watched as Luke started away, his cleats clicking on the tile, his broad shoulders straining against his uniform. Despite the circumstances, he got turned on just looking at Luke. It made him edgy, like a shot of adrenaline pumped through him.

Luke turned when he got to the exit. "It'll be okay. And remember it's not your fault."

"Sure. Have a good practice."

Like he always did lately when he felt bad for Luke or about what was happening to both of them, Jamie took his iPod out of his backpack, plugged it in his ear, and punched up a song about making changes in your life and taking risky paths. The message made him optimistic, and when he got outside the sun was shining brightly. And the mild April afternoon warmed his body and his soul.

Paul and Nick exited from another door in the school. A spurt of jealousy at their ease in being together hit Jamie so hard and fast it made his stomach hurt. He wondered why they didn't have the need to come out as a couple like he and Luke did. He waved to them and they hustled over.

"Hey, Jame." Paul cocked his head. "Where were you?"

"In the locker room talking to Luke."

Nick socked him in the arm. "We been seeing you around school with him a lot."

Paul asked, "How come, buddy?"

Glancing down, Jamie kicked at a broken piece of cement on the sidewalk. "You know why." He glanced up. "You guys mad I didn't tell you sooner? About me at least?"

"Nah. People gotta do things in their own time." Nick moved in close to Paul. "You, um, gonna be open about it, that you and Luke are a couple?"

"Yeah. Soon, I hope. I'm sick of hiding who I am." He saw traces of embarrassment on their faces. "But it's really hard to do, so, you know, you have to do what's best for you."

Paul nodded. "There's a whole crowd of kids at Sherwood High that are gay, and a lot of straight ones are down with it. But I don't know about being a couple." He glanced away. "Besides, my parents would freak, big-time."

Jamie glanced at the gym. "So did Luke's."

"What about yours?"

"My dad's having trouble. My mom's been great, though." He thought about his brother still being in the dark. "Brian doesn't know yet, guys, so don't say anything."

"It's getting out, Jamie."

"I'm gonna tell him soon. He'll do okay, but his jock friends won't be cool about this."

"Rumor has it there are guys on sports teams who swing the other way. Besides Luke, I mean."

"No shit?" Maybe it wouldn't be so bad for Luke after all. Jamie's mood lightened. "Either of you got a car? I have to leave mine for Brian."

"Uh-huh." Paul exchanged glances with Nick. "We're going to see that new horror flick. Wanna come?"

"It'll be fun, Jame," Nick put in.

"Yeah, I guess."

Suddenly Jamie didn't feel so alone anymore. He thought back to the poem he wrote earlier. Maybe he wasn't so different. He hoped his friends were right and it wouldn't be so bad with his teammates.

❖

Maggie asked Jamie to go out with her on Tuesday after school. One of their favorite shopping places was Sutton Lane by the canal that ran through Rochester. The quaint area sported a string of unique shops and restaurants lining the road. People strolled along, enjoying the spring weather and peeking into shops, busy now after a long winter. They parked the car and headed for One World Products. Jamie preferred to buy from that store because the merchandise was made in developing nations and all the profits went to the artisans. She wondered if he planned to get a gift for Luke.

He linked his arm with hers as they walked. Maggie loved how affectionate he was in public, loved so much about this boy of her heart. "It's so great Caroline called you, Mom."

"I'm thrilled. Having a sibling you're close to, can talk to is so important."

Jamie shot her a sideways glance. "Translation—I should tell Brian about me. And Luke."

"All right, yes. You've got to let him know what's going on before anybody finds out at school. When he and I had dinner the other night, I skirted his questions about why it's tense at home, but you really have to do this, Jame."

Her son stopped on the sidewalk and faced her. "Some kids already know." His eyes were wide with both anxiety and excitement, like a toddler about to test his independence who was afraid to venture out, yet looking forward to it, too. "Luke and I are going on an official date soon. It's gonna get all over school that I'm gay."

"Oh, honey, then it's even more important that Brian be told."

"I know."

"How are Luke's parents taking it?"

"They freaked when he came out to them. Not like you. And Dad, too, by comparison, I guess."

Ah, more information to feed her mother's soul. Ashamedly, she felt smug, like people get when they've done something right with their kids and other parents haven't.

"I'm sorry to hear that. How bad is it?"

Jamie started walking again. "Luke wasn't in school for a few days. They kept him home." His face paled. "Away from me, like I'm some criminal. Like I'd sell him drugs or something."

Encircling his shoulder with her arm, she pulled him close. "There is *nothing* wrong with you, buddy. I promise. There are just bigoted people in the world who have narrow views."

They walked farther before Jamie spoke again. "Anyway, I'll clue Brian in tomorrow after school."

"Good."

"Did you let Aunt Caroline know what's going on when she called?"

"No, you asked me not to. I haven't even told Gretta." She tried to keep the disappointment out of her voice.

They'd reached the door of the One World. Jamie put his hand on the knob but stopped before he opened it. "You can tell Gretta. I shouldn't have asked you not to. You need to bounce things off of her."

"It's okay. I can wait."

"Nope. I think you need her now. Go ahead."

"I'll make you a deal. I'll tell her as soon as Brian knows."

"You drive a hard bargain."

"For your welfare I do, honey."

❖

Mike had just gotten back to his office from a long meeting with the powers-that-be for his company and was drained. He liked being at work these days, though, where there was no personal conflict, no holding back what he said, no walking on eggshells. Purposely banishing those thoughts now, he took off his suit coat, loosened his tie, and sat in the chair behind his desk.

Laura Simpson came to his office door. Her smile was radiant. She was young, about thirty, with real enthusiasm for her job. "Thank you so much, Mike. I honestly thought my position was going to be cut."

"You're welcome. There's too much work to do to share assistants, and besides, you keep me organized."

She crossed to the credenza, which was littered with papers. "Mind if I straighten this out now?"

"It's after five. Don't you want to go home?"

She shrugged a slim shoulder, encased in a white blouse. "Not much to go home to." Laura wasn't married, but her family lived nearby. As if she read his mind—she seemed to do that a lot—she added, "I was supposed to go to my mother's for dinner, but she canceled. Again."

"I'm sorry."

"Did you see the note from *your* mother?"

"No. I haven't checked my messages."

Coming to the desk, she leaned in close, picked up a stack of pink slips, and set them in front of him.

His mother's note said there was no emergency, she only wanted to chat. He leafed through the other slips. "There's one from Maggie in here." God knew what had happened now! He frowned at Laura. "I asked you to tell me right away if she or the boys called."

"Oh." She tucked her sweep of brown hair behind her ear. "She said she'd try your cell. I forgot about it."

His cell had been off during his afternoon meeting with his boss. His assistant should have known that.

Without saying more, Laura went back to the credenza. Puzzled, Mike watched her for a minute. Suddenly, he felt uncomfortable in her presence, so he stood, tossed some files into his briefcase, and snapped it shut. He had a church meeting at six, but he decided to go in early and have some prayer time before. Sitting in God's house often clarified things for Mike, and he needed that now.

Again, Laura turned at the sound. "Are you leaving? Your schedule says you have church at six."

"Yeah. I think I'll knock off early." He circled his desk, and when he got to the door, said, "Don't stay too late."

"I—"

"See you tomorrow."

Once in the car, a gas-saving Hyundai that he'd thankfully purchased before the economic downturn, Mike leaned back in the front seat and faced another worry that he'd been keeping at bay. Had he been right to save Laura's job? For some time, he'd suspected her feelings for him were less than professional. He hadn't encouraged her in any way, of course, but she was young and impressionable, and lonely, he guessed. Besides, Maggie said he was still handsome as sin.

Thinking of his wife, he got out his phone. He called her cell, then the home number, and no one answered. Relieved that he didn't have to face more hostility—God, he hated that he felt that way about his own family—he was suddenly anxious to get to church. Clearing his mind, Mike drove out of the parking lot and headed to St. Mary's.

❖

Maggie emptied the dishwasher, praying that all was going well upstairs. Jamie had closeted himself in Brian's room after school to tell his brother that he was gay. She was putting the last of the dishes away when a crash came from above. Rushing out of the kitchen and up the steps, she could hear Buck barking inside the room. She rapped her knuckles on the door to let them know she was coming in, then swung it open. The dog bolted out and scrambled down the steps. Jamie was sitting on Brian's double bed, his back against the headboard, knees up, his face ashen.

Brian loomed over his desk in the corner. Everything except his computer had been flung off the surface onto the floor. His lamp was upended and the wastebasket tipped on its side, spilling out papers and candy wrappers. The chair was at an angle on the dark blue rug. Behind him was one of the many sports posters lining his walls—a boy in a wheelchair lifting weights. The caption read, "We are all different, but the same."

"What's going on here?"

Brian's eyes were wild. "You knew."

Leaning against the doorjamb, she tried to appear calm. "Jamie told me a week or so ago."

"And he didn't tell *me*." He rounded on his brother. "We shared our whole lives. I told you fucking *everything*. And you kept *this* a secret?"

Maggie understood Brian's knee-jerk reaction all too well.

Jamie started to answer. "I—"

"How could you not tell me?" Brian cut him off.

"It's complicated, Bri."

"Brian," Maggie intervened. "Listen to me. We—"

His face was flushed when he turned on her. "No, Mom, don't try to calm me down. My brother's a goddamned faggot and he doesn't even bother to let me know."

Jamie gasped.

Crossing to Brian, Maggie grabbed onto his upper arms as tightly as she could. "I understand you're upset, and I'll give you space for your anger and confusion. But don't you *ever* use that vile term in my presence, or your brother's, again." She drew in a breath and tried to soften her tone. "And be careful what you say right now. Words can't be taken back later when we regret saying them."

Brian's eyes filled with tears. "Why are you siding with him?"

"There aren't sides here."

Dear God, don't let there be sides here. She couldn't handle that.

Jamie vaulted off the bed and drew himself up to full height in front of his brother. "Go to hell. For the record, there's nothing you could have told me about yourself that would make me be so brutal to you." He stormed out of the room. Maggie heard a door slam.

"I'm outta here," Brian said, brushing past her.

Again, she grabbed his arm. "No, you're not."

With a man's strength, he shrugged her hand off. "Let go, Mom."

She literally chased after him but he reached the front door before she did. "Brian, honey, please don't leave. You're upset, you shouldn't be driving."

"I gotta get out of here."

And so Maggie stood in the foyer, helplessly, as her son banged out, got in his car and drove off. She sank down on a step, her heart a giant vise in her chest. The dog scuttled over, and she buried her face in his fur. "What are we going to do, Bucky?" After taking solace in the pet's affection, she dragged herself up, climbed the stairs, and knocked on Jamie's door. "Can I come in?"

"Yeah."

The room was shadowed by maple trees right outside his window, which allowed in a warm breeze. It stirred the hint of incense in the air. Her son was on the bed, his T-shirt and jean-clad frame stretched out, his forearm resting over his closed eyes.

"You all right?" she asked.

He shook his head.

"What can I do?"

"Nothing." The sandpapery tone of his voice made her throat clog.

"Do you want to talk about this?"

No answer. Then she saw his shoulders shake. Though Jamie was a sensitive kid, she could count on one hand the number of times she'd seen him cry as a teenager. Sitting down on the bed, she tried to pull him up. He resisted, then lurched forward and collapsed into her arms. It was an awkward position, but she held him as he wept like he was a boy half his size and age. Stroking his hair, she murmured soothing words until the catharsis passed.

Finally Jamie sat back and wiped his face with the hem of his shirt. "I, um, didn't expect this from Brian."

Shock at her son's naïveté that everyone would accept his disclosure easily left her without a response. Accompanying it was raw fear that Jamie wasn't ready for what he might encounter out in the real world. Hell, he hadn't been ready for what came at him from inside his own house.

When he peered up at her, his eyes were red-rimmed. "Remember when we were little, Mom? Brian was bigger than me then. That kid Anthony picked on me so Bri beat him up. And he always chose me for his kickball team, even though I sucked at sports."

"I know, Jame."

"Now he's turning on me. I can't believe it."

"He's not turning on you. He's upset. We don't know exactly why."

"Mom, come on, he called me a faggot."

She said loftily, "I'd prefer you didn't use that ugly word, either."

Jamie gave her what passed for a smile.

"All I'm saying, honey, is there's a lot that he could be upset about."

"Name what else besides the fact that it grosses him out that he's got a gay brother."

"Well, for one, you didn't tell him sooner. You heard what he said. You two share everything. More than you share with me or Dad, right?"

"I guess."

"So maybe that's at the root of his reaction."

Jamie studied her. "You can't *make* all this right, Mom."

"I know I can't." Melissa had told her that many times. "And if I become overbearing, you need to tell me. But we know Brian. He's a decent boy. Give him time."

In the end, Jamie agreed—he didn't have much choice. As he'd said, Maggie couldn't fix this and neither could he. She went to her own bedroom to decompress, wondering how much time it would take for Brian to come to grips with his brother's homosexuality.

CHAPTER NINE

Brian stepped on the gas pedal and the engine kicked into gear. "Fucking son of a bitch. Jesus Christ." He pounded the steering wheel with his fist. When the car fishtailed, he made himself slow down. He had to stay calm until he got to Heather's. With any luck, her mother wouldn't be home.

She was. Their ordinary SUV sat in the driveway of their house. It looked like every other ordinary suburban home. Up until a few minutes ago, Brian thought his own family was as ordinary. Perfect, in some ways.

Never again! His brother was a fag. He wouldn't say the word in front of his mother again, but he could when he was alone.

His mother.

Who'd always been on his side. Who'd always been there for him. Thinking about how she looked at him today, what she said in that horrible voice, made his throat hurt.

Heather stepped out of her house, slamming the front door behind her. She was so hot in her tight jeans and pink top, with those cute little sneakers on. So feminine. But Jamie wouldn't think so. Jamie liked... Fuck!!

When she reached the window, she leaned over. Her shirt gaped and he caught a glimpse of her breasts. Usually the sight of her rack made him hard. Today, nothing. "Hey, what are you doing sitting in the car out here?"

"I..." Jesus, he blinked a few times. "I need to talk to you."

Her smile disappeared and she touched his arm. "Are you all right?"

Unable to answer, he shook his head.

"Do you want to come in?"

"No. Let's go for a ride."

After Heather told her mother she was leaving, they were on their way. Her sitting next to him calmed him down some. "Bri, what—"

"Not yet." He grabbed her hand. "Let's go to the park." Where they often went to talk. And to do other things. Thinking about those other things, and Jamie doing them with a guy, Brian wanted to puke. He swerved a little too fast into their usual spot in between two big oak trees.

"Brian, you're scaring me."

"Today I found out…it's bad."

"God, is it your parents? Jamie?"

An ugly laugh escaped him. "Jamie…Jamie…"

"Tell me, please."

He faced her. "He's gay, Heather. My brother's gay."

For some reason, she seemed puzzled. "Is that all?"

"What the fuck do you mean, is that all? Didn't you hear me, he's a queer."

Heather was so quiet, it confused Brian. Then she took his hand. "Bri, really, it's okay. He's still Jamie. He's still the same person he was yesterday."

Out of nowhere, he thought of Grandma Lorenzo. How inflexible she was. One time when they were in Cornwall, Jamie questioned her about Caroline. Their grandma said, "She's dead to me." Brian had been horrified she'd cut her own child out of her life. So, okay, he had to get a grip here. He had to find his way through this. He was just so hurt Jamie didn't tell him. So confused about how he felt about this.

"What are you thinking?" Heather asked.

He leaned his head back on the seat. "This is gonna get all over school."

"So what? Anti-gay sentiment is very uncool these days. There are TV programs and movies that show being gay in a positive light. We've even read articles in Advanced Health on sexual orientation and discussed the issue in Psychology. Teenagers are more tolerant than you think."

"Oh, man, not jocks. They are *so* not going to think this is okay.

They're brutal to the dykes on the basketball team. They make crude remarks all the time about what girls do together."

"Susie Mason and Jill Blazek are sweet girls. There are a lot of gay students at our school, Bri."

"Yeah, sure, I know. The kids in drama club." Who were Jamie's friends. Paul and Nick were gay, Jamie said. Why hadn't Brian ever recognized the significance of the fact that Jamie hung around with gay kids? "It's different when it's your own brother. Besides, nobody cool, nobody in our crowd is gay."

Heather shook her head. "When Luke Crane broke up with Kiki Jones after the play, it got around that he might be gay."

"Crane? No way, he's the best pitcher on the team."

"Bri…come on, this is the twenty-first century. Those stereotypes are passé."

"Sherwood High is conservative, Heather. I always kind of liked that." He hit his hand on the steering wheel. "And those over-the-top Christian kids will freak." Oh, shit. Julianne was one of them. Poor Jamie.

"I still don't think this is a big deal."

"You wouldn't feel that way if it was your brother who was queer!"

Very quietly, she said, "Yes, I would."

And very quickly, he realized she was looking at him the same way, using the same tone of voice that his mother had when Jamie dropped the bomb today.

Then another thought occurred to him. "You said all those kids are gay. Did you know about Jamie? That he is?"

She sighed. "I suspected. There's been some talk."

"Why the hell didn't you tell me?"

Waiting a long time before she answered, she finally whispered, "I think that's obvious."

❖

"Mrs. Davidson, this is Heather. I wanted you to know that Brian's here at my house. He's upset and not thinking straight or he would have called you himself."

Maggie could have wept with relief. "Oh, Heather, thank you for letting me know where he is."

It was past suppertime and Brian had been gone for hours. She'd left Jamie holed up in his room, headphones in place, escaping to a world of music and the Internet. Mike was at a Contemporary Issues discussion group and tonight's session included dinner. "Can I talk to him?"

"I'll ask." There was a slur of conversation. Then Heather came back on the line. "He says no. I'm sorry."

"Tell him I love him and to come home soon."

"I will. Are you okay?"

"Yes, I'm fine."

She wasn't, of course. She was shaken and worried about her sons. For so long, she'd taken their closeness for granted, relishing the fact that they were best friends.

Mike rolled in about nine. He was whistling. The church group always made him upbeat. God, she guessed, gave him hope. She was in the kitchen, baking chocolate chip cookies, Brian's favorite, trying to sort out her own feelings.

"Hi." Mike put his keys in the cupboard and came up behind her. Sliding his arms around her waist, he nuzzled her neck. He felt strong and safe and she wanted to bury herself in his chest. "Hmm, you smell almost as good as the cookies."

"I took a bath." Her antidote to tension. Usually it worked. Not tonight, though.

Drawing back, he snitched a cookie and munched on it. "How are the boys?"

Oh, Lord, she didn't want to ruin his mood, but she had no choice.

She put the last pan into the oven then faced him. "There's a problem. Brian and Jamie talked. Brian lost it and stormed out."

The muscles of Mike's face tensed and she watched the inner peace he'd gotten from church drain from his body. "Define *lost it*."

She described the incident with as much objectivity as she could. "He's still at Heather's."

"I'll talk to him when he gets home."

"I want to, too. I was part of it." She explained what she'd said when the explosion occurred. Mike always backed her in situations like this, and she needed that support tonight.

Instead, his face blanked. "You can't side with Jamie on this."

Her arms folded across her middle, she struggled to control the churning of her stomach. "I'm not siding with either one of them. And I resent you saying that to me."

He raised his chin. "Really? You've been implying worse about me for days."

"I have not."

"With every criticism of my church, of my attitude, you have."

"I—"

He pushed off the counter and walked out of the room.

Maggie fell asleep on the couch in the living room off the foyer waiting for Brian to come home. She awoke when she heard the front door open and click closed. He halted when he caught sight of her. "You didn't go to bed?"

"No. I was waiting for you."

"I'm beat. I'm gonna crash."

"Can we talk first?"

"I don't want to. Maybe tomorrow."

Rising from the couch, she crossed to the foyer and took his hand. She cradled it in both of hers. "I'm going to tell you what I told your brother. There's nothing you could do, ever, that would make me love you any less."

Conflicting emotions played across his face. Then her big jock, who had once finished a football game with a broken wrist, her tough athlete who'd been knocked off balance by a stray pitch to his leg and went on to hit the winning run, burst into tears like a little boy.

Maggie managed to get him into the living room onto the couch, and once there, she held him, much like she'd held his brother hours earlier. Brian's sobs were as wrenching as Jamie's. When he quieted, he drew back and wiped his face with sleeve. "I don't know what to say, Mom."

"Tell me what you're feeling."

"Can I be honest?"

"Absolutely. It won't help anybody to lie."

"I guess I'm embarrassed. We've been a normal family. Now I find out my brother's *gay*?"

"Do you think that will reflect badly on you at school?"

"Maybe. With the jocks, at least."

"Why?"

"Guys don't do that stuff with each other." He shook himself. "It's gross."

"Not to someone who's gay. Jamie's feelings for a person of the same sex are as natural as the feelings you have for Heather."

"No way, Mom. It's abnormal."

"Abnormal means not the norm, not like the majority. It doesn't mean wrong or perverted."

He rolled his eyes. "That's the psychology professor talking."

"And the mom. There's nothing wrong with Jamie, Brian. He merely has a different sexual orientation than you."

"You really believe that?"

"Yes, I do."

Brian hit his hand on his forehead. "What about the church? They hate homosexuals. Dad must think something's wrong with Jamie."

"You'll have to discuss that with him. But for the record, the Catholic Church says it isn't a sin to *be* homosexual, but it is to practice it."

"So what, a gay guy can't ever have sex? Yeah, right, like that's gonna happen."

"It's my belief that a loving relationship straight or gay is not a sin. But your father's views are different. You have to make up your own mind."

Leaning back into the cushions, Brian shook his head. "I been thinking about when we were little. You know, we have that picture of all of us kids on the street playing dress-up. Some of us were in girl clothes. I keep seeing it, thinking about Jamie knowing all that time he was…"

When he didn't go further with the point, she said, "First off, I don't think Jamie would have known he was gay at seven years old. The awareness would most likely come at puberty, when sexuality emerges and starts to develop."

"All right, but when he did know, he should have told me." Emotion filled Brian's words. "How could he not, Mom? We had our first cigarettes together, we read books about the birds and the bees when we didn't know anything about it. I told him when Heather and me first…" He trailed off.

Of all the topics the boys discussed with them, sex was the most strained. She and Mike had given them both "The Talk" and Mike had gotten further with them in private man-to-boy discussions, but they wouldn't openly discuss their sexual feelings with her. Of course, she'd suspected Brian and Heather were sexually active, but hearing she'd been cut out of his confidence weakened her own as a mother. Mike had told her she was overreacting. Boys were like that. If they'd had a girl, she'd be different.

Now, however, wasn't the time to deal with that issue. "You need to discuss all that with Jamie. I'm sure he had his reasons."

He pushed blond curls out of his face. "Don't you feel bad he didn't tell *you* sooner?"

"More than I can say, honey."

"Oh, Mom. I didn't think about how hard this must be for you." He hugged her. When he drew back, his face was ragged. "Can I ask you something else?"

"Always."

"It's probably stupid."

"I don't care."

"If Jamie's gay, does that mean...hell Mom, could I have, like, some of those tendencies?"

"As a psychology professor, I can tell you we all have those tendencies. Sexual orientation is more of a spectrum. Some people are bisexual, some more hetero, some more homo. Do *you* think you're closer to the homosexual side?"

"No. I like girls. Hell, I love Heather. Everything about her."

"Then there's your answer." She watched him and saw more in his expression. "What else?"

"I guess I'm disappointed. I don't want him to be gay, Mom."

For the first time that night, Maggie didn't respond to her son's comment.

"Do you?"

"I-I'm not disappointed in Jamie."

Brian's gaze narrowed on her. "Do you want him to be gay?"

Oh, God. "I want him to be happy."

"That's not an answer."

"It's the best one I can give right now." No way was she repeating to Brian what she had confessed to Melissa, what she still felt ashamed of thinking. The grandfather clock in the foyer struck one. "I think this is enough talking for tonight." She stood and reached out her hand. "You need to sleep, buddy. But before you do, come on."

She led him to the kitchen. There, they shared cookies and milk like they used to when Brian was small and was unhappy. Maggie realized she'd give anything in the world to have those days back with both him and Jamie.

❖

Jamie waited for Luke at one in the morning in a park between his and the Cranes' house. After what happened with Brian, Jamie felt so bad, he'd texted Luke and asked him to sneak out and meet him when their respective families were asleep. He begged, really, but he couldn't help it. And he knew he shouldn't be doing this, Luke had enough to deal with, but Jamie didn't know where else to turn. He'd long since stopped confiding in Julianne, and now, his brother, his best friend, had called him a faggot. He could still hear it echoing in his head, could still see Brian's contorted face when he found out the truth. Who Jamie was made his brother sick. And knowing that made Jamie feel dead inside.

When Luke pulled up in his yellow Camaro, Jamie's heart started to beat fast. Luke buzzed the window down and kept the motor running. "Jame? What's going on?"

Gathering strength, Jamie closed the distance between them, vowing he wouldn't cry again, even as his eyes began to mist. "I'm...I..."

"Jesus. Get in the car."

Jamie slid in the passenger side and shut the door. Immediately, Luke took his hand, held it in between the two of his. "Tell me."

In halting sentences, Jamie poured out the whole story about Brian. Luke gripped his fingers tight, brushed a hand down his hair, and squeezed his shoulder until the ugly truth was all out. "That's awful, Jamie. I-I guess I thought Brian would be better about it, too."

"I shouldn't be laying this on you. You're having your own problems with your family." His voice was hoarse, as if he'd been sick for a long time. "I just didn't know where else to go."

A small smile from Luke. "You know what? I like that you came to me."

"Seriously?"

"Uh-huh. It makes us more of a couple."

"I like that, too."

"I've never had anybody I could share stuff with like you had Brian."

"*Had* being the operative word."

"I really envy you, admire you."

"Honest?"

"Yep. For that and more, Jame."

Flattered, he asked, "Like what?"

Luke leaned back against the seat and stared ahead. "Your whole family, mostly. You guys love each other so much. Work through problems. Do stuff together."

Jamie was sorry Luke didn't have what he did. "Your parents will come around."

"No, Jame, they won't. I just have to accept that." He turned to Jamie. "But Brian will. You're so close. Give him time to adjust. He'll settle down and see what's really important."

Luke's confident assertion calmed Jamie. And it was cool Luke could do that for him. Jamie needed that and more tonight. "So that's all you admire about me? My family?"

"No. You've always been yourself. You didn't come out, but you never pretended to like girls."

"I never saw myself as different from anybody else."

"That's the best thing about you. You just don't know how cool you are."

What could be better than getting the approval of a boy you liked? Jamie had never, ever experienced the emotion and it was heady. Earlier, he hadn't thought anyone could make him feel better, but Luke did.

Maybe he'd even try to flirt. "You're not so bad yourself, Lucas Crane."

"Yeah?" A really sexy tone had crept into his voice and for the first time, Jamie noticed the dark blond hair peeking out from the three open buttons on his shirt. Hoarsely, Luke said, "Come over here and prove it."

So Jamie slid as close as he could get. The gearshift between them was in the way, but he didn't care. He plastered himself to Luke and was enveloped by big strong arms. Luke couldn't make Brian's reaction any more acceptable, but at least he could make Jamie forget for a little while. Against Luke's lips, he said, "I never necked in a car with anybody, except for that night at the play. And it was only one kiss."

"It's about time, then, don't you think?"

"Oh, man, do I."

❖

The morning after Jamie told Brian he was gay, Maggie headed for the gym at RCC to meet Gretta. They worked out together whenever they could—Gretta had bought a membership in the college's facility after she quit teaching. Maggie arrived early and warmed up on the treadmill, waiting for her friend. Though Jamie had lifted the caveat on telling Gretta, Maggie had indeed waited until Brian knew.

And now he did. What happened between her sons had made her physically ill. After Brian had gone to sleep, she'd locked herself in the downstairs bathroom and cried so hard she made herself sick. She felt such raw fear, such hopelessness, she wasn't able to contain it.

Gretta entered the gym from the locker room, tall and lithe, wearing a cotton peach sweat suit, not unlike Maggie's red one. After greeting her, Gretta hiked up on a treadmill.

"How was your trip?" Maggie asked.

"Great. I took a class on small art gallery ownership at the Chicago Art Museum." She rolled her eyes. "And listen to this. Tim got mad that I was gone a week."

"Maybe he just missed you."

"I'll never understand men. He travels all the time with his job and he's impatient and preoccupied when he *is* around. Then he has the nerve to criticize me."

Tim owned a business in Rochester. He commanded a hefty six-figure salary, and Gretta made plenty of money with her artwork, but like everyone else, they had their problems.

"I don't blame you. This has been a bone of contention between you two, but I thought he was going to hire a new VP who could share some of the traveling."

"Fell through." She shook her head. "Anyway, tell me about you. How's Caroline doing?"

"It's so great to talk to her, hear her voice, learn about her life. I can't wait to see her."

"Have you told Sara or your mother yet?"

"No. I won't until Caroline says it's okay. That's what she wants."

Just then, Damien Kane walked by. Dressed in sleek black workout clothes, he was sexy and fit.

"Morning, ladies. Nice to see you, Gretta."

"Hello, Damien."

He nodded to Maggie and gave her a suggestive smile. "And, Mrs. Davidson, you look as good in sweat clothes as you do out of them."

"Go away, Damien," she said. "Girl-talk time."

When he left, Gretta frowned. "Hell, could he be any more obvious?"

"He's harmless. He flirts with everybody."

Gretta grunted. "I think it's more than that on his part. And Mike has good instincts and doesn't like the guy. Unless you want to risk your marriage—" She stopped short. "What's the matter, Mag?"

Her eyes blurred.

"Is it about Damien? Is that what you've been keeping from me?"

She shook her head, unable to get out the words.

"Sunday's Easter. Is it the prospect of seeing your mother?"

"No, it's what I wanted to talk to you about but couldn't."

"Then let's knock off here and sit down."

When they were settled in the school café at a table in the corner, Gretta's face was troubled. "Tell me."

Maggie wrapped her hand around a mug full of coffee, letting its steam warm her. "I couldn't tell you before you left. Now it doesn't matter because people at school know. Jamie told me two weeks ago that he's gay."

The plastic bottle of water slipped out of Gretta's hand and hit the table with a thud. "Wow! We talked about this before, but hearing it confirmed…oh, Mag, I'm sorry." Tears coursed down her cheeks and she swiped at them impatiently. "I shouldn't be crying. It's not a tragedy. But I'm worried about how hard life's going to be for him."

Maggie's throat felt like a sock was stuffed in it. "Me, too. I'm worried about that." She shifted in her seat. "There's more."

"Oh, God, Mike! He must be devastated."

"He's struggling. So is Brian."

"I'll bet."

When Maggie recounted what had happened after Jamie's disclosure, her spirits plummeted even more. Spoken aloud, it all seemed so stark.

"I'm sorry, sweetie."

"I never expected this, Gretta. I knew Brian and Mike might have a hard time because of the church, but not that they'd be so irrational about Jamie being gay."

Gretta sat back against the vinyl chair and sipped her water. "You know, none of this is in your control. You have to let them find their own ways, Mag."

"I'm not sure they will."

"Maybe you're not giving them enough credit."

"I don't trust Mike and Brian to handle this well. Alone, anyway, without my vigilance."

"You can't protect them. You always try, but I don't think interfering this time will work. They've got to find their own ways back to Jamie themselves."

"What if they don't, Gretts?"

Her friend waited a long time before she answered. "You'll always be Brian's mother, no matter what. But Mike? If there were sides to choose between him and Jamie, who would you pick?"

Maggie said simply, "Jamie." She buried her face in her hands. "I can't believe I'm saying that. Mike's the love of my life, but it's true. I'd choose Jamie over Mike if I had to."

Gretta took her hand, clasped it tightly. "For what it's worth, Mags, Amber will always be my top priority."

Behind Gretta, a group of students entering the café caught Maggie's attention. Each of the boys had his arm around a girl, hugging her close. Maggie was instantly jealous. They seemed so normal, so untroubled, and she longed for that kind of normalcy in her life now. She averted her gaze to her coffee cup, ashamed.

"What are you thinking?"

Her friend's compassion and matter-of-factness allowed her to admit to Gretta what she'd told Melissa. "Sometimes I wish my family could go back to how they were a month ago. Sometimes, I wish Jamie wasn't gay."

"That's normal, Mag."

"But it isn't right. It isn't fair to my son."

"You're so strong. You'll get beyond this."

Right now, the compliment fell flat. Maggie felt as vulnerable as a newborn kitten and hated it!

CHAPTER TEN

Maggie's mother, Gertrude Lorenzo, sat at the head of the table in her daughter Sara's house as if *she* was the one who'd risen from the dead on Easter Sunday. Her gray hair was cut sharply around her face, her nose long, her eyes a muddy brown. Every time Mike was with the woman he wondered how Maggie had turned out to be such a kind, sensitive person having come from a woman like that. As a Christian, he tried to be forgiving, but it was tough to be charitable about his mother-in-law.

"Michael," Gertrude pronounced with a raspy voice. "You say grace."

His gaze connected with Patrick's, who was the head of the Baker household and should be doing the prayers. Pat hid a grin and nodded. Years ago, he and Mike had agreed to give Gertrude a wide berth.

"I'd be glad to say grace." He caught Maggie's grateful expression. Though she wore a cheerful yellow cotton sweater, and her dark hair curled softly at the shoulders, she seemed tired today. Regretting his role in that, he said, "Let's all grasp hands."

The nine people around the table reached out to each other. Brian was between Allison and Haley, Sara's kids. Jamie sat as far away from his brother as he could get. The fiasco of their midweek showdown lingered over the house like a fog. Though the boys had talked to Maggie that night, Mike had tried unsuccessfully to discuss the incident with each of them. Jamie seemed to resent his probing and Brian absolutely refused any dialogue.

As always, he and Maggie had hidden Easter baskets full of

small gifts and candy, but the kids went through the ritual without any enthusiasm. Now they had to deal with Gertrude, which was tough even in the best of times. Inside, Mike was a wreck.

"Dear Lord," he began. "Thank you for this bounty. Thank you for our family. Let us heed your message to us on this day—you are here, unstoppable by sin and sinners. Reveal your will and help us to live a pure and moral life by abiding by it. Amen."

When he looked up, Gertrude was smiling. "Amen. Michael you're a blessing to this family. Mary Margaret, remember that and be grateful."

Mary Margaret did not seem grateful. The narrowness of her eyes and taut jaw told Mike she was angry. At her mother's condescension? At his prayer? He'd spoken from the heart but maybe he'd offended her. It didn't take much anymore.

They ate their turkey and trimmings, served as a buffet from the kitchen, in relative silence. Mike was the one to break it. "Are you enjoying your stay with Sara, Gertrude?"

"Yes. Except I can't smoke in the house."

"Smoking is bad for you," Patrick, the doctor, asserted. "Especially after your vocal cord surgery and the swelling that comes and goes."

Gertrude sniffled. "And Jimmy's not here. That breaks my heart."

Sara shared Maggie's dark eyes and hair, but hers was cut severely at the chin and she was thinner, a bit harder, than her sister. She covered Gertrude's hand. "Jimmy's at his in-laws'. You spent Christmas with him."

"Sons should be with their mothers."

But not daughters? Given the circumstances with Caroline, his mother-in-law's remark was unbelievable. It was as if her oldest child didn't exist anymore. The woman was in for a very big blow.

Contrary to what Mike had hoped for, Caroline's reappearance was exacerbating Maggie's negative feelings toward the church. Instead of being grateful for having Caroline back and forgiving the old priest for advising the Lorenzos to send her away, Maggie seemed even more resentful. And now Jamie's circumstances were adding to her bitterness about his faith. What was God's plan here? Mike wondered to himself for the hundredth time.

Thankfully, Allison poked Brian in the ribs and broke into Mike's morbid thoughts. "Where's your girlfriend today, Bri?"

Brian gave a half smile. "I had brunch with her family this morning. They, um, have a hard time at holidays. Her father moved out around this time."

Because her father had cheated on her mother. Mike couldn't imagine how he'd handle that happening. It was inconceivable to think of Maggie with another man. The thought led to a quick prayer to do better in supporting her.

Patrick picked up the ball. "You could have invited Heather and her mother."

"Not if the woman's divorced." This from Gertrude, in a deadly grave voice. "It's a sin."

Jamie straightened. "Grandma, I thought Easter was supposed to be a time of forgiveness and redemption."

"Some things can't be forgiven."

Sara squirmed in her chair. She was in for a shock, too, when Maggie revealed their *two* secrets. "How's work going, Mike?" she asked.

"Fine. Long hours lately, though."

"A man who works as hard as you do needs time off." Gertrude turned to Maggie. "You should take better care of him."

His wife glanced away. Avoidance worked best with her mother. Jamie scowled. "Grandma, Mom's got a job, too."

"But he's the man, and men support their families. You'll find out when you grow up and get married. Your mother should be staying home with you, like Sara did with her girls."

Though Sara rarely bucked Gertrude, she loved her sister, too. "Maggie's made choices that work for her, Mother."

Dead silence. Gertrude Lorenzo's favorite weapon.

Finally the interminable meal ended. Brian went outside, ostensibly to call Heather, and Mike and Patrick escaped to the living room, while the women began to clean up. That was the process in this house. Instead of going with the guys, Jamie picked up some dishes.

At the doorway to the living room, Mike studied his son. Images bombarded him: Jamie wanting to learn to bake with Maggie, preferring to play with the girls down the street instead of the boys, eschewing sports and loving poetry. Like helping out today in the kitchen, there had been signs all along that his son was different. Mike wondered how he'd missed them, and what he could have done to change Jamie if he'd picked up on them earlier.

❖

"Jamie, go watch baseball." Gertrude Lorenzo's voice was strident and grated on Maggie's frayed nerves.

"I don't like to watch baseball unless Brian's team is playing." He glanced at Maggie and gave her a shy smile. She knew he was thinking about Luke on the team, and how great it felt, as he said, to have a boyfriend. She winked at him.

"Well, go play on the computer."

"After I help clean up."

The most Jamie got to do was bring in plates, then Sara kicked him out of the kitchen. He left Maggie with a sympathetic glance.

"Jamie's different, Maggie," her mother said.

You don't know the half of it, Maggie thought as she scraped food from the plates into the garbage disposal. "He's considerate, Ma."

Allison, pretty and petite like her mother, was putting out chocolate mousse, flaky apple pie and a variety of Italian cookies on the kitchen table. "I'm going to marry somebody like him. I'm not going to do all the grunt work myself."

Gertrude snapped, "Wait till you're married to criticize, young lady."

Given Jamie's comments at dinner, and now Allison's, Maggie realized how the younger generation seemed to stand up to her mother more than she and Sara did. Feeling abashed by that, Maggie straightened and faced her mother. "Mike cleans up at our house. So does Brian. We all pitch in."

Her sister shot her an annoyed look. "Well, you always did have people spoil you."

"Yeah, as if Dad doesn't spoil *you*, Mom." Allison again. Her pretty eyes held a hint of rebellion.

"Maggie's *husband* needs spoiling," Gertrude said. "He seems exhausted. Probably from all he does around the house. Even the grocery shopping. In my day, I never would've made your father go to the store."

Maggie's heart rate escalated and she busied herself with drying the pans Sara was washing. But her mind hurtled back to when she was five and forced to go grocery shopping with her mother because Caroline was at school and Maggie was too little to leave home alone...

The Food Mart was huge, noisy and big people bumped Ma's cart all the time. With each nudge, her mother's face became more pinched. "We gotta hurry. Mary Margaret, go get the milk from the cooler."

"I don't wanna, Ma." The milk was up high and she couldn't always reach it.

"Jesus Christ, it's right around the corner. I can't do all this alone. You have to earn your keep. Now go or you'll get it when you get home."

Maggie's new pink sneakers, that Caroline had bought her with babysitting money, dragged on the floor as she traipsed away in search of milk. When she reached the refrigerator section she shivered in her light T-shirt.

She looked up, then to the sides, but the milk wasn't here. Somebody had moved it. Oh, no, what was she going to do?

"Can I help you, young lady?" a woman asked.

Never talk to strangers, Caroline had said.

So Maggie shook her head and ran back to find her mother. But she ended up in another aisle. Ma was nowhere in sight.

Maggie tried two more aisles—there were so many—but couldn't find Gertrude. The chatter and clangs of carts got louder and the store got noisier by the minute. Closing her eyes, Maggie dropped down on the floor and covered her ears. The tile was freezing cold on her bare legs.

Suddenly, somebody was shaking her shoulder. She peered up and saw two men from the store and her mother standing over her. "Here's your mom, sweetheart," one man said. "We found her."

Gertrude's lips thinned. "I got her now. Thank you."

When the men left, she yanked Maggie up by the arm so hard it made her wince. "How could you embarrass me like this? Everybody heard about you over the loudspeaker. Just wait till we get home..."

"Aunt Maggie, are you all right?" Allison had touched Maggie's shoulder.

"Oh, yeah. Yeah, I am, sweetie. I just zoned out."

She pasted on a smile.

Sara gave her a questioning look.

Her mother said, "I thought you were ignoring me because I scolded you about Mike." Not a trace of apology in the statement. Maggie had never heard the words "I'm sorry" come out of her mother's mouth.

"No, I'm not. But I wish you wouldn't harp on me about taking better care of him."

Gertrude's eyes slitted. For a minute, Maggie was paralyzed by the expression on her mother's face. She was right back in the grocery store, in that life, when Gertrude had complete control over her.

Her mother's hands went to her temples dramatically. "I'm getting a headache from Mary Margaret's attack. Sara, I have to lay down."

Haley approached her. "Come on, Grandma. I'll help you to your room."

After they left, Sara's face was flushed and her shoulders stiff. "Did you have to do that?"

"In some ways, yes."

"I'll bear the brunt of it, you know."

"I'm sorry."

"Tell her that."

"I'm not sorry for what I said to her. I'm sorry it will affect you."

"You can't change her, Maggie. And trying upsets everybody."

"I think it's a sin what Grandma did to your sister." Allison's tone was full of contempt. "Don't you, Aunt Maggie?"

"Yes, I do."

She asked Sara, "Mom, don't you miss your sister?"

"I hardly remember her. I think it best that we don't talk about her. When will you learn that you can't control everything, Maggie?"

Allison started to speak, and Sara held up her hand. "Be quiet, young lady. This isn't your concern."

Throwing the dishcloth on the table, Allison said, "Fine, Mother," and stormed out.

"See what you've done now."

Maggie's strength deserted her and she white knuckled the counter for physical support. First, Jamie's confrontation with Brian last week. Then the tension between her and Mike. Add that to her mother's constant criticism, and suddenly, one of the secrets she'd been keeping was too much for her. She needed to talk about Caroline. So she purposely softened her voice. "Sara, let's not fight. Something's happened that we're going to have to stand together on."

Her sister's face filled with concern and Maggie was reminded of Sara's kind streak. Once, when Maggie contracted food poisoning and was hospitalized for four days, Sara came at night after Mike and the boys left to sit with her. When Brian injured his back at baseball practice and needed a week of bed rest, she brought magazines and games for his computer over to their house throughout his recuperation.

"What is it, Mags?"

"Caroline called me. Well, her daughter phoned first, then she did."

Sara's hand went to her mouth and she leaned against the sink.

Maggie rushed on to get it all out. "Her husband died and her daughter, Teresa, that's our niece's name, called because she was worried about Caroline."

"Oh, my God. She's had a whole life we don't know about."

"And she was happy. We should be glad about that."

Sara stood stock still, staring at Maggie.

"It's okay, Sara. Caroline's a wonderful person."

Finally Sara asked, "How much have you talked to her?"

"Weekly, and we send e-mail."

"When did Teresa call?"

"At Christmas time."

"You've known since then and haven't told me?"

"I was waiting until Caroline said I could."

Sara gasped. "Oh, my God, Ma will never be able to handle this."

Maggie lifted her chin. "She's going to have to."

"What do you mean?"

"Because in May, Caroline's coming to see us."

❖

When Jamie left the kitchen, he was pissed. He couldn't stand seeing what his grandma did to his mother. What he'd just witnessed made him count his blessings. The situation with his dad wasn't good, but he had his mom's support. Bypassing the TV room because he didn't want to see Brian, he trundled down to the Bakers' finished basement, thinking he'd use the computer there. He booted it up and sent for his e-mail. He was scanning the list in his inbox when he heard someone on the stairs. He hoped it was Allison or Haley.

It wasn't. Over his shoulder, he saw his father walking toward him. Up close, his dad seemed haggard, as if he hadn't been sleeping. "Hi, Jame. Grandma give you a hard time?"

This was safe ground, one they'd bonded over for a long time. "Not me so much. She's ragging on Mom. Why doesn't Mom stand up to her?"

His dad dropped down on a stuffed chair adjacent to the computer. "You know Mom's been to therapy about this, right?"

"Yeah, sure, she always says the people who *don't* go get help are the crazy ones."

"I think she discovered that trying to change Grandma was pointless and would only cause her more pain. Grandma's what some books call an irregular person, and trying to change her basic beliefs and personality only causes your mother heartache."

Jamie felt his throat clog. "Is that a subtle message to me?"

"Excuse me?"

"Are you trying to tell me you and Brian aren't going to change your minds about me?"

His father's jaw dropped. Deep hurt etched itself out in his face. "God, Jamie, do you see me in league with your grandmother?"

"No, I don't." He sighed heavily. "Can I be honest with you?"

"Of course. I always want that."

"Sometimes, you know, your religious beliefs seem more important to you than I am."

"Oh, honey, I'm sorry you think that. Sure, my faith is important, but Mom, you, and Brian are the most important things to me."

"Not God?"

"The God I believe in would want me to love you as I do. Besides, I see God as the center of my life, as part of all my relationships. I feel one with God. He's integral to my feelings for you three."

Though Jamie didn't fully understand what his father was saying, probably because he never experienced God that way, his dad's explanation made him feel a little better.

"But I have to be honest, son. I'm still struggling with the church's views on homosexuality and how they apply to you."

"Love the sinner, hate the sin? What do you think, Dad, that I'm going to hell if I love another guy? Have sex with him?"

"There are sinners in heaven, son."

Jamie froze. The statement just about killed him. "That's how you see me? As a sinner?"

"We're all sinners."

"Not because of who we are. Other people sin by action. You think I'm sinful because of the person I am." He felt his eyes blur. "And you don't even realize how awful it feels having you say that to me." He swiveled around to the computer. "I don't want to talk to you anymore."

His father was silent, then Jamie heard him stir, and from the corner of his eye, saw him stand. He didn't come to Jamie, didn't hug him like before or even put his hand on Jamie's shoulder. He only said, "I'll never abandon you, Jamie, and neither will God."

His back to his father, he said, "In a way, Dad, you already have."

❖

The dream came to Maggie that night.

Jamie was three and Brian four. Wearing Oshkosh overalls and little blue high-top sneakers, they were strolling down their street, Autumn Lane, holding on to Maggie's hands, and suddenly the location changed. It became Second Street, where Maggie had grown up in Cornwall. On a hill, the road was lined with older homes in a predominately Italian neighborhood from which the scent of spicy spaghetti sauce often wafted. The boys were singing a song from *Sesame Street* and Maggie was laughing at their off-key rendition of Big Bird's adventures.

Then, her mother came toward them. She wore her usual house dress and her perpetual frown. "What are you *doing?*" Gertrude yelled when she reached them.

"Taking the boys for a walk."

"What will the neighbors think?"

Used to that refrain, Maggie tried to divert her mother from her unreasonable anger. "Say hi to Grandma, guys."

Breaking free, Brian raced to her mother and buried his face in the folds of her skirt. "Nana."

Her mother caressed his neck. "My boy," she murmured.

Jamie tended to emulate his brother. He ran to Grandma, too.

But Gertrude jumped back and held up the palm of her hand. "Don't."

Maggie's little son stopped short. "Nana?"

Gertrude looked at Maggie accusingly. "He's a bad seed."

Scooping Jamie up into her arms, Maggie cuddled him close. "Ma, how can you say that?"

"He is, and it's your fault. I'm taking Brian to live with me so you don't ruin him, too. Come on, darling," she said, leading the boy down the concrete sidewalk.

"No," Maggie screamed. "You can't have him. He's mine."

She tried to pick up her feet, get some momentum to rescue her son, but she was stuck, rooted to the ground. "No, come back. Bring Brian back to me."

"It's your fault," her mother called out again and kept walking.

Brian held his grandma's hand with undiluted trust. He had no idea what emotional atrocities the woman would inflict on him.

Gulping for air, Maggie found herself sitting up in bed, in the room she shared with Mike, in the home they'd made together.

He had hold of her arms. "Honey, are you all right?"

Her eyes focused. "Oh, God, oh."

"You were calling your mother's name."

"She stole Brian away from me and told me it was my fault she had to take him."

"Brian's in his room. So is Jamie. And I'm right here. Everyone's safe. We're all fine."

Maggie shivered. Even poised on the fence between fantasy and reality, she knew that statement was false. Everyone wasn't fine and she feared, like in the dream, she was losing what was most important to her.

❖

The next weekend, Mike and Maggie went to the Rochester Art Gallery where the Clothesline Art show was held every spring. They always arrived at eight to help Gretta and Tim set up a booth for Gretta's artwork display. Then they stuck around most of the day, shopped, relieved the Chandlers for lunch and enjoyed Gretta's sales.

Tim greeted Mike warmly and kissed Maggie. "Hey, guys, thanks for helping."

Mike said, "We wouldn't think of missing your exhibit."

"Let's start with the tent."

While the guys were busy with poles and canvas, Gretta pulled Maggie away to sort through boxes they'd set in the back area near a parking lot. They could hear the low hum of conversation from the men, but no words. Gretta kept glancing at them.

Maggie took a painting Gretta had done from a box. It was Picasso-esque, of a figure torn apart and put back together again. It was called *Fractured Woman*. Maggie knew how that felt. When her friend again looked at the guys, though, Maggie asked, "What's wrong?"

"I guess I should tell you before Mike does. Mags, Tim said he'd feel the same as Mike if Amber told us she was a lesbian."

Another blow out of nowhere, knocking her off-kilter. "But you guys don't even go to church."

"No, he didn't mean because of religion. He thinks fathers have a harder time than mothers accepting their kid's homosexuality."

"I've read that can be true. I never thought Tim would…"

"Don't misunderstand. He's totally supportive of Jamie, says he loves the kid to pieces, but he's worried about Mike, too."

"So am I. Craig Johnson hasn't been around much since he found out. Mike needs somebody to talk to."

"I've never been able to tolerate the Johnsons' holier-than-thou attitude."

"I thought we all were so close. I'm shocked he'd alienate Mike like this."

"How are *you*?"

"Hanging in there."

"We haven't had much time to talk. How'd Easter go with your mother?"

"Unbelievable." She dropped down on the grass after she set

the fractured woman on the stack again. "Jamie took her on about Caroline."

"Really?"

Maggie explained the circumstances.

Gretta's grin lighted her mood. "I always did love that boy. Good for him."

"He stands up to her better than I do. So did Sara's daughter. I told my younger sister, by the way, about Caroline." Maggie could still see Sara's confused face. "Poor Sara. She straddles the world between placating my mother and being true to herself."

"When will she learn there is no pleasing your mother?"

"She probably won't. She never went to get help about it." Maggie leaned against the bed of the truck. "You know what? I'm so tired of all this and was hoping for a respite, for some quality time with Mike, without the kids around. Let's not talk about it anymore."

For the rest of the day, Maggie tried hard to enjoy setting up Gretta's booth, joking like old times and sharing coffee with her friends. What started out as an effort soon became natural. When patrons began to arrive, she and Mike left to wander the grounds. They'd check back with Gretta and Tim at noon, but for the morning, they were on their own.

Given the upheaval in their lives, Maggie treasured the normalcy of the tradition. Mike held her hand as they walked through the vendors selling woodwork, jewelry, handmade clothing, and other high-quality crafts. Dressed in a sweater and jeans, like him, she snuggled into him against the slight chill in the air.

He kissed her hair. "I'm glad we did this again."

"Me, too. We need time together alone."

"Let's not talk about anything heavy. Too much is going on. We'll just enjoy the day."

"I agree, honey."

They stopped at a stand where an Italian man was selling bracelets. Stones in myriad colors winked in the sunlight. "I want to buy you a present."

"I don't need any jewelry, Mike. And we just spent all that money on Cancun."

"Still…" He pointed to the display. "Let's browse."

He insisted on purchasing a beautiful bracelet of what she thought were amethysts but was actually Murano glass from Venice. The piece was breathtaking.

"You always wanted to go to Italy," he said as they strolled away, the pretty purple stones encircling her wrist.

"We still will, Mike. Won't we?"

"Yeah, we will. I promise." He squeezed her hand. "We're going to get through this."

The assurance had her snuggling into him again. The feel of him next to her, his woodsy aftershave filling her head, made her body respond. He asked, "The, um, boys have dinner plans, don't they?"

"Yeah. Brian's at Heather's. Jamie's hanging out with some friends."

"And the Chandlers are always too whipped to go out after this."

"I know." She smiled up at him like she used to when they were college kids and decided to skip class to go to Mike's apartment to make love.

"You thinking what I am?"

"Uh-huh."

He laughed.

They enjoyed the rest of the day knowing what they had to look forward to. And that night, the lovemaking was sweet and sensual, as it had been all those years ago. Maggie fell asleep content and happy for the first time in weeks.

CHAPTER ELEVEN

His face lifted, Brian let the hot spray pummel him. It was a while before he noticed his teammates in the communal shower stopped joking and mocking each other. Just the hiss of the water sounded in the too-silent space. He opened his eyes to see Luke Crane had stepped into the area.

"Why don't you wait to get in here, Crane?" This from Eric Cummings, who'd perfected the art of being an asshole.

Luke frowned. "Why the hell would I do that?"

Cummings plopped his hands on his hips. The pose was ridiculous with water dripping off his naked body. "We don't wanna have to watch out if we drop the soap."

Heather had been right. Luke was gay. What Brian hadn't known was that he liked Jamie. Jesus, Brian couldn't believe it. It felt like a month, not just six days, since Jamie told him he was gay and was seen openly with Luke around school.

"Lay off," the catcher, Mason Edwards, said.

Cummings shot him a vicious glare. "You not tellin' us something, Mase?"

"Shut the fuck up, is all."

The water continued to steam and spit, but no one else said a word.

And it wasn't right. "That attitude's so backward, Cummings." Brian's tone of voice was as disgusted as he could make it. "Grow up and join the twenty-first century." He took the phrase from Heather, though he was still pissed off at her for criticizing his reaction to Jamie's situation.

One by one, the rest of the guys glanced away—even Edwards—but not before Brian saw the guilty expressions on their faces. Did they agree with Cummings or were they just too afraid to buck him? For some reason, Cummings's bullying always went unchecked.

Luke said, "Fuck you," turned, and left the shower.

Cummings called out to his back, "That's just what we're tryin' to avoid, man."

Hell! Were people saying stuff like this to Jamie? A huge wave of guilt swamped Brian.

Then Eric Cummings focused his attention on Brian. "So you wanted him to stay, Davidson? Didn't know *fagdom* ran in the family."

It was all too much for Brian. Hunching over like he was about to make a tackle, he charged Cummings. Several guys intercepted him and held the two of them apart. His body was slick from the water, so he got free just as Coach Perkins stepped into view.

"What's going on?" Coach shouted.

Cummings angled his chin. "Ask *him*."

Coach stared them all down then focused on Brian. "Davidson, get dressed and come to my office."

All the while he was drying off and putting on his clothes, Brian's mind whirled. He'd been right about the jocks' reaction to Luke and Jamie, though not all of them participated. But it was *silent consent*, as Ms. Carson called it. The team had been tense and tempers ran high all week. Again, Brian thought of his brother. God, he hoped Jamie's friends were treating him better. At least he had the theater kids. Brian was thinking about what Jamie could be going through—and how he'd let his brother down—when he reached the physical education office off the locker room. Coach's door was open.

The space was chock full with three desks, filing cabinets, and a couple of chairs. Sports schedules were posted on the walls along with newspaper clipping about the games. The room smelled like sweat. Coach was perched on a tipped-back chair, feet propped on his desk, drinking fortified water. "Sit down, kid."

Please, God, let Coach be okay with all this.

Brian sat. "What's up?"

"Is it true? About Crane and your brother?"

Shifting in his seat, Brian shrugged as if it didn't bother him. "Yeah, I guess."

"Hard to believe Luke's a fag. Christ, he's one hell of an athlete." Coach shook his head. "What a waste."

Feeling guilty, Brian nonetheless held his tongue.

"I gotta ask this, Davidson, even though I could get in a shitload of trouble for it. So don't tell anybody. But I gotta know if you're of the same persuasion as your brother? Two on one team would be a hell of a thing."

"Jesus, no. I got a girlfriend."

Coach seemed relieved. "Then don't stand up for Crane. No matter what's politically correct today, Cummings will bury you."

Brian's mother would freak if she heard Coach's advice. A year ago, Brian had told her about Perkins calling the gym class for kids with special needs *Phys. Ed. for Dummies*. His mom said Coach shouldn't be working with kids, not if he was that much of a Neanderthal. She wanted to report him to the principal, but Brian freaked and convinced her not to.

"I won't defend Crane," Brian told the coach. And already feeling shamed, he added, "But I'll stand up for Jamie if I have to."

"Be careful. The captain of the team has to be able to lead his men. If you're not up to the job…"

Shocked, Brian nonetheless got the message. Fuck! He worried about Coach's warning all the way to the car. Along with it, he felt the huge weight of guilt. His mother wouldn't be proud of him. No matter what she said, she didn't feel about him the way she did a few days ago.

Damn it, *he* hadn't done anything wrong. All he wanted was for his life, his family, to be the way they were before. Guys looked up to him. Girls flirted with him. He was voted homecoming prince his junior year and was a shoo-in for Senior Prom King. When Senior Superlatives came out, Brian got Best Athlete and Most Liked. He told himself to calm down. He still had all that. Coach was just saying not to go overboard in defense of his brother.

But the next morning, when he stopped at his locker to get his books, *Fag Lover* was scrawled on the inside wall. The only other people who had the combination were Heather and Brian's friend Tony. At lunch, Brian left his English notebook on the table where he always sat with his teammates, and when he came back from getting his food, the cover had filthy words all over it. Inside, somebody had drawn obscene pictures of two guys humping. By the end of the day, Brian felt like the outcast.

Tony found him at the drinking fountain before practice. "We're goin' up to the lake tonight. Wanna come?"

Brian knew all about the lake. Eric Cummings's family had a cottage there. The guys drank and screwed around. In the past, if they asked him to go along, he refused and said he was in love with Heather. The guys would rag on him that he was pussy whipped, but they'd let it go. He started to say no again when he caught the look on Tony's face.

It was challenge.

Which was why, four hours later, after lying to his parents about where he was, Brian arrived at the lake house. Outside, the water was too cold to swim in, but the air was warm enough to take the boat out for a spin. They spent an hour drinking beer and shooting the shit with the girls. Barb Atkins, Tami Smith, and Josie Giancarlo had gotten wind of the boys' night out and crashed the party, just as they were expected to.

It had all gone according to plan. And right now, everybody was pairing off. Since there were three girls and four guys, Brian had a perfect excuse for booking. He could still see Heather tonight if he left right now. Her unhappy face wavered before him. Then that cleared and Big Boobs Barbara stood before him.

"Wanna go for a walk?" she asked and blew a puff of cigarette smoke in his face.

"Hell, ditch that. It smells like shit."

Her eyes widened. With hurt?

"Sorry, Barb."

"It's okay." She stubbed out the cigarette in a nearby ashtray. "I got other stuff." She patted her bag. "You smoke pot?"

"Sometimes."

"We could sit on the dock. Smoke some. Talk."

Yeah, sure. She wanted to do more than talk, and they both knew it.

Cummings cruised by with Josie thrown over his shoulder and Simonetti behind him. "We call the first door on the left." He stopped and glanced behind him. "Davidson, get a move on. We gotta be home by midnight." Then he sneered. "Unless you're not interested..."

Brian took a deep breath.

He pictured Jamie's shock when Brian called him a faggot.

He remembered the sick looks of the guys in the shower.

He heard Heather criticize him whenever they discussed Jamie now.

But most of all, he recalled his mother's face, full of disappointment.

So he grabbed Barb's hand and pulled her out to the dock.

❖

Later that week, Maggie sat on a bench on the edge of the sprawling college lawn and pulled out her cell phone. April had dawned beautifully in upstate New York, bringing spring breezes and sunshine. Maggie needed warmth these days and the feel of the sun on her face.

The fact that she'd had little sleep the last month was catching up with her. She'd managed to get through her afternoon class and decided connecting with Caroline would cheer her up. Her sister was off from school today, so Maggie hoped to catch her.

The phone rang twice, then, "Hello."

"Caroline, it's Maggie."

"Hi, honey. What a nice surprise." They usually talked at the end of each week and e-mailed in between. Maggie wasn't crazy about texting, and Caroline didn't seem to favor it either.

"I had a few minutes so I thought I'd give you a ring. Can you talk?"

"Of course." A pause. "What's wrong?"

"Nothing. I just wanted to hear your voice."

"*Your* voice says you're lying."

Could she breach Jamie's privacy and tell Caroline about the minefield her family life had become? She'd only told Gretta because Jamie said she could.

"I, um, can't tell you what's wrong. I promised I wouldn't."

Caroline waited a beat. "Sisters don't count."

Maggie laughed out loud. "I love hearing that, but no. I promised. I'll be able to explain everything soon." She hesitated. "But I do want to talk about Easter."

A sudden, scary silence. "Did you tell Ma that we're in touch again?"

"No, no, I didn't." This was the first time Caroline had brought up their mother, so Maggie seized the opportunity. "I'll wait until you're ready to break the news to her."

"I know I've avoided discussing her. Coping with Derek's death hasn't left much room for other kinds of mourning. Besides, I've gotten used to blocking my childhood."

"I'm not sure that's bad. But, Caro, I did tell Sara. I kind of blurted it out after Ma had another of her hissy fits."

"How did Sara take it?"

"Mixed. She was so little when you left, she really doesn't remember you."

"That's sad."

"I know, but you can rectify the situation when you visit at the end of May. Are you anxious for school to be done?"

Maggie heard a sniffle. "In some ways, so I get to see you. But Derek and I always went to our cottage on a lake out here the week after I finished."

"I'm sorry, Caro."

"Oh, Mags. This is so hard."

"God, I wish I was there with you. Maybe the reunion we'll have when you come here will take the edge off what you're missing."

"You know what? I think you're right."

"Little sisters usually are."

She loved talking to Caroline, but today the loss of her for so long rubbed raw. Maybe because the threat of other potential losses loomed like a big black cloud in the sky.

❖

Mike stepped into the interior of St. Mary's Church and felt a calm descend over him. Candles flickered on the altar and the atmosphere was still and hushed. Because he was early for his appointment with Father Pete, he sat in a pew and bowed his head.

So, he said to God. *My life is in havoc mode. I need help. I need to do what's right.*

God didn't talk back, but as time went on, Mike felt His presence. *I've been making mistakes. Acting foolishly. Hurting Maggie. I'm sorry for that. Sorry for not being a better father, husband. Even friend. Help me.*

A hand settled on his shoulder. "Mike?"

He looked up at the kindly man who'd brought him closer to God. "Hi, Father Pete."

"Would you like to pray more or talk now?" The priest's expression was serene, his voice gentle. Age wrinkled his face and lines had deepened around his eyes in the years since Mike had known him. But his genuine fervor and love of God had never changed.

"Talk. I said I'd be home for dinner."

They settled into an anteroom of the church proper. Father Pete took a chair at the desk and Mike dropped down in front of it. Behind the priest, a huge painting of the Sacred Heart beamed down on them. "So tell me what's going on, Mike."

Recounting all the details of the last weeks and how he'd let everyone down to a man he admired so much made Mike feel terrible.

Father Pete waited until he was done, then gave him a benevolent smile. "God's with you in this. Don't forget that."

"I'll try not to."

"And your behavior's understandable. You let off a little steam, but your concern is well founded."

"How am I going to reconcile Jamie's sexual preference with the church's views on homosexuality?"

"First off, let's be clear on what the church believes. We no longer think of the homosexual as irredeemable. We believe being gay or lesbian is a choice. By your choice of words, I see you do, too. But even if the congregant doesn't want to change, that's workable. All he has to do is refrain from acting on those sexual impulses."

"Jamie has to be celibate all his life?"

"If that's what it takes. God doesn't give anyone a burden he can't handle."

Mike scowled.

"I see you don't think your son can do that."

"No, Father, I don't. Celibacy is an abnormal state for human beings."

Father Pete leaned over his desk, bracing himself on his forearms. "Listen, Mike, this is new to you. You don't have to decide a path to take now. I've got some literature. Some information about why people are gay and what God expects of them. There are spiritual counselors within the church to talk to boys like Jamie. And there are reparative therapy camps at our disposal as well. They're residential facilities that take kids who think they're gay and lead them back into their natural state. The state God wants for them."

The idea of sending kind, sensitive Jamie to a place like that disgusted Mike. He knew the elements of deprogramming camps. Isolation. Deprivation. Intolerance. Could Mike inflict that on his son in the name of God?

"I'll get you the literature."

He nodded.

"Do you think Jamie would come to talk to me?"

"I don't know."

"How about Maggie?"

"I doubt she'd come."

"I've been worried about her. She needs God's guidance in this, too."

When Mike thought of how his wife stood up for Jamie, and how gently she'd treated Brian, he had trouble believing that God wouldn't want her to do just what she'd done. And, as much as he hated it, the fact that she'd been searching for another church meant she still wanted God in her life.

He stood. "I'd like to pray some more before I go home."

"A balm to the soul. Go ahead. I'll bring the reading material out to you."

Mike found his way back to a pew. This time, he dropped onto the hard kneeler. He folded his hands and bent his head. *Please*, he prayed. *Please help me to do the right thing.*

It wasn't until early the next week that Maggie noticed Heather hadn't been around lately. She often stayed for supper and helped out with cooking. Thinking the girl would be safe dinner conversation, Maggie brought up her absence over a meal of comfort food—Southern fried chicken, potato salad, and corn on the cob. "Where's Heather been all week?"

Brian's light complexion reddened. Even as a child, he couldn't hide his feelings. But it was Jamie's reaction that drew their attention. He slammed down his glass on the table, startling everybody.

Brian's head snapped up. "Shut up."

"Excuse me?" This from Mike. "That's not how we talk in this house."

The boys glared at each other like sworn enemies. As far as Maggie knew, Brian and Jamie hadn't spoken much since Jamie came out to him. She'd tried to encourage some communication between them, but they'd essentially told her to back off.

She turned to Brian. "What's going on with Heather?"

"She broke up with me."

"What?" Mike shook his head. "Why?"

"Personal reasons."

Throwing back his chair, Jamie stood. "It's because of me."

Maggie's heart plummeted. "Heather broke up with Brian because she found out you're gay? I don't believe it of her."

"Not that." Jamie's stance was stiff. "It's all over school that Brian screwed around on her at an orgy at the lake."

Mike fell right into the father role he played so well. "Brian, is that—"

Brian bolted off his chair, circled the table, and launched himself at his brother. They stumbled backward and amidst the thuds and crashes, Buck flew in from the living room, barking frantically.

Fists connected with flesh as punches were thrown.

Maggie screamed, "Stop it, you two."

Mike got between them and held Brian by the arms. Maggie circled behind Jamie, dragging him back. "I can't believe you'd attack your brother," Mike shouted.

"He had no right to tell."

"Then it's *true*?"

Blood trickled down Brian's jaw from a cut on his lip. A quick glance told her Jamie's nose was bleeding.

Mike yanked on Brian's shoulders forcefully. "I asked you a question. You were part of an *orgy* at the lake?"

"I went up to Cummings's cottage, and there were some girls there." His hands curled at his sides. "I don't wanna talk about this in a goddamned public forum."

"You don't have to," Jamie spat out. "It's obvious what you were doing."

"Okay, Einstein, clue me in."

"Proving you're not like me. You really are a dumb jock." He stalked from the room.

Mike said to Brian, "Get your jacket. You're coming with me."

"I don't want to."

"I don't care. We're going to hash this out, man-to-man."

Maggie swallowed hard. She had no idea what to do, and so she stood helplessly in the center of the porch while Mike dragged Brian out of the house with him.

Trembling all over, she surveyed the room: one straight-back chair was upended on the floor, the coffee table was at an angle, and a lamp had shattered into pieces. It had broken her heart to watch her beloved sons duke it out in the home she'd created for them.

CHAPTER TWELVE

From the time the boys started wearing their adolescent shoes, the Davidsons had an unwritten rule at their house not to invade each other's privacy. That meant they always knocked on closed doors and didn't enter anyone's space unless invited. There would be no snooping in a wallet or purse, no hacking into personal e-mail, no purposeful eavesdropping on conversations.

And no parental overriding of these dictums.

"But if you leave something lying around," Maggie had warned, "like a note from a girl, or an essay you wrote for school, then it's fair game. This includes what's in your pockets when I do the laundry."

They'd all abided by that agreement for years.

Maggie recalled that conversation a few days after the boys' fight when she found Jamie's journal sitting on the coffee table. Mike was at church to help with some banners for tomorrow's Mass, and Jamie and Brian were still asleep. She had no idea what went on between Mike and Brian when they'd gone out that night of the fight, and Jamie withdrew into himself for the remainder of the week. Starved for information on how *he* was doing, at least, she decided to take a peek at the journal. Sitting in the sunlight streaming through the living room windows, she could hear the birds chirp happily outside.

She opened the leather-bound book gingerly. He'd read her some of his writing, and she smiled when she glimpsed previous entries with a mythology theme, an interest they shared. There was humor here, too, like the one about a vampire showing up at the blood drive Jamie had taken charge of this year. Leafing to the most recent ones, she skimmed them. These were not funny. They were deadly serious, about what had been happening with his coming out. "Free to Be You and Me" and "Alone" were heartbreaking. Then she came upon the poems about their family, particularly Mike and Brian.

My Father's Hands

Strong enough to move mountains,
Soft enough to wipe tears,
My father's hands were part of my life.
They had combed messy hair for church,
Tossed a ball in the backyard,
Fixed a bicycle chain
So I could ride with other kids.

Never had they fisted with anger,
Punched a hole through the wall,
Slapped a single human being.
But grasped my shoulder in support,
Clapped at my successes.

Now, he does not touch me.
It is punishment for being who I am.

I never thought I would lose those hands,
I wasn't sure I could live without them.
I can.
But I don't want to.

Lost

He was my best friend
For as long as I can remember.
Now I am a freak to him.
Who knew what lurked in a house
Which had always seemed so safe?
The unnatural silence,
The angry looks,

The deep and dark rejection
Which bludgeons my being every day.

Where did my brother go?

Those Days

I yearn for those days
When I ran barefoot through the grass,
Ate warm cherries off the tree,
Splashed in a growing boy's rubber pool.

I yearn for the bedtime stories,
The visits to the Apple Farm,
The zoo, with all its scary animals,
And Mom or Dad next to me.

Now there's *stranger danger* of a different ilk…
The beady eyes that track you down the hall,
The hushed conversation—
"Are they really?"
Or "That's sick."

Even at home, always before a safe cocoon,
There are pitying looks
And harsh words of disapproval and damnation.

The strain lays heavy on my head,
And even heavier in their hearts.

Maggie sank back into the couch pillows and stared at the journal. She'd wanted to know how Jamie was doing, and now she did. Her son was in pain, a pain born of the sickness in society that Maggie couldn't control. Hell, she couldn't even seal her own household off from this homophobic plague. It was invading all of them, weakening them, attacking her family's emotional blood cells. And she had no idea what the antidote might be.

❖

"My boys had a fistfight on the porch at dinner the other night." Maggie was back in Melissa's office on Monday afternoon, and had made arrangements to come weekly until Melissa left for a trip to Greece.

The therapist raised her brows. "Wow. That must have been devastating for you."

"It was. I can hardly bear it, Melissa. What am I going to do?"

"Tell me what you're concerned about. Start with the most important."

"I don't know how much of this conflict Jamie can take. I read his journal. He's feeling really bad about what's going on in our family."

"After Mike's and Brian's reactions, I can understand that."

A deeply buried fear surfaced, as often happened in this setting, and Maggie felt her eyes mist. "The suicide rate among gay teenagers is much higher than straight ones."

"Do you think Jamie's suicidal?"

"I never did before. Now I don't know, and I'm so scared for him."

"Has he shown any signs of suicidal behavior?"

Maggie knew what to look for: Did the person threaten to kill himself? No. Did the person start giving away personal possessions? Not that she knew. Did the person seem unnaturally happy because he knew he was going to end the pain? That certainly wasn't the case. "No, he doesn't."

"Then I think he's safe for now. Depression doesn't always indicate feelings of hopelessness which can lead to suicide. Keep an eye out for the signs. We should also think about getting him somebody to talk to." Melissa watched her for a second. "What about you?"

"Gretta asked me the other day if I had to choose between Mike and Jamie, who it would be."

"And you said?"

"Jamie."

"That's nothing to be ashamed of. It's the natural order of life."

"But what if I have to choose between Jamie and Brian? I could never do that!"

"Then we have to find ways to keep that from happening. It doesn't have to come down to a choice between your sons, Maggie."

"I wish I could believe that. Right now everything seems hopeless."

"Then it's a good thing you're here. I'm going to help you restore some of that hope."

❖

Feeling drained, Maggie dragged herself into the house after her therapy appointment. It always happened this way—she felt more optimistic than before she talked to Melissa, but totally enervated when the session was over. Her head hurt and her purse weighed down her shoulder. So she snuck in quietly through the garage, hoping to avoid whoever owned the unfamiliar car parked behind the Prius in their driveway—a friend of one of the boys, no doubt. All Maggie wanted was to retreat to the solace of her bedroom.

Voices came from the sun porch—one was female. As Maggie reached the end of the hallway, she heard, "Mom, is that you?"

So much for peace and quiet. Maggie straightened her shoulders and headed to the porch. Jamie sprawled on a chair, grinning broadly. She hadn't seen him smiling like that in a long time. Someone sat in the high-back rocker but Maggie couldn't see who it was.

Then the chair swiveled and she froze. Her purse dropped to the floor with a thud almost as loud as her heartbeat. Because sitting on her own porch was a woman she'd only seen in pictures, a woman who so much resembled Maggie in the flesh it made her breath catch. *Oh God, oh God.* "Oh, God."

Caroline smiled and stood. "Hi, Magpie."

At the nickname, Maggie's eyes welled.

"Mom?"

"I…I…"

"It's all right, honey," Caroline said. "I know this is a surprise."

One hand clapped over her mouth as years of loneliness, of feeling

abandoned, of fending for herself after Caroline left overwhelmed her.
"I…"

Caroline reached out. "Come over here."

Maggie rushed to her sister. Caroline hugged her tight. The
memory of other hugs resonated—when she fell and skinned a knee,
when she saw her father slap her mother across the face, when Jimmy
was born and Maggie was scared about who would take care of a new
baby in the house. Solid, safe arms wrapped her up. Even her sister's
scent had remained the same. And the kiss on the head, the "Shh, baby,"
were all familiar. Maggie relished the embrace.

After several moments, she was able to pull back. Caroline wiped
Maggie's cheeks with her thumbs. "Feel better?"

Over Caroline's shoulder, she saw the alarm on Jamie's face, so
Maggie forced herself to calm. Caroline took Maggie's hands in her
own. Her sister's were older now, though, heavily veined, with age
spots, reminding Maggie of how much time had passed. She smiled at
a familiar detail: Caroline still had one of the amazing manicures she'd
favored back then, one she'd tried to duplicate on Maggie's little nails
by painting them pink.

Which her mother had yelled about.

Maggie cleared her throat. "I thought I was ready for this, but I'm
overwhelmed."

"I can see that." Caroline bit her lip, a show of insecurity that
gave Maggie more strength. She wasn't eight and Caroline eighteen
anymore. It wasn't this woman's responsibility to take care of her.

They sat on the couch, side by side, and all the while held hands.
Maggie looked over at Jamie. "I guess you met my sister."

Dark eyes danced with emotion, mostly mirth now. "Yeah. We
were having a nice talk. She told me about when you were born, what
you were like as a baby and little kid. It was seriously cool to finally
hear those details about you."

"And you have a seriously cool young man here."

"She teaches high school, Mom. She's even directed some plays.
She works with kids like me."

Caroline winked at Jamie. "I don't know. I'd guess you're one of
a kind. Straight As. All the lead roles in plays. Even head of the Red
Cross blood drive."

Still smiling, Jamie stood. "I'm gonna let you two catch up." He crossed to Maggie and kissed her on the cheek. "I'm glad for you, Mom. See ya, *Aunt* Caroline."

"Later," Caroline said.

Maggie turned to her sister and, hungry for details, studied her face. Caroline's hair was straight and shorter than Maggie's, longer at the sides and wedged in the back. There was no gray visible. She wore diamond earrings, a diamond tennis bracelet, and a gold pendant with a *C* engraved on it. Her dress was light peach jersey, fitted to a still trim body. She appeared chic and sophisticated.

Caroline was studying Maggie, too. "I can't believe it. You're a grown woman," she said, soothing a hand down Maggie's hair. "Beautiful."

"You, too."

"And your son. Could he be any more precious? And astute. He asked me right away why I came out early."

"Why did you? Not that I'm not glad."

"You said something was going on with you, but couldn't talk about it. I sensed how conflicted you were. So I thought, hell, this is my sister. I took the last weeks of the school year off for what I told them was a family emergency and flew out. My daughter left Colorado a week ago with the car, so we met up here at about the same time."

"Where is she?"

"At the cottage getting Chloe settled in."

"I can't wait to meet them."

"I'll bet. And I can't wait to meet Mike and Brian."

Briefly, Maggie glanced away. "The atmosphere is a little tense here, Caroline."

"I know."

"We've—"

Caroline squeezed her hand. "I know what's going on, Mag. Jamie told me. That's what I meant about being astute. He figured out why I came, and he filled me in on what's happened so you didn't have to."

Bless that boy's heart. It was such a good one.

Maggie hurried on to say, "It's all right that he's gay. Really. It's just caused some strain here."

"I understand." The softly uttered words were rife with meaning. Caroline understood only too well how dysfunctional families could be when a child bucked the value system. "He talked a bit about school when he found out I was a teacher. I've worked with gay and lesbian teens in Colorado, Mag."

Maggie blurted out bitterly, "The Catholic Church's beliefs are hurting my family again."

Shaking her head, Caroline sat back into the cushions. With the sunlight streaming in, Maggie could see a few crow's feet around her eyes. "They did so much damage to us. I hate that they're hurting you again. I thought they softened their views but not on this, I guess."

"I'm sorry. What's happening to us is bound to dredge up all kinds of negative emotions for you."

"It does. But I knew I'd have to face them if I reconnected with you. And I chose to come here."

Maggie wanted to ask her sister why she hadn't contacted her before, if Teresa could find her so easily. But now wasn't the time. "I'm so sorry about Derek. I know I said it on the phone, but I want to reiterate it in person. And you don't have to worry about me. Just take care of yourself."

"I have been doing that. But I'm here for you now, Mag, too. I want to be." She gulped back emotion. "And I want to share Derek with you. Teresa takes after him. I brought pictures, newspaper clippings of some of his buildings."

"I'm anxious to know all about him."

A weight on Maggie's shoulders, her back, even dragging down her legs lightened; the only other person who could do that for her was Gretta. The psychology professor in Maggie knew the sense of relief was residual memory from her very formative years where, until she went away, Caroline had always made life better.

Even if her older sister couldn't change the situation they all found themselves in, just having her there would help Maggie cope.

❖

Mike picked up the picture frame he always kept on his desk at work and periodically updated. In it were the four of them, this time in Cancun. Maggie was tanned and smiled at Tim, who took the photo. The boys appeared relaxed and easy with each other. Mike himself was grinning broadly. It seemed light-years ago that they'd all been happy.

Now he'd never forget the sight of his two boys fighting on the porch and his talk with Brian after. He'd taken his son down to the church and they sat outside on a play area that Mike had helped build and Brian had spent time on when he was little. But he was no longer pushing a child on a swing; he was having an adult conversation with his almost-a-man son…

"Regardless of how upset you are, promiscuity is not an option, Brian. I'm shocked at your behavior."

Brian had gotten belligerent. "Join the real world, Dad. Guys screw around. It's no big deal."

Instead of preaching, he said quietly, "I didn't think that was the way we lived our lives."

"Maybe I wanna live that way."

"I don't believe that. I think Jamie's right. You're trying to prove that you're not like him." Mike winced at his own statement, thinking of when he and Maggie made love just after he found out Jamie was gay. He knew something about proving a point.

"I'm *not* like Jamie!"

"I know, son. But behaving badly isn't going to help you deal with your feelings about all this."

Suddenly, Brian deflated, the arrogance seeping out of him. With wide troubled eyes, he asked, "What is, Dad? What *are* we gonna do about Jamie?"

"I don't know. Father Pete has some ideas. But let's get back to you. I want your word you won't do this again. It's dangerous to your mental and physical health. As far as I know, it's the first time you've been indiscriminate, right?"

"Yeah, it is…"

The phone in Mike's office rang, halting the memory. He picked it up and heard Laura on the extension. "Mr. Davidson's office."

"Hi, Laura. It's Maggie."

"Hi, Maggie. Let me see if Mike's free."

Irked again, because Laura knew to patch Maggie right through any time, he said, "I'm on, Laura. Hi, honey."

A click. Then, "Oh, Mike," Maggie said without greeting. "You won't believe what's happened. You have to come home early."

Her tone of voice told him she had good news. "Yeah?"

"Caroline's here, Mike."

"Ah, sweetheart, I'm so glad." He eyed his calendar and saw he had a meeting at five. "I'll leave now."

After he hung up, he shut down his computer, locked his door, and approached Laura's desk, which was just outside his office. "I'm leaving. Cancel my five o'clock."

She checked the clock. "Really?"

"Uh-huh."

"I hope there's not a problem. Was it Maggie's call?"

"No, it's good news. We have company that I've been waiting a long time to meet. Feel free to knock off early, too."

"Mike—"

"Good night, Laura."

Mike drove home and tried to think positive thoughts. He hoped having Caroline here would be good for them all. It had to be. His step was light as he entered the house. Hurrying down the hallway leading from the garage, he reached the entrance to the kitchen and stopped short. They were both at the sink, staring out the window at the backyard. He noticed Caroline's arm around his wife, their heads bent toward each other. Same height. Nearly the same build. Even their dresses were of a similar style. Soft laughter, and he wasn't even sure who it came from. Yes, this was going to be good for all of them.

❖

Brian banged in through the door of his house dreading a night with his family. The atmosphere at home was so tense he could barely stand being there. But his mom had called his cell and left a message that Aunt Caroline had flown to Sherwood early and Brian had to come home. She knew him so well. He'd totally planned to blow off dinner.

Jamie would be there. They hadn't said a word to each other since the fight a few nights ago. And he'd be damned if he'd be the one to apologize. Jamie had narced on him to their parents—a mortal sin between brothers—and Brian was royally pissed.

Ditching his dirty uniform from practice in the laundry room, he went to the kitchen and found a table full of people he didn't know around it.

"Hi," he said simply.

His mom's face bloomed with a smile, causing the tightness in his chest to ease a little. He wasn't sure she was glad to see him anymore when he came home.

"Hi, honey." Crossing to him, she kissed his cheek like nothing was wrong, took his hand, and led him to the table. "Bri, this is your Aunt Caroline, your cousin Teresa and"—she ruffled the hair of a little girl the way she used to ruffle his—"this is Chloe."

Caroline stood. She looked more like his mom than Aunt Sara did. "Hello, Brian." She hugged him. "Aren't you a handsome one?"

"Hi. Thanks." He glanced at the others. "I can't believe I got a cousin I didn't know about."

Like Heather, Teresa had long thick hair and blue eyes. She stood and hugged him, too. "Hi, cuz."

Chloe climbed off the chair where she'd been drawing, stood before him, and lifted her arms. Bending down, he scooped her up.

"You're my second cousin, Mommy said."

"I am."

She wrinkled her nose. "You smell."

"Didn't take a shower after practice." Though the guys had calmed down some, and even the co-captain talked to Brian alone about what jerks Cummings and his friends were, not a lot of guys showered after practice anymore.

Pushing away the memory, he tugged one of Chloe's pigtails. "I couldn't wait to get home." He scanned the room and noticed his father, who leaned against a wall. "Hi, Dad. Didn't see you there."

"How was practice?"

"Tough. We had to do a ton of laps." He set Chloe down and asked, "So, how come you all came early?"

"It was time," Aunt Caroline said. "We couldn't wait any longer to get to know you guys."

A month ago Brian would have been happy that his aunt had come early. Now he felt like shit about even good news.

"I got time for a shower, right?"

"Sure." His dad smiled. "We're going out to the deck to have drinks."

Before he left, his mom moved in close and squeezed his arm. Brian found himself leaning into her, wanting to be close to her, like they used to be. Man, he'd screwed up so bad.

"Go shower and join us. I made your favorite lemonade."

Brian didn't know why that made his eyes sting, then it hit him. His mom had lost this part of her family—Caroline, Teresa and Chloe. People *lost* their families for a lot of reasons. His gaze went to Jamie, who'd sat on a stool and hadn't spoken to him. They exchanged looks. Jamie's said clearly, *This sucks.* He hoped his own expression matched his brother's. Suddenly, Brian wanted peace in his family more than anything else in the world.

❖

Jamie peeked out his bedroom window and saw that Brian was at the basketball hoop his dad had put up in the driveway when they were little. Though Brian didn't play the game at school, he was good at every sport he tried. Aunt Caroline and her family had just left and it was almost dark, but Brian had the garage lights on so he could see the hoop.

Thinking about the night they just spent, about lost families and forgiveness, Jamie made his way downstairs, outside and over to his brother.

Brian stopped playing when he saw Jamie.

And once again, the heat of rejection flushed him. "I can go back in if you want me to."

"I don't want you to." He held up the ball. "Wanna play HORSE?"

His brother was such a jock. Guys couldn't get together without doing something, though Jamie had missed that gene. So had Luke. Must be a gay thing.

"Sure."

Bri tossed him the ball. Jamie made the first shot from the invisible foul line. He remembered how his dad had drawn them a real one with paint and his parents would come out and watch them play. God, he missed all that closeness in the family.

"Did you have a good time tonight?" Jamie asked when Brian took his turn.

"Yeah, but it sucks that we had all this family and never got to grow up with them. Teresa's an adult."

This was safe ground, Jamie thought. "I know. Did you see Mom tonight? She was like another person. I never saw her as the little sister."

"Yeah, I noticed that, too."

"Losing Aunt Caroline must have been hell for her. It's like she never got over it." Jamie didn't think he'd ever in his life forget how she sobbed in her sister's arms. It had scared the shit out of him.

After making his first two shots, Brian stopped and stared over at him. Jamie stared back.

"I'm sorry I called you a faggot." The comment wasn't a non sequitur. Jamie knew the parallel Brian was making about Aunt Caroline without voicing it.

"Thanks for saying that. I'm sorry I narced on you. I was pissed."

Brian's arm circled the ball and held it at his side. Before he spoke, his Adam's apple bobbed. "Jame, why didn't you tell me you're gay? I thought we talked through the big stuff. Why didn't you share this?"

Jamie dropped down on the blacktop and Brian joined him. The glow of the garage lights highlighted the real confusion on his brother's face. "I was afraid to tell anybody. Do you have any idea how scary it was? Discovering who I was? Feeling so bad about it at first."

"You don't seem to feel bad about it now." Brian's tone wasn't critical, but the surprise in it hurt some.

"I don't. I'm who I am and I can finally celebrate that. Actually, it feels great."

Brian stiffened. "I'm not rejecting you, but you're asking me to believe in something, say something is right when I don't think it is."

Despite his words, a surge of self-doubt shot through Jamie. Was he so reprehensible that Brian couldn't tolerate him? "You and Dad believe all that stuff the church spouts, but Mom and I don't."

"I know. Don't you ever worry you won't go to heaven?"

Oh, God, this was so hard, just like his talk with his dad in Aunt Sara's basement. *Be careful what you wish for.* He wanted to hash this out with Brian, but hearing what his brother was thinking just about destroyed him.

"I'm not even sure I believe in heaven, Bri. Besides, I think the real issue for you is school. Your jock buddies are picking on you about me and you can't stand up to them."

"That's not true. I did stand up to them. I told them to leave Luke alone."

Jamie hadn't known any of that. He wondered if Luke did.

"All right, you want the truth? Here it is. I can't help it if seeing you two together is hard for me and a lot of other kids at school."

So much for the truce he was hoping to get out of coming down here tonight. Jamie bolted up. "Fine, if I see you coming down the hall when I'm with Luke, we'll go the other way."

Brian stood, too. "Jame, I don't want to hurt your feelings."

"You're kidding, right?"

"I…"

"I'm going in. Stay out here and practice your shots. At least you're good at basketball. Right now, you're being a really shitty brother."

CHAPTER THIRTEEN

The advent of a new baseball season was normally an up time for the Davidsons. Mike looked forward to Brian's opener and made it to a few practices. Jamie became Brian's biggest cheerleader, and Maggie eagerly anticipated seeing her son on the field. This year the initial game took on even more significance because the Ithaca College baseball coach, who'd determine if Brian got some scholarship money and a promise to play his freshman year at his first-choice school, was in attendance.

However, today held little of the spirit of previous seasons. Though they wore their traditional gear—Mike a Spartan baseball cap and Maggie a T-shirt that read *Baseball Mom*—the joy was gone. Brian kept to himself the week before the game, Jamie refused to go with them today, and Mike and Maggie drove over to the high school in strained silence. They'd seen the boys talking out on the blacktop the other night and had hoped the two of them reached some common ground. But afterward, they were even more surly with each other, which had thrown Mike into a depression. The amethyst bracelet on her arm, the one Mike had bought her when they were feeling close, mocked her.

As they made their way out of the car and to the field, Maggie wished Caroline could have come with them today. She broke the ice with everybody in the house. Her mere presence comforted Maggie. Her sister had only been in town three days, and already Maggie felt the bond they'd shared when she was little. Maybe, she liked to think, they'd never lost the connection, it remained dormant, just ready for a breath of new life. But Caroline hadn't come to the game with them because she and Sara were meeting. By tacit agreement, they'd agreed not to tell their mother Caroline had come back, but her older sister was anxious to see Sara.

Still not speaking, she and Mike reached the steps leading up to the bleachers and came face-to-face with Luke Crane's parents. Both couples stopped on a dime. Finally, Maggie said, "Lucas, Erin."

Erin gave her a weak smile. "Hello, Maggie, Mike."

"I think we need to talk, Davidson," Lucas said without greeting them. His mouth was set in stern lines, and in the harsh sunlight, Maggie realized he was older than she'd originally thought.

Mike raised a brow. "Excuse me?"

"I'd like a chance to speak with you sometime. Alone."

Maggie bristled, especially when Mike didn't automatically refuse. "What about, Lucas?" she asked.

"I think we all know the answer to that."

Mike glanced at her "That might be a good idea."

"We'd need to check with Jamie first," Maggie put in. "I'm not sure he'd like the idea."

"Perhaps letting Jamie do what he *likes* is the root of this problem."

"And what problem would that be?" Maggie pushed.

Mike started to move away from the Cranes. "Give me a call, Lucas."

Stunned by Mike's autocratic behavior, Maggie fumed as they reached the bleachers and checked out the stands. Since they were later than usual, the seats with the team parents were taken. She noticed the Cranes headed in the opposite direction. Waving to the couples they knew, Mike and Maggie found places in the top row by themselves.

They settled in but when Mike remained maddeningly silent, Maggie couldn't keep quiet any longer. "Mike, you can't possibly—"

"Could we please not get into this now? It's overshadowing every single aspect of our lives. I want to enjoy Brian's game."

"Fine."

Staring out at the field, Maggie calmed down by finding her son at third base. That *did* make her smile. He seemed so competent, so sure of himself out there. She glanced at the mound. Luke Crane was the pitcher. Maggie took the opportunity to study him. Melissa had said it was best to admit all her concerns at least to herself, and if she was honest, she had to admit she found it uncomfortable seeing Jamie's boyfriend in person. Briefly, she wondered what it would be like to watch them show affection for each other. Heather and Brian held hands and sat close all the time on the family room couch, but she couldn't picture two boys snuggling. She and Mike had only met Luke briefly at the Valentine's Ball party, but she wanted to get to know him better now. She resolved not to anticipate problems and to deal with any issue when it came up.

"What the hell?" Mike was scowling. "Jamie's here." He pointed across the field. Their younger son was sitting alone in the opposite team's section. "I thought he wasn't coming."

Actually what he'd said was that he wasn't going to the game with them. She glanced back to Luke. Of course Jamie was in attendance.

"Did you know he'd be here?" Mike asked.

"No."

She didn't mention Luke and neither did Mike. Or the fact that Heather was nowhere to be seen. As far as Maggie knew, the girl had never missed a game. Finally the first inning started. Maggie was glad to have an excuse for the silence between her and Mike.

As the team's strongest hitter, Brian was cleanup batter, and the three players before him got on base. Amidst loud cheering from the spectators, he strode to the plate, broad-shouldered, loose-limbed and imposing in his gray uniform. His swing was powerful and the crack of the bat resounded in the warm afternoon air. The ball arced high and fouled off to the right.

Mike cupped his hands around his mouth. "You can do it, Bri. Stand tall."

Maggie stole a surreptitious glance at her husband. He'd played college baseball and one of her favorite pastimes then was watching him at the plate as he hit one out of the park or on the field as he reached for a ball. He always seemed invincible, like he could control the elements, thwart gravity. The nostalgic memory hurt, made her miss their closeness, which ebbed and flowed like an emotional tide. Saddened, she turned her attention to the field.

Another pitch. Another pop foul.

Mike lurched to his feet, as did much of the crowd. In times like these, Brian pulled through for the team. He was his best in a clutch.

A pitch. A swing. And a strike.

And soon, an out—which turned into a double play.

A low mumble of disappointment rippled through the crowd. She and Mike sank back onto the bleachers and Maggie touched his arm. But he didn't lean into her like he always did to seek comfort when they were disappointed about the boys. Consequently, she couldn't take solace from him.

Yanking on the bill of the ball cap, Mike snapped, "Damn it, Brian's concentration's shot. I hope he doesn't lose out at Ithaca because of this whole thing with Jamie."

Abruptly, Maggie stood. "I'm going to get a soda." She didn't ask if he wanted one. He didn't comment.

Judy Johnson, Craig's wife and head of the Sports Booster Club, was working behind the counter at the concession stand. She smiled at Maggie. "Hi, Maggie. I've been meaning to call you but I've been swamped."

"Life gets busy." She smiled back at Judy. "If it's about the church bazaar I already signed up."

"No, it's not that." After she served the coke, Judy leaned over the counter and squeezed Maggie's hand. "Tyler told me about Jamie. I'm so sorry."

A cheer from the stands echoed around them. Birds sang happily from the trees, which swayed with a mild breeze. The day was beautiful, and Jamie's situation shouldn't mar that for anyone. "Jamie's doing fine," she said tightly.

A frown shadowed Judy's face.

"He's getting straight As. The All Star Theater Program downtown accepted him into their summer workshop. And he and Mike are checking out colleges for drama."

"You know what I mean." She was whispering, like she was discussing some criminal activity and was afraid the other volunteers would overhear. "This is so awful."

Without responding, Maggie walked away from her friend. Twenty yards down the blacktop, she stopped, trying to decide where to go, what to do. Judy caught up with her.

"I'm sorry. That came out wrong. I wanted to tell you that Craig and I are here for you like you were when Tyler was sick."

Maggie whirled around. Her anger dissipated at the genuine concern on Judy's face and suddenly Maggie realized she couldn't afford outrage. She had to be careful about alienating people who might be able to help ease their situation. She'd beg for Jamie if she had to. "Oh, Judy, please don't say that. Jamie's not sick."

The other woman cocked her head. "I...I'm sorry if I offended you. But there's a contingent of our church that believes homosexuality is an illness."

"And you agree with them?"

"Yes."

"Father Pete told Mike that Jamie could change."

"He can."

"No, Judy, he can't. Don't you have any understanding of the psychology of sexual orientation? There's no choice involved. Being gay is not a *preference*."

Judy's eyes were troubled, but something else reflected in them, too. Serenity. Certainty. And blind, blind conformity. "I know you're hurting. I'm sorry. We're praying for you every day."

Now Maggie welcomed the anger that surfaced. "And what are you praying for, Judy?"

"That God will help Jamie do what's right."

"God made Jamie like he is."

"We all have our crosses to bear."

"Being gay isn't a cross."

Her face held pity now. "Of course it is." She squeezed Maggie's arm. "I know God will be with you in this."

"I'm going to leave now, because what you've said upsets me. Please, try to think about this in a different light. For all our sakes." With that, Maggie walked away. She didn't go back to the game. She didn't feel a part of it anymore. She didn't feel a part of a lot things anymore.

❖

Wait for me after the game, Luke had said, making Jamie's heart bump in his chest. It excited him and scared the shit out of him at the same time to be in a real relationship openly.

Jamie had teased him. *What? Like Kiki used to?*

Instead of busting his balls, Luke's face had gotten serious. *I told you I admired you for not doing what I did with girls, Jame.*

Feeling bad, Jamie said, *I know. But you did what you had to do at the time.*

Luke's expression lightened and he socked Jamie on the arm. *And no, asshole, not like Kiki. Just wait down the hall outside the locker room.*

Which was where Jamie stood now, over by the trophy case, away from the chatter of girls wearing guys' spring letterman jackets who fawned over their boyfriends when they came out of the locker room, one by one, like heroes returning from war.

Heather wasn't with them, though. Jamie felt bad about that, too, and had tried to talk her into taking Brian back.

It's not your fault, she'd said. *He cheated on me and he knew I'd never stand for that after what my father did to my mother. You and me are still friends, though, Jame. I'm on your side.*

Even though Brian and Jamie's talk the other night hadn't ended so well, Jamie felt guilty about his role in what happened between Heather and Brian.

His back to the locker room, Jamie saw his reflection in the glass. He brushed back his hair and straightened the collar of the polo shirt he wore. God, it had been fun dressing for a boyfriend. Now Jamie knew what all the fuss was about when Brian got clothes-conscious for Heather, when girls told him about the time they spent primping for a date.

From behind, he heard, "You waiting for me?"

Jamie pivoted and was surprised Brian even approached him tonight. His brother's hair was wet, his face grim. He'd had a rotten game. They'd hardly spoken since the night they'd played HORSE. "Sorry you had an off night."

"Yeah, it sucks. Coach Denton was there from Ithaca."

Without thinking, Jamie reached out for Brian's arm. But Brian stepped back and Jamie felt like he'd been kicked in the gut. Images of his brother in the past came to him: Brian hugging him after one of the plays, wrestling with him on the floor, putting his head on Jamie's shoulder when he drank too much.

Now his own brother didn't even want to touch him.

"You're not waiting for me, are you?" Brian asked.

"No."

Without saying more, Brian turned and strode away.

Barely able to swallow, Jamie wanted to turn tail and run, too. But as Luke said, why the hell had he gone through all this shit if he couldn't be with Luke openly, be like all the other kids? Their relationship was different, not wrong!

Jamie had calmed down by the time Luke exited the locker room. He noticed right away that Luke hadn't showered. Jamie knew about the problems in the shower when the guys found out Luke was gay. And it bummed him out totally.

Dressed in cool jeans and a long sleeved-checked shirt rolled up at the sleeves, showing off his muscles, Luke crossed to him. "Ready to go?"

"Yeah. I don't have a car, though."

"I do. I'll—"

"Lucas?"

Luke stilled. "Fuck."

Glancing behind them, Jamie saw Luke's parents had come into the building. He swore, too. When Luke gripped his gym bag so hard his hand turned red, Jamie said, "I'll go on ahead. We can meet later," and started away.

Luke held Jamie in place. "No, you won't. Not this time." He glanced at his parents. They remained a distance down the hall. "You don't have to come with me to talk to them, though."

"Like hell."

Side by side, they covered the few yards until they reached the Cranes.

"Hi." Luke's tone was casual.

His mother said, "Terrific game, Lucas."

"Thanks."

Neither greeted Jamie.

He stood tall, though, and watched the threesome. No hug. No fuss like his family always made over one of Brian's games. He was beginning to understand why Luke had trouble showing affection.

Dr. Crane's jaw tightened. "I'd like you to come with us. We're having dinner at the club."

"Sorry, Dad. I got plans with Jamie."

Mrs. Crane brought her hand to her heart. "Please, Lucas."

"Please what, Mother?"

She whispered, "Don't embarrass us. Just do as your father says."

Luke stared at them for a minute. "Can Jamie come, too?"

"No." One word from his father, a dictum that spoke volumes more. "We won't have that."

Shaking his head, Luke glared at his parents. "That's a terrible way to feel." He turned away and started to walk down the hall, Jamie by his side.

Neither of them spoke; they held themselves as rigid as stone. When they were near the door, almost free, Jamie heard Luke's father call out, "This isn't over, Lucas. Not by a long shot."

Luke mumbled, "Didn't think it was, Dad." He gave Jamie that half-smile he loved. "But we did it this time, didn't we, Jame?"

Though they hadn't come far enough for Jamie to put his arm around Luke, or vice versa, in public, they shared that smile and leaned into each other. It was a sweet victory all the same.

❖

Two days after the game, at about six p.m., Damien Kane poked his head into Maggie's office. Today he wore a casual gray sports shirt that highlighted his eyes. "Hey, pretty lady, what are you still doing here?"

Trying to find an excuse not to go home. "Finishing some grading." She held up a paper. "What *was* I thinking to assign a research project to intro students this late in the year?"

"Told you." He eased inside and sat down across from her desk. "It's not our job to do that."

"Then who's going to teach the freshmen to write?"

"Their English teachers."

An old argument. One that was still invigorating. She leaned back in her chair and gave him a flirty grin. "The English department shouldn't be expected to teach kids to write psychology papers."

"If kids can write one kind of paper, they can write another."

"Spoken like someone who hates to grade these."

His eyes twinkled. "Now there's the smart, sassy woman I know."

"What do you mean?"

"You haven't been yourself lately, Mag. I've wanted to ask about it, but I was afraid I'd offend you."

"You wouldn't offend me."

"Are you kidding? You're like a mama lion about her cubs."

Mike would hate that Damien could read her so well. It felt intimate even to her. "How do you know this is about my family?"

"Intuition." He winked at her. "We psychology types have ESPP."

"ESPP?"

"Extra sensory perception about other psychologists."

She laughed out loud. Not only was Damien an excellent professor of psychology with an artistic bent, he had a great sense of humor.

Sheila Stone, the psychology department secretary, came to the doorway. "Hi, guys. Some of us are going over to Jinx's for cocktails. They opened a glassed-in porch area and we're christening it. Want to come?"

Damien gave her a killer smile. "I'm already in."

While Maggie thought about the offer, she pretended to straighten the light green spring dress she'd bought on a recent shopping trip with Gretta. "I don't know. I hadn't planned on it."

"Family stuff?" Shelia asked.

Glancing at the phone, she thought about whether or not she should go with her colleagues. Mike was at dinner with clients. Jamie was out with some friends. Brian had baseball practice. And she'd had lunch with Caroline—she saw her sister almost every day—so she was at loose ends tonight. "No, no family stuff."

Damien got to his feet. "You should come."

Sheila echoed the sentiments and left.

"Come on, Mag. It'll relax you. No heavy stuff preying on your mind. Nobody to be responsible for. We'll have drinks and argue about what's wrong with education today."

The offer was too good to resist. What would she do with her evening anyway? Go home and sulk about her problems? "All right. I'll call and leave a message for the guys." When Damien didn't move, she said, "I'll meet you there."

"No way. You'll duck out. If it isn't private, I'll stay right here."

"It's not private."

Punching in her home number, she waited for the answering

machine to pick up. She listened to the boys' message, which they changed periodically, often depending on the weather: *We're all out in the sun. We're probably skiing. We went to Florida.* Once in a while they groused *Mom's making us clean the house.* This time, both boys joked about school's end and Brian's graduation. Her heart felt heavy at how carefree they sounded. This particular tape was made before Jamie's disclosure.

After the beep, she said, "Hi, it's me, Mom." Hmm, was that her identity in the house? "I'm stopping for a drink after work with people from the psych department. I'll probably beat all of you home, but just in case, I didn't want anybody to worry." Then she added, "I love you."

When she hung up, Damien's face was full of approval. "What?"

"It's cool. That you say *I love you* on a phone message."

"Is it so unusual?"

"Even better that you think it isn't." He held out his arm in a courtly gesture. "Let's go. I'll buy you a glass of your favorite Chardonnay."

❖

"I think we can come to terms on the turnaround time," Mike told Jeremy Connors, the man who would decide on a five-million-dollar job for Mike's company. "Our reps are formalizing the schedule, but it's a go."

This meeting would end with dinner at the Landings, a swank restaurant in downtown Rochester, and hopefully cinch the deal Mike had been orchestrating for months. At least work was going well.

Connors was about sixty, with distinguished looks that reminded Mike of Lucas Crane Sr. "Let's see the bottom line."

From beside him, Laura put statistics up in a PowerPoint presentation. Mike said, "Notice the fall delivery dates, Jeremy. No other company is going to be able to beat them."

It took another hour to convince Connors, but the deal was closed and Mike was feeling good when six o'clock rolled around.

Connors stood. "We'll meet you two at the restaurant."

You two. Laura had not been invited to dine with them. He asked her with a casualness he didn't feel, "Would you be able to join us, Laura?"

She sent him a dazzling smile. The tip of her chin made her hair fall attractively over her hazel eyes. "Yes, but my car's in the shop today. Can you give me a lift?"

Connors left ahead of them to make some calls and Mike faced Laura. "I'm sorry you got roped into this."

"Truthfully, I'm glad to be invited. I know I'm only your administrative assistant, but I worked hard on this account, too."

Mike hadn't asked her to dinner because he didn't want to encourage any kind of socializing with her. Lately, as if she sensed trouble between him and Maggie, she'd made more outright comments like, "You're the *best* father. I *love* how you treat your employees. You look *great* today."

"I'm sorry about that. I thought you'd have more exciting things to do. A date maybe?"

"I'm not seeing anyone right now."

Too bad.

"Is the ride okay?" she asked.

"Sure. I have to call home first, but I'll be ready to go after that."

Without asking, she leaned over and picked up the phone. This close, he could smell some pretty perfume on her. She dialed his number and handed the receiver to him. As she straightened up his conference table, the answering machine came on. He said, "Thought I'd catch you, Maggie. I'm heading out to dinner. Hope your day went well. See you later."

"Not home?"

"No. She has a four o'clock class. She's probably still with students."

Laura's smile was female, flirtatious. And flattering. "I guess it's you and me."

"And Jeremy Connors, his lawyer, and his VP."

"You held your own with them, Mike. I'm amazed at how nobody intimidates you."

The compliment felt good. So did her approving perusal as he shrugged into his taupe sports coat.

His wife hadn't looked at him like that in a long time.

❖

Maggie dragged herself into the house at nine that night. The boys' car was gone, but Mike's Pontiac was parked in the garage. Normally, work dinners ran later than this.

He was on the deck, sitting in the black and gray patio furniture they'd brought out of storage as soon as the weather warmed up. Drink in hand, he stared at the backyard but swiveled around at the sound of a screen sliding open. The light breeze ruffled his hair and chilled Maggie's bare arms.

"Hi." She smiled at him. "You're home early."

"You're not." His tone was cool, distant. He was still dressed in his the taupe blazer she always thought looked sexy on him.

"I was—" She started to defend herself, but halted midsentence. Suddenly, she was weary of walking on eggshells around everyone in the house. "I left a message."

"I know. I heard it when I got in."

"When was that?"

He sipped his drink, but didn't take his eyes off her. The skitter of a squirrel running up a tree and the crickets chirping in the distance filled in the silence before he added, "A while ago." He scanned her outfit, his expression unreadable. "You wore your new dress."

"Uh-huh. To school today." Sitting down opposite him, she tried to determine his mood.

He studied her with that piercing gaze of his. The boys used to squirm beneath it when they were young and had been in the wrong. "So, you went out with *people* from your department."

"Yes. I said I did on the machine."

"Who was there?"

"The usual suspects."

"Who?"

She drew in an exasperated breath. "Look, Mike, if you have something to say, say it."

"Was Damien Kane with you?"

"He was part of the group, yes."

"Did you spend most of your night"—he glanced at his watch—"the three hours since you left the message, with him?"

She had, of course. She'd tried socializing with others. But Damien always seemed to be at her elbow with a drink, or some appetizer the restaurant had served to their group. "I spent the entire time with the nearly dozen coworkers who came along to celebrate Jinx's new addition."

"How much did you have to drink?"

Sliding to the edge of the chair, she snapped, "I'm your wife, Mike, not your child. I won't be questioned like one."

"That much, huh?"

"I had three glasses of wine over four hours. I also ate."

"You ate?"

"People have been known to do that."

"With who?"

"Stop it! If you're angry at me, don't be searching for excuses to show it. Come right out and tell me you hate the way I'm handling this situation with Jamie."

He waited only a beat. "I hate the way you're handling this with Jamie."

"Well," she said silkily, "I hate the way you're handling it, too. So that makes us even." She stood abruptly. "Don't ever question me like this again about my whereabouts."

He threw back his chair. It hit the railing so hard the sound echoed like a gunshot in the quiet backyard. "Fine, but I want to know if this is how you're going to handle the trouble between us?"

"What are you talking about?"

"You know damn well what I'm talking about. Are you going to deal with the distance between us, the strain in our lives, by turning to another man?"

"There is no other man."

"Kane has been after you since he set foot on your college campus. I've seen him sidle up to you at parties. The few times he's called here, he's been overly chummy with me. Last fall, at the kick-off picnic, he wrangled being your partner in almost every event."

Since what Mike said was true, she didn't bother to deny it. "And what did I do, Mike?"

"Nothing." He arched a brow. "Yet."

"Go to hell." She stalked into the house, marched upstairs, got ready for bed, and slid under the covers. Her guess was that Mike would sleep on the couch.

He did.

At five the next morning, she awakened to find him creeping into the room. She'd slept horribly, as she always did when they went to bed with an argument unsettled between them. Rolling over, she faced him. He closed the door and leaned against the wall. A neighbor's outside lamp was on and a sliver of light slanted in through the blinds. His face was haggard, flushed with fatigue. He crossed to the bed. Sat on the mattress. Bent over and kissed her.

Makeup sex. His hands brushing down her hair. Cupping her breasts. Sliding to her thigh with urgency. She'd been on the other side of the jealousy issue, so she knew what he was feeling. Women at Mike's workplace flirted with him at company events, and other times, too, she suspected. Afterward, she couldn't wait to get him alone.

The silk she'd worn to sleep in slipped off her like water. His lips roamed everywhere. He covered her body with his.

The tone of their contact changed to one of raw desire. She felt it rush over her and clung to him. For a while, little else mattered.

CHAPTER FOURTEEN

Maggie stretched out on her bed, exhausted from the tension between her and Mike, despite the tenderness of their lovemaking a few nights ago. When Jamie got in after school, he peeked into her bedroom and asked if she was all right. She told him she just hadn't gotten enough rest lately. Amazing how lies fell freely from your lips when life has shifted out of focus like a camera lens you couldn't quite get right no matter how many times you adjusted it.

The phone rang and Jamie answered it. From downstairs she heard, "Mom, it's for you."

"I've got it." She picked up the extension by her bed. "Hello."

A cough on the other end. "Maggie, this is John Miller."

John Miller. Did she know a John Miller?

"Darcy's brother."

Darcy Miller Larson was Maggie's best friend in high school. Maggie had a crystal-clear memory of one Christmas in Cornwall long ago, when she'd gone over to visit Darcy. She'd stood outside the Millers' quaint stone house, which resembled a Thomas Kincaid cottage, with the snow falling around her, looking through the window, watching Darcy, her mother, father, and brothers gather around their fireplace. Maggie had known a longing so strong for a family like that of her own, it almost leveled her. And she thought she'd created it, the perfect family of her dreams.

Darcy had dropped out of college to get married and still lived in Cornwall. She and her husband Dick had three kids. Their boys were close in age to hers.

"I'm afraid I have some bad news," John was saying.

"Has something happened to Darcy?"

"It's Kenny." Darcy's second oldest. "H-he was killed in Afghanistan."

"Oh, good Lord, no, John."

Kenny was a happy-go-lucky boy with a sunny smile who adored his mother. In many ways, he reminded Maggie of Brian.

"I know this is a shock."

"I'm so sorry. How did it happen?"

"He was out on a recon mission with more experienced infantry. They got caught in a firefight. You don't want to know the details—they're obscene."

"Darcy must be inconsolable."

"She is. I thought you'd like to know what's happened. In the confusion, we missed calling some people right away. They shipped his remains"—he choked on the word—"home and we buried him quietly when the coffin arrived. Just family. But we're having a memorial service at the end of this week." She heard a muffled sob on the other end. Darcy's brother was a construction worker, big, burly, bulky. She remembered him as always laughing.

"What can I do?"

"We wanted you to know the arrangements. The service is Saturday morning. I think Darcy would appreciate it if you and your mother were there."

"Of course I'll be there. Can I help out in some way? Bring food?"

"We've got plenty to eat. Her church has seen to all that. I don't know what we would have done without them." He cleared his throat. "There's a luncheon in the fellowship hall after the service."

"We'll see you Saturday, then."

After she hung up, Maggie just sat there, thinking about Darcy and Kenny, immobilized by the nature of *real* tragedy. When she could move again, she slid off the bed and opened the cedar chest where they stored their photo albums. She drew out the one marked *Brian's Toddler Days*, dropped down onto the floor, and leafed through pages until she found what she was looking for.

Darcy had come to Sherwood to visit when the boys were just shy of a year. On one glossy page was a picture of her with Kenny, and Maggie with Brian. They were bouncing the babies on their knees while someone took a picture. She studied Darcy's kind, trusting face and the innocent visage of the child on her lap. A drop of moisture hit the plastic and she blotted it with her thumb before she realized what it was. Staring down, she cried hard for Darcy's loss.

A rap on the door. "Mom?"

She didn't answer.

"Mom? Are you all right?"

"I—" She couldn't talk.

"Mom?" Jamie had come into the room. Then she felt a hand on her shoulder. "What happened?" He glanced at the photo album. "Isn't that your high school friend Darcy?"

Maggie nodded.

"Did something happen to her?" Through tears and strangled sobs, she told Jamie about Kenny.

"Oh, Mom." Sinking onto the carpet, he dragged her into an embrace and she cried on his shoulder. She hugged her living, breathing son and begged God to keep him safe.

A door slammed downstairs. Someone walked around. All the while, she and Jamie stayed on the floor holding each other.

Mike and Brian found them there.

Her husband crossed the room. "Maggie? Jame?"

Finally disentangling, Maggie and Jamie stood.

"Honey, what's wrong?" Mike asked. "What happened?"

Brian was in the background, leaning against the doorjamb, his hands stuck in his pockets. They were all alive and safe. "Kenny Larson. Darcy's son?"

Mike grasped onto her. "What about him?"

"Oh, guys, Kenny was killed in Afghanistan."

"Maggie, no."

Brian said, "Kenny? Mom, Kenny?"

Struggling with her own reaction, Maggie crossed to Brian. Tears clouded his eyes as she stood on tiptoe to hug him. In her peripheral vision, she saw Mike slide his arm around Jamie's shoulders, and Jamie lean into him.

"Yes, Bri. I'm so sorry. I know you kept in touch with him."

They went downstairs, sat in the warmth of the April day's end on the porch and made plans. They'd go to Cornwall on Saturday. Brian would miss a baseball game but that couldn't be helped. They'd drive down in the morning, pick up her mother, attend Kenny's service and the church luncheon. They'd stay overnight at her mother's house if they were too tired to head back.

Dinner was noneventful and they all pitched in to clean up. Then they found themselves in the family room watching *Jeopardy*, an excuse to be with each other.

That night, Mike and she lay in bed holding hands, staring at the ceiling fan as it whirred in the still air.

"We have to do better," Mike said into the darkness.

"I know."

"We have to help the boys do better with each other."

"I know. Seeing Zack tomorrow will be hard for them."

Zack was Jamie's age, Darcy's other son. Darcy's *only* son now.

As she dozed off, she thought of one of her mother's stern admonishments. *Stop your crying or I'll give you something to cry about.* Maggie had always hated that adage. Still, it played through her mind as she drifted off.

❖

The atmosphere in the car was somber as Mike drove to a memorial service for a dead child—the worst thing that could possibly happen to a parent. Last night, he'd meant it when he said that he and Maggie had to do better with what had been disrupting their own world. In comparison to the Millers, his family's problems seemed manageable now.

Still, there was so much he had to contend with.

Mike hadn't told anyone about his meeting with Lucas Crane at the country club...

The distinguished doctor pounded his fist on the table. "This is totally unacceptable. We need to take the bull by the horns."

Mike had been curious about the man's views. "Lucas, you're a pediatrician. The AMA takes the position that homosexuality is determined at birth. Do you disagree with them on that?"

"That and other tenets they hold. I believe abortion is immoral because the cells are human life at conception."

Mike flinched to find he had so much in common with Crane.

They'd gone on to discuss reparative therapy camps at length.

"I'm in total agreement with the premise for these places,

Davidson. Homosexuality is not an orientation, but a set of behaviors that lies at the root of the dysfunction. Therefore, it makes sense that homosexual desires can be reprogrammed."

Last week, Mike had researched the camps' methods. Primarily, the staff minimized contact with what they claimed encouraged homosexual behavior: no secular music, no more than fifteen minutes per day behind a closed bathroom door, and no contact with any practicing homosexuals.

"I'm not sure about their tactics, Lucas."

Mike thought of the frank talks he'd had with his boys about healthy sexual practices. He imagined Jamie unable to listen to the music he loved. Could God want this kind of punitive indoctrination for his son?

Lucas Crane did. He'd been unyielding, immovable, and Mike cringed thinking of what poor Luke must be going through. He knew in his heart this man would never change.

"Mike?" Maggie said, breaking into his reflection. "I asked if you wanted to stop for coffee."

"No. Your mother's expecting us at nine."

His wife's sigh was meaningful.

"She'll be fine. Darcy's situation is sure to take precedence over her own self-absorption."

"I'm not so sure. Truthfully, I'm surprised she agreed to go with us." Another sigh. "And we still have to deal with her about Caroline coming back." There was no mention, of course, about telling Gertrude that Jamie was gay. Mike couldn't fathom what his mother-in-law would do with that information.

"Caroline still hasn't talked about telling your mother she's back in your life?"

"Not much. I brought it up after she met with Sara and she said she wasn't ready yet."

"I think the only one in the family equipped to deal with your mother is Jimmy."

"No one's called him, either." She shook her head. "I hate this."

"I know, honey."

They reached Cornwall an hour before the service. Maggie always had a visceral reaction to driving up the hill to Second Street and catching the first sight of the big gray house where she'd lived. Mike noticed she placed her hand on her stomach as they pulled up to the curb. He covered that hand with his own. "It'll be okay."

Solemnly the four of them exited the car and climbed the steps to the porch. Maggie opened the front door and they went inside. "Ma, we're here."

Following her, Mike was assaulted by the putrid smell. Years of cigarette smoke settled over the house like a toxic blanket.

"She's probably upstairs." They heard mumbling, then Gertrude Lorenzo emerged from the enclosed staircase. She was wearing a blue cotton house dress and had a cigarette in her hand.

"Hi, Ma."

The guys greeted her. No hugs in this family. Mike had been lucky that God had given him to Lucy and BJ Davidson instead of the deal He struck for Maggie.

Then he noticed that Gertrude's face was beet red. She glared at Maggie, practically spat out, "I need to sit," and headed toward the bay window of the old house, where she eased down into her stuffed chair. For as long as Mike had known her, that had been his mother-in-law's throne.

The boys took the couch and Maggie a chair. Mike leaned against an archway to the television room.

"Ma, why aren't you ready for Kenny's service?" Maggie asked.

"I'm not going."

"What?" His wife's face was confused. "Why?"

"How can you ask me that?"

"Because you said you'd go."

Lifting her chin, Gertrude sniffed. "That was before."

"Before what?"

God, this was familiar. Things always had to be pried out of this woman. She withheld like a pro, and Mike couldn't imagine Maggie as a young child trying to deal with this kind of manipulation.

"You know, Mary Margaret." She butted out a cigarette and immediately lit another.

Mike exchanged a concerned look with Maggie, and from the corner of his eye saw the boys fidget.

"I *don't* know, Ma."

The chill in Gertrude's eyes even affected Mike. "I talked to Sara just before you got here."

Silent, Maggie waited. She didn't seem to understand the innuendo. But Mike did and tried to head off the explosion. "What did Sara say, Gertrude?"

"I can't talk about it." She placed her palm over her heart. "It's not good for me, Father Bingham said."

It was the mention of the priest that did it. His wife shrank back and paled. But it was the fear on her face that cut Mike to the quick. She managed to get out, "S-Sara told you Caroline was back?"

Gertrude slammed a hand on the wooden arm of the chair, making Maggie jump. "Don't say that name in this house."

"Grandma." Jamie spoke up before Mike could shield him. "All that was a long time ago."

"Shut your mouth, young man."

Straightening, Mike took a step toward his mother-in-law. "Don't speak to my son that way, Gertrude."

She rounded on Mike, but he wasn't her child and had no fear of her. He faced her squarely.

"You're a good Catholic man. How can you accept this?"

"I think God would understand. And forgive. Jesus certainly didn't hold grudges. I also believe the modern Catholic Church would want you to forgive Caroline."

"God's word is clear. I thought you understood that."

"Ma," Maggie pleaded. "We have to deal with her return."

"I don't."

Maggie sank back in her chair and stared mutely at her mother. Now the boys were watching Gertrude like she was from Mars.

Finally, Mike said, "We have to get to the service. Gertrude, there's still time for you to dress."

"I have a headache. Because of you." She pointed to her daughter. "You always did this to me."

"Oh, Ma, it would help Darcy if you came with us. She specifically asked for you. Can't you put your feelings aside for the time being?"

"I'm sick. Nobody cares about that. Nobody cares what this is doing to me."

There was dead silence, absolute stillness in the room.

Then Mike saw his wife stand, cross to her mother, and kneel down next to her. "I care, Ma." Maggie leaned over, but Gertrude turned her cheek away from Maggie's kiss. After a long moment, his wife straightened, touched her mother's arm, and walked to the door. "Let's go, guys."

Jamie and Brian flanked Maggie and linked their arms with hers. Mike followed behind.

❖

Brian watched his mom as they drove into the church parking lot. He knew her childhood had sucked, and he hated seeing how hard she still had it with Grandma Lorenzo. But today had been the worst ever. It made him feel ashamed about his own behavior and how it was hurting her, too.

The church loomed ahead of them and his heart started to pound like it did when he ran the bases. He dreaded going inside. He remembered sneaking out of the house with Kenny at night when the Larsons came to visit and going skinny-dipping in a neighbor's pool. He remembered Kenny in front of the TV when they watched R-rated movies while their parents went out to dinner. Now Kenny was dead. Brian couldn't take it in.

They exited the car and entered the church as a family. Darcy, Dick, Zack, and Mary were huddled together in the foyer. Darcy burst into tears when she hugged Brian's mom. "Oh, Mags, it's awful."

"I know, Darce. I'm so sorry."

Darcy's eyes were red and her skin pasty. "His birthday was the week before he left. He was eighteen. He'd only been gone six months."

Brian had meant to send Kenny a birthday card. Swallowing hard, he had to turn away from the sight of the two friends, though Jamie stayed right behind his mom. Brian pretended to study a bulletin board, but he could still hear their conversation.

"We fought about his enlisting," Darcy was saying. "We weren't on the best of terms when he left."

"Darcy, sweetie, don't feel guilty about that."

"That's what our minister said."

After a few minutes, his dad came over to him and placed a hand on his back. "Say hello to Darcy, Bri. Just say you're sorry."

Brian barely got out the words, but he noticed that Jamie managed to murmur a few good things about Kenny.

As they made their way downstairs to wait for the service to begin, Brian tried not to think of what was happening. Tried not to think about Grandma Lorenzo and his mother. Or about Aunt Caroline, who Grandma hated, and Jamie, who Brian couldn't find any common ground with. He spotted the picture boards lined up in the fellowship hall. Crossing to them, he studied the short scope of Kenny's life.

Jamie saw his brother go to the other side of the room. The sports coat he'd gotten for Christmas made him seem big and sturdy but Jamie could guess what he was thinking. Brothers could be lost in a heartbeat. So, after a few minutes, Jamie walked over and put a hand on Brian's shoulder. Brian stiffened and Jamie thought he was going to blow him off again. Then Brian squeezed his hand and left his own on top of Jamie's for a minute. "Hard to believe, isn't it?"

Somber, Jamie looked at the photos. The one of Kenny in his uniform stood out among the rest. "What a waste."

"Ever think what it would be like if we had to go to war, Jame?"

Jamie thought about the antigay polices and sentiments of the armed services. "It makes me sick, thinking of something happening to you."

Brian dug his finger and thumb into his eyes. "Me, too. To you. I've been a shit about, you know, all this with you."

Jamie thought about saying it was okay, but it wasn't. "I hate that we fight all the time now."

"I gotta be better."

"Okay. Let's not think about that today, though. Let's just get through this." He glanced across to where his mother sat on a chair. She looked fragile and alone. "Can you believe how Grandma acted?"

"I never saw her be so awful. Poor Mom."

"I knew what Grandma did to Aunt Caroline hurt Mom, but I never realized how much."

"Me, either."

Their dad appeared at their sides. "It's time to go up."

Maggie saw the guys coming toward her. Together they headed to the sanctuary. As she'd done when she was growing up, she had to literally force from her mind the recent damage her mother had inflicted on her. She would *not* let it intrude on this service. She would *not* let it level her as an adult. She'd deal with all that later and concentrate on Darcy in the present.

The service was lovely, but the ritual was so final, so utterly sad. She could barely watch Darcy cling to Dick, or their oldest child, Mary, cuddle her younger brother Zack to her side. Other things registered amidst the grief and sorrow she felt for her friends...the smell of candles, the murmuring of prayers, the singing of a beautiful hymn about the light of Christ shining in the darkness.

Listening to the poignant words of a pastor who had known Kenny well was uplifting. He spoke of the boy's joie de vivre, of his faith in God, of his earnest love for his family. Kenny wanted to be a teacher once he got out of the military and was planning to attend college on the army's scholarship plan.

Maggie studied the altar, the pews filled with people, and thought about the denomination of this congregation, the United Church of Christ. Once again, she longed for a place to get close to God, to get some help in dealing with her own problems.

They left after the luncheon and walked to the car. As they got on the road and drove away from Cornwall, Maggie let herself acknowledge that it was obviously too late for any change to occur in her mother—and God, why, *why* had she been thinking maybe Gertrude would be different? But, picturing Darcy mourning her son, Maggie also acknowledged they all might not have as much time to fix their family's problems as they thought they did.

CHAPTER FIFTEEN

Mike was sitting with his boys on the deck of his parents' home, which overlooked Conesus Lake, when Maggie came around the side of the house with Caroline and her daughter and granddaughter. This Sunday brunch had been planned before they'd gotten the news about Darcy's son. Still, they'd decided to go through with it. Lucy's genuine affection for Maggie always soothed the rough edges of her own mother's treatment. Those edges were jagged after yesterday's ordeal.

Looking drawn and tired, his wife nonetheless smiled at the assembled group. She was putting up a good front, but had let down with him last night and cried in his arms when they were alone.

She said, "Mom, Dad, this is my sister Caroline and her family, Teresa and Chloe. Ladies, this is BJ and Lucy."

His mother stepped forward. "Hello, Caroline. And Teresa." She bent down and ruffled Chloe's hair. "Hi, there, sweetheart."

The child peered up at Mike's mother with wide blue eyes; her blond hair was in pigtails. "Can I call you Great-Grandma?"

For a few moments, only the lap of the water and the buzz of a faraway motorboat could be heard.

Teresa touched her daughter's shoulder. "Honey, Lucy's not your grandma."

"Aunt Maggie calls her Mom." Chloe's lower lip trembled, as if she knew she'd made people uncomfortable. "And she's Grandma's sister. Don't they have the same mom?"

Lucy, bless her heart, took over. "I'd be honored if you called me Grandma, Chloe." She pointed to Mike's dad. "And that's Great-Grandpa."

Mike studied Caroline as she digested the exchange between the child and his mother. Everyone assembled knew that there would probably never be a maternal great-grandmother in Chloe's life.

Standing, he crossed to Lucy and slid an arm around her to show his appreciation. When everyone was seated, she asked, "Can I get anyone a drink?"

"Coffee for me," Caroline said.

The boys asked for soda and greeted their cousins warmly.

Caroline had taken a chair at the umbrella table right next to Maggie. Mike noticed that whenever they were together, Caroline was always in the closest proximity she could get with her sister. It touched Mike's heart and made him even more aware that Caroline had lost a sister, too.

After he helped his mother serve coffee and juice, Jamie asked, "Can we take Terry and Chloe out on the boat before we eat, Grandpa?"

"Sure, if they want to go. Everybody in life vests," BJ said winking at Chloe. "Especially this little precious cargo."

Brian hiked up Chloe in a piggyback, her arms looped around his neck and her pink-clad legs encircling him as if it was the most natural thing in the world. Jamie walked ahead with Teresa as they descended the stairs down to the dock. Mike took pleasure in seeing the boys get along with each other, as well as their good-natured teasing of Teresa and their tenderness toward Chloe. Yesterday had sobered everybody.

Always adept at small talk and putting people at ease, his mom addressed Caroline. "How are you enjoying the Simons' place?"

"It's a lovely home." She crossed her legs and sipped her coffee. "I'm surprised it was available so late in the season."

"It wasn't supposed to be," BJ put in. "Jack and Mary's son and daughter-in-law were going to spend July and August there, then their son's National Guard unit got called up. The daughter-in-law didn't want to come to the lake alone, so she stayed in South Carolina to be with her parents."

"How long has the house been for sale?"

"A year, at least," Lucy told her. "The Simons moved south last winter."

Settled in his favorite deck chair, BJ shook his head. "The house is beautiful, but too expensive for this lake. They overbuilt and now they're having trouble getting their investment back."

"I have a place on Hollow Lake in Colorado. It's not as big as this one, though."

Maggie reached over and squeezed Caroline's hand. Hollow Lake was where Caroline and her husband went every year after school finished.

"I'm so glad you could come over today," Lucy said. "We invited Sara, too."

"She went with Allison to a tour of Bard College this weekend," Maggie was quick to put in. Though Sara was totally against the innovative teaching methods and liberal course of study, Allison had insisted on at least seeing the school.

Mike wondered if Sara would have come anyway. Not everybody was as grateful as Maggie to have the Dean family in their lives.

The day went well, though Maggie seemed distracted. She had yet to tell her sister that their mother knew about her return and Gertrude's bitter reaction. The time came after brunch. Teresa was on the lower deck with the boys, who were trying to teach her to fish, and Chloe was sitting on his mother's lap, playing with the boondoggle Lucy had bought for her.

"I thought I might take Caroline out on the boat, Mom," Maggie said. "Is that okay?"

"Of course."

"Can I come?" This from Chloe. "I liked it with Bri and Jamie."

Lucy wrapped her arms around the child. "I was hoping you'd walk down to the ice cream stand with me and Grandpa."

Mike smiled. Yep, he'd really lucked out in the mom department.

❖

The sun sparkled off Caroline's dark hair and kissed her bare arms. Wearing white capris and a peach top, Maggie noticed the Birkenstock sandals on her feet, like the ones Maggie herself wore. Sometimes their tastes coincided so much, it made her think of twins separated at birth marrying similar types of men, taking the same job, or giving their children identical names.

As casually as she could, Maggie said, "Let's stop at the little cove over there and enjoy the sun."

Caroline gave her a knowing look. "You've been trying to get me alone all day."

When the anchor was down, Maggie smiled at her sister. "Am I that obvious?"

"Uh-huh. How'd it go with Darcy?"

"Horrible. I...just can't imagine losing a child."

Caroline took off her sunglasses and stared out at the water. "Me, either. It was bad enough losing a spouse." She focused on Maggie. "Then again, some people choose to lose a child, Mags."

Her sister was giving her an opening, so she blurted out, "Sara told her you were here."

"I'm not surprised. When we talked she didn't like keeping my return from Ma." Caroline sighed heavily. "I guess you and I have to have this conversation."

"We do. I can't bear to tell you what happened, though."

"She didn't handle it well, did she?"

"No. As a matter of fact, she handled it the same as she did when you told her you were marrying Derek."

Despite the hot weather, Caroline shivered. "I guess I knew that would happen. It's why I've been dodging the subject since you and I connected this spring." She gave a half-smile. "I wanted to enjoy you for a while."

The disappointment in her sister's tone stirred up Maggie's emotions. "Damn her, Caroline."

"Well, you know what? She's been out of my life for years. It's really no loss for me." Caroline sat up straighter. "And this time, she can't keep you away from me, Magpie. That is truly a blessing."

"I just wish she was different."

For a moment, they both stared out at the water, the cottages, the blue sky.

Maggie restarted the conversation. "Can I ask you a question?"

"Sure."

"If she'd been willing, would you have been able to forgive her?"

"I think so. I'm not sure you ever get over wanting to make things right with a parent. Wanting to please even an abusive mother or father, an emotionally challenged one. I see it in my students all the time, longing for the approval of absent parents, neglectful fathers. Even as adults, we still have that need."

"I guess."

"It's why I feel so sorry for Sara. She seems to crave Ma's approval more than any one of us."

"Ma can be so mean to her, too. To all of us."

Caroline studied Maggie. "That's because part of her personality was shaped by the hard life she had."

Which Maggie had talked about in her own therapy sessions with Melissa in an effort to put her upbringing in perspective. "I know Ma's background. That she had to quit school in the eighth grade to work in a box factory. And that she was clinically depressed and her condition was never treated."

"Actually, it *was* treated." Caroline frowned. "Though I think that did more harm than good."

"There weren't antidepressants then, Caro. She's on some now, you know. Patrick talked her into taking them."

"Oh, good. But I didn't mean with pills. Mags, she had a nervous breakdown before you were born."

"I never knew that."

"Dad and I kept it a secret because of the stigma. She went to a mental hospital about two hours away for six months."

Maggie clapped a hand on her chest. "Oh, no, Caroline. In the fifties those places were so backward."

"They did their best, but yes, the treatments weren't as advanced as what we have now. She had electric shock therapy, and it was a lot different from the gentler method used today."

Maggie felt a sudden, acute sense of sadness for her mother. She must have been terrified. "How was she when she came home?"

"Better, for a while at least. Then day-to-day life wore her down. Part of that was Dad's fault. He was never home." She scowled. "I remember like it was yesterday how his brother and sister-in-law would come to pick him up to go to the race track after he got out of work and Ma standing on the grass, watching the car full of people go out for the night while she stayed back with the kids. It happened a couple of times a week, at least."

Maggie's stomach cramped. "I never knew any of that, either."

"Would it have mattered?"

"In understanding her, yes."

"I'm sorry I wasn't around to tell you, kiddo."

Maggie decided to get it out in the open. "You could have been around, Caroline, when we were both adults, at least. I tried to find you when I was in college, then later on when I married Mike. Why didn't you ever call me? You knew where we were."

Caroline blew out a heavy breath. "I guess it's time to confess all this. Promise me it won't make you think less of me."

"Nothing could."

"After we got married, Derek put me through college and I got my degree, then taught for a few years. I was doing okay with Ma and Dad disowning me until Derek wanted to have a baby. I panicked. I had a kind of meltdown, too, and needed a lot of help."

"Oh, Caro."

"After the counseling, I decided to have a child and concentrate on my own family, to live like the rest of you never existed. It was my way of coping and a hell of a lot easier than facing the loss. For what it's worth, I missed you so much. And now, seeing you again, I wish I'd done it differently."

Forcefully, Maggie tamped down her disappointment. "I understand. And, like you said, we should concentrate on the present. We have each other again. That's what matters."

"You've become a lovely person, Maggie Davidson. And a wonderful wife and mother."

Now Maggie scowled. Because of the upheaval of Jamie's coming out, she questioned how well she fulfilled both those roles every day.

❖

Jamie whipped off his red T-shirt with the golden dragon on the front and pulled a long-sleeved black shirt out of the closet. No, too hot for today. He checked out his jeans. Should he put on shorts?

Once again he was obsessing over clothes, over his looks, which never mattered too much to him. He laughed out loud and turned up the CD by a gay boy band, which was playing a song about loving your first guy. And for Jamie, that guy was coming to dinner. His mom had been enthusiastic, his father *said* the right things, and Brian had pretended he was cool with it. But in his heart, Jamie knew this was a big deal for his whole family. He was beginning to feel better, though. After Kenny's death, they were all trying to work their problems out, so he decided to enjoy tonight. As a safety net, he'd asked Aunt Caroline to come. He thought maybe she'd keep things light. He liked her a lot—she reminded him of Ms. Carson.

Pulling on the T-shirt again, he checked his appearance in the mirror and left his room. Brian's door was still closed, so Jamie trundled down the steps and out to the back of the house. Aunt Caroline was on the deck with his mom. "Hey. I didn't hear the bell."

"Your mother said I don't have to use it. I'm family."

Oh, good, she was upbeat today, too.

"Hey, buddy." His mom's expression was serene. That expression had calmed him when he was five and broke his leg, when he was ten and his dad had a car accident, and when Brian was caught with alcohol. Jamie breathed easier.

He noticed a white plastic bag on the glass table. "What's that?"

His aunt smiled. "The last time I was here, I noticed you had a Wii. This is their new game that just came out."

"Turbo Jet?"

"Uh-huh."

"Sweet. Brian and I have been saving to go in on it."

"I thought we might play after dinner. With your friend Luke."

Grinning, Jamie said, "He's awesome at games, Aunt Caroline."

She sniffed. "So am I. My students were always dead meat when we played."

"You played those kinds of games with your kids?"

"Uh-huh. Our high school has alcohol free after-prom parties and other carnival-like events and we bring in all sorts of entertainment."

They were still talking about Aunt Caroline's teaching experiences when someone came around from the side walkway to the back of the house. Luke. He was wearing jeans, like Jamie, and a T-shirt that showed off his wide shoulders. Jamie's heart stuttered in his chest and he got turned on by just looking at Luke, which happened all the time now.

Luke stopped at the bottom of the stairs. "Hey. I rang the bell out front but nobody answered."

Jamie jogged down the steps. He would have hugged Luke, but he knew Luke would be embarrassed. Instead, he squeezed his arm. "Hey, you. Come on up."

His mother stood and when they climbed the steps, she went right up to Luke. Taking his hand between both of hers, she said softly, "Hi, Luke. We met before the Valentine's Ball, but didn't have a chance to talk. I'm looking forward to getting to know you better." She sounded like she meant it.

"Thanks, Mrs. Davidson."

His mom's smile bloomed brighter than the sun. "And this is my sister, Caroline Dean."

"Hi, Mrs. Dean. Jamie talks about you a lot."

"Hello, Luke."

"She bought Turbo Jet for us."

"Shut up! I didn't know it was out."

Jamie socked him on the shoulder. "Good, so we stand a decent shot of beating you."

Luke blushed. Jamie loved it when he did that.

From inside, the door to the garage slammed and Jamie tensed. His dad was home. Again, Jamie's heart began to gallop in his chest but for a different reason.

Like a little kid, hoping for approval, Jamie looked to his dad as he came to the doorway of the porch. He smiled genuinely, clapped a hand on Jamie's shoulder and faced Luke, his other hand extended. "Hi, Luke. I didn't have much of a chance to talk to you the last time you were here, but I've seen you on the ball field a lot. You're a hell of a pitcher."

Jamie wanted to cry with relief at his father's overture.

"Thanks, Mr. Davidson. Good to meet you."

"Welcome to my home, Luke." He glanced over and smiled at Jamie's mom. "Hi, honey."

"Hi, Mike. Work go okay?"

They were trying to be normal, Jamie realized. Blessedly normal.

"Uh-huh." He touched Caroline's shoulder. "And here's my sister-in-law. I didn't know you were coming tonight."

"Last-minute decision. It's okay, isn't it?"

"Of course. Let's have a drink?"

Jamie stood. "I'll get sodas for us."

"No, I'll do it. Enjoy your friend. Caroline? Mag?"

They asked for wine and his dad started through the porch just as Brian came into it from the kitchen. Jamie saw his father speak to Brian, clap a hand on his shoulder, then Brian came to the doorway. "Hey, everybody." His smile was phony, but he zeroed in on Luke. "Nice to see you, Luke."

"Hey, Bri."

"Good practice today, huh?"

"Yeah. You hit really well."

"That's right, you guys play baseball together." Caroline smiled at Maggie. "Did you know I taught your mom to hit a ball when she was little?"

His Mom's laughter rang out through the yard.

And Jamie thought maybe, just maybe, this was going to go okay.

❖

Later that night, Maggie was washing her face in their bathroom. As she lathered her cheeks with soap, she felt good about the way the evening had gone. Caroline had beaten the pants off all three guys in Turbo Jet and they'd been stunned.

"I thought that went well with Luke," she called out to Mike.

Her husband sat on the cedar chest at the end of their bed. He'd taken off his shirt and belt and wore blue jeans. He'd removed one shoe and was holding it. "He's a nice boy."

"I feel bad for him having to deal with a father like the one he has."

No confirmation. No response at all.

"We need to talk about Lucas Crane asking to see you."

A pause, then, "I already met with him." He rushed on to say, "I didn't want to tell you before because you were upset about Darcy."

Her good mood fizzled like the mist off her in-laws' lake in the morning. "I thought we decided you wouldn't meet with Luke's father unless we discussed it with Jamie first."

"No, you decided that all on your own."

Drying her face slowly, Maggie tried to summon patience. She wanted that feeling of closeness they'd had just a few hours ago when, by tacit agreement, they bonded to make the night go smoothly. So she said, "Oh, honey, I think that was a mistake."

A size twelve shoe hit the floor with a thud. "I don't. I'm trying to support Jamie as best I can in all this. I welcomed Luke into our home. But there are still a lot of problems we have to address. Lucas Crane and I discussed some options."

"Options?"

Now his face showed guilt. "We both think we should to try to get the boys to change."

Maggie walked into the bedroom and sat beside Mike. "Even if Jamie could change, which you know I don't think is a possibility, Jamie doesn't *want* to."

"He says that now. But if he could be shown the right path..."

"Haven't you been listening to him? He doesn't see his being gay as a problem to be solved. As a matter of fact, he's celebrating who he is. I think that's all good."

"His being gay certainly has *caused* a lot of problems in our lives."

"It's not Jamie's sexual orientation that's created the stress around here, Mike." An edge crept into her voice. "It's because he came out, and now that's an issue for you."

"I can't help how I feel about this or what my church teaches!"

"And Jamie sees your conflict. He sees that you believe he has an illness and it can be cured."

"Nobody's putting it that way."

"Those were Judy Johnson's exact words."

"Is that why she hasn't been around?" He scowled. "Have you alienated her, too?"

"You'd have to ask her that. All I know is that it's too hard to hear her preach sentiments I think are harmful, murderous, really. Hate crimes against gay people are *not* a thing of the past."

Mike studied her as if deciding whether to go further. "Father Pete gave me some brochures on reparative therapy camps where Christian parents send their children to be deprogrammed."

"Oh, my God, Mike. Those camps do unconscionable harm to

teens. Their experiences at places like that can damage them irreparably *and* take thousands of dollars from misled parents." Her voice ratcheted up a notch. "And it doesn't even work! Gay people who undergo the process just suppress their homosexual behaviors. The therapy doesn't actually change them into heterosexuals."

"Father Pete says otherwise. He's seen some real successes with the camps."

"Kids coming out of places like that have been known to commit suicide because they're trying to be what they aren't. Christ, Mike, suicide rates are high among gay teens as it is."

A muscle in his jaw pulsed. "Do you have reason to think Jamie's suicidal?"

"No, and I discussed it with Melissa. She doesn't think so either. But those camps could push anybody over the brink. Even adults."

"Or they could help Jamie get out of a bad situation he's in."

"Most psychologists wouldn't agree. The AMA and the APA declared decades ago that homosexuality is not a psychosis."

He shook off her hand. "I *hate* when you do that."

"Do what?"

"Use your psychology degree to win an argument."

"Psychology is important in this discussion."

"Faith and spirituality are more important."

"To you maybe."

He bolted up and towered over her. "That's at the crux of this, isn't it? You're using Jamie as an excuse to leave the Catholic Church."

"I don't need to look for additional reasons to leave that institution. I made all this clear when I started checking out other churches. I can't ignore the doctrines I don't believe in."

He swallowed hard but he didn't answer.

So she kept going. "We decided we couldn't abide by the birth control edict so, like millions of other Catholics, we ignored it."

His face tightened.

"And we conveniently accepted Craig Johnson's annulment and never discussed it with him or Father Pete. We also don't openly object to the church's position on women, but I should hope you don't actually subscribe to that thinking. When *are* we going to deal with the fact that we don't agree with the Vatican on most issues?"

Usually Mike was fair and backed down if someone out-argued

him. Not when the debate involved his religion, though. "I agree with the church's position on homosexuality."

The lines had been drawn, and Maggie felt any promises they'd made to each other after Kenny's death evaporate.

So she said bitterly, "Then I feel sorry for you. It might very well cost you your son."

CHAPTER SIXTEEN

The United Church of Christ on Clayton Avenue was a modern brick building, striking in its simplicity. Its inviting interior consisted of high ceilings, pews and benches made of oak wood and an intimate altar. The faint smell of candles and flowers scented the air and Maggie noticed beautiful groupings of them decorating the sanctuary as she entered and sat in a pew halfway down the carpeted aisle. She was surprised to see that the modern cross on the wall behind the altar didn't have Jesus nailed hand and foot to the wood. And there were no kneelers anchored to the floor, either. The entire structure was the antithesis of the Catholic Church they attended. St. Mary's had peaks that arched and loomed above its congregation and a forbidding altar sectioned off with a railing at which people used to kneel to receive communion.

Maggie's discussion two nights ago with Mike had brought her here. And to some degree, so had Caroline's return. She couldn't stay in a church that had taken her sister away from her and was threatening harm to her son.

The door to the sanctuary whispered open and a few people entered. They scattered themselves in different pews. One of them approached her. "Hello," a woman said from the aisle. "I'm Anabelle Brooke. The minister here."

"I'm Maggie Davidson. I e-mailed you to see if it was all right to come to Centering Prayer today."

"I was hoping you would." Anabelle's short blond hair framed her pretty face. Her smile was easy, her blue gaze direct. "If you'd like to talk afterward, I've cleared my calendar."

"I'm not sure but I'll let you know."

Reaching out, Anabelle touched Maggie's arm. "No worries." The reverend found a seat farther down the aisle and five more people joined the group.

One of the women switched on a tape recorder. Stringed instruments filled the open space and voices sang in harmony, asking God for insight and inspiration. Maggie let the spiritual melody soothe her. Then the music went off and there was absolute quiet.

After Maggie had contacted her, Reverend Brooke had e-mailed back and explained the process of Centering Prayer. Participants were encouraged to simply clear their minds and let God's spirit fill them. But sometimes, people worked out issues in their own lives or simply talked with God about what they were feeling.

Maggie had chosen to come to this informal event before attending a worship service on Sunday. Besides, it had been a while since she talked to God.

Maggie prayed that she'd made the right decision when she'd telephoned Darcy's minister after the debacle with Mike over reparative therapy camps...

"Reverend Jones? This is Darcy's friend, Maggie Davidson. You told me I could call you."

"That's right. You were inquiring about our denomination at the luncheon."

"I wondered if I could ask you some questions about it."

He cheerfully agreed and gave their history. The United Church of Christ, with its roots in the Protestant Reformation, took a liberal view on most issues. They believed in God, Jesus Christ, and the Holy Spirit. But each person in the congregation was encouraged to wrestle in his or her own mind about the particulars of their faith understanding. She and Darcy's pastor spoke a long time about theological freedom and the responsibility that comes with it, about sin and grace, and about a loving God.

"I can recommend a UCC church in your area for you to visit."

"That would be great."

"Hang on." Computer keys clicked in the background. A minute or two passed. "There's a small United Church of Christ not far from Sherwood, on the west side of Rochester." He gave her the address. "It's open and affirming, Maggie."

"Which means?"

"Everyone is accepted regardless of race, gender, income level, physical ability or sexual orientation."

"Sexual orientation?"

"Yes. Gays, lesbians, bisexuals, and transgender people are embraced by the congregation." He paused, then added, "As a matter of fact, the minister there is a lesbian."

"Oh."

"Is that a problem?"

"No, it's not a problem, it's a godsend."

He chuckled. "Go to their Web site. Visit the church and give them a try…"

Maggie was so deep in her own thoughts that she was shocked when the music began to play again, signaling the end of the session. And pleased to find herself feeling better, which was why she waited in the narthex for Reverend Brooke to exit the sanctuary.

"Would you like to talk?" the minister asked.

"Yes, I would."

"Fine, let's go to my office."

As she followed the woman down the hall, Maggie had a strong sense of God being with her, a feeling she hadn't had in a very long time.

❖

For the first time since Jamie came out, he wished he hadn't told anybody he was gay. He wished he *wasn't* gay.

He wished he was dead.

"I gotta go."

His father, on the edge of his bed, grabbed for his arm. "No, Jame. We have to talk about this."

Jamie backed away from him. "I gotta find Mom."

"Forget Mom. You and I need to talk about this." His dad's tone had turned anxious, panicky, which made Jamie even more scared. He was always the rock of the family.

"I need Mom." Jamie stampeded down the staircase and skidded to a halt at the doorway to the laundry room where his mother was doing the wash. Where he'd started this whole thing. Had he been wrong to trust them?

Buck was at his side, wagging his tail.

Jamie said to his mother, "Did you know about this?"

"About what?"

"Dad thinks I need a shrink. To turn me straight." His whole body cramped at saying the words, the truth, out loud. "He thinks I'm broken, Mom."

His mother's eyes widened. "Oh, honey."

"I didn't say that, Jamie."

He rounded on his father, who'd followed him down. "You and Dr. Crane think Luke and I should be shipped off to one of those *camps*. I read about them on the Internet—they brainwash people!" His voice cracked. "They treat you like a pervert, monitoring your behavior, watching every move you make."

"You're taking all this wrong, Jame. I just wanted to talk to you about the camp."

His mother was silent, and suddenly Jamie couldn't breathe. "Mom, do you agree with him?"

His father's voice was ragged. "Jamie, this is between you and me. Leave Mom out of it."

Like a little boy, waiting for approval, he watched his mother.

"No, Jamie," she said finally. "I don't agree with Dad or Father Pete or Dr. Crane. I don't believe a person's sexual orientation can be changed, and I'd never let you go to one of those camps"—she glanced at his father with anguish in her eyes—"no matter what your dad says."

His father grabbed his arm and forced him around. "Jamie, I'm not sure a reparative therapy camp is our best option either. Father Pete also suggested you could get some therapy from their spiritual counselors, but only out of deep love for you and this family." His dad ran a hand through his hair. "Maybe Mom's right with her psychological theories. Maybe people are born with a sexual orientation and it can't be changed." He took Jamie by the shoulders, his grasp gentle in contrast to his words. "But the Catholic Church is adamant about practicing homosexuality. I wish you'd at least give the spiritual counseling a try."

"Fuck the Catholic Church."

Always in the past, Jamie feared disappointing his dad. He wanted to puke when he saw moisture fill his father's eyes.

Could this get any worse?

The door to the garage, just a few feet from the laundry room, slammed. And Brian walked in. "What's going on?" he asked glancing from Jamie to their dad.

Nobody spoke.

"Mom?"

Jamie faced his brother head on. "Dad thinks I can change. He *wants* me to change. He thinks I'm defective."

"I didn't say that, son."

Jamie glared at his father. "By implication you did." He faced Brian. "Do you agree with him?"

Brian looked like somebody had hit him in the stomach with a baseball bat.

His mom stepped forward. "Jamie, it's not fair to draw Brian into this."

"I want everybody here to say out loud what you think of me!"

Brian's Adam's apple bobbed and he grasped Jamie's upper arm. "I'm Catholic, Jame. I believe what the church teaches. But I love—"

Jamie shirked off his brother's touch. "Quit saying you love me." He glared at his father. "Both of you. If you want me to change who I am, you don't love *me*." He looked around wildly. "I-I never expected this. From either of you."

Knowing he had to get away, he slammed out the back door. Behind him he heard his father shout, "Jamie, don't leave like this."

But he did. He jumped in the car Brian had parked in the driveway and made it to the end of the street, where he pulled over, put his head down on the wheel, and cried.

❖

Brian leaned against the wall as if it was holding him up. "Is this my fault?"

"No, honey," Maggie said, "it's nobody's fault."

He turned to his father for help, for the guidance that the boys always sought from him. In the past, Maggie had loved that about Mike's parenting. "What should I have done, Dad?"

"I don't know, buddy."

Reaching out to him, Maggie smoothed down her son's hair. "You got ambushed, Bri. It wasn't fair. Want to talk?"

"No, I'm going to my room." Before he left, he glanced from her to Mike. "Why can't our life be like it was before?"

No one attempted to answer that query.

Brian headed upstairs and Mike stood there, staring at her. "You don't think that this was nobody's fault, do you? You think it's mine."

Try to stay true to yourself but don't alienate your husband or your son, Anabelle had advised yesterday during their two-hour conversation. Once Maggie had started talking, she'd poured out the whole dilemma to the reverend.

How do I do that?

Be honest. Don't imply anybody's wrong. Then she squeezed, Maggie's arm. *God will be with you if and when the time comes.*

Well, Maggie hoped God hung out in laundry rooms.

"I think you did what you had to do and it didn't work out."

"No *I told you so*?"

"No, none."

"God, Maggie, what am I going to do now? How can I reconcile all this with my religion?"

"I'm not sure you can. I went to check out another church yesterday. I talked to the minister. She said believing in God, loving God, is different from following a religion."

He leaned back against the wall just like Brian had and closed his eyes. "I can't believe you'd go to another church at a time like this."

"I'm sorry. I felt I had to." She folded her arms across her chest. "I'm planning to attend their services Sunday. I'm asking Jamie to come along."

"I suppose they're liberal. Their belief is that God accepts"—he made a sweeping motion with his hand—"all this."

"It's called being open and affirming, Mike. They embrace people who are marginalized by society. No judgments are made on anyone."

Now wasn't the time to tell him Anabelle was a lesbian.

"Including any judgment of Caroline, I might add."

"You can't divide our family like this because of past issues."

Despite Anabelle's advice, Maggie snapped, "I'm not the one who's dividing us."

"I can't believe this is happening to us."

How you work out this difference between you will affect your marriage for a long time to come.

Maggie was struck by a memory. In their younger days, she and Mike fought like most newlyweds trying to navigate the murky waters of marriage, filled with disagreements over money, sex, how they'd spend their time. Once, after they'd made up, Maggie told him she was sad because she'd read somewhere that relationships were like vases. Every time a couple had a fight, the vase cracked. Over the long haul, the cracks would destroy the vase. Mike had come home not long after with a copper vase. "Indestructible," he'd said confidently. "Like our marriage."

"I'm going out." He pushed away from the wall. "I have to think about this."

As Maggie watched him take the same path Jamie had, she wondered for the first time how she could accept a man who wanted to send his son away to a place that could very well destroy him.

❖

Feeling like his insides had been shredded, Jamie sat on the edge of Luke's bed in a room twice the size of his own, with a private bath attached. One whole wall was filled with a desk, computer system, and stereo equipment from which blared some hard rock. Jamie had ended up here after he called Luke from the car and Luke told him to come over. His parents were at the country club playing in a Scotch tournament.

"No way am I going to one of those camps," Luke was saying. "I'll run away first."

At his words, Jamie's pulse began to beat fast. "I hate when you talk like that."

Luke paced the room without responding.

"Maybe my mom can help. She disagrees with my dad."

"I can't believe our fathers met to discuss sending us to one of those places." Luke's fists curled at his sides and his blue eyes were wild. "At least your father told you what he did."

And assured Jamie he loved him. Poor Luke never got any of that.

"I'm sorry. My mom could talk to your mom, and she can work on your dad."

"My mom always agrees with my father. She always takes his side."

Jamie was beginning to realize how lucky he was. He remembered times in his house when his parents didn't agree on issues about him and Brian but respected each other's opinions and compromised. And now that he'd calmed down, he thought of some of the ways his father had tempered his words.

"We have to plan."

"Plan what?"

"How we're gonna get away from them."

Even though things were a mess at home, Jamie wasn't sure he wanted to get away from his parents, especially his mother. "Luke, you're not thinking straight."

"I don't give a fucking rat's ass." He picked up a CD Walkman from his desk and flung it across the room. It smashed into pieces and gouged a hole in the drywall. Then he began to pace again.

Now, Jamie's heart raced. "Luke, settle down. Think about this in another way. You'll be gone in a few months."

The comment made Luke stop, though his face was still grim. "Yeah, I guess. If they let me go to college."

"You got tons of scholarships. You've been accepted at top schools. They can't keep you from college. You're eighteen."

The notion seemed to calm him and his body relaxed. "So how do we deal with them until then?"

"I don't know. We could talk to Ms. Carson. She might be able to help us."

"Jamie, talking about this won't make my parents hate me less."

"They don't hate you."

"You're so naïve sometimes. Because your parents' love is unconditional, doesn't mean everybody's is."

He thought of Grandma Lorenzo and what she'd done to Aunt Caroline, what she was still doing to his mother.

"Let's get out of here," Luke said. "We'll get some beer and go for a drive. My parents will freak if they come home and find us together."

"I guess."

"I gotta take a leak first." He crossed the room, leaned over, and kissed Jamie on the mouth. "Sorry I'm not dealing with this as well as you, Jame."

"I'm bummed, too."

When Luke left, Jamie couldn't sit still so he slid off the bed and wandered over to the desk. It was neat and tidy, but the drawer beneath it was ajar. Inside, he saw pills.

Prescription pills.

Several bottles of them.

CHAPTER SEVENTEEN

At the end of the day after another confrontation with his family, Brian was totally whipped. And he still had practice for two hours. He hadn't slept much last night because he waited until he heard Jamie come home. One of their parents went into his room and then the low murmur of voices drifted through the walls. Whoever it was didn't stay long.

Brian lay awake long into the night, trying to figure out how to accept his brother and how to avoid the explosions at their house. This hadn't ever happened before. Sure, his family had the normal conflicts about where he and Jamie were allowed to go, about pitching in with chores, but nothing so big. Now his parents were edgy and moody, which worried the hell out of him because he never saw that, either.

So this morning, he'd taken a risk and knocked on Jamie's door. When there was no answer, he'd gone inside anyway. Jamie had left early for school for a blood drive meeting, his mom told him later, but while he was in the empty room, Brian caught sight of a loose leaf sheet of paper on Jamie's desk—another one of his poems. Brian knew he wrote this for class, and also to vent his feelings. For that reason, Brian had stuck it in his pocket, but hadn't read it yet.

With no energy at all, he entered the locker room. The guys were trading jibes while they dressed for practice. Heather had been right about some things. After the initial flurry over Jamie and Luke being gay, the kids at school pretty much went off with some other bit of gossip. There were a few groups who still made nasty comments, but Brian hadn't seen any overt bullying. The team was doing okay, too, he thought as he changed into his uniform and sat on the bench to put on his cleats. They were having a winning season, and when Coach Denton visited again, Brian had scored two home runs and done some awesome fielding. Denton had been encouraging about him getting a place on the Ithaca team and some alumni scholarship money. Now, if he could just make peace with Jamie.

As he was putting his clothes in his gym bag, he felt the paper in his pants pocket. What the hell? He couldn't feel any worse. He pulled it out and read it.

The Dragon

The Dragon comes alive again,
Ambushing me when I think
All will be well.
In stealth it stalks and slithers
Searching for my suffering soul.
Then it morphs! Becomes a priest,
A dad, a brother.

Why do I not just give in?
Maybe I will.

Brian had to battle back the moisture in his eyes. He wasn't as good as Jamie in English, but he got the metaphor. And the message. He was responsible for much of the pain that his brother poured out onto this page. He couldn't stand it, so he bolted up from the bench and strode to end of the row. Just then, Luke entered the room late. His locker was way at the end of the aisle and he had to pass all the guys to get to it. He nodded to Brian, and suddenly, Brian wondered if Jamie had told him about the latest trouble at home.

When Luke disappeared down his own row, Brian heard Eric Cummings say, "Wonder if gay boy was getting a blow job in his car. God, that stuff makes me sick."

The guys around Brian went still. Everybody knew he was a couple rows over, so he'd hear Cummings's comment. *Fuck this*, Brian thought. He wasn't going to sit on the sidelines any longer. He could slay this dragon for Jamie, at least. He stalked down the aisle, his cleats echoing loudly in the open space. Grabbing Cummings from behind, he slammed him against his locker, banging his head hard against it. Brian fisted his hands in the front of Cummings's uniform and said in a deadly quiet voice, "Shut your mouth about Luke and my brother or I'll knock your goddamned teeth down it."

Cummings's face reddened, and he seemed scared, too, so Brian moved in even closer. "You hear me, jerkoff?"

The guy glanced to either side of him, probably for help from his posse, but none of the other teammates intervened.

So Cummings battered his arm. "Let me go, Davidson."

Brian stepped back and dropped his hands. "Just remember what I said."

One by one, all the guys left, not supporting Brian, but not defending Cummings, either. That was progress, Brian guessed.

And he felt better. He'd let Jamie down yesterday, but not now.

Practice went as usual, though nobody talked much, just played extra hard. The workout energized him and at six, when they finished, Brian jogged ahead to the locker room, just changed his shoes, got his bag, and went out into the school hallway still in his uniform. He didn't feel like sticking around for more fighting.

A flash of pink and white off to the side caught his attention. Heather. She'd moved her stuff out of his locker and her new one was down two halls. Seeing her drained some of the good feelings he'd gotten from standing up to Cummings. But he said, anyway, "Hey, Heather."

Her head whipped around, sending dark locks everywhere. "Hi, Bri."

"How come you're here this late? Cheerleading's over, isn't it?"

"Yeah, I had chorus practice for the spring concert." She studied him with sad eyes. "You okay?"

"Like, are you kidding?"

"I'm sorry."

"That's my line," he joked. She didn't laugh. Behind her on the wall was a poster announcing the sale of Junior Prom tickets. It made him ask, "I don't suppose I should be buying some of those? Since I was supposed to take you?"

She glanced over her shoulder, then back to him. The expression on her face was his answer. He couldn't stand it so he closed the distance between them and put his hand on her arm. "Please don't do this. Give me another chance."

"I can't." Her voice was shaky. "You know my dad cheated on my mother. I couldn't forgive him and I can't forgive you. You and I are over as a couple, Brian."

"You still going to the prom?" His throat clogged at the thought of another guy dancing with her, holding her.

"I don't know." She stepped back. "I have to go. My mother's waiting for me." She started away then stopped. "Brian?"

He prayed for a miracle. "Yeah?"

"It's too late with me, but not with Jamie. You don't have to lose your brother, too."

Leaning against the wall, he watched her walk away, feeling rotten again. Before he could make himself move, somebody else came up to him, and when he turned, he saw it was Luke.

Without greeting him, Luke said, "What happened with Cummings before practice? Edwards said you got into it."

"I'm sick of his bullshit. He's such a prick."

Luke smiled. "We agree on that. You gonna tell Jamie you confronted the asshole?"

"I don't know. I'm not his favorite person right now."

"It could take the edge off what went down at your house last night."

Of course Jamie would have confided in Luke. No longer did he turn to Brian with his problems. And that knowledge made his chest hurt as much as it had when Heather refused to get back with him. "I keep blowing it with Jamie, Luke. Sometimes I say the wrong thing and don't even know it."

"Give him some space, Bri. He's getting it from all sides, too." Then Luke walked away.

Miserable, Brian laid his head against the cold steel locker, wishing he could crawl inside. He'd never felt so alone in his whole life.

❖

After Thursday night, the tension in Maggie's house was so bad that none of them were talking much. They'd been polite to each other, but communication was zilch. She was worried about Mike, of course, but he was an adult and had developed coping skills. She was more concerned about Jamie and Brian. They'd never had to deal with a schism among the four of them and suddenly, Maggie wondered if she and Mike had protected their sons from the realities of real life. Thinking of her mother, she knew why she'd always wanted a calm, conflict-free home, but she still worried about the boys. So she'd called Melissa late Friday afternoon and now, Saturday morning, was waiting for them to get up.

Jamie stirred first. He came downstairs and out to the porch. All the doors were open and spring warmth filtered in through the screens.

"Morning." Jamie's face was relaxed. When he was a baby, waking up was the best time for him and he'd coo and babble until they got him out of the crib. Contrary to Brian, who screamed his lungs out.

"Hi, honey. Come sit with me."

"Let me get some juice first."

He returned in a moment and they watched the birds in the feeder, oohing and ahhing over red-breasted robins and blue jays and particularly a hummingbird that buzzed in the flower boxes.

When Jamie seemed fully awake, Maggie pulled a paper out of her bathrobe. "I have something for you."

His features went taut. "Mom, please, I'm not up for a serious talk. I told you Thursday night I didn't want to discuss Dad or Brian."

"You don't have to talk to me. But *I* have to do this. Then we can go back to the birds and enjoy the day." She slid the paper over to him.

He picked it up. "What's this?"

"I can't sit by while you and Brian are at each other's throats and getting more and more depressed. I thought about individual counseling, but Melissa suggested the Gay Alliance. They have support groups for gay youths and a counselor on hand to talk individually to kids."

"You can't fix the problems we're having, Mom. Neither can a counselor."

"I think you're looking at this wrong. I know the value of having a trained clinician clarify and frame situations in a different light. I also know how support groups can help ease some burdens." She patted his hand. "I've seen a counselor all my life, honey, and she's helped me immensely. I also did a few groups."

"Yeah, but your family was so screwed up."

Her throat got tight. She'd always been proud that the four of them were the opposite of the Lorenzos.

"Mom? You okay?"

"I think *our* family needs help now."

"Maybe." Jamie waited, staring out at the birds. "Did you, um, find somebody to help Brian? Even though I'm mad as hell at him, I know he's having a hard time."

Her heart swelled in her chest. Jamie was such a good person and loved his brother enough to set aside his own anger. "There's a group at the Alliance for brothers and sisters of gay teens. But I'm also giving him the name of a private psychologist."

An idea popped into Jamie's head. She could see it by the slight raise of his brows, a light in his eyes. "Is there a cost to this, Mom?" He held up the paper.

"No, the Alliance is free." At the relief in his expression, she added, "Honey, we can afford private counseling if you'd prefer that."

"I was thinking about Luke. But his parents wouldn't pay for him to see somebody."

"They might surprise you."

"I doubt it."

"Well, let's get back to you."

Clasping the note, he stood. "I'll think about it." He kissed her cheek. "I'm gonna watch some TV."

Not much later, Maggie went upstairs. Brian's door was ajar and she could see him at his computer. She knocked and went inside. "Morning, honey."

"Hi, Mom."

"Do you have a minute?"

His face tightened exactly as Jamie's had. "I don't feel like talking," he said. "Please."

"Neither did your brother. But *I've* got something to say. It'll only take five minutes." Crossing to the desk, she stood behind him and kissed his head. "I love you, Brian, and I'm going to help you." She placed a second paper on the desk and went through the same explanation as she had with Jamie.

But her older son surprised her. Staring down at the number, he said, "I don't have anybody to talk to. I used to have Heather and Jamie." His voice cracked.

"I know, baby. You still have me and Dad, and don't ever forget that. But if talking to us is too hard, which I suspect it is, here's another option."

"Thanks."

Maggie went back to the kitchen, poured more coffee, then settled out on the deck. She sat under the umbrella table and prayed to God she'd done all she could for her boys. For today, at least.

❖

Before church on Sunday, Mike planned to pray silently about the war zone his household had become. But as soon as he knelt down, one of the deacons came over and told him Father Pete wanted to see him in his church office. So Mike headed there. Inside he found Craig Johnson sitting in an empty chair in front of the desk, the priest behind it. "Hey, Craig. Father."

"Good morning." Father Pete's smile was warm, but there was an expression in his eyes that disturbed Mike. Or maybe he was reading more into the priest's demeanor because he felt so bad about himself today. He'd made some serious mistakes last week.

Dropping into a chair adjacent to Craig and facing Father Pete, Mike asked, "What's up?"

"I'd like to talk to you about the schedule for the Contemporary Issues group."

Mike frowned. "I thought we had it all set. Tomorrow night is divorce." Ironic, given Caroline's reappearance and what Maggie had said about Craig's annulment the other night.

"It's the following week I'm concerned about you leading."

Again, Mike tracked the list in his memory. "Ah, homosexuality."

Folding his hands in front of him on the desk, Father Pete held Mike's gaze. "Given your situation, I'm not sure you should be in charge of that session."

Craig leaned forward in his chair. "It could be hard for you, buddy."

"It might be, but not impossible."

"I was thinking we should reorganize the order of the issues. Maybe put the topic last. By then," Father Pete said in a stern voice Mike rarely heard, "you'll have a better handle on your family life."

That stung. Was he losing credibility in his own church? With two men he admired for their deep faith? "I'm shocked you don't think I can handle the church group objectively."

"It is what it is, son."

"I see. Well, then, let's reschedule."

"Would you like to talk more after church?" the priest asked. "Maybe your whole family could come in with you."

"Only Brian will be here."

Disapproval etched out on the holy man's face. "I'm very sorry to hear that."

"Me, too." He stood. "I'm going pray about it before the service."

Mike hurried out of the office, conflicted by Father Pete's decision and his obvious disappointment in Mike. The priest's questioning his leadership ability made him feel even worse than when he'd come to church. He'd let down Maggie, Jamie, and even Brian on Thursday. Now Father Pete was losing confidence in him.

In a blur of recrimination, he made it to the vestibule before Craig caught up with him. "Mike, wait."

He stopped. The man was his best friend and Mike could trust him. What's more, he needed *somebody's* support now. Maybe God had sent Craig out after him.

"I'm sorry if that upset you," Craig said earnestly.

"I'm glad you were there. Did Father Pete ask you to come to the meeting to be there for me?"

Craig's expression was pitying. "No, Mike. *I* asked for this meeting. It was my idea to postpone the topic of homosexuality."

❖

Jamie sat in the parking lot of the United Church of Christ at eleven o'clock on Sunday morning, having asked his mother to take him to church. After what happened with his father on Thursday, then finding the pills in Luke's drawer, he needed some spiritual comfort. Staring at the cars on the blacktop, he realized he wasn't the only one seeking out God today.

In the car next to him, his mom reached over and squeezed his arm. "You ready for this, buddy?"

At least he could answer that. "Yeah, Mom, I am. I've had trouble with the Catholic Church for so long, and not just about gay issues, but I never, you know, wanted to leave *God.*" He gestured to the building. "Maybe this was supposed to happen."

"I feel the same way. Let's go see."

When they entered the foyer, people were everywhere—chatting by a signup board, where big lettering said COFFEE HOUR and FOOD SHELF, socializing in small clusters by an office. Most everyone was smiling.

To the left of the entrance there were greeters wearing name tags. A woman held out her hand as they walked in. "Hi, I'm Patty Ames. These are my sons Brendan and Chris, my husband Brian and my daughter Beth. Are you new to UCC?"

His mother introduced them, then Jamie heard, "Oh, Maggie, I'm so glad you came."

Jamie turned to find a woman in a white robe behind them. So this was the minister. The *lesbian* minister. Her short blond-streaked hair was highlighted by the sun streaming in from the big front door. She wore a white robe with a button reading *Another woman for peace* and a stole embroidered with abstract children of different races. She also had some color on her eyelids and wore lipstick. He wasn't used to a female pastor, let alone one who wore makeup.

"Hi, Anabelle. This is Jamie."

Without inhibition, the minister took Jamie's hand in both of hers and held on. "Glad to have you here, Jamie." Her grip was firm and her eyes met his directly.

"Thanks, Reverend."

"Call me Anabelle. We don't stand on formalities at UCC."

"Sure, okay."

"Come with me," she said, tugging his mom by the arm. "I've got someone for you to meet. They're members who want to sit with you."

Becky and Dave Banks greeted them warmly, then accompanied them into the sanctuary to a pew halfway down the aisle. Organ music filled the air and people were quieting down. As minutes passed, the chatter dwindled to silence.

Up front, Anabelle addressed the congregation. "I'd like to welcome all of you this morning, especially our visitors." Her smile, aimed at them, was brilliant.

The service had some similarities to the Catholic Mass, but it was more informal, more personal. They started with an opening hymn, followed by a children's sermon, where people laughed at the antics of their offspring while Anabelle tried to teach them a lesson from the Bible. Then the choir sang a piece about spring and rebirth. Jamie was impressed by the professional quality of the performance.

Differing from the Catholic service was Anabelle's request for the congregation to share their joys and concerns aloud. One woman asked for prayers for her sister who had cancer. A man spoke about a career change. Joys abounded—two people who'd been South for the winter were back, someone graduated from college, another person had relatives visiting. A tiny white-haired lady with a smile the size of Texas thanked the choir for sharing their amazing talent.

Then there was time to meditate on concerns the congregation kept to themselves. And Jamie couldn't avoid his own major-league worry any longer. He'd stuffed it for a few days, but now he had to think about it...

When Luke came back from the bathroom after Jamie had found the pills, Jamie had held out a bottle. "What the hell are these?"

"Did you go into my drawers?" Jamie had recognized the offensive tactic because Brian always used it.

"The drawer was open. Answer my question."

"Get the fuck out of here."

"No."

Luke strode over to him. His big frame was imposing, making Jamie want to step back. But he didn't. Instead he stood in front of the drawer, a shield between it and Luke.

Finally Luke blew out a breath and his shoulders slumped. "I wasn't gonna take them."

"Then why do you have them?"

"The night I told my parents? They looked at me like I was pond scum. I *felt* like pond scum." He flopped on the bed and sprawled out spread-eagle. "I-I thought about taking those."

"Jesus Christ." Then, "Why didn't you?"

"You really want to know?"

Jamie nodded.

"Because of you. You're so strong. Your family's great. I kept thinking maybe if I was more like you, I'd get through this. Maybe if I waited long enough, my parents would be more like yours."

Jamie scooped the rest of the bottles out of the drawer and put them in a plastic bag that was tucked behind the pills. "I'm taking these when I leave."

"Go ahead."

"You need to talk to somebody."

"Listen, I'm not suicidal. It was a crazy thought."

Crossing to the bed, Jamie sat on the edge of the mattress. "Promise me you won't hurt yourself, Luke."

"If you promise not to tell anybody about the pills, I'll promise, too."

So they'd made their pact and Jamie had let go of the issue...

He glanced over at his mother, guilt heavy in his gut. He hadn't told her about Luke and the prescriptions, and he'd had the perfect opportunity Saturday morning. He was afraid to tell her too much because she'd take matters in her own hands. His parents had always said, *You can have your privacy unless we think you're in danger, physically or mentally.* He was pretty sure that would extend to Luke, which was why he kept his concern to himself.

He dipped his hand in his pocket, where the paper his mother had given him yesterday rested. He planned to show it to Luke when they met up later today. Maybe they could even go to the Alliance together.

Anabelle was at the pulpit now and Jamie transferred his attention to her. She read from the Bible, then gazed out at the congregation. "There are passages of scripture that make theologically progressive Christians wince. Let me propose a few. 'Wives, be subject to your husbands.' 'Slaves, obey your earthly masters.' Or the ultimate cry of vengeance, 'Happy is the one who seizes the enemy's infant children and smashes their heads.'"

Her expression was wry. "It's my belief that those passages should be challenged, as well as this other one, which is often held up as proof of the superiority of Christians. 'I am the way, the truth, the light. No one comes to God except through me.' In other words, only those with an intentional relationship with Jesus will be saved. That means, folks, that Buddha, Mohammed, Confucius, anybody living or dead who finds truth in a non-Christian faith is out of luck. However, I'm here to tell you that to make that claim, based on this text, is flat-out wrong."

Wow! Jamie thought. That took guts.

Anabelle went on to the time period in which Jesus spoke the words. She emphasized that the message was meant to be taken in context, for a small band of people who were struggling with how to follow a Messiah that led them away from all they knew—the Jewish faith.

"In today's modern society, many progressive Christians refuse to make sweeping, imperialistic claims about the superiority of Christianity and condemn our sisters and brothers of other traditions. Today, as Christians, we must simply follow Christ, and that means embracing everyone, welcoming everyone who follows his or her spiritual path, even if it's different from our own. Christianity can be an inclusive and transforming faith. That's my dream, that Christ will be our light. That Christ's light shine in our hearts, shine through the darkness, in this church and in all churches."

She left the pulpit, stepped down from the altar, and picked up her guitar. Placing the strap over her shoulder, she began to strum. The members of the congregation took an insert out of the bulletin. On it was "Christ Be Our Light," the same hymn sung at Kenny Larson's funeral.

As both Jamie and his mother sang along, he felt that God was with him. He rubbed the paper in his pocket again, grateful for a way to maybe help Luke. For now, this was enough.

CHAPTER EIGHTEEN

Maggie was abruptly awakened by the phone ringing at six a.m. on Monday. She panicked. Both boys were home and Mike was sleeping next to her, but still... She snatched up the phone. "Hello."

"Maggie? It's Sara. I'm in Cornwall. Ma went to the hospital in an ambulance last night. Paul and I drove down about midnight."

"Oh, no. What happened?"

"She couldn't breathe. The doctor said it was the cigarettes and that botched vocal cord surgery. When she got here her throat was closing up. She had an emergency tracheotomy."

"Oh, my Lord."

Maggie felt a hand on her arm. "What is it?"

"My mother," she told Mike.

"She can't stay by herself after this, Mag. I'm bringing her back to Rochester as soon as she gets released from the hospital."

"Oh, Sara. I'll come over today to help out."

A long pause. It took Maggie a minute to decipher it.

"She doesn't want me there, does she?"

"She's still upset about Caroline." And probably blaming this latest trauma on Maggie. Then she remembered Caroline filling her in on Gertrude's background, and her heart softened somewhat toward her mother.

"What *can* I do, Sara? I don't want you to take care of all this alone."

"Nothing, yet. Paul says the tracheotomy tube will need special care. We'll have to hire a nurse. I don't think I can clean it." Her voice cracked on the last word.

"You don't have to do that." When Sara didn't respond, Maggie added, "I'll help financially."

"Her insurance covers the cost. And Paul will be there, of course." Her sister's voice got teary. "I…I'm just not sure I can handle her on a daily basis, Mags."

"Oh, Sara. Couldn't she go to a rehab facility up here? We could visit every day."

"No! I will not put my mother in one of those places."

At a loss, Maggie said, "All right. But I'll be there for you and her, I promise."

"If she lets you." Sara's tone of voice indicated she didn't hold out much hope for that.

"We'll work something out."

"I'm going to call Jimmy now."

Maggie sighed. "She wants to see him, of course."

"Of course."

Sara's tone was lighter, and Maggie thought about how Paul and Mike joked that when Jimmy visited, it was like the pope coming to town.

"Please, keep me informed."

"Sure. Oh, and could you call Caroline?"

At least Sara was thinking about their other sister, a good sign. "Sure."

When she hung up, Maggie lay back down into the pillows and stared blindly at the ceiling.

"Honey?"

The endearment calmed her. Despite what was between them, she moved to his side, cuddled in, and told Mike what had happened. Their disagreements were once again forgotten in the wake of this newest development.

❖

Later that week, Jimmy swung into town on his way back from Asia and stayed at Sara's house to be near their mother. He called Maggie to come over the day after he arrived. This was the first time she'd see her mother with the tracheotomy, since Gertrude hadn't allowed her to visit. Maggie went alone, not wanting to inflict more on the boys. Mike had protested that he should be with her for moral support, but he wasn't doing well himself so Maggie declined his offer.

She'd gone straight from work and pulled her car into Sara's driveway at about four in the afternoon. As she switched off the engine, the front door of the Bakers' sprawling colonial opened and out jogged her baby brother. Emotion filled Maggie as she watched him, dressed in casual shorts and a golf shirt, come toward her. His dark hair was cut shorter than when she'd seen him last, accentuating his incredibly dark eyes. He was a few inches shorter than Mike, but muscular. She had a flash of him as a child with curls and long lashes, riding on the back of her bike and accompanying her to her summer job at the swimming pool in Cornwall.

Circling to the side of the car, he opened her door and dragged her out. And Maggie burst into tears. Jimmy encompassed her in his arms. She nestled in, vaguely aware of how she used to comfort him as a boy when he skinned his knee or their father yelled at him. Now his man's strength was giving her the solace she needed. "Shh, it's okay. I've been talking to Ma. She's scared and vulnerable, so I don't think she's going to be on the offense with you, Mags."

"It's not just that."

"The situation with Caroline will work out, too."

She peered up at him. "How, Jimmy? Ma won't even see her."

"I have a plan."

Of course he did. He was head of human resources at a multibillion-dollar company and negotiated contracts with six-figure employees and union bosses.

Her brother waited, then tipped her chin. "Something else happen?"

"Uh-huh."

Drawing back, he checked his watch and took her hand. "Come on, let's walk down to the park." Which was only a block away.

"Okay." She fished a tissue out of her purse and wiped her eyes. "I'm a mess."

"You're as beautiful as ever."

They headed down the winding driveway and onto the tree-lined street. A soft breeze fluttered the leaves and the sun slanted through them. They strolled hand in hand for a while but Jimmy didn't say anything more until they reached the small park and sat on a bench off to the side of the children's play area.

"Is it the boys?"

Staring wistfully at the jungle gym and sandbox, Maggie nodded. "Jamie told us this spring he's gay."

"Wow." Jimmy was thoughtful for a moment. "And it's been hard for you."

"For everybody, for different reasons."

Again, he took her hand and squeezed it. "I wish you'd called me. I might have been able to help."

"Jamie didn't want anybody to *be told.*" She went on to explain his reasoning.

"Who else knows?"

"Caroline. We talked on the phone and she sensed something was wrong, so she came to Sherwood earlier than she'd planned. I haven't told Sara yet, but I'll have to before Brian's graduation party." When he gave no response, she said, "You're still coming, aren't you?"

"Of course. Tammy and the boys, too." His pretty blond wife and two gorgeous kids. She envied their normalcy.

He didn't comment on his feelings regarding Jamie's disclosure.

"This must be really hard for you. You love those boys to pieces."

"Uh-huh." She hedged, waiting to discover where he was going to fall on the acceptance scale. *When* had she begun to see life that way?

"Mags, you know I couldn't love Jamie more if he was my own kid. He is who he is—a creative, bright, interesting boy. His sexual orientation makes no difference to me. My concern here is that it's caused problems for you and you're worrying like a mother hen."

Again, she burst into tears. Too much was happening and she felt weak and vulnerable, like her mother.

Jimmy tugged her close. "Aw, Mags. Don't cry. This will be all right."

Finally, she said, "There's more."

Dark brows furrowed. "What?"

The whole story of her conflict with Mike just tumbled out.

After she finished, Jimmy sighed heavily. He adored Mike, who'd played basketball with him when he was little, taught him to drive, and bought him his first suit for a job interview. They'd also sent him money when he was at Cornell and strapped for cash.

"This is serious."

"I know."

"I've always envied your relationship with Mike. It's not a tragedy that Jamie's gay. But it would be catastrophic if you and Mike lose what you have together."

Put so starkly, Maggie realized Jimmy was right. "Oh, Jimmy, when did you get so smart?"

A chuckle. "I've got this terrific older sister who rubbed off on me."

Jimmy's unconditional support buoyed Maggie, but there was more to deal with today. "Okay, enough of this. What about Caroline? And Ma?"

"As I said, I have a plan."

"What?"

"I called Caroline and asked her to come over, too. Ma's had enough time to deal with the tracheotomy and so I thought I'd get us all together."

"You can't fix everything, honey."

His brown eyes filled with confidence. "I can try."

❖

It was surreal, sitting at Sara's table, across from Jimmy and between her sisters. All four of them had dark hair and eyes, but there were differences, too. Jimmy's nose was sharper, Caroline and Sara had the same chin and shape of the jaw, but Sara was more slender than either Maggie or Caroline. Right now, the three older sisters were waiting to hear their little brother's plan. Caroline couldn't seem to take her eyes off him.

"What?" Jimmy asked boyishly. "Am I that ugly that you can't stop staring?"

"I can't believe you're all grown up. And so accomplished. I bought you a cowboy hat right before I left and you were too small to wear it."

"I wore it for years, though. Mags never let me forget where it came from."

"Oh, how sweet." Caroline touched Maggie's hand.

Jimmy grinned. "She kept you alive for both of us, right, Sara?"

"Yes." Sara gave a weak smile. "And I'm truly glad you're back in our lives, Caroline." Her face was so taut Maggie's heart went out to her. Despite her earlier comment—*I don't even remember her*—Maggie could tell she wanted to be part of this reunited family. "What are we going to do about Ma? I don't mean to complain, but it's been hard enough having her here. I can't fathom dealing with her reaction to you coming into our lives again."

"As I told Maggie, I think now is the best time to bring it up," Jimmy put in. "Ma's feeling vulnerable and insecure. Maybe she'll be more open-minded."

"I don't know, Jimmy." Sara shook her head. "I'm worried."

"Hey, sis, I've always been able to sway her. I'm sure I can help this process along, too."

"Your approval always means more to her than anyone," Maggie said hopefully. "So it could work."

Caroline sipped her coffee and Maggie noticed her hand shaking. "Caro?"

"I want to do this. It's just hard to imagine coming face-to-face with her after almost four decades."

"She kicked you out, Caroline." Jimmy the negotiator surfaced. "You have a right to be upset."

"I know. I've worked on forgiving her. At understanding her."

"What do you mean?" Sara asked.

"There's a lot you two don't know about Ma's life." Caroline recounted the same stories about her growing-up days she'd already told Maggie. She also talked about how she'd wrestled with the past and why she never contacted them before this. "I'm not sure how I'll handle it if she rejects me again."

The air was so solemn it hurt to breathe.

"We never knew." Sara's voice was hushed.

Jimmy frowned at the information.

And Maggie tried to let her family deal with their feelings without interfering.

Finally, Jimmy stood. "Let's leave all that in the past and try to bring this family together now."

With no small measure of reluctance, the girls pushed away from the table and stood.

"I'll go first. Ladies, come right behind me."

Cowardly though it was, all three Lorenzo women agreed to let their baby brother lead the way.

❖

Maggie's heart was beating so fast, she could almost hear it. She wanted this to go well, for Caroline mostly, but also for Sara and herself, too. She wanted a sane, normal extended family and wondered briefly if it was because her immediate one was falling apart.

Jimmy knocked on the spare room door and when their mother said, "I'm awake," in a gravelly voice, he opened it.

From behind Jimmy in the hall, Maggie could see her mother, propped up in a mound of pillows, remote in one hand, listening to a cooking show. Gertrude's smile bloomed when she saw her only son. Maggie noticed her gray hair was combed and she wore a pretty print bed jacket Sara probably bought for her. "There's my boy." She had to cover the tracheotomy hole while she talked. "Come sit with me. I don't get to see you enough."

"Ma, I brought somebody with me."

Gertrude glanced over when Jimmy stood aside. "Mary Margaret, it's about time you came."

"Hi, Ma."

"Sara, why are you hiding out there?"

Jimmy said, "Come on in, girls."

Tentatively, Maggie stepped into the room. Sara let go of Caroline's hand and followed close behind.

There was no one in her way now, so Gertrude Lorenzo had a clear view of the daughter she hadn't seen in thirty-seven years. "Who's this? A neighbor?" The scowl she directed at Sara was all too familiar. "I'm not ready for company."

Caroline came fully inside. "I'm not a neighbor, Ma."

Gertrude clutched her throat.

And then the miracle Maggie had been praying for, the miracle Jimmy was so sure he could pull off, did not happen. Instead, her mother's face flushed with rage. "Jesus Christ, how could you…" She reached out for her son. "Jimmy, why would you let them do this to me?"

"Because it's time, Ma."

"No. Never." Her mother started to breathe fast.

Sara moved in closer. "Ma, are you all right?"

"All right?" Her voice was thready. "You would do this me when I'm on my deathbed?"

"You're fine, Ma," Sara said. "Paul agrees."

"Paul wouldn't…" Her eyes were wild. "You're all ganging up on me."

"Ma—" Jimmy began but was cut off when her mother started to cough.

"I can't breathe."

Calmly, Jimmy stepped over to an oxygen tank in the corner. He picked up the nose attachment and crossed to his mother. "Here, put this on."

She batted his hand away, hard, and the line fell to the floor. "Help me, Sara. I…can't…" Gertrude began to gasp.

Panicking, Sara reached for the phone on the nightstand and punched in three numbers.

Jimmy said, "Sara, don't, she's okay."

But Sara said into the receiver, "We need an ambulance right away at 56 Camden Place. My mother can't breathe."

The three other people in the room froze and just stared at Gertrude.

Then color came back into her face.

A gleam came into her eyes.

Gertrude Lorenzo had won this face-off. Suddenly, they were all kids again, reduced to powerlessness and once more under this woman's control.

CHAPTER NINETEEN

The psychology department at Rochester Community College met in a conference room every Monday morning and kept to their schedule, even though classes were over for the semester. Nancy Schultz, the chair, had switched off the air-conditioning and opened the windows. The teachers seemed to be enjoying the mild May weather and were cheerful as they gathered around an oval table with doughnuts and coffee. Nancy passed out an agenda and gave members a chance to peruse it. "Any new courses for the fall of next year will need to be in before you go on summer vacation."

Someone murmured, "What vacation?"

Many of the staff taught summer school sessions. Maggie had, too, when Mike was in graduate school and once when he was in danger of losing his job. She'd missed the time off with the boys and was grateful every year not to have to teach again.

Nancy joined in the chuckles. "Suggestions for curriculum?"

Damien lounged back in his chair, all masculine grace and charm. "I'm going to propose a full semester course on the psychology of art. Several of my 101 kids took a real interest in the mini unit I did with them."

Nancy smiled at Damien. "Give it a shot." She scanned the others.

One person suggested Spirituality and Psychology: do they cancel each other out? Again Nancy encouraged the teacher to forge ahead with a proposal. Maggie thought maybe *she'd* like to take that class.

"I have one." That she'd been considering since winter. "A class on the gay and lesbian experience in the teens and twenties. It would be for gay students and straight ones who might be dealing with their friends and family members who are gay. I might call it The Ups and Downs of Coming Out."

"We have courses on gay issues in our Women's Studies Program." The professor who made the comment taught one of them. "Lesbianism as a feminist issue. The History of Women and Sexual Orientation."

"I wouldn't take a feminist view, Lee."

"What tack would you take?" The other teacher's tone wasn't challenging. It held interest and a trace of support.

"An inclusive view of the psychological ramifications of coming out, the effects on a person's whole life, the ups and downs, as the name suggests." Maggie shrugged. "I'm not sure exactly where I'd go with it. I've got to think it through. And I'd seek your input."

"Don't overlap with their courses." This comment came from an older man Maggie didn't like. "And don't make it some *gut course* with no substance."

Damien leaned over in his seat, his shoulders stiff. "I can't fathom Maggie Davidson ever teaching fluff, Harold." He shot her a quick smile. "Your course sounds great to me, Mag."

The meeting ended and, as the others filed out, Nancy asked Maggie to stay. When they were alone, she leaned back casually in her armchair. "Interesting course." A pause. "Can I ask you a personal question?"

"Sure."

"You've had a rough few months. I haven't brought it up before because it hasn't affected your work, but I've noticed you've lost weight and seem anxious lately. Want to talk about what's bothering you?"

Hating that the effects of her family troubles were so obvious, especially to her colleagues, Maggie shook her head. "No, thanks. I'm working it out."

"All right. I hope the course you suggested flies." Nancy's expression turned soft, understanding. "I'm sure my daughter would enroll."

Ah, interesting subtext. "My son Jamie would like it, too, but he's still in high school."

"And he's gay, right?"

"He told us this spring."

Nancy stared over Maggie's shoulder. There was a distant

expression in her brown eyes. "I remember when Callie came out. She was a sophomore in college. Boy, did it throw our family into chaos."

"Ours, too. There's so much to deal with once it's out in the open."

"It's really tough for even supportive, loving parents to work through. There's still significant homophobia in our society today."

"Mike and I are trying really hard to handle this right."

"And Jamie will grow up the better for it." She studied Maggie for a few seconds. "You know, sometimes people in the field of psychology won't seek professional help when they need it. I saw a counselor after Callie's disclosure and he saved my sanity."

"I got some help initially. Now I'm waiting for my therapist to get back into town. Unfortunately, she left for a month's vacation in Greece not long after this broke."

"Do you know about PFLAG and the Gay Alliance?"

"Yes, I've been to their Web sites and I gave Jamie some information on both."

"There are terrific local resources. And if you need to talk to a mom who's been where you are, just holler."

"Thank you, Nancy. I might do that."

"Let me leave you with one thought. There will come a day when Jamie's being gay is a fact of life and not an *issue* anymore. Your family will discuss it openly, joke about it. At least that's what happened to us."

The thought of Brian or Mike joking about Jamie's sexual orientation was so farfetched Maggie couldn't imagine it. The atmosphere around the house was stifling. "I hope so."

"You can't see that now. But I know you, your boys, and I have a feel for the kind of man Mike is. This will work out."

Thinking about support coming from unexpected places, Maggie was bemused when she reached her office—where Damien waited in the corridor.

He slouched against the wall, arms crossed. His black jeans fit him well and the gray striped golf shirt accented his broad chest. "Hi, gorgeous."

Maybe his greeting was inappropriate, but with people telling her she'd lost weight and seemed haggard, it felt good. "Hi. Do you need something from me?"

He winked. "Now there's a question."

She gave him a scolding look.

"Okay, I'll behave. I wanted to talk to you."

"Come on in."

They took seats on the couch again, with Damien sitting a little closer than usual.

"So, you won't be teaching summer school?"

"No, thankfully."

"What will you do for three months?" Damien asked.

Referee, she thought. "My sister, who I haven't seen in years, is in town for the summer, so I'll get to spend time with her."

"Really? Why did you lose touch?"

"Long story."

One she couldn't bear to tell today. She could still see her mother, gasping for breath, as the paramedics treated her with oxygen and albuterol, and the vulnerable expression on Sara's face when she had to ask Maggie and Caroline to leave.

"I got time," Damien told her.

"No, it's too painful right now."

"Tell me about your sons, then. Talking about them always makes you happy. What's happening with Brian and college?"

The notion made her heart heavy. She'd yet to deal with Brian leaving home. "He got a nice chunk of change from Ithaca College. It's a good school and he'll fit right in."

"You'll still have Jamie at home, right?"

"Yes. He's a joy to be with."

Damien's seemed sad. "You're a terrific role model for parents, Mag."

Oh, Lord. Talk about irony. "Thanks."

"Though something's wrong, isn't it, at home? Or is it just your sister's reappearance that I'm reading now."

Once again she hesitated to answer. He'd asked this before, and she'd dodged the issue.

"You wheedled out of answering that question weeks ago." Maybe he did have ESPP. "Talk to me."

What the hell? "Our family has had some upheavals other than Caroline in the last month."

"And is that fairytale marriage of yours in trouble?"

"No, of course not."

His gray eyes focused on her. "I don't believe you. Like I said, I have a sense about these things. Especially with you."

Grasping her hand, he held it tightly. Damien and she had shared some collegial hugs, a squeeze on the shoulder, pats on the back. And hand holding wasn't really a *move*, was it?

"All right, Mike and I are having problems. But I love my husband."

He didn't let her go. "A fact I truly bemoan."

"Damien—"

"Shh. Let me say this, then I'll drop it. A lot of men find you very attractive, and if your marriage is deteriorating, you have choices. I think you know what I'm saying, Maggie."

For a brief moment, she let herself spin out the fantasy of what it might be like to have an affair with a dynamic man like Damien. It would feel good. Do her ego good. Maybe that was why she didn't pull back when he leaned over and kissed her cheek.

A sharp knock on the open door, then, "Maggie?" Father Pete stood at the entrance to her office.

As unobtrusively as she could, she extricated her hand from Damien's and rose. He followed suit.

"Hello, Father," Maggie said.

Damien introduced himself, then left.

In his traditional collar, black shirt, and pants, the priest's eyes were troubled. "I hope it's all right that I dropped in. I was driving by the college and had you on my mind. I decided God steered my car this way, telling me I should come see you." He glanced to the couch. "Now I'm glad I did."

Purposely, she ignored the innuendo. "It's fine that you came, Father."

Ushering him inside, Maggie offered coffee, which he accepted. When she returned with a mug, she slid behind her desk and he took the chair in front of it.

"What can I do for you?"

"I was hoping it was more what I could do for you."

"In what way?"

"Maggie, you weren't at church Sunday, nor was Jamie. Mike and Brian attended Mass alone. When I asked your husband how you were, he told me where you'd gone."

"To a new church."

"Yes. He also said that you'd been visiting other congregations, which I wish I'd known then, so I could have counseled you."

She gripped the edge of the desk so she wouldn't fidget. "Is that why you're here now?"

"I'm here because I care a great deal about you and your family."

He did. She knew that. "I appreciate that, Father."

"And I'm advising you not to seek answers in another church."

Maggie remained silent, waiting for him to go on.

"I imagine you're confused right now. But leaving God isn't the answer."

"I'm not leaving God, Father. I'm leaving the Catholic Church."

Father Pete frowned deeply. "Don't let this new place seduce you away from us."

She thought of the comforting atmosphere of the UCC's sanctuary. The genuine wisdom of Anabelle. The cross without nails. "It doesn't feel like we're being seduced. It feels like Jamie and I are being embraced."

"Often sin is disguised that way."

"Do you really think it's a sin to go to another church?"

"You know from our teachings that the Catholic Church is the chosen one of God and all others are false. God sent you to us, Maggie. He made you a Catholic."

"I'm sorry, but I don't believe in your church anymore."

Father Pete cocked his head. "Does this rejection have to do with your sister Caroline? Mike told me about her coming to Sherwood."

They'd never discussed Caroline's situation with the priest because Maggie was fearful he'd be judgmental.

"Maybe." She lifted her chin. "The church deprived me of my sister for thirty-seven years."

"I was sorry to hear that. Some clergy, especially back in the seventies, were overzealous about issues."

"Then you wouldn't have advised my mother to disown Caroline?"

His brows rose. "No, just like I'd never advise you or Mike to disown Jamie. All problems can be worked through, Maggie. I've been praying for your mother, sister, and you since Mike told me about this."

"Thank you," she said, surprised by his support. "We need it."

"Let me know what else I can do."

Maggie cocked her head. "Even though I won't be coming back to St. Mary's?"

"Of course. I'll always be here for you. Besides, I haven't given up on you." He gestured to the couch. "But I have to ask. Is there someone in your life besides Mike? Is that was this is all about?"

"No, of course not."

"I found you in a compromising position."

"You misunderstand what you saw. I love Mike and have never been unfaithful to my vows."

"Perhaps you could come back to the church for Mike. You made those vows with him. One of them was to obey."

"You know, I could do that for Mike. But I could never sacrifice Jamie to your church, Father, not even for my husband."

Now the priest's eyes were warm and sympathetic. "God won't ask you to sacrifice Jamie. You'll find a way through this."

"I'm sorry, I can't do what you're asking me to do."

"Aren't your worried about Jamie's soul?"

"Oh, Father, Jamie has a wonderful soul. He's kind and loving. God must be very pleased with him."

"Not if he practices homosexuality. You know I think that his orientation can be changed, but even if you don't have the same set of beliefs, can you at least convince him to remain in the Catholic Church and work on his sexual preference within our boundaries?"

Coming to the edge of her chair, she said crisply, "This isn't a preference, Father. It's the way God made him. I'll never allow your church to make him think he's a sinner for following his natural instincts."

"Then you're giving up on your faith?"

"No, never on faith. But on your church. It's not an institution I can embrace anymore." If she ever really had.

The priest stood. "I'm sorry to hear that. I came today because I want you to be healthy and happy. I want that for all God's people. I'll pray for you, and especially for Jamie."

Suddenly, Maggie was ten again, being admonished by a priest from the pulpit for her sinful ways. It silenced her for a moment. But she shook the sensation off. She wasn't ten. She was a mother with her own child to protect. "I love my son, and maybe we've found a church that can accept him, one that has an understanding of God which is more in line with our beliefs."

"Just be careful of the choices you make, Maggie." Now he gestured to the couch. "Especially other kinds of temptation." He walked out of her office.

She sank onto her chair and, putting her head down on her desk, she prayed. Not for Jamie this time, but for her husband, who had an unwavering faith in a church that could never accept his son. What would Mike do if he was forced to choose between them?

❖

Searching for a cage in the garage, Mike banged old cans of paint around, kicked the lawnmower in his way, and knocked some tools to the floor. His frustration with his home life was affecting all his actions. Jamie's accusatory stares, Brian's pressure on Mike to fix all this, and Maggie's cold shoulder were getting to him. Today, his wife was foremost in his mind. It was amazing to him how couples picked on what they used to let go, or even help with, when they were angry about something else.

"Let me put the dishes away, you're exhausted," had become, "I'm going upstairs. It's your turn to clean up."

"Honey, the faucet's leaking," translated into, "Can't you fix that before your damn golf game?"

And sliding sweetly into each other's arms in the darkness was precluded by, "I'm too tired," or worse, a lie on her part, "I have my period."

The last memory brought back what Father Pete had told him. Infuriated all over again, Mike picked up a piece of wood for the fireplace and threw it against the pile...

I went to the college to speak with your wife...she's in dangerous water, Mike. We have to help her.

Is it more than Jamie's situation? Caroline's?

I'm telling you this, son, for your own benefit. Maggie was with another man in her office. They seemed close. Too close. He went on to give Mike the details. *During hard times, people seek out others. Take comfort in someone who doesn't disagree with them. Talk to your wife.*

But Mike hadn't broached the subject of her and Damien Kane because he was trying to get control over his feelings first. So the silence had simmered between them like a pot ready to boil over, and the tension had become intolerable.

As he found the cage he needed, he thought about the raccoons he was going to trap. He'd spotted them weeks ago before life fell apart. Maggie was out and Mike was cooking dinner. He'd called Jamie and Brian from their rooms to catch a glimpse of the visitors…

"Guys, come and see this. Quick."

They'd trundled down the stairs and over to the window where Mike stood. "We have raccoons living under our deck."

"Oh, man," Jamie had said. "She has a baby."

"Cool." This from Brian. "Let's go get a better view."

They raced out onto the deck. The baby had been trying to climb the small hill behind their house, but kept slipping back down the incline. It didn't yet have its sea legs, and the mother was nudging it along. Suddenly, the big raccoon's head snapped up. She froze, seemed to stare at Jamie and Brian. Then she abandoned the baby and scooted under the deck.

"Aw, shit," Jamie said when they came back in.

Brian's shoulders sagged. "It's my fault. We shouldn't have gone out there."

The boys worried all evening about the baby, who remained on the hill alone. They kept peeking out the window to see if the mother had rescued it yet. She hadn't reappeared by the time they went to bed.

That night, at two a.m., Mike was awakened by a noise. His and Maggie's bedroom faced the back, and he went to the window. Outside in the yard, the full moon caught his boys in its silvery net. He didn't think he'd ever forget the images of Brian and Jamie, on the hill, one holding the flashlight, one bending down and scooping up the baby raccoon and carrying the tiny fur ball back its mother.

Mike remembered that incident even as he put sardines in the cage and carried it to the backyard. The steel glistened in the sunlight. It was an animal-friendly contraption that he set on the grass and propped open at one end.

Before he started up the steps to the deck, the mother raccoon sneaked out into the light of day. Behind her was the baby, a cute little bundle of energy. She must have spotted Mike because they both scurried out of sight.

He hadn't seen Maggie on the deck until she called out, "What are you doing?"

He glanced up. She was gilded by sun, its rays making a halo around her, making her dark hair appear lighter. The pink shirt and shorts fit her nicely and he longed to hold her.

That feeling led to thoughts of her with Damien Kane, so he said, "We have to get the raccoons out from under the deck," with more edge than he intended.

Leaning over the railing, she examined the cage. "You can't trap the mother. What about the baby?"

"We'll trap it, too."

"This isn't right."

He climbed to the top and stood before her, full of righteous anger and bitter jealousy. "She can do harm to the deck. Or she could be rabid."

"She isn't rabid. I've seen her cleaning her baby, nuzzling it. And what's she going to do, gnaw through pressure-treated wood? Don't separate them."

Too late. The mother inched back out and approached the trap. Smelling the bait, she darted inside. The cage snapped shut with a loud clang.

"Oh, no, Mike."

He'd always loved this kind of sensitivity in his wife, but today it irritated him. "Maggie, they aren't mother and child like you and Jamie."

Before they could discuss the situation further, a door slammed inside. Jamie strode to the porch and slid a screen door aside. His gaze whipped from Maggie to Mike. "What's going on?"

"We were just talking." Maggie's voice was gravelly with concern.

"You mean you're fighting about me again."

"As a matter of fact," Mike put in tightly, "this doesn't concern you."

Jamie dropped down on the wooden bench. His whole body

slumped and his eyes closed briefly. Mike's heart went out to the boy and the weight he was carrying. Knowing he added to it caused him deep pain.

"Is something wrong, honey?" Maggie asked.

"Julianne's being weirder than usual. We were supposed to hang out..." He slanted a glance up at Mike, his expression wary. "Never mind. I'll deal with it." He got to his feet. "I'm beat. I'm gonna go take a nap."

Maggie smiled at him. "Okay."

Mike grabbed his son's arm before he could get away. "It's not okay. I want to talk about your life with you like we used to."

Ignoring the overture, Jamie shrugged Mike off. He noticed the cage and the raccoon clawing from inside it. Even from up on the deck, they could hear a gurgling, growling sound. "What the hell?" He looked at his father. "Did you do that?"

"Only temporarily. I'm taking it to the wildlife preserve."

"You shouldn't cage a live thing." His voice rose a notch. "You can't lock it up and ship it off to an unnatural environment because you think it should be somewhere else." Then he spat out, "Oh, fuck," and stormed into the house.

Weary, Mike sank onto a chair. "That wasn't about the raccoons."

"No, it wasn't."

"Did you know about Julianne?"

"Jamie mentioned he was having issues with her."

"You didn't tell me."

She glanced away from him. "No."

"Why?" When she didn't respond he said, "You didn't trust me to handle the situation well."

"I guess I didn't." Her tone was raw. "I thought maybe you'd side with Julianne. She's using her faith against Jamie, too."

"That's not what I've done."

"I think it is."

"So this is what our relationship has come to?"

"I don't know. Sometimes, I'm afraid to talk to you."

"You're afraid I don't put my own children's welfare above my own?"

"I'm...not sure anymore."

He could swear his heart stopped beating in his chest. "You know, don't you, there isn't anything you could say that would hurt me more than what just came out of your mouth?" He glared at her. "Except maybe that you've turned to another man."

She shifted uneasily, her dark hair swinging into her face. She pushed it back impatiently. "What are you talking about?"

"Father Pete filled me in on the cozy little scene with Damien Kane in your office."

"There was no cozy little scene."

"He said you were holding hands. He witnessed a kiss, damn it."

"It was colleague stuff."

"Fuck it, Maggie, you don't kiss your colleagues."

Guiltily he recalled dropping Laura Simpson off from the business dinner a few nights ago and the peck on his cheek she gave him. But Kane had been hovering on the fringes of their relationship for years, and Mike was sick of it.

"Are you finally going to take him up on his veiled offers?"

"I won't dignify that with an answer."

He stood and faced her. Suddenly, Mike had the awful thought that they were squaring off like adversaries on an emotional battlefield. Deflated by the notion, he said softly, "Listen to us. I hate how we're acting."

"Me, too." She gripped the railing behind her. "Maybe we should get some marriage counseling. If for no other reason than we might be able to help Jamie. And Brian. I'm worried about him. He's a mess, and I can't talk to you about him."

A gasp came from the lawn at the bottom of the stairs. Brian was standing near the cage with a frown on his face. He catapulted up the steps. "You two are going for marriage counseling?"

Mike took Brian by the shoulders. His son's face was taut with worry. "It's no secret I'm having a hard time reconciling Jamie's homosexuality with my faith. But make no mistake, Bri. I love Jamie and you, more than I love anyone in the world."

"What about Mom? Don't you love her, too?"

Silence. Then, "Of course I do."

"She said you should go to marriage counseling. Because of me. Because I handled this so bad."

Maggie stepped forward. "No, honey, this discussion has nothing to do with you."

He went on as if they hadn't spoken. "You're gonna get a divorce over the problems we're all having, aren't you?"

"No, no." She soothed his arm. "We're working out our differences. Don't worry about a divorce. It's not going to happen."

Brian seemed unconvinced. Mike wished that his son was a toddler again and he could drag him onto his lap and make everything all right for him with calming words and a big hug.

"I'll be better. I promise. I know you're disappointed in me. But don't..." Then he, too, rushed off through the doors.

Staring after his son, Mike knew exactly how he felt about disappointing Maggie. So be it.

He didn't go into the house. Instead, he walked down the stairs and stood over the trapped raccoon for a minute. With his wife watching, he bent over, picked up the cage, and headed around to the side of the house.

❖

Brian took the steps two at a time to the second floor. His whole life was a freaking train wreck and he didn't know what to do. He couldn't believe his mother and father were having problems! Jamie and him used to joke about how they were an indestructible force. Now Brian had split them up because he couldn't accept who Jamie was.

He knocked on Jamie's closed door. "Jame, it's me."

"Come on in."

His brother was at the desk, online, probably talking to Luke. Jamie scowled. "What's wrong?"

Brian shrugged. "It'd be easier to tell you what's right."

Like a little boy on a playground trying to make friends, Jamie asked, "Wanna talk?"

"Yeah." Brian went inside—where he hadn't been since Jamie told Brian he was gay. He started to tell Jamie about their parents, but he noticed his brother's face. Jamie seemed so sad, Brian couldn't do it. Once again, he wondered how much shit his brother was getting at school.

"Is it about Heather?"

"Heather's history." He dropped down on the bed.

"You tried talking to her?"

"Yeah, she won't take me back. I knew when I did it what I was risking. What her father did hit her hard. Cheating was a deal breaker."

"I'm sorry. It was my fault."

"No, Jame. I acted stupid." He picked up a CD and studied the face of Emm Gryner, one of Jamie's favorite musicians. "Eric Cummings asked her to the Junior Prom."

"Fuck."

He swallowed hard. "Mom gave you a psychologist's name, didn't she?"

"Uh-huh."

"You gonna go?" Brian asked.

"I'm not sure. You?"

"I wasn't, but now…" He thought about his parents. "Anyway, I'm gonna try to be better, Jame. About you. I said it at Kenny's service, but I didn't do it. I can change, Jame."

"From what I hear, you already did something. Luke said you slammed Cummings into a locker. I wish I'd been there for that one."

"The team's been better about all this."

"Yeah, Luke told me that, too."

Feeling really jealous of the guy Jamie talked to now, Brian stood. "Okay. I gotta go."

Jamie stood, too, and put out his hand.

Hell. Bypassing it, Brian hugged Jamie.

Jamie held on tight.

Neither spoke again. Then Brian left.

CHAPTER TWENTY

On Melissa Fairchild's advice, Maggie decided to attend a meeting of PFLAG in downtown Rochester. All along, she'd had it in the back of her mind she might visit the group, and now seemed the time to do it.

She asked Gretta to go with her. Not Mike. He'd never give an organization like this a fair shot, and she was tired of begging him to be more open-minded. So she drove with her girlfriend to a meeting one Thursday night. On the way, Maggie was preoccupied.

"What are you thinking about?" Gretta asked.

"The list of *Dos and Don'ts* on the PFLAG Web site. It's for parents to use when their kid comes out." She shrugged. "I did some of the *don'ts*."

"Like what?"

"For one, I rushed the process. Our family needed time to internalize the whole issue of Jamie coming out and I intervened too much."

"You know what I think is most important? That Jamie understands you love him for the person he is. Now that has to be a *do* on the list."

"It is." She smiled at her friend. "Thanks for being here for me."

"You didn't ask Mike to come?"

"No."

"Maybe that wasn't such a hot idea, sweetie."

"Maybe not. But I didn't."

"Well," Gretta said pulling into the parking lot, "let's go see what they have to offer."

The meeting was held in an old building that housed the Gay

Alliance offices in downtown Rochester. Up on the fifth floor, they found five men and twelve women gathered around a table. They all said hello, then Maggie and Gretta took seats. Brochures, newspapers, and flyers advertising certain events were in display racks around the room.

Sam, an attractive, prematurely gray-haired guy with a friendly smile, was the leader that night and introduced himself as a staff member of the Gay Alliance. Others followed suit, giving their names and situations. One woman had two gay sons, another had a lesbian daughter, the treasurer was a lesbian herself, and a woman with dark hair was just dealing with her son coming out. All of them spoke of how they were advocating for gay rights locally and nationally. Sam said, "The mission of PFLAG is threefold, Maggie: support, advocacy, and education."

He went on to give her a brief history of the organization. PFLAG was headquartered in Washington, DC, but currently had 200,000 members with affiliates in more than 500 communities. One of them was in downtown Rochester on Main Street. The group was started in 1974 by a mother who marched in the Gay Pride Parade in New York City. Afterward, she was surrounded by walkers asking her for help in enlisting their parents' support. The nationwide group grew from there.

Maggie especially liked how they stated their mission—to celebrate diversity, envision and work toward a society that accepts people's differences, and advocate for an end to discrimination. Their goal was to create a society respectful of everyone.

"So, that's the overview." Again, the warm, gracious smile from Sam. "Tell us what brought you here."

Maggie explained her situation and ended with why Gretta was with her. "My husband wouldn't come to a meeting like this."

Joan, the woman with the two gay sons, leaned forward. "Mothers are quicker to accept than fathers."

With a glance at Gretta, who'd said the same thing when she told Maggie about Tim's reaction, Maggie confessed, "That certainly applies to us."

An older man asked, "And you're angry about that?"

"I guess." Then, "Yeah, I am."

The male participants launched into a spirited discussion on how they had handled the discovery of their children's homosexuality. They ranged from fathers of lesbian daughters to those of gay sons.

One man became teary-eyed. "I went through the typical stages of finding out: shock, denial, guilt, and grief. The old thinking, 'If I'd been a better father, more of a man, my son wouldn't have become gay,' haunted me for months."

Maggie wondered if Mike had been having those kinds of recriminations. She'd never asked him about it because, after years of being in tune with his needs, with helping him to deal with problems, they weren't there for each other. She felt even more rotten about the state of her relationship with her husband than before. How on earth had they come to this?

"Any other kids?" a woman wanted to know.

"Yes, another son. An athlete. He's having a hard time, too. I'm worried about him."

They filled her in on their experiences with sibling reaction, some similar to Brian's and some not.

"What can we do for you Maggie?" Sam asked.

"I don't know. I'm floundering and thought maybe this organization could help." She shrugged. "Actually, knowing my experiences are common *does* help."

Gretta spoke up. "I have a question. What about Catholics? Are they welcome in PFLAG?"

She must be asking for Mike.

"Yes, of course. We have a table over there displaying pamphlets about community life where we're active. On it is a brochure about DIGNITY."

"What's that?" Gretta wanted to know.

Another man sat forward. "I can answer that, seeing as my wife and I are Catholic. DIGNITY is a group which seeks to reform the Catholic Church from within."

Gretta's brows rose. "I don't think that works very well."

The guy cocked his head. "Actually, we believe it's the only way reform comes about. It used to be forbidden to eat meat on Fridays. And women had to wear hats to Sunday Mass. People *inside* the church worked to get those things abolished. That's how change occurs in organized religion."

After a long discussion, Sam checked the clock. "We're going to take a break, then get into the advocacy part of our meeting." He pushed a paper over to Maggie. "Here's what we're going to talk about next."

On the list was the Gay Pride Parade in a few months, a fall March on Washington, a list of speakers who were going to area high schools to talk about gay rights, and the Day of Silence, where students nationwide spent the school day in silence as a protest of discrimination.

Gretta went to talk to the people who'd mentioned DIGNITY and Maggie picked up a brochure on education by the Gay Alliance, thinking of Sherwood High and also of her new college course proposal.

A woman named Patty approached her and nodded to the pamphlet Maggie held. "I head a subgroup on reform in schools, if you're interested."

Scanning the information, Maggie noted that some of it was not so radical—Sherwood High had antidiscrimination polices and library resources on gay issues. But she wondered if her sons' school would ever have support groups for parents of gay children, or gay/straight alliance groups for students, or workshops on tolerance for teachers. Would her kids' school ever sponsor a Day of Silence?

Patty had some insights. "Some of the larger districts in Rochester have already incorporated a lot of this."

"Yes, but we're more conservative in Sherwood."

Patty smiled. "That's why we need people from towns like yours to effect reform."

When the break was over, the members had a spirited discussion of the advocacy efforts, surprising and pleasing Maggie with what was going on to help the gay community, particularly kids. She and Gretta left PFLAG with a pile of brochures and hope in their hearts.

"Will you join?" Gretta asked in the car on the way home.

"I think so."

"Maybe I will, too. It's for friends."

"I appreciate this support more than I can say. I'd love it if you joined with me."

"Then I will."

As they drove away, Maggie was bombarded by a deep sense of sadness for not asking Mike to come along so that he might have found some solace, as she had. That notion led her to wonder if she no longer had her husband's best interests at heart.

❖

It exhausted Maggie to watch everybody tiptoe around each other. Since the raccoon incident and the inadvertent mention of divorce, all four of them had been cautious. Brian especially was putting up a brave front. As far as she knew, neither boy had taken her up on her suggestions for counseling. If something didn't break soon, she was going to nudge them.

At least last night they'd gathered around the computer to make up invitations to Brian's graduation party, which would be held at the end of June. They tossed out ideas, teased Mike about his typing skills, and joked around—just like old times. To add to the excitement was the knowledge that Caroline, Teresa, and Chloe would be in attendance this year. The jury, of course, was still out on Gertrude Lorenzo, who, after the fiasco with Jimmy, once again wouldn't see Maggie.

"This is fun," Brian said about the format Mike had been playing with—the invitation was in the shape of a baseball and on the stitching were the details of the party.

"How many of them will we need?"

Maggie was thinking about Sara and Mike's siblings who would attend the party and what had to be done before that happened. If Jamie brought Luke as his date, people would have to be told he was gay. She was hit by a flash of resentment—against the world, she hoped—that having a simple get together wasn't even easy these days.

"I want fifty," Brian told them. "All the kids won't come, but most of them will." He grinned, the old Brian surfacing from the sullen teen he'd become.

"Jamie, do you want any?" Mike asked.

"A couple, maybe."

Brian shot a quick look at his brother and Maggie tensed. Would they argue over Jamie bringing Luke? Instead, her older son let the matter drop. However, Maggie couldn't ignore the reality of who Jamie might have as a guest. The responsibility of parenthood drove her to his room later that night.

"Honey, I know you said you don't want us to announce your sexual orientation to anyone, but if you're going to ask Luke to Brian's party, our family has to be prepared."

Jamie shrugged. "I guess it's okay if we tell some of them. Who?"

"Grandma Lucy and Grandpa BJ. Any of Dad's sisters or brothers who are flying in. And Aunt Sara and Grandma Lorenzo."

He gave a typical teenage snort. "Wear armor if you talk to the last two in person."

"It won't be that bad."

"Don't bet on it, Mom."

So that night she decided to get the confrontation with Sara over with. She sat staring at the phone, thinking about their differences on issues: Sara was still working in organizations to get abortion banned and had participated in pro-life marches on Washington. In the past, she'd devoted much of her time to get two ultraconservative justices appointed to the Supreme Court.

Disconcerted by the knowledge, Maggie nonetheless punched in the number and was glad Sara answered. "Hi, it's Maggie."

"Hi."

"How's Ma?"

"Still in martyr mode." There was weariness in Sara's tone. And a sense of resignation that cut to the quick. "She goes on and on about us ganging up on her. Allison particularly is having a terrible time with her rants."

"I'm sorry. I'd try to help but she won't even see me. Right?"

"Yeah. I guess we have to give it time. Is that why you called?"

"Partly. I need to talk to you about something else. Could we have lunch tomorrow? Just you and me?"

"What's wrong?" Genuine concern resonated in her sister's voice.

"I just need to see you. We'll talk then."

"All right. Meet me at noon at Alex's by the canal. I'll make a reservation."

Mike had come into the bedroom while Maggie was on the phone. He'd removed his shirt and Maggie could see the definition of muscles in his chest. His back was tanned from working in the yard. At odd moments like these, she missed being physically close to him with an acuteness that bordered on pain. She wanted to reach out and touch him, take him into her body.

"What was that all about?" he asked when she hung up.

"I'm having lunch with Sara tomorrow."

"Why?"

"Mike, Jamie will most likely bring Luke to our graduation party. They could act like a couple. Sara would pick up on it. As would my mother, though I doubt she'll come now that this has happened with Caroline. In any case, people need to be forewarned."

His face darkened, but he joined her on the edge of the bed and took her hand between his two big ones. The gesture brought tears to her eyes. She missed *this* Mike. "Want me to come along?"

"No thanks."

"I wish you wouldn't cut me out of your problems with your family."

"Have I been doing that?"

"Yes."

"I'm sorry. I'll be better." She held tight to his hand. "*Your* family needs to be told about this, too, honey."

He let go of her and stretched his big frame out on the mattress, crooking his elbow and resting his head on one elbow. "This will be hard for them. Mom, especially, has a soft spot for Jamie."

Once again, Maggie bristled when Mike spoke as if there was something wrong with Jamie.

Still, one battle at a time. "Wish me luck with Sara."

They met the next day. Sara had secured a table in the outdoor section of the restaurant. Maggie arrived first and tried to enjoy the cool breeze that wafted off the water. She watched the ducks glide around in circles, tiny ones following their mama. She'd read once that two weeks after the mother duck had its babies, the mallard took off and was never seen again. Gretta and she joked about the unreliability of all male species, but today the notion was far from funny.

Dressed in a chic white pantsuit, Sara arrived and kissed her on the cheek. She squeezed Maggie's arm, too, which made Maggie's throat tight.

A young waiter approached. He was handsome and had an easy manner. Would Jamie find him attractive? "Mrs. Baker, how are you today?"

"I'm doing well, George. Thank you for asking."

"Can I get you a drink?"

Sara asked for an iced tea and Maggie ordered a glass of Chardonnay.

"You're having wine at noon?" Sara sounded like a little girl wanting to try her first drink with the big kids. Maggie remembered Caroline's words about Sara trying to find her place in the family.

"Uh-huh. Go ahead."

"All right. I'll have the same."

They discussed their mother again, and Maggie told Sara about Father Pete and his offer. Both thought calling on the priest was a good idea if Gertrude continued to behave badly. They made chitchat while they sipped their wine and waited for their food. Maggie was hesitant to bring up the issue of Jamie until lunch was over, and truthfully, she was enjoying the camaraderie with her sister. Maybe God had heard her prayers and this wouldn't be a disaster after all.

Eventually, Maggie set down her fork and braced her elbows on the table. "I need to talk to you about a personal matter."

Sara's face was stricken. "You're not sick, are you? Any of you?"

"No, no. It isn't that."

Her eyes widened. "Don't tell me Mike's fooling around with another woman."

"No." She toyed with the stem of her wineglass. "I assume you're coming to Brian's graduation."

"Of course. Though Ma probably won't, given the fact that Caroline will be there."

"Maybe she'll change her mind."

Sara's face was so torn, Maggie was sorry she was going to add to her problems. "In any case, I told you I'd bring the desserts. I've found this bakery that makes terrific cakes."

"I'm sure it will be great." She hesitated. "Sara, I have to tell you something before then. And I really hope you can support me in this." She swallowed hard. "I need you to."

"What is it?"

"At Brian's party, Jamie may very well have a date."

Her sister's dark eyebrows raised. "That's not exactly breaking news."

"It is, in a way. Jamie's going to be bringing a boy to the party."

"Excuse me?"

"Jamie's date is a boy."

"He has a date with a *boy*?" Awareness dawned. Genuine concern filled Sara's eyes. "Oh, Maggie, I'm so sorry."

What to say? There was no reason to be sorry? Somehow that didn't ring true. Maggie was sorry that her marriage was strained, her sons in turmoil, her life in flux.

After she thought for a moment, Sara seemed confused. "But I don't understand. Why would you allow him to bring a boy to the party? I mean, you're not *encouraging* him in this, are you?"

"I support my son being who he is."

"This isn't who he is, Maggie. This is an illness." She sat up even straighter, so sure of her views Maggie envied her. "And illnesses can be cured."

"Being gay isn't an illness." She was getting tired of making this argument. "It's who Jamie is."

"All right. It's a sexual orientation, but it can be changed. Surely you believe that."

"No. And besides, Jamie doesn't want to change. He's happy with who he is."

Sara sat motionless for a moment. Then she said, "He only thinks that now, Maggie. When he tries to live this way, he'll only find suffering." On her face was Father Pete's expression, Judy Johnson's expression, Lucas Crane's expression. Even Mike's. Maggie was bombarded by insecurity. All these people were on the opposite side. Was *Maggie* wrong?

No, no, she wouldn't think that way! "Let's not argue philosophy here. I'm really not asking for your approval or your acceptance, though I would have liked the latter."

"Then why did you tell me?"

"I thought you'd want to be prepared for all this before Brian's party."

Sara was silent.

"What?"

"Maggie, I'd feel really uncomfortable if I came to the party and Jamie was there with a boy."

"Oh, Sara, please don't stay away. Jamie would know why you didn't attend."

"It isn't just me. My girls would be even more unsettled."

"One out of ten people is gay, Sara. I'm sure Allison and Laura have been in contact with gay people before. They probably have friends who are gay."

"Not that I know of. It's not part of our family values."

"I think your girls might surprise you."

"What do you mean?"

"Just that it was obvious on Easter Sunday that you and Allison don't agree on everything."

"Don't look for trouble in my family because there's so much in yours."

Maggie felt moisture well in her eyes at Sara's disapproval. Maybe she'd wanted her approval after all. And because Maggie's emotional armor was dented, she couldn't withstand another attack by her sister.

"I'm sorry. I don't mean to hurt you," Sara said. "But I can't condone what goes so much against what I believe in."

"Not even for me?"

Sara sighed. "Maggie, I'd be a hypocrite if I went to Brian's party and saw Jamie like that. I tried to get a gay group banned from Allison's high school when I was the president of the PTA a few years ago. We only got it delayed—they instituted one this year—but I'm still working against it behind the scenes. I think we have some sympathy from the new superintendent to find a way around this."

"Why didn't you tell me about that?" Anger started to mount.

"Because you're so liberal in your views, I knew you'd disagree with me and I didn't want to fight with you." Maggie stared at Sara as her face closed down. "I'll still get the desserts for the party."

Scraping back her chair, Maggie stood. She drew some money out of her purse and tossed it on the table. "Don't bother. I'll provide what's necessary for my sons."

"Maggie, please..."

But she didn't hear the end of Sara's comment as she hurried out of the restaurant. Instead of going to her car, she took the steps to the footpath by the canal, thinking a walk would help.

It didn't. After ten minutes, she dropped down on one of the benches and watched the water flow by her. A crew boat whizzed past with a dozen smiling teenagers rowing it. Staring at the kids, she wondered if Jamie would ever again be as carefree as they were.

CHAPTER TWENTY-ONE

Jamie loved Sherwood High. The school had provided him with good friends, great learning experiences, and the opportunity to perform in shows. To give back to it, this year he'd volunteered to head up the Red Cross blood drive held in the spring. Area high schools around Rochester competed to see which district could donate the most pints. Though Sherwood was half the size of some of the major suburban schools, they'd won hands down every year. For months, Jamie had worked hard with the faculty, staff, and the Red Cross administration to make the drive a success this time, too.

Even Brian was upbeat at breakfast. After he'd come to Jamie's room that night, Jamie knew his brother was trying to mend fences and he appreciated the effort. He hoped it was a good sign that they'd dressed alike in Spartan T-shirts and jeans.

"He's pestered everybody, Mom," Brian said as he poured himself a bowl of Cheerios and slanted Jamie a big-brother look. "He's set up competitions between the junior and senior classes, made bargains with teachers, and enlisted all the secretaries and aides."

"You mockin' me?" Jamie asked.

"Nah, I think it's great that you do things like this for the school."

"I'm glad the drive's going so well," their mom put in. The delight in her voice warmed him. "I'll be there to volunteer."

Brian shoveled cereal into his mouth and said around it, "When?"

"Noon. I can stay as long as they need me."

"Maybe I'll wait until you come before I let them suck the life out of me." Brian shivered. "Man, I'm not looking forward to that."

He had never given blood before because he was skittish, and Jamie had just become old enough to do it. Jamie razzed Brian. Big, brawny guys turned into dweebs when they donated.

"You'll be fine," their mother told them.

"How do you know?" Brian asked. "You've never done it." His mom had a genetic anemia problem that kept her from donating.

"I just do."

Jamie and Brian drove to school together, which didn't happen much anymore. Jamie had been riding with Luke, but he had to go in early today. And Jamie used to hitch a ride with Julianne, but not lately. Probably never again after their last conversation...

I'm sorry you're gay, Jamie. He'd told her right before he and Luke went public. *I know you don't want to hear that, but I am. It's morally wrong. I love you still—love the sinner, hate the sin, you know—and I'm praying for you.*

For a brief minute, Jamie had questioned who he was, what he was doing. She did that to him a lot...

"You okay?" Brian asked across the car.

"Yeah, I just want today to go good."

When they got to school, Jamie went directly to the gym. He'd been excused from all classes today to keep the drive running smoothly.

The Red Cross had set up six stations. Each consisted of a nurse, a long rectangular table, and the equipment to draw blood. Before students could donate, there was a check-in area where they'd stop to give information to the Red Cross staff, who filled out a questionnaire to make sure the student was eligible to donate. They asked for name, weight—you had to be at least 110 pounds—grade level, previous donation history, and a series of other questions Jamie hadn't seen.

Because kids were prone to weakness and/or fainting after giving blood, an area to rest had also been set up and was staffed by parents who came in to serve juice and cookies.

His mother showed up around noon. She headed for the volunteer section and was talking to the school nurse when Jamie crossed to her. He heard one of the nurses say, "Nice to see you here, Maggie. Jamie's done a fantastic job with the drive."

He had. The place was wall-to-wall people. He'd decided on a separate line off to the side for teachers who had to get back to work quickly. Kids were late to classes all day long because of delays in the process, but no one seemed to mind, as they were supporting an important cause. Jamie was proud of what he'd done and feeling better about himself than he had in weeks, months, maybe even years. He was whistling when he reached his mom and kissed her on the cheek. "Hi, Mommykins. Thanks for coming."

"Wouldn't miss it."

"Did you see the tally?" He pointed to the wall where an oversized poster of a thermometer showed a count of how many pints were given every hour. "We're gonna beat last year's total easy."

"That is so great, honey."

"Yes, it is." The principal had come to stand behind them. Jamie liked Mr. Thomas. A huge guy with linebacker shoulders, he was tough and fair-minded, though Jamie heard some of the teachers bitch about him being too controlling.

His mother greeted the principal warmly. "Hello, Steve." They were on a first-name basis because she'd worked on committees with him.

Jamie smiled at him. "Mr. Thomas."

"You've done a terrific job, Jamie. We all appreciate your hard work."

"I love this school," Jamie said without reserve. "I wanted to help out."

"You raised two super kids, Maggie." Mr. Thomas glanced across the room to where Brian entered through the gym's double doors. "I hear Brian got a couple scholarships to Ithaca."

Brian had received the official notice of two alumni scholarships that covered half his tuition. The school didn't give athletic scholarships, but coach had written a letter that the money was a show of faith that Brian would play baseball his freshman year. They'd all gone out to dinner to celebrate the news. That had also made Jamie feel better. It was sort of like things were back to normal again.

The principal left and Brian reached them. He, too, kissed their mom. Facing Jamie, he asked, "Ready?"

"Yeah, sure. I still can't believe I gotta hold your hand. You're such a wuss about this."

"Zip it, little brother. Just come with me."

Brian was the first to donate. He sat down at a table and talked with the Red Cross representative, who recorded his answers on a computer.

She took his temperature, checked his blood and blood pressure. From the sidelines Jamie gave him a thumbs-up.

While Brian was still answering questions, Jamie went to the next open station. He'd gotten the sober faced older guy who could have been an ex-Marine. The man went through the same routine as Brian, and asked the requisite stats about name, age, weight. Then, still staring at the computer, he began a series of questions. "Do you or have you ever had hepatitis?"

"No."

"HIV?"

"No."

More medical disease questions.

"Have you had sex with another male, even once, after 1977?"

Jamie stilled. The chatter around him went on, the laughter, the excited hum. But his mind filled with images of him and Luke. "Um, is it legal to ask me that?"

The worker peered up at him from behind thick glasses. "These are all standard questions set by the FDA. Everyone gets asked them, son."

Son. Would his dad condone this interrogation? Or would he stand up for Jamie's rights?

"Did you ask the girl before me if she had sex with a male?"

The guy sat up straighter. "In a way. We asked her if she had sex with a male who had sex with another male after 1977."

"That's not the same thing. Did you ask her if she had sex with another female?"

"I don't believe that question is on here."

Of course, he knew the origin of the question, that HIV could be transmitted through certain types of sexual activity performed by gay men. But straight couples did those things, too.

Jamie's hands got clammy and his throat clogged. *Don't tell*, his mind shouted. *Lie. Don't embarrass yourself or your family.* "I-I won't answer your question. It's discriminatory."

The guy stared at him like Dr. Crane had. "Then you can't give blood."

Anger now, which was better. "What if I answer yes, can I donate then?"

"I'm afraid not."

Heat flushed Jamie's face. There was a buzz in his ears. He threw back his chair harder than he thought. When the metal hit the floor, it banged and echoed in the cavernous gym, causing people to stare at them.

Run, get away. He raced out of the gym, spotted an alcove with a drinking fountain down the corridor, and strode to it. His breath came in gasps and he closed his eyes to steady himself.

He'd never seen this coming. How stupid of him.

"Honey, what happened?"

Oh, God, his mother. She didn't need this. He didn't want to lay this on her. But he didn't know what else to do. Facing away from her, he said, "They won't let me give blood."

"*What?* Why?"

"They asked me if I'd, if I'd..." His face reddened at the thought of admitting private stuff to her.

Tugging him around, she held onto his arm. "Jamie, you can tell me anything. I won't question you right now about it. Please, I need to know what went on in there."

"They asked if I had sex with another male."

Silence. "And you said yes."

"Uh-huh. So they told me I couldn't give blood." He leaned against the wall and closed his eyes. "Mom, the question is unfair. Sexual disease is transmitted by both men and women."

"Oh, baby, I'm sorry. I didn't know about this because I can't donate." And of course, nobody in Sherwood talked about those issues.

"It's not your fault. It's mine. I should never have done this. Started this."

"By *this* you mean?"

"Told everybody who I am. What I am."

"I know it seems that way to you now." His mother was so calm, so sure of herself. "But Jame, you have to be who you are. Keeping your sexual identity a secret has its own set of problems, as you know."

Her affirmation helped him breathe easier. He thought about Luke, who never got an inkling of support or understanding from his parents. Oh, God, Luke! He was going to give blood in a half hour. He'd never donated before, either, because he was sick last year on the day of the drive. Would his father have told him the caveat, as he was a doctor?

No, of course not, they'd never discuss male/male intimate contact. So Luke must not know about the questions either. Jamie remembered the pills.

"Would you like to go home, honey?" his mom asked. "I can make excuses."

Fuck that. "I'm not leaving. The drive is my responsibility." He shook his head. "You know, Ms. Carson would call it irony. I set up the whole blood drive and now I can't donate because I'm gay."

"What can I do for you now?"

"Go back in there with me so I can finish this out." He squeezed her hand. "Will you stay until it ends?"

"Of course. And I'm sorry if this ruins the drive for you."

"You told me once nobody can ruin anything for you if you don't let them."

"Did I?" She linked his arm with hers. "Then let's go back inside and not let your success be tainted."

They reached the gym door from the hallway just as Brian came up to it. His face was pinched. "I just finished giving blood and found out all the kids are talking about you in there. The person behind you heard your conversation. Jesus Christ, Jamie, did you have to tell the Red Cross people you did stuff with other guys?"

Jamie gripped his mother's arm. "Yeah, Bri, I guess I did."

As Brian stormed past them, Jamie saw all the progress they'd made in the last few days go with him. Shaking his head, he walked into the gym—and gasped.

Luke was seated at the table Jamie had just vacated. His face was tight as he stared at the man asking questions.

❖

Maggie felt like a ping-pong ball, being batted back and forth between Jamie and Brian. Today had been horrific. The rest of the blood drive had passed in a blur of worry, but after she took Jamie home, she made an excuse to go out again and was waiting in the parking lot at school for her other son. She'd done her best with Jamie, but like before, she had to help both kids. Her conversation with Melissa about choosing between them came back to her.

Support Brian, too…validate his mixed emotions…talk out what's bothering him and don't let problems fester…

Her son came out of the gym, his face grim. She'd pulled in right next to the Prius but he didn't see her until he was almost at his car.

The window was down and she said, "Hi, honey."

"Mom? What are you doing here?"

"I came to see you."

He swallowed hard. "I…I don't think I can take another lecture."

Her mother's heart twisted in her chest that he now saw her in that role. "Oh, Bri, I'm not here to lecture you. I'm worried about you, too."

"You are?" His eyes misted.

Hers did, too. "Of course. I told you that when I gave you the counselor's name. Get in my car."

Tossing his bag in his trunk, he circled the Civic and got inside. She started the engine. "Where we going?"

"To get ice cream."

A small smile. "It's dinner time."

"Let's live dangerously."

Maggie drove to the closest ice cream store. Both she and Brian ordered chocolate cones and sat at an outdoor picnic table. It was warm today, but shady under an oak tree. They sat in silence until they finished the treat.

"Are you disappointed in me, Mom?" he asked.

Reaching across the table, she grasped his hand. "No, I'm not. I'm just worried about you."

"I didn't know any of that stuff about giving blood."

"Teenagers don't tend to think about those things. But I should have investigated this. I feel foolish not to have known."

"Why is *everything* so hard?"

"I wish it wasn't, Bri. Did the team harass you about what happened today?"

"No, but they knew. They all stopped talking when I came into the locker room. I thought this had blown over. It's like a cut that keeps getting the scab pulled off."

"I'm sorry, honey."

"How's Jamie?"

"Understandably upset."

"I made it worse."

She wasn't going to lie to him. "If you did, you can make it better. We can fix things with each other. It's not too late like it is with Darcy's family."

"I know. I said I'd do better."

"This was a big blow to all of us. Did you think more about getting some counseling, using the name I gave you?"

"I did, but then I started to feel better. Jamie and me were doing okay." He shrugged. "I guess not, though."

They talked more about the counseling and Brian's feelings in general, then drove back to school. When Brian got out, he came around to her side. "Thanks for this, Mom. I wasn't sure you even liked me anymore."

"I told you before, there's nothing you could do that would make me love you less."

"I know you love me. But you always liked me, too."

"I still do. We're all feeling our way in this, honey. We just have to try to do our best."

He kissed her on the cheek. "Thanks."

And for the first time since that horrible bang of the chair resounded in the gym, Maggie could feel the constriction in her chest ease.

❖

The day after the blood drive, Jamie and Luke walked to the cafeteria at the beginning of fifth period. Luke had been rejected as a donor by the Red Cross, too, but wouldn't talk about it. His MO, Jamie knew, but it bothered him to see Luke going back into himself. Jamie had also suggested again they go to the Gay Alliance support group, but Luke was resistant. So, if he didn't talk to Jamie, there was no one else for him to unload on.

"You sure you want to do this?" Jamie asked trying to keep up with Luke's brisk pace.

"Yep. Fuck the Red Cross. We're not hiding what's between us." He stopped short and focused wide eyes on Jamie. "Unless you don't want to. You backing out on me?"

"No, I'm just not sure of the timing." When Luke seemed

unconvinced, Jamie said, "Hell, Luke. I'm worried about you. After yesterday—and the pills—I don't know how much more you can take."

Instead of getting angry, Luke sighed. It was the very first time Jamie realized how much Luke cared about him. Jamie took a second to savor the moment, to revel in the joy of having this guy in his life.

Luke said, "I'm okay. As long as you are."

"Let's go, then. It can't get much worse, can it?"

As they neared the table outside of the cafeteria, they found Julianne selling the tickets. Oh great. He watched her as she took care of the few people ahead of them. But instead of the pretty teenager sitting there, he saw the two of them when they were three, playing dress-up and having tea parties; at five, learning to swim together; in junior high, going to their first formal dance as a couple. So many years of closeness insignificant now because of who Jamie was.

When their turn came, Jamie stepped up. "Hi, Jules. We need Junior Prom tickets."

"You do?"

He whipped out the money for one ticket and Luke stepped up next to him with his own cash in his hand.

Julianne looked down. "Okay, um…" She fumbled with the metal box, her hands shaking as she took their money and then gave them tickets. She picked up a pen. "You guys are going stag, right?"

"Why?"

"Because I need to write down who your dates are. If they're from a different school, they have to sign a statement of agreement with Sherwood High's polices."

"No, Julianne," Luke said coldly. "We're not going stag. Jamie and I are going together."

"As a couple?"

"Yes."

"Jamie, you can't do that!" She'd dropped her voice to a whisper. Luke's entire body stiffened.

"We can, Jules," Jamie said with calm he didn't feel. He wanted to puke. "And we are."

"I-I told you it's okay you're"—she couldn't even get the word out—"but you can't, you know, be with a guy."

"Who the hell are you to decide that for me?"

Behind him he heard a buzz of voices. Several kids were waiting for tickets. Among them were jocks from Luke's team and some of Jamie's friends from the play, including Nick and Paul. The two of them got out of line and came to stand behind Jamie and Luke.

"What's up?" Nick said casually.

No one spoke.

Paul asked, "You okay, Jame?"

"Yeah. It's Jules here who has a problem."

Julianne's face hardened as she scanned all four of them. "I don't have a problem. I'm a Christian. I stand for Christ."

"Christ hated bigotry." Jamie spat out the words. "He loved everybody."

Her voice rose a notch. "The Bible says homosexuality is a sin."

"Forget it, Jame." Luke grabbed his arm. "Let's go. We got the tickets."

Julianne grasped his other arm. As an actor, the staging didn't elude him. Two sides of his life were literally tugging at him.

She said, "If you do this, Jamie, have this relationship, we can't be friends. God wouldn't want me to associate with you." She glanced at Nick and Paul. "Any of you."

Speechless, Jamie was rooted to the ground. Nick and Paul didn't say more either. Now that he'd caused such a scene, Jamie didn't blame them.

Ms. Carson, who was senior class advisor, came out of the cafeteria. "Hi, guys, Jules. Is there a problem here?"

"Yes. With them." Julianne's confidence further assaulted Jamie.

Frowning, Ms. Carson cocked her head.

"We're done here." Luke yanked on Jamie's arm, began dragging him down the hall. Everybody stared openly at them.

And at that moment, Jamie understood why Luke had collected all those pills.

CHAPTER TWENTY-TWO

Maggie entered the cool interior of their house, relishing the quiet. It still smelled of bread she'd baked yesterday and of fresh potpourri she'd placed in bowls scattered throughout the rooms. For some reason, she thought of the smell of the house she'd grown up in—stale cigarette smoke, old coffee and mildew, in the dark corners, which she was expected to clean but could never completely remove.

Today, she needed the serenity of her home after the upheaval of the last weeks, and especially after the debacle of the blood drive. Mike was away on a business trip so she had some blessed time alone. Setting her bag down in the den off the front foyer, she headed upstairs to her bedroom, hoping an hour's sleep would refresh her.

But when she passed Jamie's room, she heard sobs. Somebody was crying. Hard. She knocked on his door. "Jamie, are you in there?"

No answer.

"Jamie, it's Mom. Are you all right?"

A muffled "Yeah."

"I need to see for myself. Can I come in?"

"No."

She gripped the doorknob. "I'm afraid I have to insist."

A longer pause. "All right."

The room was dark for midafternoon because Jamie had drawn the blinds, casting the room in shadows. His computer hummed eerily in the half-light, flashing a screen saver of one of his favorite rock stars. Some of his treasured pictures, those he'd matted and framed, lay on the floor. The wood was broken. Shards of glass dug into the carpet.

Scanning the room, she recalled a time when she'd babyproofed it. She wished she could babyproof the world for him, but she'd come to realize she could no longer protect Jamie.

He was stretched out on the bed, propped up on pillows.

"What's going on, honey?"

No response.

Maggie picked up a shattered frame. The picture had been torn by the glass—one of Jamie and Julianne at the Valentine's Ball they attended together last winter. She'd thought how masculine Jamie looked in the tux, a complement to Julianne's feminine frills.

"Did something happen with Julianne?" He'd mentioned she'd been acting weird and now the destroyed pictures of her.

And once again, Jamie burst into tears.

Sidestepping the mess, she sat on the bed and dragged him up. For longer than she thought possible, he cried in her arms. Not sniffles. Not a burst of emotion. But deep, wrenching sobs from his gut. She wondered how much more of this he could take. For a stark moment, she thought again about the statistics on suicide among gay teens.

"Shh, shh," she said, rubbing a hand over his back. "It can't be that bad."

"It is."

"All right, then, we'll work through it together." When he drew back again, she nodded to the floor. "Julianne let you down?"

He slouched onto the bed. "Uh-huh."

She took his hands. "What happened?"

Her son didn't look at her when he spoke. Instead he stared at the Van Gogh poster on the wall across the room. "Before it got around I was gay, I told her about me. She seemed okay with it. Said she'd pray for me." His hand tightened on hers. "It sucked but she's entitled to her beliefs."

Maggie waited when he paused.

"She belongs to that fundamentalist church on Parson Road. They're really conservative. They believe all that shit about women being subservient to men. Their service is practically a gospel rally."

"Yes, I know."

He closed his eyes. Finally, he asked, "Can you rub my back?"

"Sure. Scoot over."

He yanked off a shirt that said *Carpe Diem* and lay down on his stomach. She stretched out beside him and began the ritual that he always asked for when he was upset. "Tell me the rest, Jame."

When she began to knead his shoulders, he continued. "Luke and I went to get our tickets to the prom. Luke was so pissed about the Red Cross, it was like he wanted to do something to fight back, or thumb his nose at the school, or…I don't know. Anyway, we're going to the prom together so I thought, why hide it? What can they do?"

Maggie panicked. They were going to the prom together? Oh, dear Lord. Would they be safe? As far as Maggie knew, no one had openly taken a person of the same sex to a Sherwood High prom. Though kids often went in groups of girls or guys, an honest-to-goodness boy/boy date hadn't yet happened. Jamie's foray into that uncharted territory would be trailblazing and possibly dangerous. Her mother's heart beat faster at what he might endure. On the heels of that, though, she felt pride in his courage to be who he was, especially after the knocks he'd taken lately.

"How does Julianne fit into this?"

"She was selling the tickets. She looked like she was gonna barf when we told her we were going as a couple."

"Oh, buddy."

"She sounded worse than Dad."

Maggie rubbed his neck, where the muscles were knotted. "About the Bible and homosexuality?"

"Yeah." He buried his face in the pillow. She had to strain to hear what he said. "She doesn't think we can be friends anymore, which I knew she might do, but still…" He trailed off.

"Jame."

Turning slightly on his side, he raised his head to see her. His young face was ravaged. "What did I do to deserve this, Mom? I'm just trying to be who I am."

"There is *nothing* wrong with being yourself. I told you that at the blood drive. Julianne and anyone else who makes you feel bad about being gay are the ones who are wrong."

"Even Dad and Bri?"

"Even them."

"I'm so mad at all of them."

"That's okay, too."

He lay back down. "Thanks for not saying this will all work out."

"It might not, honey."

Neither of them voiced who it might not work out with—Julianne or Mike and Brian. Maggie couldn't bring herself to entertain the thought that it might be the latter.

"I have no idea what's going to happen, Jame. But you can count on this. I'll be here no matter what happens."

❖

Early the next afternoon while Maggie was waiting for Mike to return from his business trip, the phone rang. Neither boy was home, so she answered the call.

"Maggie? This is Shirley Lewis." Shirley was a neighbor of theirs who had a son Jamie's age. She had her own set of friends and Maggie didn't often socialize with the woman, so she knew there must be a reason for the call.

"Hi, Shirley. How are you?"

"I've been well." A hesitation. "I have to talk to you. I'm on my way home from playing golf and was wondering if I might stop by your house."

"Sure, come over."

"Don't fuss. I can't stay. I'm exhausted."

The woman arrived a few minutes later, dressed in what Jamie called the country club uniform—a white collared shirt and a golf skirt. She'd exchanged her cleats for tennis shoes.

"Come out to the deck, Shirley. There's a nice breeze." Maggie added, "Do you want a drink? Iced tea, maybe?"

"No, thanks. I'm fine." She followed Maggie to the deck.

When they were seated, Maggie noted her neighbor's youthful face—Gretta said she'd had cosmetic surgery—was almost blank. Maggie couldn't fathom why the woman had come to see her.

"What's going on?"

"I've come to ask for your help."

"With what?"

"You know we're having the party before the Junior Prom."

Like the one Maggie and Mike had had for the Valentine's Ball. "Yes, of course. Brian went to your house last year when Susan was a junior. Your gardens are a lovely backdrop for picture taking."

Her hand twisted in the fold of her skirt. "Well, I've heard, I know..." She cleared her throat.

Maggie's heart started to thud as awareness dawned.

"I don't know how to phrase this."

"Just say it."

"Kyle came home and said it's all over school that Jamie's..." Again, she trailed off, her face reddening.

"Jamie's gay, Shirley. You can say the word."

"It's more than that. Kyle said he's going to the prom with another boy."

Maggie held her gaze unflinchingly. "Yes, he is."

"I wanted to make sure he wasn't coming to our house with, you know, a *boy*, for pictures. I mean, that would be awkward."

"For whom?"

"Oh, come on, Maggie. You can't be serious. Sherwood isn't a big city like Rochester where these things are accepted. My parents will be there, for God's sake. Some people from the club are coming. Natalie Anderson told me her husband would never attend if there were two boys—" Shirley cut herself off, probably realizing she'd just admitted she'd gossiped about the situation. "Of course, if they brought more people, we could try to pass it off as a group of boys going together."

"I don't think Jamie would want that. He and Luke are clearly a couple." She couldn't help but add, "They're even exchanging boutonnières."

"You're joking, right?"

"I'd never joke about this, Shirley."

"You don't approve of it, do you?"

"Of what? My son being who he is? I absolutely approve."

"I can't believe Mike does."

"Mike loves Jamie as much as I do. Tell me, Shirley, what would you do if you found out one of your boys was gay? Or your daughter was a lesbian?"

Her eyebrows skyrocketed. "They aren't, thank God. I'd die of embarrassment. And I certainly wouldn't let them flaunt it."

"Then thankfully you weren't given a gay child. But I was, and I'll love and nurture and cherish him until the day I die."

Shirley's face had turned red. "They're not welcome at my house. Well, Jamie is, but not if he comes with his *friend*."

Oh, dear Lord, Jamie didn't need this complication right now. Battling back her real feelings, swallowing her anger as she'd done at the baseball game with Judy Johnson, Maggie softened her tone. "Shirley, please, reconsider what you're saying. Your position's going to hurt everybody."

"I won't reconsider." She stood abruptly. "Please tell your son."

Damn her. Maggie rose, too. "I'd like you to have Kyle call and tell Jamie what you've decided."

"Kyle? He can't do that."

"Does he know you're here, doing this awful thing?"

"Of course not. I'm trying to protect my boy."

"So am I. In any case, I suggest you tell Kyle what decision you've made. He's a nice kid. I don't think he's going to be very proud of his mother right now."

"I can't believe you're being so unreasonable." She stalked down the deck steps and took the slate path around to the front of the house.

Dazed, Maggie sank onto the chair. Shirley Lewis had rubbed in her face what had been her greatest fear since she began to suspect Jamie was gay. This was the kind of prejudice her son would encounter all his life. Sickened by the thought, she sat outside, pondering what to do, until she heard noise in the house, people calling, "Maggie," and "Mom, where are you?"

"Out here."

Jamie was first to reach the deck. He studied her face and frowned. "You okay?"

"No, I'm not."

Brian came in behind Mike. "What's going on?"

"Sit down, all of you. We need to talk."

Jamie dropped down at the table, but Brian and Mike remained standing.

"Is anyone hurt?" Mike asked.

"Not like you mean, though this is going to hurt us all." She faced Jamie. "Jamie, sweetheart, Mrs. Lewis came over tonight."

"Kyle's Mom?"

"Yes. She's concerned about the party they're having before the Junior Prom."

It didn't take him long. The resignation on his face came quickly, all the more heartbreaking that he'd gotten the message so fast. "Let me guess. She doesn't want me and Luke to come to her party."

Brian's face blanked. "You're going to the prom with Luke?"

"Yes."

"Like on a date?"

"Uh-huh."

Maggie saw the struggle etch itself on Brian's face. He was trying to be better. Instead of storming off, he held his brother's gaze a long time but said no more.

Mike said, "Tell me exactly what happened with Shirley. She doesn't want Jamie and Luke at the party?"

"That's right. I tried to reason with her, but she was adamant."

"Does Kyle know about this?" Jamie's voice was raw. "He's my friend, Mom."

"No, honey, he doesn't."

"He'll be pissed."

Crossing to Jamie, Mike squeezed his shoulder. "I'm sorry, son."

Brian managed to get out, "Me, too, Jame." Then he left the three of them on the deck.

Maggie tried to content herself with that little bit of progress, but in light of what else was happening it was small comfort.

❖

The day of her encounter with Shirley Lewis, Maggie drove to the lake to visit Caroline. All three of her men were home. Jamie was reeling from two big blows. Brian had been quiet but at least he wasn't sulking, and Mike was holed up in the den paying bills. Maggie couldn't stand the stifling stress coming from everywhere, and she thought a dose of her older sister might help.

The May evening was hot as she pulled up in front of the Simons' lovely house. Its backyard was larger than most of the other lakefront properties and the structure itself was cedar. Exiting the car, she crossed the lawn to the porch, but before she could press the buzzer, the door flew open.

Chloe flung herself at Maggie, who scooped her up. Her bathing suit was wet and her hair smelled like lake water, but Maggie savored the child's embrace. "Hi, Aunt Maggie."

Teresa, also in a suit, came to the door. Her hair was up and soft blond strands floated around her face. "Sorry, she's wet," Caroline's daughter said.

"No worries. I love her hugs." Tears threatened but she battled them back. "Enjoy these years, Terry. You can never recapture them."

"Come on in." Teresa kissed Maggie's cheek and gave her a concerned look, much like Caroline's. "You okay?"

She nodded.

"Was Mom expecting you?"

"No. This was a spur-of-the moment decision."

"She's on the phone."

"I'm done." Caroline appeared in the kitchen, dressed in a black net bathing suit cover-up. She seemed younger than her fifty-five years and less sad than when she arrived in town. "Hi, Mags. This is a surprise."

"I hope I'm not interrupting."

"No, we took a swim after supper. Want coffee?"

"Yeah, sure."

Teresa placed a hand on Chloe's shoulder. "Okay, cowgirl, time for a bath."

"I wanna see Aunt Maggie."

"You can, after."

As Caroline's daughter dragged her own child down the hall, Maggie said, "That was thoughtful of her to leave us alone."

"You're upset."

"I am."

"Is it Ma?"

"Not this time."

"Mike again?" Caroline asked, leading Maggie to the kitchen and pouring them coffee.

"The world in general, I guess. I can't believe how much happened this week."

They took their mugs to a sunroom with walls of glass and screens facing the lake. The water lapped right beyond it and the low sun glistened off the surface. Maggie felt soothed by the calm setting.

"What is it, Magpie?"

"Jamie's had a lot to deal with." She told Caroline about the blood drive.

"Honey, I'm not blaming you, but didn't you know about those questions? There's been a huge uproar from the gay community over them. Our school considered not having a blood drive because so many people objected on principle."

"Astonishingly, I didn't know. I have a kind of anemia that keeps me from giving blood. Brian was always scared to donate and Jamie wasn't old enough. The issue just never came up." She thought about Mike. He gave blood, but never mentioned this. It wasn't anything he'd think about. "That's not all." She recounted Julianne's tirade and then Shirley Lewis's dictum.

Caroline's dark gaze narrowed. "Shirley's behavior is abominable. I guess small towns like Sherwood *are* different."

"You know, now that Jamie's come out, I notice discrimination against gay people everywhere. It's just more prevalent in Sherwood."

"I'm sorry. Truthfully, I love this place, your town, the lake, the surrounding areas." She glanced out at the water, distracted by its soft whooshing. "Is it always this beautiful?"

"In the spring, summer, and fall it's breathtaking. Winters can be tough, like in Cornwall."

Caroline focused back on her. "Have you told anyone in our family about Jamie?"

"Not Ma, of course. But I did talk to Sara. Which was another issue with Jamie."

After Maggie finished *that* story, Caroline sighed. "I feel sorry for Sara, like I said before. But she should have overcome her prejudices to support you."

"You think so?"

"I do. I'm sorry she reacted badly to Jamie's situation."

"At least Jimmy pulled through."

A grin. "What a guy, even if he did overestimate his influence on Ma." Caroline swallowed hard. "I missed so much."

"But no more," Maggie said helpfully. "You'll be back certainly for holidays, maybe next summer."

"I'm not sure that's soon enough. Earlier, when you arrived, I was talking to the Simons' realtor."

It took a minute for Maggie to internalize the meaning of her words. Her eyes filled. "Oh, my God. Oh, Caroline!"

"We're just in the beginning stages, so don't get your hopes up.

But if I retired from teaching, sold our place on the lake and my home in Colorado, I *could* swing this house."

"What about Teresa and Chloe?"

"Well, it would be a moot point if they wouldn't move here with me."

"They might?"

"Yes. Though the divorce was amicable, Terry's ex remarried and it's hard for her to be around them. He doesn't pay a lot of attention to Chloe, either, since he's got a son now. My granddaughter will be starting school next year, so this would be a good time to change residences. A small lake town would be a nice place to raise her."

"Just the possibility of this cheers me up."

"Me, too. It even tempers Ma's reaction last week." After a moment, Caroline asked, "What do you think will happen now with her?"

"I have no idea."

"If Jimmy couldn't change her mind about even seeing me, I don't know who can."

Maggie was about to agree, when she recalled Father Pete's comment. "When I was talking to Mike's priest about Jamie, he brought up what happened with you and Ma. He said he'd pray for us."

"I think we need more than that."

"He offered to talk to Ma."

"And what? Beg her to change her mind?" Caroline's tone was bitter. "I don't think so."

"No, to tell her it's okay to forgive." When Caroline looked askance, she added, "Not that you need forgiveness, but maybe Ma might be able to see your coming back in a different light if the Catholic Church tells her it's okay."

"It sounds so manipulative."

"Hey, you were the one who said Ma had a hard life, that much of her personality was formed by it. It made me think a lot about forgiveness."

"Maybe. I guess we should consider it."

Maggie's spirits were lifted by the thought of her mother coming to terms with Caroline almost as much as the thought of having Caro back in her life full-time.

CHAPTER TWENTY-THREE

Jamie and Luke were wrestling in the Cranes' basement, which was bigger and fancier than the Davidsons' whole first floor. Thick Berber carpet sprawled over a huge recreation room and there was a full kitchen off to the right and two bedrooms and a bath. Luke's parents were at a charity event, and though Jamie planned to be long gone before the Cranes came home, it was fun having some alone time with Luke. And being physical.

"Gotcha," Luke said, flipping Jamie to his back and straddling him.

His weight felt good, and Jamie's whole body tightened when Luke's muscles pressed against him. An edgy kind of need raced through him. "No fair. I was thinking about something else."

"Gotta concentrate." Luke grinned down at him. He was mellow tonight, probably because he'd smoked up earlier. Jamie wanted no part of it.

Your brother does it, Luke had said.

I didn't know that.

Hunching forward, Jamie tried to throw Luke off, but he was pinned to the floor. "Let me up."

Luke didn't move. Then he bent over and kissed Jamie. Hard on the mouth, with a lot of tongue. Jamie got really turned on. When Luke started to sit up again, Jamie grasped the back of his neck and kept him close. The cologne Luke used, now familiar and exciting, filled Jamie's head. "I like when you do that."

"What?"

"Take the initiative. Physically."

That crooked half-smile of Luke's did Jamie in, like always. They'd gotten their shirts off when they heard noise on the steps. There was no time to cover up what they were doing before Luke's father burst through the doorway.

"What the *hell* is going on here?"

Shirtless, Luke bolted up. The top button of his jeans was undone.

His father's fists clenched. "This is sick."

"Dad, it's—"

"Not a word out of you."

Behind him, Luke's mother placed a hand on his father's arm. "Lucas, don't fly off the handle."

"Off the handle? It's bad enough we had to leave the club because Shirley Lewis can't keep her mouth shut. I'm not going to ignore what's going on under my own roof."

Luke's stance became taut, belligerent. "Yeah, Dad, like you'd be upset if this was happening with a girl."

Shrugging into his shirt, Jamie buttoned it and stood. "I should go."

"No!" Luke had raised his voice.

"Not only will he go, he's never coming back here again."

Jamie felt his throat close up.

"You are never to see this boy again. There will be no prom. And I'm signing you up for the summer reparative therapy camp Mike Davidson and I talked about."

Bending over, Luke picked up his T-shirt and slid it over his head, then rounded on his father. He moved in close, in his dad's face, fists clenched, chin raised. "I'd rather die than go to one of those places." Luke's voice was deadly cold.

"You have no choice."

"Lucas." His mother tried to draw his father away. "We haven't thought this out."

Jamie felt suffocated, and it wasn't even *his* father saying these ugly things.

Finally, Luke stepped back. "Come on, Jame, I'll take you home."

"You are not to leave this house, young man."

Ignoring the command, Luke grabbed Jamie's arm and brushed

past his dad. His mother reached for him. He stopped and said, "I'm sorry, Mom."

Jamie wondered what Luke was apologizing for.

❖

When Casey Carson called Maggie and asked to meet her for coffee at the Starbucks near the college, Maggie gladly accepted. She knew both boys confided in this woman and was happy to spend time with an ally.

Entering the store, Maggie caught sight of Casey in the corner and made her way through half-empty tables to the teacher. Her dark hair was shoulder length and styled into a mass of thick waves. She was wearing a pretty peach dress. Maggie got coffee at the counter first, then approached the teacher. "Hello, Casey."

"Hi, Maggie."

Maggie sat down and slid her purse over the back of the chair. "Nice to see you again."

One reason she liked this woman was that she included the parents in activities and kept up contact with them throughout the year. She even conducted reading/writing workshops for adults. The seminars were an attempt to have parents experience how their children were being taught language arts. Maggie enjoyed them and Mike had always looked forward to going, too. All that seemed very far away now.

"How are you?" Casey asked.

Maggie bit her bottom lip. "I assume you know the latest with our family."

"Yes, I do. Some kids came to see me after the blood drive. For the record, they were upset about it. And I was there when the prom tickets incident happened. I'm sorry. I would have intervened if I'd suspected Julianne would go off on them like she did."

"This is all so hard to deal with. I never quite know if I'm doing what's right for Jamie and Brian." Maggie waited a beat. "I realize it's personal, what they write in their journals, but are they handling this?"

Casey gave her a comforting smile. "In my opinion, yes. Brian's struggling, but he's trying to find his way, I think because of your support. I advised him to go see the counselor you suggested, too. And Jamie's upset by all these things happening, but he's doing as well as can be expected." She frowned. "I do worry about Luke Crane, though. The boys have you and Mike, but he's alone in all this."

"I know. I wish we could help him."

"Jamie's lucky to have you. So many kids keep being gay a secret from their parents until they're adults. Jamie told you when he was still vulnerable to you, when you can control so much of what happens to him. You've given him the emotional support he needs for what life's throwing at him right now. Believe me, I've seen the other side way too many times."

"Thanks for telling me that. We keep hitting walls like we did with the blood drive."

"I understand the Red Cross needs to adhere to FDA standards, but those questions are blatantly homophobic. After what happened with Jamie, a group of teachers wants to put in a formal protest of the questionnaire. The principal isn't sure that's the way to go, but we feel if schools don't speak up, nothing will ever change."

"I'm grateful that you care."

"Most of Jamie's teachers are crazy about him and are standing by him. We'll be at the prom, too. We'll watch over him and Luke."

"Thanks. That means a lot to me."

Casey sipped her coffee, as if she was waiting before she said more. "Maggie, I want to share a personal experience with you, if that's all right."

Maggie was sure Casey was going to tell her she was a lesbian.

"My brother's gay. He came out to my parents at twenty-seven. More than ten years later than Jamie told you."

"How did your parents deal with it?"

"Not well. They've seen little of him over the last decade. And because he wanted to bring his partner home with him at Christmastime, and they said no, he doesn't come for holidays anymore. I've taken to spending most vacations with Joel and Tom—who is a wonderful guy, by the way—and not my parents."

"I'm sorry this happened to your family."

"Maybe knowing that will make you feel better."

"Is that why you asked to talk to me?"

"Partly. But there's another reason, and that's why I wanted to meet here and not at school." She fiddled with a stray napkin on the table. "I'm on the committee to choose National Honor Society members. Jamie's applied."

No, no, not this, too.

"A teacher made a comment about Jamie and Luke getting prom tickets together. Specifically, she's questioning Jamie's suitability for NHS. And she's head of the committee."

Maggie clutched her mug. "Oh, Casey, Jamie can't withstand another blow from the school he loves so much. And I'm sure Luke can't either."

"Luke's already in NHS. It would be a lot harder to get a student out than to keep one from getting in."

"Even though it's clear discrimination?"

"She's being nuanced about it. Not saying it outright."

"Did you talk to Steve Thomas about it?"

"I was going to, but then I heard he was dragging his feet about registering a formal protest with the blood drive. If he doesn't act quickly on NHS, the committee's decision will be a fait accompli." She shrugged. "So I decided to tell you. Steve won't put this on hold if a parent complains."

"I'll call him right now."

Casey waited while Maggie phoned the school. The principal's secretary told her he was free in two hours, at five, and Maggie made an appointment.

As she left Starbucks, she glanced at her watch. She had time to call Mike to go with her. She *should* call Mike. She hadn't told him about the blood drive or about Julianne. But, though he'd tried to hide it, he was upset by what the Lewises had done, too. Would he handle the NHS situation right?

In the end, Maggie did errands instead of calling her husband, and at five, she faced Steve alone over his massive cherry desk. Afternoon sunlight slanted in through a double window that faced the courtyard. On the credenza behind him was a picture of a petite blond woman with two-black haired boys. "What can I do for you, Maggie?"

"One of your teachers on the NHS committee told me something troubling. It seems the chair has hinted that she isn't in favor of my son becoming one of the inductees."

Steve's dark brows knitted and he steepled his hands. "First of all, this teacher should have come to me. Did she say why she called you instead?"

"She said you were dragging your feet registering a formal complaint from the school concerning the blood drive eligibility policies and she didn't know if you'd deal with this issue in a timely manner. And please don't ask me who the teacher is."

His face flushed. "All right. Still, I hate to think one of my staff is afraid to talk to me." He braced his massive arms on his desk. "So, are you saying this NHS concern is related to Jamie being gay?"

"Of course I am. My son is a straight-A student. He's active in several extracurricular groups and has had lead roles in all the school plays. He almost single-handedly organized the school blood drive. If he doesn't fit your definition of Scholarship, Leadership, Character, and Service, no kid does."

"Keeping him out of Honor Society for his sexual orientation is against everything our school stands for." Steve's tone was neutral, but there was fire in his dark eyes.

"Nonetheless, someone is blackballing Jamie."

"That's a volatile word to use."

"Maybe so. I'm not out to cause problems, Steve. Please, help me here." Maggie's voice cracked. "Honor Society is important to Jamie. He's still fragile in so many ways I'm not sure he can handle something like this."

"I understand." He studied her. "And thanks for coming right to me. It's better to do this without lawyers."

"I'll go to them," she said. "If I have to."

"I hear you." He glanced at his watch. "I'll get to the bottom of this as soon as I can contact the people involved. But it will be today. I'll call you myself tonight."

"When will the notices of induction go out?"

"The end of this week. The ceremony is in ten days."

The principal stood. "Just for the record, if I'd gotten wind of this before you did, I'd do exactly what I'm going to do now. And I'm not stalling on the blood drive protest. I have to run it by central administration first because the teachers want it to come from the school in general. But I have to say the FDA has been operating this way for years and hasn't budged in the face of the gay community's complaints."

"Thank you. And one more thing, if this turns out as I hope, I'd like to keep what happened or could have happened from Jamie."

"Agreed," Steve said. "I'll be in touch."

Ferreting out a business card from her purse, she scribbled her cell phone number on it and handed it to Steve. "Use this, please. Then no one will accidentally overhear our conversation."

Maggie drove home, totally drained. She, Mike, Jamie, and Brian had a blessedly uneventful dinner that night. At ten, her cell phone rang. The boys were in their respective rooms and Maggie was in the den when she picked up the call.

"Maggie Davidson."

"Maggie, Steve Thomas."

Her heart began to pound. If this went wrong, the sky was going to fall.

"Jamie will be notified on Friday that he's being inducted into NHS."

"Oh, thank God." She cleared her throat. "I appreciate you looking into this."

"I'll tolerate no discrimination in my school."

Translated, there *was* a problem.

"Thank you again, Steve."

"Would you do something for me, Maggie?"

"Yes, of course."

"I'd like confidentiality on your end, also."

"I understand. I won't tell anyone."

"And if there are more problems in school around Jamie coming out, please contact me first."

"I will. Good-bye, Steve."

She clicked off and leaned back in the chair. *Another bullet dodged*, she thought.

"What the hell was that all about?"

The comment came from Mike, who stood in the doorway his eyes blazing.

An insidious feeling crept into Mike as he watched his wife, who'd just had a conversation with Jamie's principal. She was keeping secrets from him.

She held his gaze unflinchingly. "I was talking to Steve Thomas."

"I gathered that. It's a little late for a call from the principal."

"I know."

"You're keeping things about Jamie from me."

"Come in and sit down. Close the door. I don't want to be overheard."

His pulse rate sped up, but he did as she asked. Once again they faced each other over her desk like enemies from different camps. He had to struggle against the swell of emotion that notion brought out in him.

"Jamie's had a rough few days at school." She recounted the blood drive fiasco.

"Poor Jamie."

"It gets worse. Julianne flipped out when Luke and Jamie bought prom tickets. She says she can't be friends with him because he's gay."

"God wouldn't want that."

A ghost of a smile. "No, I don't think God would."

"Is that what Steve wanted to talk about?"

"No. Casey Carson called me today and I met her for coffee. She said there was a chance of Jamie being excluded from Honor Society."

"No, Maggie, that can't happen."

"It's all taken care of. I met with Steve, too, and he got to the bottom of it. Jamie will be inducted in a couple of weeks."

Mike was relieved. On the heels of that came a blinding slice of anger, which he tried to keep out of his voice. "Let me get this straight. You dealt with the blood drive and met with a teacher and the principal all by yourself?"

"Yes."

"And Jamie must have told you about Jules."

"Yes."

"What else?"

Her chin raised. "I went to a PFLAG meeting. It's an organization—"

"I know what PFLAG is. Did you go alone?"

"No, Gretta went with me."

His chest began to ache, like his heart was being squeezed to death. "You didn't tell me any of this because I have a faith issue with Jamie being gay?"

"No, it's not that."

"Are you punishing me for my beliefs?"

"No, of course not!"

He slapped an open palm on the wooden surface of her desk. "Then why am I just finding out about all this? Why didn't you call me to meet with Casey?"

"She didn't ask to meet with you."

"I could have gone with you to see Steve, then. That was my right, damn it."

"There wasn't time to contact you."

"Bullshit. You didn't want me to go."

"All right! I didn't want you to go."

Utter silence.

She broke it. "It's…it's hard to talk to you these days."

"So you completely took charge of our son's life. You had no right."

She raised her chin. "I have to protect him."

"From me?"

"No, that came out wrong."

He bolted off the chair. The back of it hit the wall, hard and harsh like the emotional words between him and his wife. "I can't believe you'd do this to me. To us."

"Mike, you've been dividing us for weeks now. I feel like I'm in this all by myself. Worse, that we're on opposite sides. It's why I asked you to consider marriage counseling."

He loomed over her, his fists clenched and his mind whirling. "Fuck marriage counseling, Maggie. Fuck everything."

Stalking to the kitchen, he grabbed his keys and strode out of the house. He got in the car and made it to the main road before he pulled over to the shoulder. His head back against the seat, he prayed. For guidance. For patience. For humility.

None of it came.

He felt calmer, though, so he drove the half hour to his parents' place on the lake. His father came out the front door when he pulled into the driveway and got out of the car. It was eleven at night.

"Mikey, is that you?"

His dad's use of the old nickname choked him up. "Yeah. I hope it's not too late."

BJ walked over to him. "No, of course not. Something wrong?"

"Yes." He stepped closer to his father.

Then his dad opened his arms and Mike walked into them.

❖

"Do you want to be alone with your father?" Mike's mother asked. She was ready for bed in pajamas, her face washed, her hair combed off her face. When he was little, his mom's nightly ritual made him feel safe, as it was constant and predictable.

Despite the gravity of his situation, Mike smiled. "Why? He'd just tell you later what I said." Mike understood that from being a child in this house. There were no secrets between his parents. They settled into the family room, which faced the lake. "Anyway, I need a woman's perspective. And a mother's."

"What happened, son?" his father asked.

"Several weeks ago, Jamie told us he's gay."

His mom and dad exchanged looks.

"You knew?"

"We suspected." His dad leaned forward in his chair. "We were going to talk to you about it, but you never brought it, up so we waited."

"Did Jamie tell you, honey?"

"He told Maggie, of course." Mike hadn't realized that he resented Jamie telling Maggie first. Or that Jamie hadn't told them together.

"You're upset about his sexual orientation?"

"Hell, Dad, of course I'm upset. It's against our religion."

A shock of white hair fell over his father's forehead when he frowned. "Some people in the Catholic Church think that homosexuality is a sin. Some don't."

"What about you two?"

His mother spoke first. "Jesus loved everybody. He wouldn't expect Jamie to live an unnatural life."

"Celibacy."

"Yes. It's crazy for the church to believe that lifestyle is healthy."

"Maggie agrees." Mike's heart twisted in his chest. "You're on her side."

"There aren't sides here," his dad told him. "Jamie's our concern. And you."

His mother studied him, her eyes full of sympathy. "You feel as if you and Maggie are on different sides?"

"Are you kidding? We're on different planets when it comes to this." He gave them the broad strokes of how his marriage had suffered in only a few weeks.

His mom got up and came to sit next to him. She took his hand in both of hers. "I'm sorry to hear that."

"How's Brian?" his dad asked.

Mike swallowed hard. Those details were harder to relate, but he managed to get them out.

"Brian's taking his cue from you." His father's words were like a bucket of cold water in the face.

"Oh, God. I've caused all this?"

"No. I didn't mean it that way. I think your pastor is influencing you negatively."

"He's a good man. He has our family's best interest at heart." When his father just stared at him, Mike added, "I believe in him. In our church."

His dad waited before he commented, "Then you have a tough road to hoe."

Lucy said, "A man's family should come first."

"God should come first," Mike responded.

"God wouldn't want you to hurt Jamie." His mother's voice was so sure, so confident. "He wouldn't want you to hurt your family. Anyone who advises you differently is wrong."

Torn, Mike sighed. "I'd like a drink. A strong one."

"You've got to drive back."

"No, I don't. I'd rather spend the night here."

"Do you think you should do that?"

"Who the hell knows?"

❖

Maggie heard the garage door go up, drained the rest of her coffee, and rinsed the cup out in the sink. She glanced at the clock. She was done with classes but she usually went in at this time to finish up the paperwork.

Hers and Mike's phone conversation last night was curt.

I'm staying out here with my parents.

Fine.

They'd hung up simultaneously. Luckily the boys had been in bed before Mike stormed out, and they'd left for school this morning thinking their dad had gone to work.

Mike halted at the entrance to the kitchen. "I thought you'd be at school."

"I'm sure you timed coming home so that you wouldn't see me."

His shoulders sagged and he eyes were bleak. Suddenly, she wanted to rush to him, wrap her arms around his neck and tell him everything would be all right. But they both knew it might not.

"Don't harp on me. I'm wiped."

Staring at her husband, she took a deep breath. "I'm sorry I kept what's been happening with Jamie from you. You're right, I didn't trust you with it."

"That's the problem."

"No, Mike, the problem is you can't accept your son for who he is. So it's sent us all into a tailspin. We're acting out of character."

"I'm not the one keeping things from you."

"You were the one who stayed out all night."

"At my parents'."

"You ran away."

Pique flushed his cheeks. "I told them about Jamie. You've been nagging at me to do it. I did."

"And?"

"I don't want to talk about this now." He glanced at his watch. "I've got to get to work. I have a meeting shortly."

"Then you'd better get going."

He left without saying good-bye.

At noon, Maggie was on the porch, trying to get some final papers graded, when the doorbell rang. She didn't answer it, fearful of what new crisis lay on the other side.

But she heard the front door open and went into the foyer to find Mike's mother, Lucy, holding the key to their home that they'd given her long ago. Without saying a word, she set her bag on the corner table, crossed to Maggie, and embraced her in a warm hug.

Maggie began to cry.

"Shh. There now, sweetheart." Lucy rubbed her back. "It'll be all right."

"I'm not crying because he's gay," she said adamantly, though the effect was diluted by the sobs. She buried her face in Lucy's shoulder.

"I know you're not. With Caroline coming to Sherwood and your mother handling it so badly, along with Jamie's revelation, I think the stress you're under is unbearable."

"But I'm not crying about my boy."

"You're crying about *my* boy."

When Maggie finally composed herself, Lucy took her hand and led her to the porch. Instead of choosing the stuffed rocker she favored, her mother-in-law sat down on the couch with Maggie and didn't let go of her.

Maggie was glad for the contact. She loved and respected this woman so much, admired her grit, her unerring faith in God, and her love for her five children. Today, in comparison to Lucy Davidson, Maggie felt like the worst kind of mother and wife.

"Honey, I'm going to tell you something. And I want your promise that you won't share this with anyone."

"Of course, Mom."

"When Tommy was five, I got pregnant again. We had a brood by then and I was so overworked, I was miserable. I was also in my forties. Your father-in-law had refused to use birth control because of the Catholic Church's stance on contraception. I knew in my heart having another baby was not right for us at that time of our lives."

"Did you have a miscarriage?"

Blue eyes so like Mike's clouded. "No, Mag, I had an abortion."

"What?"

"I had an abortion. My doctor was worried anyway about my emotional well-being. We did the procedure in his office."

"What did Dad say?"

"I didn't tell him. You're the first person I've ever told."

"I'm—"

"Shocked. As you should be." For a moment, Lucy stared out at the backyard. "It was against my religion, my ethics, my belief system. Yet I did it for myself and for my family. I suffered over it, confessed to God, but I didn't even tell our priest."

"I'm sorry you had to go through that alone."

"Oh, honey, I didn't. God was with me, even though I'd sinned."

"Why are you telling me this?"

"Well, for one, I want you to know that protecting your family and doing what's best for them and yourself are important. But I haven't finished the story."

"Oh, okay."

"Like I said, I never told your father-in-law, but I did confront him on the issue of birth control. He blew up at me. Flatly refused 'to wear one of those rubber things,' he called them. We'd practice abstinence, he said, as we always had. Like *that* had worked."

"What happened?"

"I wouldn't sleep with him until he agreed to use birth control. That's probably more information than you want about your in-laws, but it's necessary to make my point. Dad was mad as a hornet, but he finally caved. Now he thinks back on that time in our lives and wonders why he ever got so angry. Why he couldn't see that God would want him to protect his family." She smiled. "When you get older, I guess you can see the gray areas."

"He couldn't see them then because he was blinded by his faith in the church."

Lucy sat back. "The Catholic Church has done harm to your family. But that doesn't mean there aren't a lot of good Catholics out there, good Christians in the fold. Us. Your husband. But sometimes, it's a difficult church to live under."

"I know. I can't go back there after how it's affected Mike's attitude toward Jamie."

"He told us. We're glad you found God elsewhere. Someday, I'd like to go to a UCC service with you. And maybe to an event or two."

"Oh, Mom."

"Now, don't get weepy on me again." She squeezed Maggie's hand. Her self-possession was calming. "There's a message in all this. You and your husband can disagree, but you have to stay close and try to work through it. Fix it, Maggie, and don't do anything to make it worse."

She wondered if Mike had told Lucy about Damien, but she couldn't broach the subject with her mother-in-law.

"At the same time, never, ever sacrifice Jamie for Mike. It's not the natural order of life."

Laying her head on Lucy's shoulder, Maggie was glad for the reassurance. "Thanks so much for telling me this. For coming here today."

In a motherly gesture that had been missing in Maggie's life since Caroline left, Lucy soothed down her hair. "You can repay me by being the wonderful wife, mother, and human being you've always been."

CHAPTER TWENTY-FOUR

Suit coat off, the sleeves of his light blue shirt rolled up, Mike sat behind his desk at work unable to concentrate on the contract before him. He'd been distracted for two days. His visit with his parents had only served to make him feel worse. Regardless of how supportive of him they were, he sensed they disapproved of how he was handling the situation at home. He'd slept badly because he was away from Maggie, but even last night, when he shared the same bed with his wife, the distance between them was like an ocean.

A rustle at the doorway. Laura Simpson stood there in a raincoat. He'd heard the droplets ping against his windows for the last hour. "Leaving?"

"Yes, and you should, too."

"What time is it?"

"Seven." She gave him an understanding smile. "Don't you need to get home?"

"Hardly." He had no idea what either boy was doing tonight or where his wife was right now. He hadn't called her and she hadn't made contact either.

"Are you all right, Mike?"

Leaning back in his chair, he watched the lovely woman before him. "No. I guess not."

Uninvited, she came inside and perched on the edge of the chair in front of his desk. "You've been preoccupied all day. Actually, for a couple of days."

"I know. I almost blew that phone conference with China."

"You did fine." Again, she smiled. The red of her dress peeked out from her coat and, he noticed, went great with her coloring. "You could run circles around those guys using half your brain."

Compliments rolled easily off her tongue and it made him feel good. "You didn't have to stay this late."

"I had paperwork to catch up on." She gave him a suggestive wink. "Besides, any assistant worth her salt doesn't leave before the boss."

"Then I better get out of here."

"I'll walk out with you."

That seemed harmless. They made small talk on their way down the hall, riding the elevator. When they reached the entrance, she pulled out her cell phone.

"What are you doing?"

"My car's in the shop again. They didn't fix the problem last time and it stalled out. I hope I can get a cab in this weather."

"Did you have a ride arranged earlier?"

"I was supposed to go home with Ginny."

"But you stayed because I was here?"

Now she gave him a level stare. "Yes, Mike, I stayed because you were here."

He waited only a beat. "I'll give you a lift."

The drive to her apartment was filled with work chatter. When he pulled up to her apartment building, she faced him. The front seat of his Taurus seemed to have shrunk, and her perfume, sweet and flowery, filled it. "Want to come in? For food. Or a drink." She shrugged one shoulder daintily. "Anything."

Don't do it, his conscience warned.

But this time, Mike didn't listen. He was tired of being sensible Mike. Mike the father. Mike the husband. Tonight he wanted to be Mike the man. So he smiled back and realized he hadn't forgotten how to flirt. "Sure, I'll come up. I'm not hungry but I could use a drink."

❖

Maggie had been in a funk for two days. She'd dressed for work today in a buttercup yellow skirt and knit top, one of her favorite outfits, hoping the bright color would cheer her up.

Gretta had gone with Tim on a business trip, and Melissa wasn't due back from her vacation until next week. So when Reverend Anabelle called and wanted to meet, they'd chosen tonight at eight. After Maggie finished grading papers, she decided not to go home.

Instead, she headed out of her office to the student café. The trip across campus lightened her spirits—the sprawling, picturesque grounds, coordinated architecture, quiet now because most of the students were gone and summer school hadn't yet started. At the door to the building, she bumped into Damien. In tailored slacks and a beige linen shirt, open at the collar, he was handsome, attractive, alluring.

"Hey, pretty lady, you're usually long gone by now."

"Usually."

"Nobody to go home to?"

Tears threatened. "Um, no."

Damien grabbed her arm. "You all right?"

"I can't talk about this, Damien."

"Then eat with me."

"I was heading in there."

"Nah, not in there. Come on, we'll go to Jinx's."

Maggie knew she shouldn't go with him. But then she recalled Mike's black moods and the turmoil in her marriage. And bitterly, a thought came to her. *Maybe I'll give Father Pete something to worry about.*

"I'll go on one condition. That we don't discuss my problems."

"If that's what you want."

The atmosphere at Jinx's was pleasant.

Damien was a terrific conversationalist.

The wine they ordered was rich and it went down smooth.

When they left, both she and Damien were feeling mellow. He walked beside her to her car, which was parked at the far end, overshadowed by some trees. He opened the driver's door and Maggie slid behind the wheel.

Then Damien rounded the hood and got in the passenger side.

"What are you doing?"

"Just this."

Leaning over, he grasped her shoulders. His lips were soft, tender. At first. Then they became more insistent. He deepened the kiss. Drew her to him.

Maggie moved in close. Closer.

And let herself go.

❖

Jamie was alone in his house, which never happened, so he took advantage of it and lit incense and cranked up the volume of his stereo. His brother was at a baseball meeting and had called Jamie, pissed that he hadn't gotten the car back before Brian had to leave, forcing him to catch a ride. His mother was having coffee with Anabelle, and his father was…he had no idea where his father was. All he knew was that his dad hadn't come home a few nights ago. His parents were fighting. He'd be more worried about them if he wasn't so preoccupied with Luke.

So much had gone wrong lately—the blood drive, the prom tickets. But the run-in with Luke's parents that night in the basement was almost too much to handle. He could still see the disgust on Dr. Crane's face. Two guys getting physical with each other made him sick. When Luke's father ordered Jamie out and said he was never welcome in their home again, it shocked both Jamie and Luke. They'd left together and sat in the car in front of Jamie's house talking about it. They'd decided that Luke didn't have to go to that camp no matter what his parents said, so there was no reason to be upset. And they could still see each other as much as they did now. Like with college, Luke was eighteen and his father couldn't *force* him to do anything. Luke seemed to have calmed down, but Jamie knew when he went home, his parents would work him over.

Yet then in school today, Luke seemed happy. He'd told Jamie his mother had been reasonable and he was feeling better. He'd also given Jamie a present. A meaningful one. His school letter jacket. Jamie asked why and Luke shrugged, said he wanted Jamie to have it, wear it. Then he put his arm around Jamie—right out in the open at school—and whistled all the way down the hall. They'd caught people's attention but Luke didn't even seem to notice.

Jamie's cell phone rang. Grabbing it from the desk, he checked the caller ID. "Hey, Luke," he said clicking on.

Mumbles. A sound in the background.

"Luke, is that you? I can't hear you."

"Jame…"

"Luke? You sound funny."

"Come over…"

Some coughing. Rustling. Jamie couldn't place the noise in the background.

It took his brain a minute to catch up. Something was really wrong. Luke's words were slurred. Was he drunk? Jamie yelled Luke's name into the phone. Though the line hadn't gone dead, Luke wasn't talking anymore. Jamie bolted out of his desk chair, grabbed his car keys, and hurtled downstairs. He was in the Prius and on the road in a few minutes. Thinking about the pills, about Luke's fights with his father, he drove as fast as he could to the Cranes' house and came to a halt in the driveway. He leapt out of the car. The windows were all dark. The garage doors were closed and as he passed them, he heard an engine running inside. *Heard* an engine? *What the hell?*

Oh my God.

Stay calm. Stay calm. He put his ear to the first of three bays. A car was definitely running behind it. He banged his fist on the metal. After a few seconds, he remembered that he and Luke had been out late one night and when Jamie dropped him off, Luke realized he had forgotten his key. The Cranes sometimes left open the side door to the garage, and Luke got in that way.

Jamie bounded around the house. He tried that door. It was locked. *Fuck*! But it had a window. He could see two cars inside.

Frantically scanning the lawn, Jamie caught sight of a big decorative rock. He hefted it up and smashed in the glass. The shattering sound was loud in the still night air.

Jamie yanked open the door and rushed inside. His eyes stung and he began to cough. There was an empty spot where Dr. Crane would park, then Mrs. Crane's BMW, then Luke's car. Which was running. *Oh God oh God oh God.* He vaulted onto the BMW, walked over it, and circled around to the driver's side of Luke's Camaro. He opened the door and found Luke, cell phone still in hand, head back against the seat.

No, no, no, no.

"Luke!" Jamie pressed his ear to Luke's chest. He was still breathing.

Spotting the three automatic garage door buttons on the wall, Jamie sprang toward them and hit the first one open-handed. The single bay where Luke's car was parked screeched up. Jamie reached inside the front seat for Luke. He was dead weight. No, no, not dead. He was breathing. He was heavy anyway, but now… *Please God, please let him be okay.* Finally Jamie managed to pull Luke out of the car. He fell onto the hard cement floor and Jamie went to his knees with him. He maneuvered Luke so he could grab him under the arms, then stood and dragged him out into the fresh air. The cell phone dropped out of his hand on the driveway. Jamie scooped it up and punched in 911. "There's been an incident. 987 Lark Lane. My friend was in the car. There was a lot of carbon monoxide. Please hurry."

"Stay on the line," the woman said. "An ambulance will be right there."

Jamie dropped the phone. He'd taken Advanced Health last semester and had gotten his CPR accreditation.

Tilt the head.

Clear the passageway.

Take a breath.

Cover his mouth.

Until the ambulance arrived, Jamie gave his own air to Luke and prayed that he would be all right.

❖

"Thanks for asking me to coffee." Sipping her latte, Maggie sat across from Anabelle at the same Starbucks where she'd met Casey Carson. "I know you're busy."

"I wanted to see you, Maggie. You're one of us, even if you haven't officially joined our congregation." She gave Maggie a comforting smile. "And I want to help any way I can."

Maggie and Jamie had been back to UCC on several Sundays. Jamie talked about joining their youth group. Maggie helped with a coffee hour and signed up for the book club.

"How's it going with Mike?" Anabelle asked.

"Can you read minds, too?"

Her slate blue eyes twinkled. "Comes with the collar." Which she didn't often wear but had on tonight because she'd been to the hospital to visit a sick member of the church.

"Not good." Maggie thought about what she'd done earlier and cringed. "We've never been so distanced before. Not for so long, anyway."

"Is that all you're feeling?"

"No, I'm mad at him, too. He should be doing better with Jamie." Anabelle waited. "And I should be doing better, too. I've withheld a lot from him."

"Why?"

"Because I don't trust him to handle what's happening to Jamie anymore."

"That must hurt you both."

Moisture filled Maggie's eyes and she blinked it back. "I did something tonight, before I came here."

When she hesitated, Anabelle said, "Maggie, I'm not here to judge you, and I might be able to help."

"I let another man kiss me. I kissed him back. It was more than friendly and would have led straight to a motel room if I'd let it."

"Why didn't you?"

"Because I love Mike. And I know he could never forgive infidelity. I'm not sure I could either." She ran a hand through her hair. "I just want my family back, Anabelle."

"Have you thought of marriage counseling?"

"I suggested Mike and I go to a therapist, but he balked at the idea." Actually, he'd said *fuck marriage counseling*.

"Men." Anabelle shook her head. "Can I help?"

Maggie shrugged. "You're helping by being here with me. Listening. You make me feel closer to God."

She smiled. "Well, if that isn't the nicest thing anyone has ever said to me!"

Maggie admired so much about Anabelle and wondered about her life. What was it like to be a lesbian? To have a female as a partner, a woman who thought more like you, felt the way you did? Would that preclude the majority of arguments?

So Maggie asked her.

Anabelle chuckled. "Sometimes it does. Especially if you have as much in common as Lisel and I do."

Maggie had met Anabelle's partner at some UCC activities and seen her from afar at worship services. A tall, light-haired woman with a beautiful smile, she always seemed serene, which Maggie envied. Maybe Lisel's calm came from working with special education students and the patience that demanded.

"I—"

Maggie's cell rang. Briefly she closed her eyes. "I hate to answer my phone these days."

Anabelle squeezed Maggie's hand. "Answer now while I'm with you."

She fished her phone out of her purse. "Hello."

"Mom, oh, God, Mom."

"Jamie, what's wrong? Are you okay?"

"I am. Luke's not. Mom, Mom, he tried to… I found him in his garage with the car's motor running."

"Honey, no. Is he all right?"

"He's alive. But he tried it, Mom, he tried to kill himself." Jamie began to cry.

"Where are you?"

"Memorial Hospital." Hiccups. "In the emergency department waiting room. I followed the ambulance here."

"I'll be right there. Hang on, buddy. Ten minutes." She added, "I love you," and clicked off.

Maggie stood and filled Anabelle in while she gathered her belongings.

"Call Mike," Anabelle said. "Don't shut him out of this."

"All right." As they made their way out of Starbucks, she punched in Mike's number. The cell rang and rang and rang. Then the answering machine picked up. She shook her head at Anabelle. "No answer."

"Leave him a message."

"Mike, it's me. Jamie's at Memorial Hospital. Luke Crane tried to commit suicide tonight. I don't know how bad it is. I'm heading there now." Her voice quavered. "Meet me in the ER when you get this. Please."

They'd reached the parking lot by the time she finished the call. "I'm coming with you," Anabelle said. "I'll drive. You're too upset."

As she got into Anabelle's gold Saturn, Maggie prayed for Luke Crane.

❖

The emergency department waiting room was crammed with people, filled with low moans, an occasional raised voice, and the ringing of phones. On one of the couches, Jamie clutched Luke's cell phone and tried to be strong. The ambulance attendants had been hopeful.

His heart's steady, they'd said as they put an oxygen mask over Luke's mouth and nose. The woman had glanced at the house. *It's a good thing the garage is so big because it would take longer to fill up. And you got him out of there fast. That was critical.*

Jamie closed his eyes, reliving the heart-stopping moment when he realized what Luke had done, the terror of getting him out of the car and the garage, the nightmarish ride as he sped over the roads behind the ambulance to the hospital. To block the images, he stood and began to pace. It was then that he saw his mother and Anabelle come through the double glass doors. When his mom reached him, he threw himself into her arms. They felt solid and strong.

"Oh, Jamie, sweetheart, I'm so sorry." Finally he was able to draw back.

"Thanks for coming."

"Of course I came." His mom brushed a hand down his hair.

Anabelle was standing behind her. She asked, "How is he, Jamie?"

"I don't know. Nobody's come out to say. I'm not sure they'll even tell me, I'm not family."

"Did they contact his parents?"

"They just rushed him in without talking to me. After, somebody came out asked me his name and address, that kind of information. They know his dad, from working here. I gave them the home phone number, but I don't know if they got in touch with the Cranes."

Anabelle motioned to the chair. "Let's sit."

When they were settled, Jamie felt his chest tighten. "It's my fault, Mom."

"Oh, honey, no. You had every right to be friends with him."

"It's not that." God, he could hardly say the words. "I knew he was thinking about this. A couple of weeks ago, I found pills." His face felt like it was on fire, he was so ashamed at what he'd done, but he told her anyway. "I gave him the Gay Alliance information and we were both thinking about going. I should have pushed him harder to see the counselor there."

His mom grabbed his hand. "Jamie, don't beat yourself up about keeping Luke's secret."

Anabelle said, "You should have told an adult about the pills, Jamie, but it's understandable why you didn't. You made a mistake. And in the end, Luke called you, probably because he could trust you."

"You think?"

"I do." She pointed to the cell phone. "Is that Luke's?"

"Yes."

"We should try to get in touch with his parents. Their cell numbers are probably in there."

"I don't think I can do it."

His mother held out her hand. "Give it to me."

As she found the number in the menu, a doctor appeared in the doorway of the examining area. "Is the family of Luke Crane here?"

Jamie stood. "I'm not family. But I brought him in."

The doctor walked over.

"Is he okay?"

"I have to speak to the family. His father is Lucas Crane, correct?"

Anabelle came to Jamie's side. "Yes, we're contacting him now. Please, at least tell us if Luke's going to be okay."

The doctor's face was grim. "He's stable. But he's unconscious."

"What does that mean?" Jamie asked.

"I really need to speak to Dr. and Mrs. Crane."

His mom said, "I've got them on the line."

The doctor took the phone. "Dr. Crane?"

Someone must have spoken.

"Your son's here at Memorial Hospital. There's been an incident. He's stable but you need to get to emergency right away."

After the doctor clicked off, he addressed Jamie. "The EMT said you found him and got him out of the garage. If he lives, you very well could have saved his life."

"*If* he lives?" Jamie whispered to his mother as the doctor strode away.

"We'll have to wait and see." She glanced over his shoulder. "Oh, thank God."

Jamie pivoted. His dad burst through the doors and hurried to them. He put his arms around Jamie and pulled him close. Jamie buried his face in his father's chest.

"How is he?" his dad asked his mom.

"We're not sure."

His father kissed his head. "I'm sorry, Jame. I'm so sorry."

❖

Mike hadn't answered his cell phone until an hour after he heard it ring because at the time of the call, Laura Simpson had been all over him. But he wouldn't think about that now. Instead, he forced himself to be there for Jamie. And Maggie.

When his son let go of him, Mike gathered Maggie close. "Let's sit. Tell me what happened."

As they sat, he noticed another woman with Maggie. Her clerical collar told him who it probably was. She said, "I'm Anabelle Brooke."

"I guessed. We'll talk later."

He kept his arm around Jamie while his son recounted the whole incident. When he was done, Mike took him by the shoulders. "Look at me, Jame. This isn't your fault. Concentrate on the fact that Luke changed his mind about wanting to die and called you."

"Okay, Dad."

He clasped his wife's arm. "You all right?"

She leaned into him. "Better now that you're here."

They kept vigil in silence until he felt Maggie nudge him. The Cranes had entered the emergency department. Dressed in a tux, Dr. Crane scanned the area. When he located them, he headed over like a bulldozer, ready to level whatever was in its way. In formal wear, too, Erin followed meekly behind.

"What the hell is going on here?" Crane asked.

Erin touched his arm. "Lucas, please, calm down." To Maggie she said, "The doctor said an incident. And that Luke is stable. Was there a car accident?"

"No." This from Jamie, who cowered next to Mike. "Luke... he..."

"Spit it out, boy."

Mike circled his arm around Jamie's shoulders again and answered for him. "Apparently Luke got in his car tonight, closed the garage doors, and started the engine. It looks like a suicide attempt, but he must have changed his mind because he called Jamie. My son went over and got him out. The ambulance brought him here. He's stable but still unconscious. That's all we know."

Erin burst into tears and dropped down into a chair. Anabelle went to her side.

"You little bastard, this is your fault." Crane lunged for Jamie, but Mike stepped in front of his son and grabbed Crane's shoulders. "Lucas, this is not Jamie's fault."

Shrugging off Mike's grasp, Crane was wild-eyed. "The hell it isn't. If he hadn't lured my boy into some perverted relationship, this wouldn't have happened."

"You're upset. That's understandable. Calm down and go see if you can find out what Luke's condition is."

"Get out of here," Crane said, ignoring Mike's advice. "All of you."

"Dad, please, don't let him make me go."

Luke's mother stood. "Stop this! For God's sake, Jamie saved our son's life. Now go find his doctor."

Crane glared at them but finally stormed away. He disappeared into the emergency treatment areas, and the rest of them sat down again. After several minutes, Crane came back out with another doctor. They all stood in unison as he approached them. The doctor addressed Erin.

"Your son is in stable condition, but he hasn't woken up yet. It's odd, as I understand he was initially given mouth-to-mouth resuscitation and the ambulance got there in a timely manner and administered oxygen. His carbon blood content is below thirty, which is manageable, and he's breathing on his own now. But we just have to wait to see what the damage is."

"D-damage?" Erin asked, gripping Anabelle's arm.

"There are aftereffects of carbon monoxide poisoning. We don't know how much he inhaled or for how long. At best, he'll have nausea and headaches. Worst-case scenario—brain damage and organ failure. We're lucky he changed his mind and alerted someone. And that he didn't take any alcohol or drugs before he attempted this."

"Alcohol or drugs?" Maggie asked.

"In most cases, when people chose to terminate their lives by carbon monoxide poisoning, they take drugs or alcohol so they fall asleep in the car before the fumes overcome them. They never have a chance to change their minds, like Luke did. The fact that he's in top shape helps. But we'll have to wait till he wakes up to see how he fared."

"Will he wake up?" Jamie asked.

"I hope so." He nodded to Dr. Crane. "I'll be back out as soon as I know more, Lucas."

When the doctor left, everyone except Lucas sat back down. Instead, the man crossed to the entrance to the treatment rooms and leaned against the wall adjacent to it.

Anabelle scanned the group. "Would you like to pray, Mrs. Crane?"

"Yes, please."

They all linked hands. As they bowed their heads, Mike held on to Jamie and Maggie, and Anabelle grasped hands with Erin and Jamie.

Two hours later, the doctor came through the doors for the third time. Anabelle roused Maggie and Erin, and Mike shook Jamie's shoulder. Lucas, who'd gone inside the treatment area to check for news several times, followed the doctor over. "How is he?"

"He's awake." The doctor gave a weary smile. "There's no visible damage, though we're still running some tests. I think he's going to be all right. The suicide attempt has to be dealt with, though. A social worker is on her way to talk to you."

"I want to see my son," Crane said.

The doctor focused on Jamie. "He wants to see this young man first."

"That's ridiculous." Crane again. "His parents should be with him."

"I'm sorry, Lucas. He doesn't want to see you now. He's eighteen and can make that decision. Besides, we don't know the extent of his injuries yet, so I'm not going to upset him." The doctor finished, "Come on Jamie, I'll take you back."

Mike watched his son go through the doors. Then he watched Lucas Crane's face pale at the fact that his own child had tried to kill himself and wouldn't see his parents in the aftermath. The notion was staggering.

❖

Maggie and Mike lay in the darkness of their bedroom, side by side, staring up at the ceiling. The drive from the hospital had been somber and the three of them had said little. When they'd gotten home, they'd filled Brian in on where they'd been and what happened. He wasn't answering his cell earlier when they called him and left a message, simply saying they'd be late. Brian was shocked and horrified when he was told that Luke had tried to kill himself. They'd all talked some, then both boys finally went to bed.

"I can't believe it, Mags," Mike said into the darkness.

"The poor kid."

"It makes me wonder about Jamie." Mike's voice was hoarse.

"I know, me, too. Before you got there, Anabelle took him aside and asked him point-blank if *he* was suicidal. He came right over to me to assure me he wasn't."

"That's a relief. Still, maybe he should get some counseling. Not for being gay," he was quick to add.

"We'll talk to him tomorrow."

Mike was silent.

She rolled on her side so she faced him. A sliver of moonlight filtered in and she could see the outline of his body. "Where were you tonight when we couldn't get hold of you?"

A longer silence. "I was at Laura Simpson's apartment."

"Your assistant?" Maggie fell back into the pillow. "Oh, God, are you having an affair?"

Sitting up, he switched on the night table light, leaned over her and braced his arms on either side of her. "No. I'm not having an affair. She made an overture. I rejected it."

"What were you doing there?"

"I don't know." His gaze was dark and direct. "Maybe I was tempted."

"I see."

"But I'd decided not to let the situation go further with her before I got your call."

She stared up into the bloodshot eyes and unshaven face of her husband. A man she'd loved for more than twenty years. "I believe you. And I hope you'll believe me when I tell you what I did tonight."

His expression grew more serious. "It's about Kane, isn't it?"

She nodded.

"What happened?"

"We went out to dinner and things got out of hand."

"How out of hand?"

"Not very. I stopped it, too."

A few moments passed, the whirring of the overhead fan the only sound in the room.

"All right. It makes me sick to think about you with him, but I can't, as they say, cast a stone. We will have to deal with this, though."

"Will you reconsider counseling?"

"I'll reconsider a lot of things now."

He switched the light off and lay down. His body was stiff next to hers. Unable to bear the loneliness she was feeling, Maggie inched over and turned her back to him. After a moment, he slid his arms around her waist. As they had so many times—but not much in the last two months—they fell asleep spoon-fashion.

❖

Jamie lay on his bed in the dark, alone. He was shaking all over. His mom and dad had made him feel better, but now, in the silence of his own room, terror washed over him.

Luke had tried to off himself. Jamie had known about the pills, that at least once before, Luke had considered suicide as a way out. Now Jamie was overwhelmed by guilt. He heard Anabelle's voice: *Jamie, don't take this on. It's the worst you can do for yourself or Luke or your family. You're not at fault.* He'd believed her then. But nothing was clear when you were alone in a room at three a.m. He wished he was five and could crawl into bed with his parents.

His door creaked open. Jamie could make out his brother's silhouette in the doorway. Without speaking, Brian crept inside. Jamie heard a thud from what Brian dropped to the floor. It was his sleeping bag. They'd always slept in the same room when one of them was hurting or afraid. Choked up, Jamie whispered, "I'm awake."

A hesitation. "This is okay, isn't it?"

"Yeah, I want you to."

Silence, as Brian stretched out. After a few minutes, he said, "I'm sorry about Luke. Really sorry about how all this went down."

"It's okay, Bri."

"We'll talk tomorrow, like Mom said. But Jame, I gotta know, you aren't..." Jamie heard sniffles. "God, I can't even think about it. You aren't gonna hurt yourself, are you?"

"No, Bri, I'm not."

"Promise?"

Jamie smiled into the darkness. "I promise."

"Okay, 'cuz the rest of it can be fixed."

Minutes earlier, Jamie hadn't believed that. But now with his brother on the floor next to him, the room didn't seem so dark and he didn't feel as alone. "Night, Bri."

"Night, Jame."

CHAPTER TWENTY-FIVE

The church was filled with the smell of flowers and candle wax when Mike stepped inside three days after Luke Crane's suicide attempt. He slid into a pew in the back and knelt down. First, he prayed for Luke and his parents. The boy had been released from the hospital. Mike let Jamie miss two days of school to be with Luke. Erin Crane had kept Jamie's visits from Dr. Crane, who went back to work once they knew their son was going to be all right. Jamie said Luke's suicide attempt had only exacerbated his father's negative attitude toward his sexual orientation.

Bowing his head, Mike spoke to God. *Please let Jamie be safe. Don't let anything bad happen to my son.* He'd talked to Jamie about that, too. Jamie had assured Mike he was not suicidal. *And give Maggie and me the strength to work through our problems.* His inadequacies as a father and a husband swamped him; he was deluged by a flood of failure.

When Mike glanced up, Father Pete was on the altar. The light behind him cast the priest in an ethereal glow. Mike watched the man he admired, in the church he loved surrounded by a God he adored. He rose and made his way down the aisle.

Perhaps sensing his presence, Father Pete turned around. "Mike, hello. I haven't seen you in a few days."

"How are you, Father Pete?"

The priest seemed troubled. "I've been concerned about you. And your family."

Mike sat in the front pew. Father Pete came down from the altar and joined him.

"We've been through some bad times." He recounted what happened with Luke.

"I am so sorry. This often occurs with gay teens. It's why I've been worried. The child can't tolerate himself and how he's behaving."

Mike thought about Jamie and how good he was, how well he handled the ordeal with Luke, how he loved deeply.

"I have to protect my son, Father Pete."

"Of course you do and I want to help. But we *must* act within the parameters of the church."

"My father gave me some information on the organization DIGNITY. I've been thinking maybe they can help me find a way to stay within our church and accept my son's sexual orientation."

Father Pete shifted in the pew. He seemed older today, a bit worn. Standing up for Catholicism couldn't be easy. "What did the information say about that group?"

"They believe it's not wrong in the eyes of God to ignore tenets of the Catholic Church that you can't abide by."

"Some would say that's heresy."

"They believe that the Catholic Church encourages a person to think for himself and decide his own morality on issues."

The priest frowned deeply. "The Catholic Church does not recognize DIGNITY. At first, we had dialogues with them about homosexuality, but when we discovered they weren't advocating celibacy, the church refused to let them meet in our buildings."

"It doesn't seem right."

Like a comforting parent dealing with a wayward child, Father Pete touched his shoulder. "I think it's important you don't stray from your beliefs now, son."

"I have to take care of my family."

"You *have* to do God's will."

"I'm sorry, Father, I'll never accept that caring for my family isn't God's will."

Father Pete's expression was full of pity. "Then *I'm* sorry I have to tell you this now, with all you're going through, but since it's imminent I have no choice. In light of your decisions regarding Jamie, you won't be allowed to lead the last three Contemporary Issues groups."

"The last three?" He could feel fear seeping into him. "Perhaps I'm not the best leader for the homosexuality study, but why the others?"

"Because you aren't in line with us anymore, Mike. What's happened with your son has pulled you away from our strongest doctrines."

"On homosexuality, maybe." But lately, he'd been thinking about the other issues Maggie kept bringing up and was seeing them in a new light.

"I've put Craig Johnson in charge. You're still welcome to attend. I think it would do you good."

"Did Craig agree to do this?"

"Yes."

Mike stared at him blankly.

"I'll pray for you. And for Maggie."

Swallowing hard, feeling like he'd just lost a piece of himself, he said only, "Thank you, Father."

The priest shook his hand. "Don't let the church down, Mike."

Mike glanced at the altar. "I won't let God down."

❖

Side by side, Jamie and Luke entered Sherwood High a week after Luke's suicide attempt. Both were worried about Luke's return to school, though Jamie hadn't encountered any negative reaction from his classmates in the three days *he'd* been back. As a matter of fact, some of the kids had sought him out, asked about Luke, and seemed concerned about him. Even Tony Simonetti, Brian's friend, confessed he felt bad about how he'd treated Luke.

Through it all, Jamie's parents had been great. He'd taken his mom's advice and he and Luke had gone to a couple of meetings at the Gay Alliance. The counselors were cool but the support group was the best. Jamie's dad had encouraged Luke to spend time at their house so they could get to know him better. Not much more had been said about the Catholic Church, or the one he and his mom had been going to.

Dressed in jeans and a cool light blue shirt his mother bought him when he got out of the hospital, Luke stopped short three feet in front of his locker. "Ms. Carson?"

Their favorite teacher pushed off the wall. Her smile was broad. "Hi, Luke." She squeezed Jamie's shoulder. "Jamie."

Luke swallowed hard. "Hi."

"Hey, Ms. C."

Red-faced, Luke said, "I-I'm embarrassed."

"Which is why I'm here." Ms. Carson hugged Luke, then stood back. "I want you to know that the school has been affected by what happened to you. Kids have been encouraged to talk to teachers."

Luke swallowed hard. "About me?"

"About the issues of tolerance and prejudice."

"No kidding? That's great." He shot a glance at Jamie. He did that a lot lately, looked to Jamie for support. "Right, Jame?"

"You bet."

"That's all I wanted you to know. Enjoy the day, guys."

After Ms. Carson walked away, Luke leaned into Jamie. Since the suicide attempt, Luke had been more affectionate, more intimate with his thoughts and feelings. He was seeing a private counselor in addition to the support groups, but his father didn't know about it. Luke was bummed about the secrecy, and so was Jamie. Unfortunately, Dr. Crane still hadn't budged on his position, and Luke believed he never would. His mother, though, was trying to be there for her son.

Nick and Paul came down the hall.

Paul socked Luke's arm gently. "Great to have you back, Luke."

Though he'd been uncomfortable around Jamie's friends before, Luke smiled. "Thanks, Paul."

"Sorry about all the trouble," Nick added.

Jamie and Luke got their books from the locker and started down the hall together. They hadn't made it five feet when Jamie saw Eric Cummings headed in their direction. Simultaneously, Jamie and Luke slowed their pace. Cummings stopped, gave them a disgusted look and went the other way to avoid them.

"Guess not everybody's into tolerance and acceptance around here," Luke said quietly.

"Guess not."

They were walking by a poster advertising the Junior Prom just two weeks away. Luke halted at it and faced Jamie. "So, we still on for this?"

"I didn't think you'd want to go after all that's happened."

Again the cute half-grin. "What? And miss slow dancin' with you in public? Yeah, I wanna go."

Jamie felt like somebody had given him a gift. "Then we're on."

"What kind of tuxes should we get?"

And, for the first time in ages, Jamie felt like an ordinary kid.

❖

Brian was in his room on the computer, looking at Ithaca College's Web site, trying to do normal stuff again. He was okay with everything that had gone down, but he still worried about Jamie. Brian couldn't get it out of his head that it could have been his brother in that hospital bed. Jamie was spending most of his time with Luke. And Luke was at their house a lot, too, which was cool. Brian always thought he was a nice guy and had forgotten that.

There was a knock on his door.

"Yeah, enter."

His mom came inside dressed in jeans and white blouse. She had her hair pulled up. She took a seat on the bed, where Buck was snoring softly. "What are you doing?"

"Cruising Ithaca's Web site."

"We haven't made much of a fuss about college, have we?"

"What, in between Jamie telling us he's gay, Aunt Caroline coming, the baseball team falling apart, and Luke's suicide attempt?"

She smiled at his dry humor. "I'm going to miss you, buddy."

"Are you, Mom?"

Buck woke up and nuzzled into her lap, so she petted him. "Of course I am. Why would you even ask?"

Turning back to his computer screen, he just shrugged.

"Bri?"

He didn't face her and could barely say the words. "Maybe you'll be glad to see me go after how I behaved."

There was a rustle, then Brian felt his mother's arms encircle him from behind. Close to his ear, she whispered, "It will be like losing a piece of my soul when you go. Our family will be incomplete without you. Never doubt that."

His eyes got watery. Then his mom did something she hadn't done in a long time. She swiveled him around, pulled him to her chest and wrapped her arms around his neck. He held on tight.

When he composed himself, he drew back.

She smiled down at him. "Want to go out with me tonight and talk?"

"Yeah, but can it not be about anything serious?"

"Absolutely." She cocked her head. "Here's the deal. We'll go to Bill Grayson's and get a hot dog and some of their spicy fries. We won't even mention Jamie or Dad or Luke."

"Sounds like a plan."

She walked to the door.

"Mom?" She looked back. "I love you."

"I love you, too, buddy."

❖

The day after her dinner with Brian, Maggie followed through on one of the hardest decisions she'd ever had to make in her life. But Luke's suicide attempt had sobered her and she knew she couldn't let the strife in her extended family go on. There was only one way she could think of to fix it. So she climbed the steps and knocked on the heavy wooden door of the rectory. When Father Pete opened it, he smiled. "Hello, Maggie. Come in."

She stepped into what she'd always referred to as the inner sanctum. She'd been there before, of course, but today the house seemed bigger, darker, maybe even holier with its high ceilings, ornate wood trim, and hushed atmosphere. Father Pete led her to his office, which complemented the hallway décor. "Sit down, please."

Maggie took a chair. Father Peter didn't circle the desk but sat next to her instead. "I was surprised to get your call. You said this wasn't about Jamie and Mike, though."

"No, it's not. It's about my mother."

"I've been praying for her. And you."

"You said if you could ever help me with my mother to call you."

"I meant that. What is it you think I can do?"

Though it galled her to ask, she'd beg on her knees if she had to. So much was clearer lately. "I was wondering if you could visit her at Sara's house."

He cocked his head. "And?"

"Tell her it's all right to forgive Caroline."

"Everyone should forgive, Maggie. I can do that easily. But I can't tell her what Caroline did in marrying a divorced man was acceptable to the church."

"I figured that, but I don't think it matters. All I want is for her to see Caroline, get to know her and her family, to let my sister back into our lives. I think if you give her permission to do that, she will."

He waited a long time, and Maggie was afraid she'd made a mistake to come here. "I truly believe that's what God would want her to do."

Tears filled Maggie's eyes.

"I can see you're surprised. Did you think I'd punish you for not agreeing with me about Jamie?"

"That's the Catholic Church I know, Father."

"It's not what I preach or believe in." He checked his calendar on the desk. "I can go tomorrow, if it's all right with your family."

"I'm sure it will be. I'll call Sara and let her know."

He faced her again. "How will we do this?"

"I'm hoping Mike will drive you over."

"Not you?"

"She won't see me."

"Hmm, maybe I can help with that, too."

"Thank you so much, Father Pete."

His smile was serene when he gazed down at her. "God would want this, Maggie. And I'm simply here to do His work."

❖

Melissa Fairchild returned from Greece and Maggie set up an appointment with her as soon as possible. When she entered the office, they hugged. Melissa drew back and studied Maggie. "I wish you'd agreed to the phone sessions. You look worse for the wear, I'm afraid."

"I probably should have." They sat in their usual spots and Maggie was glad for the sun streaming in the window and warming her.

"Tell me what's going on. Last time I saw you, Caroline had come into your life again and right afterward, Jamie told you he's gay. What's happened since then?"

"We've been dancing in the dark, fumbling our way through Jamie coming out."

"What's happened?"

Where to start? She told her therapist about Jamie's boyfriend and how that relationship had developed. "Luke tried to commit suicide, Melissa."

"Oh, no. Is he all right?"

For a half hour, Maggie filled Melissa in on the school incidents and Lucas Crane's actions that led to Luke's attempted suicide.

"Dear Lord. I hope the boy's getting some help."

"He is. Jamie, too."

When Maggie didn't continue, Melissa took the lead. "What about Mike?"

Maggie started to cry as she described what had happened in her marriage since the counselor left. Melissa passed her the Kleenex box. "Things between us are better now. But it's been a real mess."

When Maggie confided what almost happened with Damien Kane and Laura Simpson, Melissa said, "Close call. But I think the operative word is *almost*."

"Maybe. Mike and I are coasting. I've mentioned counseling. He's thinking about it. No decision as of yet. It's making me crazy but I'm trying not to push him."

"Which is hard for you but probably for the best."

"He's really put himself out for my extended family. I asked Father Pete to go over and see my mother and Mike took him."

"That's a huge step for you to turn to the Catholic Church for help."

"These days I'll do anything if it eases the strife in my family."

"How'd it go?"

She told Melissa of Mike's visit…

Maggie had been waiting nervously in the kitchen for Mike to return. When he came through the door, he said, "It went well, Maggie. Father Pete told your mother the church, God, would want her to forgive Caroline for her sins—his phrase—and that a real Christian woman would take her family back into the fold." He rolled his eyes. "It was all that religious and biblical language that he knew your mother would like."

"W-what did she say?"

"That she'd do whatever Father Pete suggested. Truthfully, I felt sorry for her. She seemed relieved. Like somewhere in her heart she wanted to do this all along."

"Mike, will she see me, too?"

"Yes, honey, she'll see you…"

"What did Caroline say about all this?" Melissa asked when Maggie had finished.

"That she'd go along with it. She told me no one ever really gets over their need to please a parent and she's willing to swallow a lot to make some kind of peace."

"Has that happened yet?"

"No."

"Not to put a damper on the good news, but don't expect it to be smooth sailing with Gertrude, even now."

"I know, but it's a start."

"Will you tell her Jamie's gay?"

"No, not now, anyway. She couldn't handle it without causing more havoc, and I won't do that to my son." She thought of Lucas Crane, of Judy and Craig Johnson, of Julianne and Eric Cummings. "I've realized not everybody will accept our family as it is. I'm done trying to change all that."

"I think—"

The doorbell downstairs rang. Melissa startled and glanced at the clock. "Who on earth would that be?" She whipped out her appointment book. "I didn't schedule anyone else for the next hour. I've got you down for two."

"Go check if you need to."

"Sorry for the interruption."

She left the room. Maggie could hear her footsteps on the stairs. The door open. A male voice. Melissa's voice. Then noise on the steps again.

Melissa came through the doorway—with Mike behind her. "Look who's here."

"Mike? What are you doing?"

He stuck his hands in the pockets of his jeans. He wore a taupe blazer with a brown T-shirt beneath, a style she'd always loved. "I knew you had this appointment and it was two hours long. I waited outside in the car for an hour so you could talk to Melissa alone. Then I came in."

"Why?"

"Because I took what you said to heart about marriage counseling."

"Oh, Mike."

His expression sheepish, he sat down and grasped her hand in his big, safe, comforting one. "We need help, honey. I know that."

"Well," Melissa said.

Maggie glanced over at her. It was the very first time she'd ever seen tears in her therapist's eyes.

❖

A week before the prom, Jamie and Luke sat in the back seat of his mom's car on their way to the Gay Pride Parade and Festival in the city. He'd followed the event on the Internet for years and gone down last summer to stand with the crowd. Aunt Caroline and Terry and Chloe had planned to march, too, but Chloe and Terry got sick, so his aunt had stayed home with them. Still, they had the two most important women in their lives with them.

His mom glanced in the rearview mirror. "You guys doing all right back there?"

He and Luke exchanged an indulgent look. Both moms in the front seats were pretending to be casual about this, but he could tell they were nervous.

"Yeah, we are," Jamie said.

She glanced at Erin. "Let's enjoy ourselves."

Every time his mom showed this kind of support, Jamie felt good inside. His dad was doing better, too, though he couldn't quite bring himself to come today. Same for Brian. Jamie had decided to settle for their acceptance even if he couldn't change their beliefs. His dad *had* surprised them all, though...

They were eating supper one night when he announced, "I went to see Shirley Lewis today."

"Really, what for?" his mom asked.

"I tried to talk her into changing her mind about the pre-prom party."

"What did she say?"

"No." He sighed. "So I told her we were going to have a party of our own."

Jamie stared open-mouthed at his father.

His mom stared open-mouthed at her husband.

His dad's eyes narrowed on them. "I suppose I deserve those shocked expressions on your faces." He'd addressed Jamie directly. "I'm working on my issues with the church, Jame, but in the meantime, I won't sit on the sidelines while anyone discriminates against you."

Jamie had stood, crossed to his father and hugged him. "Thanks Dad. I-I love you," was Jamie's response.

"I love you, too…"

Luke interrupted his thoughts. "I've read about this parade before. It gets political—there'll be protestors here."

"Ah, like the old days." His mom smiled. In her college years, she'd fought for Roe vs. Wade, campaigned against the conservative candidates for the presidency, and picketed the spending of money on weapons of war.

Jamie chuckled. "My mom, the activist."

Surprising them all, Mrs. Crane said, "Me, too."

Luke's jaw dropped. "Honest?"

His mother sniffed, faking insult. "Yes, Lucas, honest. When I was in college I protested against poverty. I even marched on Washington and worked on a small Democratic campaign in my hometown before I met your father."

It was fun, listening to both mothers recount their younger days. Luke held Jamie's hand and they smiled most of the way downtown.

They met people from their church at the designated site. They were all wearing the bright yellow UCC T-shirts and the organizer had brought extras, which Luke, Jamie, and their mothers donned. The church group was made up of both gay and straight people. There were kids ranging from fourteen to seventeen in the group, and an eighty-year-old man named Al and his wife Janet were set to follow the group in a truck, the outside of which sported UCC slogans. When Anabelle arrived, wearing her collar with tan shorts and sandals, he and Luke helped her get the big banner out of her van.

Someone handed their mothers buttons. His mom pinned hers to her shirt. Luke pretended not to notice his mom didn't do the same with hers. He turned away to watch the float in front of them, which consisted of a gay men's choir in drag. Jamie knew Luke's father had shown no support at all for him, but he thought his mother was beginning to come around.

Jamie started toward him when he saw Erin Crane grab her son and turn him around. "Luke?"

"Yeah?" he said hoarsely.

His mother smiled. "I thought you could help me with this."

Luke's Adam's apple bobbed. His hands were shaky as he pinned the same button on his mom as Jamie's mother wore. It read *Proud mother of a gay son.*

"Ready, guys?" Anabelle asked.

"Yeah, we are," Jamie answered.

Anabelle glanced at a woman approaching them.

"Lisel, there you are." Anabelle slid her arm around her partner and kissed her on the mouth. Right out in the open. Luke smiled at them, his mother tried to hide her surprise and even Jamie's own mom seemed a bit taken aback about the public display of affection.

They formed lines and got ready to march. Anabelle carried a sign that read PRIDE IN THE PULPIT. A pretty blond parishioner named Gwen, with her gay brother, Ron, took either side of a long banner announcing their church contingent. Another woman, Penny, who'd asked Jamie to be on a committee at church that needed a teenager, held up a sign that read OUR FAITH IS OVER 200 YEARS OLD, OUR THINKING IS NOT. The kids made up candy favors, attached to cards with the church's information on them, and tossed them out to the scores of people who lined the streets. Others from the congregation held signs that read WE DON'T SING "COME SOME OF YE FAITHFUL" and DIVERSITY WITHOUT DIVISION; UNITY WITHOUT UNIFORMITY.

A guy caught up with his mom and Jamie recognized him from the Gay Alliance. His mother hugged him, then brought him over to meet Erin Crane. "This is Luke Crane's mother. Sam's from the Gay Alliance."

"Hi, Erin." He turned to Jamie. "Hey, kiddo. I met your father, you know." His dad *had* gone to a PFLAG meeting, which Sam was also involved in.

"He liked it."

"Maybe you and your husband can join us at PFLAG sometime," Sam said to Luke's mother.

Mrs. Crane cleared her throat. "I'd like to come, at least."

When they started to march, Jamie walked beside Luke, both of them flanked by their mothers, which was totally cool. Music wafted back to them from a float ahead of them bearing a *Grease* theme. A small marching band playing patriotic songs was in the mix. Walkers greeted onlookers and lagged back to talk to other participants.

Another man came astride with them. His shirt read *Sorry, I don't do girls*. "Jamie, Luke, hi."

"Mr. Markham!" Jamie couldn't believe their social studies teacher was there. He was one of two African American people who worked at Sherwood.

His teacher must have caught Jamie's surprise, because he grinned. "Didn't know, did you, kid?"

"Nope."

"I wanted to say something when you two came out, when all that happened at school. But a long time ago, I made a choice to keep my private life separate from my professional one, so I didn't. Since I have a house in the city, my decision was easy to live with."

"It might not be so private anymore, if you do this." Jamie gestured to the TV cameras shooting footage.

He shrugged. "I know. Hiding who I am doesn't seem right anymore."

After Mr. Markham left, Jamie asked Luke, "Did you suspect anything about him?"

"Not a clue."

A screech came from the sidelines. A woman screamed into a bullhorn, "Christians unite against homosexuality. Reform, sinners." Among her group were people raising signs that read FIND THE CURE AT UNITED MINISTRIES and GOD WILL JUDGE YOU.

Jamie and Luke turned away from them. He caught sight of Anabelle staring at the protestors. Tears sparkled in her pretty blue eyes. Lisel tugged her close. And Jamie got scared for a minute. Then his mother moved in nearer and linked her arm with his. Erin did the same with Luke.

And Jamie didn't feel afraid anymore.

But the piéce de résistance came when they saw someone waving to them from the side. It was Allison, his cousin. She was with a group of girls who she left and started walking with the church group.

Jamie asked, "Al, what are you doing here?"

She pointed to her button. It said *Ally*, which meant she was straight and supportive. "I was hoping to see you." She linked arms with him, too, and walked along as she spoke. "I know Mom reacted badly to you coming out, and I'm pissed as hell at her for it. Of course, I don't share her feelings, so I came here, hoping to find you."

"Cool."

"Yeah." Gesturing to the other side of him, she whispered, "Is that your guy? He's seriously hot."

Jamie laughed and said out loud, for the first time in his life, "Yeah, that's my guy."

❖

The day after the pride parade, Maggie was in the laundry room, finishing up the week's loads when Jamie came down the hall with Buck. It was in this place that their family's journey had started all those months ago. She knew from his face that this was an easier visit for him. Her son seemed happy, at peace, and that made the past turmoil in their lives worth it.

"Hey, buddy! What's up?"

Jamie scanned the laundry room. "Nothing like the last time we talked here."

She smiled.

He held out a white envelope. "This is for you." He rolled his eyes. "It's sappy, but I wanted to do something just for you, because of how you helped me through the last few months."

She took the envelope. It was stiff, like a card.

"Shall I open it now?"

"As soon as I leave." He kissed her on the cheek. "Thanks, Mommykins."

Still smiling after Jamie, Maggie leaned against the dryer and opened the envelope with total joy in her heart. The card was handmade and on the front was a Photoshopped depiction of the myth of Hades and Persephone and Demeter.

The myth was about the god of the underworld who had stolen a young girl, Persephone, from her mother, Demeter, the goddess of the harvest. Demeter had gone crazy over the loss of her daughter and cursed the earth with famine. The story was used by the Greeks to explain the seasons. Zeus, the king of the gods, resolved their conflict by allowing Persephone to spend three-fourths of the year with her mother—when crops would grow—and one with Hades, when the earth would be barren.

It was, basically, an allegory about a mother's love and the lengths she'd go to for her child.

Maggie opened the fold, and inside was one of Jamie's poems. Once again, she smiled.

My Mother's Journey

Like Demeter, my mother went to hell and back for me.
She battled Hades and challenged Zeus.
She brandished the sword of a mother's wrath
At any who stood in her way.

Like Demeter, my mother suffered.
Her religion abandoned her,
Her family fell into the depths of darkness,
But she held the lantern as she led them out.

Like Demeter, my mother wept
In the privacy of her own domain.
Her world turned upside down,
The unfairness of life too great a foe.

But, like Demeter, my mother triumphed.
Because of her bravery, her family reunited,
Because of her grit, four became one,
Because of her determination,
I can walk in the naked light of day.

Was Persephone as grateful as I am?
Did she get down on her knees

And thank a mother who would have sacrificed all
To save her blood and flesh?

There is no love like a mother's for her child.
The universe revolves around it,
The gods revere it, respect it, yield to it.
My mother stands tallest among
Those women who have walked this earth,
A pillar of the Amazons,
Harboring a well of courage
Mere mortals cannot fathom.

After reading the poem, Maggie shed a few tears and thanked God
for all she had in life. Then a crucial insight came to her. Maybe Mike
couldn't go to the pride parade, maybe the prom was hard for Brian, and
maybe the homophobic people in her world would never come around.
She didn't have the perfect family, the perfect life, but she didn't need
that anymore. She was genuinely happy with what she had now.

CHAPTER TWENTY-SIX

The day of Sherwood High School's Junior Prom and the Davidsons' pre-prom party dawned bright and warm and full of sunshine. Maggie chose to see the beauty of the Saturday afternoon as a good omen and was looking forward to the event.

"You did a terrific job with the lawn," she told Mike as they stared through the window to the backyard. She'd already set out trays for snacks and small desserts on the umbrella table, reminding her of the Valentine's Ball. That seemed a lifetime ago, which in a way it was.

Mike slid his arms around her from behind. "The guys helped with the yard." His smile was the old Mike's. "They're going to be okay, Mag. Maybe Brian will have a tough time with this"—he swept a hand to encompass the lawn and therefore the party—"but they seem pretty at ease with each other. You should have seen them joking around like old times while they raked and weeded."

"I'm glad."

"And I can't believe the change in Jamie's attitude about the prom. He's so excited about going."

She hadn't told Mike about the card their son had given her. She wasn't keeping much from him anymore, but she didn't want Jamie singling her out to hurt her husband. She did share it with Gretta, though, who cried. Maggie leaned into Mike. "I have a good feeling about this party."

"Since we're expecting multitudes, we're off to the right start."

In an odd twist of fate, the majority of Jamie's friends had decided to come to *their* party after Shirley Lewis's proclamation that Jamie and his date weren't welcome in her home. She'd called their house about a week ago...

"Maggie, I don't know how to say this tactfully, but I would like to re-invite Jamie to our pre-prom bash."

"Re-invite him? Why? Just last week you told Mike you wouldn't do that."

"Kyle's furious at me for hinting that Jamie would be better off not coming to our party. Now none of the other kids in their circle want to come to our house. Apparently they think I'm prejudiced!"

Maggie bit her tongue.

"In any case, Jamie's welcome here with anybody he wants to bring. Jim's done fantastic work in the gardens and I'm planning a big spread."

"I'm not canceling our party. We've done a lot of preparation, too."

There was a long silence. "Are you punishing me for what I said about Jamie?"

"Shirley, this has nothing to do with you. We're simply having a pre-prom party for Jamie and his friends."

"What will I tell Kyle?"

She paused for a moment, thinking about how precious sons were. "That he and his date are welcome in my home. So are you, to take pictures, if you like..."

The doorbell chimed, dragging Maggie from thoughts of the unpleasant conversation. Buck barked from the family room and scurried to the front of the house. Somebody had put a bowtie around his neck.

Maggie checked the clock. "Oh, Lord, who's that?" Neither of them had showered. "It's not time for guests yet."

Mike kissed her head. "Let's go see."

They crossed through the kitchen into the foyer together. Mike opened the door.

And there stood Maggie's big sister. Dressed in a printed sundress, she held a big plate of Italian cookies in her hands. "Hi, there."

"You don't have to ring the bell, Caroline."

"I know. The door was locked."

She handed the cookies to Mike. "Hey, there." Then she hugged

Maggie. "My girls are coming in an hour and bringing the cake, but I wanted to get here sooner." She smiled and Maggie found more comfort than she could express in her sister's moral support.

"What can I do?"

"It's all pretty much done."

"Great timing." She angled her chin upstairs. "Is Bri in his room?"

"Yes."

"All right if I go see him?"

They hesitated. Caroline gave them a knowing smile. "I'm good with guys like him, Mags. I can hang with him awhile. He must feel bad about not going to the prom with Heather."

"He won't talk to me about it."

"Ah, well, aunts are different." She kissed Maggie's cheek. "Go get ready."

Mike and Maggie cleaned up in record time, and Jamie trundled downstairs before the guests arrived. Dressed in a raven tux, a snowy white shirt, and a green cummerbund, he was so handsome, and grown-up, Maggie got all misty-eyed. "Oh, my Lord, do you look beautiful."

He gave her a sham frown. "Guys aren't beautiful, Mom."

From next to her in the kitchen, Mike punched his shoulder. "My gay son can make a statement like that?"

Both Jamie and she froze.

"What?" Mike asked.

"You joked about me being gay, Dad."

"I did?" He held up the digital camera. "Move in closer with Mom and smile." Without fuss, the camera recorded that quiet hallmark in their lives.

"Where's Luke's boutonnière?" Jamie asked.

It had been odd buying the single rose for Luke instead of a corsage for a girl, as Maggie had done for previous proms. But that was okay, too.

Luke arrived next, holding his own flower box. Maggie was in the living room when Jamie answered the door. She recognized traces of the jitteriness of first love manifest itself in her son as his date stepped inside. "Hey, guy."

"Hi, Jame." Luke's tux was black, too, and she noticed his and Jamie's cummerbunds matched in color.

Coming to the foyer, Maggie motioned to the outside. "Is your mother in the car?"

"She's not coming." His eyes were sad. "My dad made her go to a dinner at the country club." He shrugged. "I told her it was okay."

"No matter," Mike said smoothly as he joined them. "We'll make doubles of all our shots."

Jamie stood there for a minute, darted an anxious glance to his father, then hugged Luke. It was a big, warm embrace, full of support and sexual pull. Mike turned away and Maggie admitted to herself that it *was* still hard watching Jamie with a boy. But some things were longer in coming and she accepted that, too.

By four thirty, Gretta, Lucy, and BJ had arrived, as well as Caroline's family, who'd picked up Allison. They socialized with other parents and kids on the deck and in the backyard. Mike and Maggie were outside when Anabelle came around the outdoor walkway on the side of the house with Lisel in tow. Anabelle gave Maggie her characteristic hug when she climbed the stairs to the deck.

"Mike, you remember Anabelle. And this is her partner, Lisel."

Mike smiled at them. "Nice to see you again, Anabelle." His words were genuine, his handshake firm. He didn't let go, either. Instead, he brought his other hand up to hold hers in both of his.

"You, too, under better circumstances."

"I read your sermon on family last week. Maggie brought it home. I liked what you said. It was meaningful for me."

"That's God for you—letting us hit the mark, now and then."

He was equally gracious with Lisel. "Welcome to our home."

When Jim and Shirley Lewis arrived, Mike barely spoke to them. Caroline and Gretta took over, ushering them to the backyard. An even tenser moment came when Heather showed up on their doorstep wearing a yellow satin gown, strapless and sexy with her dark hair and eyes. Maggie panicked. Brian's ex-girlfriend coming to their house with another boy would be disastrous.

"Heather, hi." She glanced anxiously at the driveway.

Heather smiled. "I'm here with my girlfriends, Mrs. Davidson. I wouldn't hurt Bri by showing up at your house with a date. But I wanted to go to the prom, so when Jamie gave me the invitation to this, I thought, what the heck? Why let Brian being a tool keep me away from you guys?"

"Oh, honey." Maggie hugged the girl.

She glanced to the second floor at the still-closed door. "Is he here?"

"Yeah, you want to go up?"

"No, thanks. I'll find my friends."

Maggie drew in a deep breath. Poor Brian. When Caroline had come back down from his room, she said he was doing okay, but Maggie seriously doubted that.

Right behind Heather was Casey Carson with two other teachers, one of them the man from the Gay Pride Parade. Lisel, of all people, answered the door when Craig Johnson showed up to take pictures of Tyler and his date. Judy didn't come, but that didn't surprise Maggie. The Johnsons were no longer their best friends, and she felt bad for Mike, but Judy and Craig had made their choice. Lisel took him out to the deck and chatted amiably with him. Craig had no idea who she was, which made Maggie smile at the moment of irony.

At about five thirty, the kids started making noises about leaving for dinner. Mike approached her. "Mag, look."

Turning, she saw Brian come out of the porch.

He was dressed in a spectacular white tux. His hair was curling around his face and his shoulders were relaxed. There was a self-effacing smile on his lips.

"Honey, what are you doing?" she asked when he reached them.

"I'm going to the Junior Prom, hopefully with Heather." He nodded across the deck, where Heather stood agape at him. "She invited me weeks ago and I got tickets even after she broke up with me. Just in case. I'm gonna—what's the word, Dad, when you gotta make something up to a girl?"

"Grovel," his father told him dryly.

"Yeah, grovel. In front of everybody, so maybe she'll let me be her date."

Maggie smiled but wondered how Brian would handle seeing Jamie with Luke, arms around each other, dancing. Would they kiss on the dance floor like the other couples?

"Besides," Brian added, "I wanted to be there, just in case, you know, for Jamie." He gestured to his brother. "Come on, let's get a picture." He led them both over to where Jamie stood with Luke. Brian greeted Luke with a warm handshake, but Jamie stood speechless, staring at Bri. Then he hurtled himself at his brother and they hugged, too.

Brian said, "How about a picture of Mom, Dad, and us two, Jame?"

Jamie barely got out, "Sure."

The four of them posed by a hydrangea bush, arms linked. Gretta snapped the photo.

After, Mike embraced both of his sons. Then Brian walked over to Heather.

When Gretta tried to hand the camera back to Mike, he shook his head. "Wait a second, I want one more." Mike motioned to the figure standing off to the side. "Luke, come on. Let's get a shot of you and Jamie and me."

Maggie's sister stood beside her as she watched Mike take his place behind and between the two boys. A bit taller than both, he placed a hand on each of their shoulders. Before he faced to the camera, he winked at Maggie. "We're ready now," he said, smiling at Gretta. "Save this for posterity."

Maggie turned her face into Caroline's shoulder to hide her tears. Funny, how you could cry at one of the happiest moments of your life.

About the Author

Kathryn Shay is a lifelong writer. At fifteen, she penned a short story about a female newspaper reporter in New York City and her fight to make a name for herself in a world of male journalists. She never stopped writing, even as she went on to build a successful career in the New York state school system—a true vocation for her. But by the early 1990s, while still teaching, she began her first novel. Despite enduring two years of rejections, she persevered. And on a snowy December afternoon in 1994, Kathryn Shay sold her first book to Harlequin Superromance.

Since that sale, Kathryn has written twenty-five books for Harlequin, nine mainstream contemporary romances, and two novellas for the Berkley Publishing Group. More books are contracted and on the way!

Kathryn has become known for her powerful characterizations and her heart-wrenching, emotional writing. In testament to her skill, she has had one of her books serialized in the December 2003 *Cosmopolitan* magazine and has been quoted in *People* magazine and *The Wall Street Journal.* For her romances, she has won five RT Book Reviews Reviewers Choice Awards, three Holt Medallions, four Desert Quill Awards, the Golden Leaf Award, and The Bookseller's Best Award.

Even in light of her writing success, that initial love of teaching never wavered for Kathryn. She finished out her teaching career in 2004, retiring from the same school where she began. These days, she lives in upstate New York with her husband and two children. "My life is very full," she reports, "but very happy. I consider myself fortunate to have been able to pursue and achieve both my dreams."

Books Available From Bold Strokes Books

The Long Way Home by Rachel Spangler. They say you can't go home again, but Raine St. James doesn't know why anyone would want to. When she is forced to accept a job in the town she's been publicly bashing for the last decade, she has to face down old hurts and the woman she left behind. (978-1-60282-178-1)

Water Mark by J.M. Redmann. PI Micky Knight's professional and personal lives are torn asunder by Katrina and its aftermath. She needs to solve a murder and recapture the woman she lost—while struggling to simply survive in a world gone mad. (978-1-60282-179-8)

Picture Imperfect by Lea Santos. Young love doesn't always stand the test of time, but Deanne is determined to get her marriage to childhood sweetheart Paloma back on the road to happily ever after, by way of Memory Lane-and Lover's Lane. (978-1-60282-180-4)

The Perfect Family by Kathryn Shay. A mother and her gay son stand hand in hand as the storms of change engulf their perfect family and the life they knew. (978-1-60282-181-1)

Raven Mask by Winter Pennington. Preternatural Private Investigator (and closeted werewolf) Kassandra Lyall needs to solve a murder and protect her Vampire lover Lenorre, Countess Vampire of Oklahoma—all while fending off the advances of the local werewolf alpha female. (978-1-60282-182-8)

The Devil be Damned by Ali Vali. The fourth book in the best-selling Cain Casey Devil series. (978-1-60282-159-0)

Descent by Julie Cannon. Shannon Roberts and Caroline Davis compete in the world of world-class bike racing and pretend that the fire between them is just professional rivalry, not desire. (978-1-60282-160-6)

Kiss of Noir by Clara Nipper. Nora Delany is a hard-living, sweet-talking woman who can't say no to a beautiful babe or a friend in danger—a darkly humorous homage to a bygone era of tough broads and murder in steamy New Orleans. (978-1-60282-161-3)

Under Her Skin by Lea Santos Supermodel Lilly Lujan hasn't a care in the world, except life is lonely in the spotlight—until Mexican gardener Torien Pacias sees through Lilly's facade and offers gentle understanding and friendship when Lilly most needs it. (978-1-60282-162-0)

Fierce Overture by Gun Brooke. Helena Forsythe is a hard-hitting CEO who gets what she wants by taking no prisoners when negotiating—until she meets a woman who convinces her that charm may be the way to win a battle, and a heart. (978-1-60282-156-9)

Trauma Alert by Radclyffe. Dr. Ali Torveau has no trouble saying no to romance until the day firefighter Beau Cross shows up in her ER and sets her carefully ordered world aflame. (978-1-60282-157-6)

Wolfsbane Winter by Jane Fletcher. Iron Wolf mercenary Deryn faces down demon magic and otherworldly foes with a smile, but she's defenseless when healer Alana wages war on her heart. (978-1-60282-158-3)

Little White Lie by Lea Santos. Emie Jaramillo knows relationships are for other people, and beautiful women like Gia Mendez don't belong anywhere near her boring world of academia—until Gia sets out to convince Emie she has not only brains, but beauty...and that she's the only woman Gia wants in her life. (978-1-60282-163-7)

Witch Wolf by Winter Pennington. In a world where vampires have charmed their way into modern society, where werewolves walk the streets with their beasts disguised by human skin, Investigator Kassandra Lyall has a secret of her own to protect. She's one of them. (978-1-60282-177-4)

Do Not Disturb by Carsen Taite. Ainsley Faraday, a high-powered executive, and rock music celebrity Greer Davis couldn't be less well suited for one another, and yet they soon discover passion has a way of designing its own future. (978-1-60282-153-8)

From This Moment On by PJ Trebelhorn. Devon Conway and Katherine Hunter both lost love and neither believes they will ever find it again—until the moment they meet and everything changes. (978-1-60282-154-5)

Vapor by Larkin Rose. When erotic romance writer Ashley Vaughn decides to take her research into the bedroom for a night of passion with Victoria Hadley, she discovers that fact is hotter than fiction. (978-1-60282-155-2)

Wind and Bones by Kristin Marra. Jill O'Hara, award-winning journalist, just wants to settle her deceased father's affairs and leave Prairie View, Montana, far, far behind—but an old girlfriend, a sexy sheriff, and a dangerous secret keep her down on the ranch. (978-1-60282-150-7)

Nightshade by Shea Godfrey. The story of a princess, betrothed as a political pawn, who falls for her intended husband's soldier sister, is a modern-day fairy tale to capture the heart. (978-1-60282-151-4)

Vieux Carré Voodoo by Greg Herren. Popular New Orleans detective Scotty Bradley just can't stay out of trouble—especially when an old flame turns up asking for help. (978-1-60282-152-1)

The Pleasure Set by Lisa Girolami. Laney DeGraff, a successful president of a family-owned bank on Rodeo Drive, finds her comfortable life taking a turn toward danger when Theresa Aguilar, a sleek, sexy lawyer, invites her to join an exclusive, secret group of powerful, alluring women. (978-1-60282-144-6)

A Perfect Match by Erin Dutton. The exciting world of pro golf forms the backdrop for a fast-paced, sexy romance. (978-1-60282-145-3)

Father Knows Best by Lynda Sandoval. High school juniors and best friends Lila Moreno, Meryl Morganstern, and Caressa Thibodoux plan to make the most of the summer before senior year. What they discover that amazing summer about girl power, growing up, and trusting friends and family more than prepares them to tackle that all-important senior year! (978-1-60282-147-7)

The Midnight Hunt by L.L. Raand. Medic Drake McKennan takes a chance and loses, and her life will never be the same—because when she wakes up after surviving a life-threatening illness, she is no longer human. (978-1-60282-140-8)

Long Shot by D. Jackson Leigh. Love isn't safe, which is exactly why equine veterinarian Tory Greyson wants no part of it—until Leah Montgomery and a horse that won't give up convince her otherwise. (978-1-60282-141-5)

In Medias Res by Yolanda Wallace. Sydney has forgotten her entire life, and the one woman who holds the key to her memory, and her heart, doesn't want to be found. (978-1-60282-142-2)

Awakening to Sunlight by Lindsey Stone. Neither Judith or Lizzy is looking for companionship, and certainly not love—but when their lives become entangled, they discover both. (978-1-60282-143-9)

Fever by VK Powell. Hired gun Zakaria Chambers is hired to provide a simple escort service to philanthropist Sara Ambrosini, but nothing is as simple as it seems, especially love. (978-1-60282-135-4)

Truths by Rebecca S. Buck. Two women separated by two hundred years are connected by fate and love. (978-1-60282-146-0)

High Risk by JLee Meyer. Can actress Kate Hoffman really risk all she's worked for to take a chance on love? Or is it already too late? (978-1-60282-136-1)

Spanking New by Clifford Henderson. A poignant, hilarious, unforgettable look at life, love, gender, and the essence of what makes us who we are. (978-1-60282-138-5)

Missing Lynx by Kim Baldwin and Xenia Alexiou. On the trail of a notorious serial killer, Elite Operative Lynx's growing attraction to a mysterious mercenary could be her path to love—or to death. (978-1-60282-137-8)